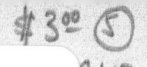

MASARYK STATION

Also by David Downing

The John Russell Series
Zoo Station
Silesian Station
Stettin Station
Potsdam Station
Lehrter Station

The Jack McColl Series
Jack of Spies

MASARYK STATION

DAVID DOWNING

For Sacha

Published in the United States in 2013 by

Soho Press, Inc.
853 Broadway
New York, NY 10003

Library of Congress Cataloging-in-Publication Data

Downing, David, 1946–
Masaryk Station / David Downing.
p cm
HC ISBN 978-1-61695-223-5
PB ISBN 978-1-61695-373-7
eISBN: 978-1-61695-222-8
1. World War, 1939–1945—Fiction. 2. Historical fiction. 3. Spy stories.
I. Title.
PR6054.O868M37 2013
823'.914—dc23
2012042044

Printed in the United States of America

10 9 8 7 6 5 4 3 2 1

MASARYK
STATION

Abbreviations

BOB
Berlin Operations Base (of US intelligence services), originally run by military intelligence, from September 1947 by the new CIA

CIA
American Central Intelligence Agency

CIC
Counter-Intelligence Corps of the US Army

CPSU
Communist Party of the Soviet Union

DEFA
Deutsche Film-Aktiengesellschaft, German film production company founded in 1946 with Soviet encouragement and support

GRU
Soviet Military Intelligence

K-5
German security police in Soviet zone, the nascent Stasi

KI
Soviet organisation set up in 1947 to coordinate intelligence services

KPD
German Communist Party

MGB	Soviet State Security service responsible for intelligence and counter-intelligence between 1946 and 1953
OUN	Organisation of Ukrainian Nationalists, founded in 1929 and later allied to the Nazis
SPD	German Social Democratic Party
UDBA	Yugoslav State Security
YCP	Yugoslav Communist Party

February 11, 1948

They were on their way to bed when the two Russians arrived, but the lateness of the hour was apparently irrelevant—she and her sister were to come at once. She asked if they knew who she was, but of course they did. Refusal wasn't an option.

Their destination was also secret. 'Very nice house,' the one with some German told them, as if that might make all the difference. He even helped her into the fur coat. Nina looked terribly scared, but the best she could do was squeeze her older sister's hand as they sat in the back of the gleaming Audi.

Soon the car was purring its way eastward along a dimly lit and mostly empty Frankfurter Allee. The men in the front exchanged an occasional word in Russian, but were mostly silent.

Like thousands of others she'd been raped in 1945, but only on the one occasion. The three soldiers had been too excited by her house and possessions to do more than satisfy their immediate lust.

And now, she feared, it was going to happen again. In a 'very nice house.'

She could feel her sister quivering beside her. Nina had only been twelve in 1945, tall for her age, but luckily still with the chest and hips of a child, and so the soldiers had left her alone. She had blossomed since, but was still a virgin. This was going to be so much harder for her.

They were leaving the city behind, driving through snow-covered fields. Three years after the war, the road signs caught in the head-lamp beams bore Cyrillic script, and she had only the vaguest idea where they were. Not that it mattered.

They turned off the road up a tree-lined drive, and swung to a halt before a large three-storey house. There were soldiers on guard either side of the door, and another inside who gave them both a curious look. There was only one man in civilian clothes and he had a classic Russian face. This was an enemy camp, she thought. There wouldn't be anyone there to whom they could appeal.

They were hustled upstairs and down a richly carpeted corridor to a door at its end. One of their escorts tapped it lightly with his knuckles, then responded to words from within by pushing it open and ushering them inside.

It was a large room, with several armchairs and a large four-poster bed. A fire was burning in the grate, and several electric lamps were glowing behind their shades, although the light was far from bright. She had never been in a brothel, but she imagined the better ones looked like this.

And then she saw who it was, and her heart and stomach plummeted.

He was wearing a dressing gown, and probably nothing else. The smile on his face was only for himself.

After calmly locking the door, he walked to a table holding several bottles, poured himself a tumblerful of clear liquid, and gulped half of it down. As he turned back to them the fire briefly glinted in his spectacles.

'Zieh dich aus,' he said. Take off your clothes.

'No,' Nina almost whispered.

'We must do as he says,' she told her sister.

Nina stared back at her. There was fear in her eyes, and pleading, and sheer disbelief.

'Take me,' she begged him. 'She's only a girl, take me.'

If he understood her—and she thought he did—all it did was increase his impatience.

They slowly stripped to their underwear, pausing at that point without much hope.

He gestured for them to continue, and then stared at their naked bodies. She watched his growing erection strain at the dressing gown, then finally break free. Nina's gasp made him smile. He took two steps forward, grabbed her wrist, and tugged her towards the bed.

Nina jerked herself free and ran for the door, which rattled loudly but resisted her attempt to pull it off its hinges. As he crossed the room in pursuit, she tried to block his way, but he grabbed her by the arm and casually threw her aside.

Nina grabbed a convenient ashtray, and hurled it in his direction. She didn't see where it struck him, but the grunt of pain as he doubled over left little room for doubt.

For a few brief seconds the world stood still.

Then he gingerly walked to his desk, and took a gun from the drawer.

'No,' she screamed, scrambling towards him.

He lashed out with the barrel, catching her across the cheek as it knocked her to the carpet.

Nina had sunk to her knees, and now he stood before her, his penis dangling in front of her face. He lifted her hair with the gun, and slowly moved around her, his erection returning.

She thought he would force the sobbing girl to take him in her mouth, but what could she do to step in that wouldn't make things worse?

And then he had the barrel of the gun in the nape of Nina's neck, and his finger was pulling the trigger. There was no explosion, just a coughing sound, an almost derisory spurt of blood, a silent Nina crumpling on to the carpet.

She tried to speak, to rise from the floor, but both were beyond her.

He came across the room, gun in hand. Expecting to die, she felt almost disoriented when he pulled her up by her hair, and threw her face down on the bed. There was cold metal in the back of her neck, but his hands were wrenching her legs apart, and she knew there was one last thing to endure before she joined her sister.

And then he was ramming himself inside her, urgently pumping away. It only lasted a few seconds, and once he was out again, she lay there waiting for an end to it all, for the blackness the bullet would bring.

It didn't come. After several moments his hands reached down for one of hers, and cradled it around the butt of the pistol. At first she didn't resist, and by the time she realised the implication, he had taken it back again.

'You're too famous to kill,' he said in explanation.

Crusaders

The Russian was almost certainly lying, but John Russell had no intention of sharing this suspicion with his British and American employers. If there was one thing he'd learnt over the last few years, it was never to divulge any information without first thoroughly assessing how much it might be worth in money, or favours, or blood.

The British major and American captain who shared command of the Trieste interrogation centre seemed less inclined to doubt the Russian. A kind reading of the situation might have them lacking Russell's suspicious nature, although one would have thought that a necessary qualification for intelligence officers. Being about half Russell's age and coming from two different realms of Anglo-American privilege, they certainly lacked his experience of European intrigue. But having said all that, a third explanation for their naivety—that both were essentially idiots—seemed by far the most likely.

The Brit's name was Alex Farquhar-Smith, and Russell would have bet money on a rural pile, minor public school, and Oxford. At the latter he had probably spent more time rowing than reading, and only been saved from a poor Third by a timely world war. The Yank, Buzz Dempsey, was a Chicago boy with a haircut to suit his name, and a brashness only slightly less annoying than his English colleague's emotional constipation. Usually they spent most of their working hours getting up each other's noses, but today they were both too excited.

The source of their exhilaration was the tall, rather elegant, chain-smoking Soviet major sitting on the other side of the table. 'I have some information about the Red Army's battle order in Hungary,' Petr Kuznakov had casually mentioned on arriving in Trieste the previous day, as if unaware that such intelligence was the current holy grail of every American and British officer charged with debriefing the steady stream of defectors and refugees from Stalin's rapidly coagulating empire. That had made Russell suspicious, as had the Russian's choice of Trieste. Had his superiors calculated that the chances of encountering real professionals would be less in such a relative backwater? If so, they'd done their homework well.

The Russian lit another cigarette and said, for the fourth or fifth time, that the MGB would be frantically looking for him, and that he would be of no use to 'the great world of freedom' if his new friends allowed him to be killed. Surely it was time to move him somewhere safe, where they could discuss what sort of life they were offering in exchange for everything he knew?

Russell translated this as faithfully as he could; so far that day he had seen no potential benefit in concealing anything specific from the two English speakers.

'Tell him he's quite safe here,' Farquhar-Smith said reassuringly. 'But don't tell him why,' he added for the third time that morning, as if afraid that Russell had the attention span of a three-year-old.

He did as he was told, and was treated to another look of hurt incomprehension from Kuznakov. Russell had a sneaking feeling that the Russian already knew about the tip-off, and the two Ukrainians in the Old City hotel. He said he was worried, but the eyes seemed very calm for a man expecting his executioners.

With that thought, the telephone rang. Dempsey answered it,

while the rest of them sat in silence, trying in vain to decipher the American's murmured responses. Call concluded, they heard him go outside, where the half-dozen soldiers had been waiting all morning. A few minutes later he was back. 'They're on their way,' he told Russell and Farquhar-Smith. 'They'll be here in about ten minutes.'

'Just the two of them?' Russell asked, in case Dempsey had forgotten.

'Yeah. You take Ivan here out to the stables, and we'll come get you when it's all over.'

'But don't tell him anything,' Farquhar-Smith added. 'We don't want him getting too high an opinion of himself.' He gave the Russian a smile as he said it, and received one back in return.

They deserved each other, Russell thought, as he escorted the Russian across the courtyard and down the side of the villa to the stable block. There were no horses in residence; all had been stolen by the locals three years earlier, after the Italian fascist owner's mysterious plummet down the property's well. A horsey odour persisted still though, and Russell took up position outside the entrance, where the sweeter smell of pine wafted by on the warm breeze, his ears listening for the sound of an approaching vehicle. Kuznakov had asked what was happening, but only belatedly, as if remembering he should. There was watchfulness in the Russian's eyes, but no hint of alarm.

In the event, the two Ukrainians must have parked their car down the road and walked up, because the first thing Russell heard was gunfire. Quite a lot of it, in a very short time.

In the enduring silence that followed, Russell saw the look on Kuznakov's face change from slight trepidation to something approaching satisfaction.

The birds were finding their voices again when Dempsey came to fetch them. The two would-be assassins were lying bloody and crumpled on the courtyard stones, their British killers arguing ownership of the shiny new Soviet machine pistols. Neither of the dead men looked particularly young, and both had tattoos visible on their bare forearms which Russell recognised. These two Ukrainians had fought in the SS Galician Division; there would be other tattoos on their upper arms announcing their blood groups. Strange people for the MGB to employ, if survival was desired.

There was no sign that Dempsey and Farquhar-Smith had worked it out. On the contrary, they seemed slightly more respectful toward their Soviet guest, as well as eager to continue with the interrogation. Not that they learned very much. Over the next three hours Kuznakov promised a lot but revealed little, teasing his audience with the assurance of a veteran stripper. He would only tell them everything when he really felt safe, he repeated more than once, before casually mentioning another cache of vital intelligence that he could hardly wait to divulge.

It was almost six when Russell's bosses decided to call it day, and by that time the four of them could barely make one another out through the fug of the Russian's cigarette smoke. Outside the sky was clear, the sun sinking behind the wall of pines which lined the southern border of the property. Leaving Farquhar-Smith to sort out the nocturnal arrangements, Russell and Dempsey roared off in the latter's jeep, and were soon bouncing down the Ljubljana road, city and sea spread out before them. There was already an evening chill, but the short drive rarely failed to raise Russell's spirits, no matter how depressing the events of the day.

He had been in Trieste for two months now, having been loaned out by the American Berlin Operations Base—'BOB' for short—for 'a week or two,' after the local Russian interpreter's wife had been taken ill back home in the States. At this point in time, all the American intelligence organisations in Europe—and there were a bewildering number of them—had only three Russian speakers between them, and since Russell was one of two in Berlin, a fortnight's temporary secondment to the joint Anglo-American unit in Trieste had been considered acceptable. And by the time news arrived that his predecessor had died in a New Jersey highway pileup, a veritable flood of interesting-looking defectors had stumbled into Trieste with stories to tell, and Russell had been declared indispensable by Messrs Farquhar-Smith and Dempsey. A replacement was always on the way, but never seemed to arrive.

In truth, Russell wasn't altogether sorry to be away from Berlin. He missed Effi, of course, but she was currently shooting another movie for the Soviet-backed DEFA production company, and he knew from long experience how little he saw her when she was working. The German capital was still on its knees in most of the ways that counted, and over the previous winter the threat of a Soviet takeover had loomed larger with each passing week. Having failed to win control of the city's Western sectors through political chicanery, the Russians had opted for economic pressure—exploiting the Western sectors' position deep inside the Soviet Zone, and their consequent reliance on Russian goodwill for all their fuel and food. Until a couple of weeks ago, it had all seemed little more than gestures, but on April Fool's Day—a scant twenty-four hours after the US Congress approved the Marshall Plan—the Soviet authorities in Germany had upped the stakes, placing new restrictions on traffic using the road, rail and air corridors linking Berlin with the Western zones. This had continued for several days, until a Soviet fighter had buzzed an American cargo plane a little too closely and brought them both down. Since then, things had got back to normal, although no one knew for how long.

Berlin's intelligence outfits would still be in a frenzy, and that was something worth missing. His American controller Brent Johannsen, though a decent-enough man, was handicapped by his ignorance of Europe in general and the Soviets in particular, and his misreading of the latter's intentions could be downright dangerous to his subordinates. Russell's Soviet controller Andrei Tikhomirov was usually too drunk to bother with orders, but in January he and Yevgeny Shchepkin had been farmed out to one of the new K-5 whizkids, a young Berliner named Schneider, who seemed to think the best way to impress his Russian mentors was to behave like the Gestapo.

No, Effi might be calling him home, but Berlin most definitely wasn't.

Trieste was a monument to failure, a city crowded with people who only wanted to leave—it often reminded Russell of a film called *Casablanca*, which he'd seen during the war—but the food and weather were a huge improvement on Berlin's. And the 'Rat Line' story Russell had been working on for over a month was making him feel like a journalist again. Over the last three years he had almost forgotten how much he enjoyed digging up such stories, sod by clinging sod.

'This okay?' Dempsey asked him, breaking his reverie. The American had stopped outside a tobacconist's about halfway down the Via del Corso. 'I need a new pipe,' he added.

In the distance there was some sort of demonstration underway—in Trieste there usually was. Yugoslavs wanting the Italians out, Italians wanting the Yugoslavs out, everyone keen to see the backs of the Brits and the Yanks.

Russell thanked Dempsey for the lift, and took the first turning into the Old City's maze of narrow streets and alleys. His hostel was on a small plaza nestling beneath the steep slope of St Giusto's hill, a Serb family business which he had judged much cleaner than its Italian neighbour. The supply of hot water was, at best, sporadic, and his clothes always came back from washing looking remarkably untouched by soap; but he liked the proprietor Marko and his ever-cheerful wife, Mira, not to mention their seven or eight children, several of whom were almost always guaranteed to be blocking the staircase with some game or other.

There was no one at the desk, no letters for him in the pigeonhole, and only one daughter on the stairs, twirling hair between her fingers and deep in a book. Russell worked his way around her and let himself into his home away from home, a room some five metres square, with an iron bedstead and faded rug, an armchair that probably remembered the Habsburgs, and, by day, a wonderful view of receding roofs and the distant Adriatic. The bathroom he shared with his mostly Serbian fellow guests was just across the hall.

Russell lay down on the over-soft bed, disappointed but hardly surprised by the lack of a letter from Effi—even when 'resting,' she had never been a great correspondent. To compensate, he re-read the one from Paul which had arrived a few days earlier. As usual, his son's written language was strangely, almost touchingly, formal. He was marrying Marisa on Friday the 10th of September, and the two of them hoped that Effi and his father would do them the honour of attending the ceremony at St Mary's in Kentish Town. Solly Bernstein, Russell's long-time British agent and Paul's current employer, would be giving the bride away, Marisa's parents having died in a Romanian pogrom. Solly also sent his love, and wanted to know where the new story was.

'I'm working on it,' Russell muttered to himself. London, like September, seemed a long way away.

He looked at his watch and heaved himself back up—he had a meeting with a source that evening, and was hungry enough to eat dinner first. There was still no one on the desk downstairs, and the drunken English private hovering in the doorway was looking for a less salubrious establishment. Russell gave him directions to the

Piazza Cavana, and watched the man weave unsteadily off down the cobbled street. Removing his trousers without falling over was likely to prove a problem. The restaurants on the Villa Nuova were already doing good business, with some hardy souls sitting out under the stars with their coats buttoned up. Russell found an inside table, ordered *pollo e funghi*, and sat there eating buttered ciabatta with his glass of Chianti, remembering his and Effi's favourite trattoria on Ku'damm, back when the Nazis were just a bad dream.

An hour or so later, he was back in the Old City, climbing a narrow winding street toward the silhouetted castle. A stone staircase brought him to the door of a run-down delicatessen, whose back room doubled as a restaurant. There were only four tables, and only one customer—a man of around forty, with greased-back black hair and dark limpid eyes in a remarkably shiny face. He wore a cheap suit over a collarless shirt, and looked more than ready to play himself in a Hollywood movie.

'Meester Russell,' the man said, rising slightly to offer his hand after wiping it on a napkin. A plate with two thoroughly stripped chicken bones sat on the dirty tablecloth, along with a half-consumed bottle of red wine.

'Mister Artucci.'

'Call me Fredo.'

'Okay. I'm John.'

'Okay, John. A glass,' he called over his shoulder, and a young woman in a grey dress almost ran to the table with one. 'You can close now,' Artucci told her, pouring wine for Russell. 'My friend Armando tell me you interest in Croats. Father Kozniku, who run Draganović's office here in Trieste. Yes?'

Russell heard the woman let herself out, and close the door behind her. 'I understand your girlfriend works in the office,' he began. 'I'd like to meet her.'

Artucci shook his head sadly. 'Not possible. And I know every-thing from her. But money talks first, yes?'

'Always,' Russell wryly agreed, and spent the next few minutes patiently lowering the Italian's grossly inflated expectations to some-thing he could actually afford.

'So what you know now?' Artucci asked, lighting a cigarette that smelled even worse than Kuznakov's brand.

Russell gave him a rundown. The whole business had come to his attention while on a fortnight's secondment to the CIC office in Salzburg the previous year. The Americans, having decided not to prosecute a Croatian priest named Cecelja for war crimes, had started employing him as a travel operator for people they wanted out of Europe. As he investigated the latter over the next few months, it became clear to Russell that Cecelja, far from working alone, was just one cog of a much larger organisation, which was run from inside the Vatican by another Croatian priest named Krunoslav Draganović. Using a whole network of priests, includ-ing Father Kozniku here in Trieste, Draganović was selling and arranging passage out of Central and Eastern Europe for all sorts of refugees and fugitives.

The Americans called the whole business a 'Rat Line,' but Russell doubted they knew just how varied the 'rats' had become. In addition to those thoroughly debriefed Soviet defectors whom the American CIC was set on saving from MGB punishment, Russell had so far identified fugitive Nazis, high-ranking Croat veterans of the fascist Ustashe, and a wide selection of all those Eastern European boys' clubs which had clung to Hitler's grisly bandwagon. The Americans were paying Draganović $1,500 per person for their evacuees; but the oth-ers, for all he knew, were charity cases.

Artucci listened patiently, then blew out smoke. 'So, what are your questions?'

'Well, first off—are Draganović and his people just in it for the money? Or are they politically motivated, using the money they get from the Americans to subsidise a service for their right-wing friends?'

'Mmm,' Artucci articulated, as if savouring the question's complexity. 'A little of both, I think. They like money; they don't like communists. All same, in the end.'

'That's not very helpful,' Russell told him, putting down a marker.

'Well, what I say? I no see inside Draganović mind. But Croat people he help—they kill for fifteen dollar. They only see fifteen hundred in dreams.'

'Okay. So, as far as you know, have the Americans only bought exits for Soviet defectors and refugees? Or have they shelled out for Nazis and Ustashe as well?' This was the key question in many ways. If the Americans, for whatever twisted political reasons, were helping certain war criminals escape Europe and justice, then he had a real story. Not one his American bosses in Berlin would want published, but with any luck at all they would never know the source. For more than a year now, Russell had been using a fictitious by-line for the stories which might upset one or both of his Intelligence employers, and the elusive Jakob Brüning was becoming one of European journalism's more respected voices. As far as Russell knew, only Solly and Effi were aware that he and Brüning were one and the same.

Artucci was pondering his question. 'Is difficult,' he said at last. 'How I say? All these people—the Americans, the British, Draganović and his people—they all have agenda, yes? This Rat Line just one piece. I don't know if Americans pay Draganović for Nazis or Ustashe to escape, but they all talk to others—Americans here in Trieste; and British, they talk to Ustashe, give them guns. And everyone know they help Pavelić escape, everyone. Why they do that, if not to please his Križari, the men they want to fight Tito and the Russians?'

He was probably right, Russell thought. It was hard to think of the Ustashe as acceptable allies in any circumstances—they had routinely committed atrocities the Nazis would have shrunk from—but, as Artucci said, the Allies had indeed spirited the appalling Ustashe leader Ante Pavelić away to South America. And what were the Americans' current alternatives? When it came to potential allies, they were understandably—if somewhat foolishly—reluctant to put their faith in Social Democrats, which only left the parties of the tainted Catholic right. Nazi collaborators, fascists in all but name, but reliably anti-Communist. Everyone knew the Križari—the Croat 'Crusaders'—were Ustashe in fresh clothes, but as long as they took the fight to Tito, they had nothing to fear from the West.

Asked for names, Artucci grudgingly provided two—young men from Osijek with lodgings near the train station, who had been hanging around Kozniku's office for the last week or so. They were waiting for something, Artucci thought. 'And they pester my Luciana,' he added indignantly. He offered to provide more names on a pro rata basis, provided Russell could guarantee his anonymity. 'Some of these people, they think murder is nothing.'

But he didn't seem worried as he walked off into the darkness, Russell's dollars stuffed in his money-belt and a definite spring to his step. Russell gave him a start, then headed down the same street. Artucci was probably less informed than he thought he was, but he might well have his uses.

Reaching his hostel, Russell decided it was too early to shut himself away for the night, and continued on towards the seafront. Halfway along one narrow street, he became aware of footsteps behind him, and carefully quickened his pace before glancing over his shoulder. A man was following him, though whether deliberately was impossible to tell. There was no sign of hostile intent, and the footsteps showed no sign of quickening. Keeping his ears pricked, Russell kept walking, and eventually the man took a different turning. Russell sometimes got the feeling that putting the wind up strangers was a hobby among Triestinos.

He ended up, as usual, in the Piazza Unità. The city's social hub boasted a well-kept garden with bandstand, and five famous cafés established in Habsburg times. Russell's favourite was the San Marco, where writers had traditionally gathered. According to legend, James Joyce had worked on *Ulysses* at one corner table, from where he was frequently collected by his furious mistress, the exquisitely named Nora Barnacle.

The café was about half-full. Russell ordered a nightcap, filched an abandoned Italian newspaper from an adjoining table, and idly glanced through its meagre contents. Nothing looked worth a laborious translation. When the small glass of ruby-red liquid arrived he sat there sipping, and thinking about the next day. Another eight hours of Kuznakov and his cigarettes, of Farquhar-Smith and Dempsey and their stupid questions. Russell didn't know which he loathed the more—the Army intelligence types thrown up by the war, who had no idea what they were doing, or the new professionals now making their mark in Berlin, who were too dead inside to know why or what for.

Russell was nursing an almost empty glass when the door swung wide to reveal a familiar figure. Yevgeny Shchepkin looked around the room, betrayed with only the faintest curl of his lips that he'd noticed Russell, and took a seat at the nearest empty table before removing his hat and gloves. A waiter hurried towards him, took his order, and returned a few minutes later with a cup of espresso. Taking a sip, the white-haired Russian made eye contact for the first time. As he lowered the cup a slight movement of the head suggested they meet outside.

Russell sighed. He hadn't expected to see Shchepkin here in

Trieste, but the Russian had a habit of appearing at his shoulder, both physically and metaphorically. He rarely brought good news but, for reasons he never found quite convincing, Russell was fond of the man. Their fates had been intertwined for almost a decade now, first in working together against the Nazis, and then in a mutual determination to escape the Soviet embrace. His family in Moscow were hostages to Shchepkin's continued loyalty, while Russell was constrained by Soviets threats to reveal his help in securing them German atomic secrets. As far as Stalin and MGB boss Lavrenti Beria were concerned, Russell was a Soviet double-agent, Shchepkin his control. As far as the Americans were concerned, the reverse was the case. All of which gave Russell and Shchepkin some latitude—helping 'the enemy' could always be justified as part of the deception. But it also tied them into the game that they both wanted out of.

After paying his check Russell wandered out into the square. A British army lorry was rumbling past on the seafront, offering material support to the Union Jack that fluttered from the top of the bandstand. The sky was clear, the temperature still dropping, and he raised his jacket collar against the breeze flowing in from the sea.

Shchepkin appeared about five minutes later, buttoning up his coat. Russell had a sudden memory of a very cold day in Krakow, and the Russian scolding him, almost maternally, for not wearing a hat.

They shook hands, and began a slow circuit of the gardens.

'Have you just come from Berlin?' Russell asked in Russian.

'Via Prague.'

'How are things? In Berlin, I mean.'

'Interesting. You remember the big shake-up last September? Someone at the top had the bright idea of merging the MGB and the GRU, so KI was set up. It felt like a bad idea then, and things have only gotten worse. These days nobody seems to know who they're accountable to, or who they should be worrying about. Different groups have ended up trying to snatch the same people from the Western zones. Some of our people in Berlin recruited KI staff as informers without knowing who they were.'

Shchepkin was always exasperated by incompetence, even that of his enemies. 'And the wider picture?' Russell asked patiently. He hadn't had the trials and tribulations of the Soviet intelligence machine in mind when asking his question.

'Serious,' Shchepkin said. 'I think Stalin has decided to test the Americans' resolve. It won't be anything dramatic, just a push here, a push there, nothing worth going to war over. Just loosening their grip on the city, one finger at a time, until it drops into our hands.'

'It won't work,' Russell argued, with more certainty than he felt. He didn't doubt the Americans' will to resist, just their ability to work out the how and when.

'Let's hope not,' Shchepkin agreed. 'We might both prove surplus to requirements if Stalin gets his way. But . . .'

A shot sounded in the distance, several streets away. This wasn't an uncommon occurrence in Trieste, and rarely seemed to have fatal consequences.

'You were saying?'

'Ah. Your absence has been noticed, even by Tikhomirov. And young Schneider misses you greatly,' he added wryly. 'He suspects you're prolonging your stay here for no great reason.'

'You can tell Schneider I'm prolonging my stay here to avoid seeing him.'

'I don't . . .'

'But the real reason is, they won't let me go. So many of your countrymen are turning up here uninvited, and I'm the only person they have who can talk to them.'

'I see. Well, maybe I can do something about that. A local volunteer, perhaps.'

'It would help if your people stopped planting fakes among the real defectors. Kuznakov will probably keep me busy for the next week.'

'Ah, you spotted him, did you?' Shchepkin said, sucking in his thin cheeks and sounding like a gratified teacher. 'You didn't give him up, though? He's an idiot anyway, and I can tell my people you helped smooth his passage. We need every success we can get.'

'We do? I thought we were doing rather well.'

'Well, Tikhomirov and Schneider don't agree. They know that building your credit with the Americans requires the occasional sacrifice of one of their own, but they still don't like doing it, and they need the occasional reminder that your uses extend to the here and now.'

'All right. But getting back to the original topic—the Americans are sending me to Belgrade in a couple of weeks, so Berlin will have to wait at least that long.'

Shchepkin was interested. 'What do they want you to do there?'

'They're still deciding. As a journalist, they want me to sound out who I can, find out how real the row is between Tito and Stalin. But if past experience is any guide, they'll also have a list of people they want me to contact. Potential allies, if they have any left, that is.'

Shchepkin was silent for a few moments. 'There's not much difference between journalism and espionage,' he said eventually, sounding almost surprised.

'One is illegal,' Russell reminded him.

'True,' Shchepkin acknowledged. 'Needless to say, we'd like copies of any reports. And there may be people we want you to see. I'll let you know.'

'Sounds ominous. If Tito and Stalin really have fallen out, then my Soviet "Get out of jail free" card won't be worth much.'

'Your what?'

'It's a board game called Monopoly,' Russell explained. 'If you land on a particular square, you end up in jail. But if you already have a "Get out of jail free" card you're released straight away.'

'Fascinating. And what's the object of this game?'

'Bankrupting your opponents by buying up properties and charging them rent each time they land on one.'

'How wonderfully capitalistic.'

'Indeed. But returning to the point—I won't be much use to Berlin if I'm stuck in a Belgrade prison.'

'I'll bear that in mind,' Shchepkin said, with a smile. They had completed one circuit, and were halfway through a second. Away to their left, two British warships were silhouetted against the sea and sky. 'I was in Prague a few days ago,' Shchepkin said, surprising Russell. The Russian rarely volunteered information about himself or his other activities.

'Not much fun?' Russell suggested. The Communists had taken sole control only six or seven weeks earlier, and shortly thereafter the pro-Western foreign minister Jan Masaryk had allegedly jumped to his death from a window in the Czernin Palace. According to Buzz Dempsey, the borders had been effectively closed ever since, as the Party relentlessly tightened its hold.

'You could say that,' Shchepkin said.

'I expected better of the Czechs.'

'Why?'

'You know your Marx. An industrial society, rich in high culture—isn't that supposed to be the seed-bed of socialism?'

'Of course. But the Czechs have us to contend with, the peasant society that got there first. And the more civilised the country, the tighter we'll need to screw down the lid.'

Shchepkin was right, Russell thought. It was the same everywhere.

In Berlin his friend Gerhard Ströhm was continually complaining that the Soviets were destroying the German communists' chances of creating anything worthwhile.

'Look,' Shchepkin said, 'I understand your reluctance to come back to Berlin . . .'

'You do?'

'I know what you were doing before you left; and you're probably doing the same thing here. Neither side has been choosy about whom they recruited, and they're getting less so with each passing month. Both have taken on a fair proportion of ex-Nazis. To retain your credibility as a double-agent, you have to offer up people on both sides— American agents to us, our agents to the Americans. But as far as I can tell, every last one you've betrayed has been an ex-Nazi. You're still fighting the war.'

'And what's wrong with that?' Russell wanted to know.

'Two things,' Shchepkin told him. 'One, eventually each side will start wondering just how committed you are to fighting their new enemy. And two, you'll soon be running out of Nazis. What will you do then?'

'Whatever I have to, I suppose. I was hoping you'd conjure us out of all this before I reached that point. Three years ago you talked about uncovering a secret so appalling that it would work as a "Get out of Stalin's reach" card. Didn't some innocent birdwatcher accidentally take a photo of Beria pushing Masaryk out of his window, which we could use to blackmail the bastard?'

'It was three in the morning.'

'Pity.'

They both laughed.

'We'll meet again on Thursday,' Shchepkin decided. 'Here at the same time.'

It was almost midnight, but Russell still felt more restless than sleepy. He walked north up the seafront, passing groups of huddled refugees, and one suspicious stack of crates guarded by a posse of Jews—more guns for the Haganah's war with the Arabs. Hitler had been dead for almost three years, but so many of the conflicts his war had engendered were still unresolved. A line from a long-forgotten poem came back to Russell: 'War is just a word for what peace can't conceal.'

It was snowing in Berlin, not hard, just a light flurry to remind the city that spring wasn't fully established. Effi was near the back of the people gathered around the grave in the Dorotheenstadt Cemetery, among a crowd of others who had worked with the dead woman—directors and writers, producers and cameramen, other actors. She had shared three film sets with Sonja Strehl, and one theatre run back when they were both in their twenties. Effi hadn't seen Sonja for years, and had never known her well, but still she found it hard to imagine the woman committing suicide. Sonja had always seemed so positive. About life, work, and even men. And no doubt about the children she'd eventually had, the boy and girl now standing by the open grave, looking like all they wanted to do was cry.

'Are you coming back to the house?' Angela Ritschel whispered in Effi's ear.

'For a little while.' They were working on the same film out at Babelsberg and, like the rest of the cast, had grudgingly been given the afternoon off to attend the funeral.

'She was good, wasn't she?' Angela said, a few moments later.

'Yes,' Effi agreed. She'd been remembering Sonja backstage at the Metropol, frantically searching through a pile of bouquets for a note from the man she currently fancied. The look on her face when she'd found it.

If truth be told, Sonja hadn't had much range as an actor. But she could make demure look sexy, light up a screen with joy in life, weep until you had to weep with her. And maybe that was enough. People had paid to see her, which had to mean something, Effi thought.

The service was apparently over, the crowd of mourners breaking up. There were two cars for close family, but the rest of them had to walk down Oranienburger Strasse to the house on Monbijou Platz, past the still-closed S-Bahn station and the wreckage of the old Main Telegraph Office.

Inside Sonja's house, her father was greeting the guests, looking suitably heartbroken. Two of the ex-husbands were there, but not the father of her children—he had been killed entertaining the troops at Stalingrad.

There was a table groaning with food, supplied by her recent Soviet employers, and enough unopened bottles of vodka to induce the traditional Russian stupor. Fortunately, the Americans had also deemed it politic to send their respects in liquid form, and so Effi chose a small glass of Bourbon to wash down the Russian hors d'oeuvres. Angela had wandered off, and Effi scanned the crowd for another familiar face. She caught the glance of Sonja's first husband, the actor Volker Heldt. He and Effi had worked on a DEFA project only the previous year.

He walked across to join her. 'A good crowd,' he said.

'Yes,' Effi agreed. 'Don't look now, but who's the man leaning against the wall in the grey suit? He keeps staring at me.'

'Who wouldn't?' Volker said gallantly, taking his time to look around. 'Oh him—he stares at everyone. He's one of the Russian culture people. MGB most likely. It was their police who found her, you know.'

'I didn't. I still can't believe she killed herself.'

'Oh, I don't think there's any doubt, despite what some people are saying.'

'How did she do it?'

'Sleeping pills. And there's no doubt she bought them. She paid a fortune for them on the black market.'

'Did she leave a note?'

'No, and that was strange. But she'd only just broken up with her last boyfriend—the one almost half her age—so who knows what was going through her mind. And anyway what reason would the Russians have for killing her?'

'Is that what people are saying?'

'A few. Like Eva here.'

The blonde joining them had done the costumes on several of Effi's films. Eva Kempka was in her forties now, and thin enough to look a little stretched. She had been married once, but according to Berlin's cinematic grapevine, had since changed her sexual proclivities.

'What are you accusing me of?' Eva asked Volker, with more than a hint of disdain.

'Of believing the Russians killed Sonja.'

'I've never said that. I just don't believe she killed herself.' The way she said it made Effi think there'd been some emotional involvement, either real or unrequited.

'Well, maybe not you,' Volker admitted, 'but there are a lot of people out there who think the Russians are behind every mysterious happening. Good or bad. And the Russians are really not that smart.'

'Yes, but Sonja was . . .' Eva began, then, for some reason, suddenly stopped.

'Sonja was what?' Volker asked.

'Nothing,' Eva said quickly. 'And you're right about everyone blaming the Russians for everything. But they are in control. They closed down all the help stations on the autobahn yesterday—it took a friend of mine eleven hours to reach Helmstedt.'

'Are they still closed?' Effi asked. She had the feeling that Eva had only just realised that she was talking to one of Sonja's ex-husbands, and was eager to change the subject.

'I don't think so,' Volker answered her. 'But they could be again tomorrow, and there doesn't seem much we Berliners can do about it. Appealing to the Americans is a waste of time—they're too scared of starting another war.'

'A good thing to be scared of,' Effi argued. 'But we can't complain about what the Russians have done for our business—if it hadn't been for them, there wouldn't have been any new German films. The Americans would have been happy to sell us theirs, and make the occasional one here using their own crews and actors.'

'Like *Foreign Affair*,' Eva suggested.

'Exactly. Marlene was the only German with a decent part.'

'True,' Volker agreed, 'but things seem to be changing over the past few months. Last year the Americans were only interested in propaganda, while the Soviets were encouraging thoughtful movies, but these days the roles seem almost reversed. I've no idea why.'

'Neither have I,' Effi said, having just noticed that the grey-suited Russian was listening intently to their conversation, a dark frown on his face. Russell had actually explained it all in a recent letter—the Russians, having interpreted the American Marshall Plan as a declaration of hostilities, were busy battening down every hatch they could, including the cinematic ones.

Another group called Volker away, and Eva seemed to breathe a sigh of relief. But instead of returning to the subject of Sonja, she asked Effi what she was working on.

'Another film with Ernst Dufring. I agree that the Soviets are becoming less open, but they haven't stopped people like him making thoughtful films. Not yet, at least.'

'What's this one about?'

'It's the history of a family, and one woman in particular—Anna Hofmann. The film's named after her. She starts off as a serving girl in an officer's family around the turn of the century, has a family of her own, loses her husband and son, and ends up making a dress for her granddaughter's graduation—they're the only two left. But it's not depressing, not really. And it asks a lot of questions.'

'And who do you play?'

'The woman in middle age. It's not a big part, but it's a good one. Anna Jesek wrote the screenplay, and some of the lines are heavenly. What about you?'

'Oh, nothing at the moment. No one's making period dramas—I guess the Nazis made too many—and films set in the last few years are pretty easy to clothe—any old rags will do.'

'I suppose so.'

'So what's next?'

'No idea. I've got an audition at the American radio station— they're planning a serial about ordinary Berliners which sounds interesting. And DEFA have offered me a film which doesn't, although I haven't seen the script yet.'

'Will the Russians be happy to let you go?' Eva wondered.

'They don't own me.'

'No, but they can make life difficult for people.'

'Well, if they do, I just might take an extended holiday. I need to spend more time with my daughter anyway.'

'I didn't know you had one.'

'We adopted Rosa after the war. Both her parents had been killed.'

'How old is she?'

'Eleven and a half.'

'A difficult age.' Eva opened her mouth to say something else, closed it, and then took the plunge. 'Look, I don't want to talk about it here, but the Russians were making life difficult for Sonja, and I just have to tell someone what I know. Could we meet for a coffee or something? I know you're busy, but . . .'

'Of course. But why me? I hardly knew her.'

Eva smiled. 'I don't know. I've always thought you were more sensible than most actors.'

A back-handed compliment if ever she'd heard one, Effi thought an hour or so later, as she waited for the tram to carry her back across town. But a coffee with Eva would be pleasant enough. She wondered if the woman had had an affair with Sonja, and what secrets she had to tell. Nothing dangerous, she hoped.

There was no point in worrying about possible problems in the future when she had enough on her plate already. Rosa might be almost twelve, but she could act anything from age six to sixteen. Most of the friends Rosa had made in their neighbourhood were a lot older, and though none of them seemed like bad children, some were definitely on the wild side, with no obvious signs of parental control. At school, where her marks remained high, Rosa's friends seemed mostly the same age as she was.

Effi's sister, who looked after Rosa when Effi worked early or late, insisted there was nothing to worry about, and she was usually right about such things. But these days Zarah's attention was so focused on her new American lover that she wouldn't have noticed a visit from Hitler. And bringing Rosa back to Berlin had always felt risky to Effi as the girl had lost both her parents here.

By this time the number of people waiting for the tram exceeded its capacity, but the only alternative was a six-mile walk. Two Soviet soldiers were standing on the far pavement, ogling a young woman in the queue. She was aware of their attention, Effi noticed, and was looking worried. The soldiers hadn't yet said or done anything, but of course they didn't need to—the legacy of the mass rapes that followed the capture of the city was still very much in most women's minds. And even now, there was nothing to stop those two men walking across the street and simply taking the girl away. The Soviets had no compunction about abducting people from other sectors, and this was their own.

Effi walked over to the young woman, and stood between her and the soldiers. 'Try and ignore them,' she urged.

'That's easy to say,' the girl said. 'I have to get the tram here every day after work, and most days they're there.'

'Well, if they haven't done anything yet, they're probably too nervous,' Effi encouraged her. 'But you could try another way home.'

'I could. But I don't see why I should have to.'

'No,' Effi agreed.

Two trams arrived in tandem, and sucked up most of the waiting crowd. Effi stood in the crowded aisle, catching glimpses of the still-ruined city, asking herself how long it would be before rebuilding started in earnest, before the foreign occupiers all went home, before it was safe for a woman to walk the streets. She knew what John would say: 'Don't hold your breath.'

She got off on Ku'damm, and walked up Fasanen Strasse to the flat which Bill Carnforth had procured for Zarah. It was on the first floor of the middle house in an undamaged row of five, had four spacious rooms, and was only a few minutes' walk from Effi's own apartment on Carmer Strasse.

Zarah was cooking dinner in one of her prettiest dresses. Like most Berliners she had been on a forced diet for several years, and in her case the benefits had almost outweighed the cost—she looked better than she had since her twenties. Through the living room door Effi could see Lothar and Rosa hunched over their homework.

'How was it?' her sister asked.

'Depressing. Are you going out with Bill tonight?'

'I hope so. I've cooked you and Rosa dinner in the hope that you'll babysit Lothar.'

'Oh all right.'

'I won't be late.'

'I said all right.'

'I don't know why you don't both move in while John's away. There's plenty of room.'

'I . . . I don't want to move Rosa again. And John should be back soon.'

'Have you heard from him?'

'No, but they can't keep him down there forever.'

Waking up alone, Gerhard Ströhm remembered that Annaliese was on early shift that week. She must have left at least an hour earlier, but her side of the bed was still warm.

He clambered out, walked to the window and drew back the makeshift curtain. The previous evening's snow had melted away, and the sun was shining in a clear blue sky. Maybe spring had arrived at last.

He made himself a small pot of coffee—one Party privilege that he would find hard to give up—and stood by the window as he sipped from the enamel mug, watching the activity on the street below. The damaged houses opposite were finally being demolished, prior to replacement, and a team of men were piling rubble into three horse-drawn carts. A year ago the workers would all have been women. This had to be progress, of a sort.

Coffee finished, Ströhm washed and dressed, tying a tie in front of the bathroom mirror with his usual lack of enthusiasm. He wasn't sure why he found the ritual such an anathema. Was it that he'd spent the first fifteen years of his working life in ordinary working clothes, and couldn't get used to looking smart? Or had spending the first ten years of his life in America—until his parents' deaths had seen him repatriated—given him a lifelong penchant for informality? Whichever it was, it would no longer do. Party officials were supposed to set an example, particularly the high-ranking ones like himself.

Outside it was colder than he'd expected—the horses' breath should have told him as much—and he set out on his two-kilometre walk to work at a brisker pace than usual. He could have taken the U-Bahn, but Ströhm welcomed the exercise, and the chance each day to notice signs of the city's revival. Some houses here, some offices there, a pothole filled in, a leaking water main repaired. This might be the American sector, but these days Germans ran the local town hall, Social Democrats and Communists in the main, and they were putting Berlin back together.

He worked in the old Reichsbahn Head Office building on Hallesches Ufer which, considering its location so close to the Anhalter Station and goods yards, had suffered remarkably little from the bombing. What damage there was had been quickly repaired by their Soviet liberators, who still ran all of eastern Germany's railways from the building, despite its location in the American sector. Ströhm, like most senior officials who had spent the war either underground or in a camp, had an office on the second floor, overlooking the Landwehrkanal and the elevated tracks running into Potsdamer Station. The third floor was home to the highest echelon of the railway administration, almost all of them comrades now returned from years of exile in Moscow.

Ströhm had barely sat down when his secretary, a young comrade from Leipzig, put her head around the door and told him a Red Star meeting had just been called. As he took the stairs up to the Director's office, Ströhm wondered what the Russians wanted this time. Red Star meetings were only open to Party members above a certain grade.

The conference room was next door to the Director's office, and most of Ströhm's fellow deputies were already seated around the table. There was only one Russian present, Alexander Klementeyev, the so-called Sovcom Liaison Officer, whom everyone knew was MGB, or whatever it was they called themselves these days.

The Director Arnold Marohn had the usual pained look on his face, a consequence, he had once told Ströhm, of eating and drinking like a Russian for six long years—his stomach had never recovered. Now, he outlined the reasons for the meeting, with occasional glances in Klementeyev's direction, as if keen that no one present should be under any illusion as to who had really called it. But no one was, Ströhm thought; they all knew the score. The differences lay in how much they liked it.

Orders had arrived from Karlshorst, the southeastern suburb where the Soviets had their headquarters, to make rail travel between Berlin and the Western zones significantly more difficult. Traffic on the only autobahn had already been seriously affected by the closure of the emergency stations earlier that week, and now it was the turn of the railways. More vehicles would be subject to inspection, more discovered to be unsafe. There would be fewer officials available to check papers, and their increased conscientiousness should guarantee longer queues and delays. And there was more— each department was asked to prepare a series of appropriately graded measures, with everything from minor inconvenience to a total cessation of traffic in mind.

'Are these measures likely to be permanent?' Uli Trenkel asked, not bothering to conceal his disapproval. Like Ströhm, he had spent the Nazi years in Germany, and they shared a jaundiced view of the Russians.

Marohn looked at Klementeyev.

'There are no plans to make them so,' the Russian said carefully. 'A little pressure, to see how the Americans and British react—that's all we're anticipating at the present.' Klementeyev beamed at the assembled company. 'Not too difficult, I'm sure.'

Walking back to his office, Ströhm found himself wondering how the Western allies *would* react. So far, the messages had mostly been mixed, especially from the Americans. Their commander in Berlin, General Clay, seemed only too happy to pick up a gauntlet, but his superiors in Washington were obviously divided, with many openly voicing their unwillingness to fight another war for half a ruined city. If they were shown a graceful way out, Ströhm thought, then they might really leave. And if they did, the Russians would feel more secure, and might eventually depart themselves, leaving their German comrades free to build their own version of socialism.

Improbable perhaps, but surely possible.

Back in his office he spent the next two hours dreaming up reasons for future interruptions. The Western authorities would know what was really happening, but they had to be given scope to pretend.

At lunch, Ströhm shared a table with Trenkel and one of the more pro-Soviet deputies, a middle-aged Dresdener named Hadewicz who had spent the war in Moscow, but had worked on the railways in his youth, and distinguished himself in the anti-Nazi struggles of the early '30s. Hadewicz had the latest Cominform bulletin with him, which gave Ströhm the opportunity to ask them both what they felt about the rumoured disputes between the Russians and the Yugoslavs.

Hadewicz was dismissive—it would soon blow over—while Trenkel just shrugged, as if uninterested.

'But think,' Ströhm persisted, 'if Moscow and Belgrade can reach an agreement on each pursuing their own course in a comradely way, then so can Moscow and Berlin.'

Hadewicz just shook his head, and Trenkel flashed Ströhm a warning glance. Ströhm took the hint and changed the subject, but the conversation, or lack of it, haunted him for most of the afternoon.

Walking to the Elisabeth Hospital later, where Annaliese would be nearing the end of her shift, he realised that the number of comrades with whom he could share a frank conversation had shrunk to almost zero—even those whom he knew shared his views found it safer to say nothing these days. The only person he could really talk to was his friend John Russell, and that was in spite of their political differences. Russell had turned his back on the Party more than twenty years earlier, but their analyses of what made the world tick were similar, and they didn't have to look over their own or each other's shoulder. All of which made for much more productive conversations than those Ströhm endured with his KPD comrades.

Russell, however, was away, and there was no one else. Ströhm loved Annaliese dearly, and her time in an American camp had made her more willing than most Berliners to give the Soviets and their KPD allies the benefit of the doubt, but talk of ideologies bored her.

He was, Ströhm thought, remembering the phrase of a long-dead comrade, suffering from political indigestion. Maybe he should just stop eating contrary ideas, like the ones in the pamphlet he was reading at home, which was an extract from Arthur Koestler's 'The Yogi and the Commissar.' Koestler was also an ex-Communist, and some of his arguments were hard to refute. But even if he was right, and Stalinism was the antithesis of all Marx had intended, what practical relevance did such thoughts have? They were where they were. Both in power and not in power, neither wholly disciples nor wholly slaves. They were struggling with the art of the possible.

Ströhm turned off the canal towards the hospital entrance. As always, the thought of seeing Annaliese cheered him up. He had met her in Thomas Schade's garden, and been smitten at first sight by her smile. They had both been invited to a family picnic, he by Russell, who had once been married to Schade's late sister, she by Russell's actress wife Effi, who had met and befriended her during the war.

Schade was a bourgeois businessman and SPD supporter, but a decent man according to John, and Ströhm had seen nothing to contradict that assessment. If all the Social Democrats were like Thomas, then half their problems would be solved.

He saw Annaliese the moment he passed through the doors. She and Effi were sitting in the patient waiting area, sharing something that made them both laugh. Annaliese jumped up when she saw Ströhm, and enfolded him in a happy embrace. Effi followed suit, with her usual spontaneous warmth.

'I just dropped in on my way home,' she told him. 'Mostly to invite the two of you to Thomas's house for lunch on Sunday week. He doesn't trust the post anymore, and he didn't dare ring you at work, in case someone listened in and thought you were plotting with the SPD.'

Ströhm smiled. 'As if. And we'd love to come, wouldn't we?' he asked Annaliese.

'I've already accepted.'

'And you can bring us up-to-date on Soviet intentions,' Effi said, tongue in cheek. She liked Ströhm, but he was sometimes too serious for words.

'Of course. Will John be there?'

She shook her head. 'Not as far as I know. He's still in Trieste.'

'What's he doing down there?'

'Researching a story on Nazi escape routes. Or so he claims. Every letter he sends me, he boasts about the beautiful weather. He keeps saying he'll be back in a week or so . . .' She changed tack. 'Gerhard, I went to Sonja Strehl's funeral on Tuesday, and there were all sorts of rumours doing the rounds. About how she died, I mean. You haven't heard anything?'

'No.'

'I just wondered. She wasn't exactly a friend, but I knew her for a long time, and I liked her.'

'I'll keep my ears open,' Ströhm promised. 'But don't expect too much. The last rumour I heard was about a missing coal train, which someone claimed the French had taken back to France. He might have been right—we still haven't found it.'

At the villa above Trieste, Thursday proved depressingly similar to previous days. Perhaps even less entertaining, as Kuznakov and his interrogators were each growing increasingly irritated with the other's refusal to give way. Dempsey and Farquhar-Smith wouldn't move the Russian westwards until he'd proved he had something to give; and Kuznakov refused to offer anything tangible until he was safe, as he put it, in American territory. Trieste, though nominally under joint control, was apparently too close to Yugoslavia to qualify. 'Full of MGB,' Kuznakov insisted, with almost a hint of pride. He was more than ready to talk about life in the Soviet Union, and here his script seemed somewhat inconsistent, mixing fervent denunciations of communism with occasional, almost compulsive, mentions of Soviet achievements. And throughout it all Kuznakov puffed away on his dreadful cigarettes, of which he seemed to have an endless supply.

The only excitement of the day came late, when a vehicle was suddenly heard entering the compound. This time Kuznakov did look alarmed, and so did Farquhar-Smith. 'It's the CIA guy,' Dempsey told them, 'I forgot to tell you he was coming. It's Russell here he wants to see.'

'What for?' Russell asked, heart sinking.

'He'll fill you in. We might as well wrap this up for today.' Dempsey went to the door, summoned a soldier to take Kuznakov back to his room, and disappeared. A minute later he was back. 'The Colonel'll see you on the terrace,' he told Russell.

The man in question was tall, grey-haired, probably in his early forties. He was wearing civilian clothes—quite a smart suit, in fact.

He rose from a wrought-iron chair, offered Russell a hand, and introduced himself as, 'Bob Crowell, CIA.'

The terrace was at the side of the villa, overlooking a steep drop, and with a distant view of the sea through the pines.

As Russell sat down, a soldier appeared with two bottles of beer. 'If you don't want one, I'll drink both,' Crowell told him. Despite being middle-aged, he had the air of a grown-up kid.

'I think I could manage one,' Russell said. 'So what brings you here?'

Crowell ignored the question. 'How's it going with Kuznakov?' he wanted to know, as if Russell was doing the interrogating.

'He's eager to leave the Balkans behind. I don't think we'll get anything out of him until he feels he's on safer ground.' Russell found himself wondering which story Kuznakov would end up telling them, that the Red Army was ready and willing to attack, or that the threat was all in the Western powers' imagination? Did Stalin want to scare the Americans, or provide them with a false sense of security? Not that it would be false—as his friend Ströhm had pointed out, what country intent on moving its armies further west ripped up half the European railway network for reparations?

Crowell shrugged. 'Ah well, I expect that's what we'll do then. But I have another job for you. It's all been cleared with your control in Berlin, by the way. Nothing dangerous,' Crowell added, mistaking the look on Russell's face. 'Just a bit of escort duty—what with the Italian elections, we've run out of manpower.'

'I thought they'd been bought and paid for,' Russell said dryly, and immediately wished he hadn't. Not because it was untrue— the only real question was whether they'd used cash the Nazis had confiscated from their victims—but because he really had to rein himself in. Like Shchepkin had said, Russell knew he should offer at least the pretence of commitment.

He needn't have worried in this instance as Crowell just ignored his comment. 'There's a Russian—Ukrainian actually, but he speaks Russian—who we're taking out. Of Europe, that is. He's being brought down from Salzburg to Udine on Saturday—you know where that is?'

Russell nodded.

'Well, you'll meet him there. But before you leave Trieste, you have to collect a visa for him.' Crowell took a folded piece of paper from his pocket, which Russell opened. The name and address belonged to Father Kozniku—Draganović's man in Trieste.

'The local forger?' Russell asked flippantly. He was curious as to whether Crowell would come clean about the Rat Line.

'No, the papers are official,' was all the other man said.

Russell raised an eyebrow.

'You don't need to know,' Crowell said shortly.

'Okay.'

'Just get to Udine, the Hotel Delle Alpi, and babysit the man for one night. Someone will collect him the following morning.' Crowell reached for the briefcase beside his chair, and extracted a large envelope. 'You'll find a DP passport in there, some supportive papers, fifteen hundred US dollars for Father Kozniku, and some lira for your own expenses. When you pick up the visa, check the details against the passport, just in case someone fucked up. We've asked the Army for a jeep, but they haven't got back to us yet. Someone'll contact you.'

'Who is he? Or do I call him Mr. X?'

'His name is Maksym Palychko.'

'That sounds vaguely familiar. And not in a good way.'

'I'm told some of the tales about him have been exaggerated,' Crowell said. 'But that's neither here nor there. He'll be more use to us in America than he would be gumming up a tribunal or rotting in a Soviet grave. So our job is to get him there. Right?'

Russell nodded, and drained the last of his beer. The sun was still shining in a pure blue sky, the clouds all in his mind.

Later that evening, Russell was early for his appointment with Shchepkin. The Russian, when he arrived, had instructions for Russell—he would be meeting a Comrade Serov ahead of his trip to Belgrade. A note would be left at his hostel with the time and place.

Russell nodded his agreement, and asked Shchepkin if he'd heard of Maksym Palychko.

The Russian gave him a look. 'What a name to drop on such a beautiful night.'

'So who the hell was he? I know I've heard the name before, but I can't remember where.'

'He called himself a Ukrainian nationalist, and I expect he still does, even though most Ukrainians would be as happy to shoot him as I would. I don't know exactly where he came from—somewhere in the western Ukraine—but as a young man he fought for the Whites in the Civil War, and in the '20s he joined the group that became the OUN—the Organisation of Ukrainian Nationalists. They made no headway in the USSR, but they grew quite strong in Poland, and Palychko was one of the men who assassinated Pilsudski's Interior Minister in, I can't remember, was it 1934? He was caught, given the death penalty, but then reprieved—he was still in jail in Krakow when the Germans arrived. They released him, and he joined in the celebrations—several thousand Jews were tortured and murdered over the next few weeks. And he must have stood out, because the Nazis sent him to Gestapo school. When the Germans invaded us, the OUN went in with the *einsatzgruppen*, and did more than their share of the killing. They were expecting to be put in charge of Ukraine, but Hitler didn't trust them that much, and those OUN leaders who complained were arrested. Not Palychko, though. He managed to stay on good terms with the Germans, mostly by selling them information about us and his former friends. He put together a small army of his own, and waged a parallel war against our partisans. You've heard of Lidice, Oradour?'

'Villages the Nazis destroyed?'

'Along with their inhabitants. Everyone has heard of them,' Shchepkin added, a rare hint of bitterness in his voice. 'But Olyka, Mlinov, Grushvitsy, and at least ten others . . . no one in the West knows about them, but they were all villages accused of helping our partisans, and then destroyed by Palychko and his men. The OUN tortured and raped whenever the mood took them, and they left no one alive.

'When the Nazis retreated, Palychko went with them, and somehow managed to disappear, though half the world was looking for him. Until this moment I assumed the Americans would feel honour-bound to hand a man like that over.'

Russell winced. 'They don't. I'm one link of the chain passing him out of Europe.'

They walked on in silence for several seconds.

'I can tell you where . . .' Russell began.

'Don't,' Shchepkin interjected. 'I don't trust myself, and we can't risk it. We'll have to let him go, at least for the moment. But you must be careful. The Americans are hopeless at keeping secrets, and word may be out.'

'Oh good,' Russell murmured. Crowell, he remembered, had assured him there was 'nothing dangerous' involved in this particular job.

A Walk into the Future

Effi arrived at the RIAS building on Winterfeldstrasse a few minutes early, which would have surprised most of her friends. She had taken the U-Bahn from Zoo, and her dress—one of her finest—had drawn several admiring glances on the train. 'Why do you care what you look like,' Rosa had asked with her usual maddening logic, 'when it's an audition for radio?'

Which was true enough, but the man conducting the audition—it was bound to be a man—wouldn't be at the other end of a wireless connection.

His name was Alfred Henninger, and she assumed from his accent and fluency that he was an American of German descent. He was about forty, with short but untidy blond hair, and a habit of flexing his fingers as he spoke. 'Have you done any radio?' was his first question.

'Never,' Effi answered cheerfully.

'But you're willing?'

'Eager, you might say. I really liked the outline and script you sent me.'

'Oh, good. We have a name for it now: "The Islanders". In a Soviet sea,' he added in explanation.

'I got it.'

'Of course. I'm always spelling it out for the people back home—they don't understand what it feels like here. Anyway . . . the part we have in mind for you is the *portierfrau*, Frau Dorfner. It's not the most glamorous role, of course . . .'

'It's the one I was hoping for,' Effi told him truthfully. Trudi Dorfner was a character that most Berliners would instantly recognise, but the writer had managed much more than a stereotype.

'Oh excellent. Well, let's go through to the studio and have you do a reading.'

Ensconced in front of a microphone, Effi went through one scene, with Henninger voicing the other part.

'Excellent,' the producer said again once they were finished. 'You, I mean, not me. We'll be broadcasting live, of course. You'll be okay with that?'

'I've done a lot of theatre,' Effi assured him. The hours might be a problem—she wanted to spend more time with Rosa, not less—but there was no point in worrying about things like that until there was a contract to sign.

It had all been a little too easy, she thought. After three years of dealing with DEFA and their Soviet backers, Henninger had seemed refreshingly straightforward. Famous last words, she told herself.

She was back home just in time for the DEFA studio car—asking it to pick her up at RIAS had seemed like tempting fate, and she'd resisted the temptation to say she'd make her own way. Journeys through the Soviet sector were normally safe, although women were still sometimes assaulted by drunken Red Army soldiers, and more lasting abductions were far from unknown. Before signing up for this film, Effi and the other Western-sector-based actors working on *Anna Hofmann* had insisted on being chauffeured to and fro, and the Russians, rather to everyone's surprise, had conjured up a fleet of old government cars to do the ferrying. The one she was sitting in now had probably taken Goebbels on philandering expeditions.

They reached the new Weisensee studio complex just as the cast and crew broke for lunch, and Effi spent the next hour in makeup, having the years added on. When the girl was finished, Effi smiled at herself in the mirror. This was how she had looked for long stretches of the war, when the world knew her as Erna von Freiwald, dressmaker and milliner. In those days she had applied the makeup herself.

She only had one scene to play that afternoon, but it seemed to take forever. It was with her supposed granddaughter, but the young actor playing the part just couldn't get her lines right. The girl was nice enough, but not very talented, and Effi found herself wondering how she'd landed the part. A Party official's daughter, or a Party official's object of lust. She was growing as cynical as John.

She was just removing the last of her makeup when a DEFA secretary put her head around the dressing-room door, and told Effi that someone from the Soviet Propaganda Department wanted a word before she went home.

'About what?' she asked.

The woman shrugged. 'He's waiting in the manager's office.'

'All right. But don't let the car leave without me.' Effi had no idea what the Russian might want, but it was unlikely to be her autograph.

The official in question was one she hadn't seen before, which made her doubt that he worked for the Propaganda Department—she had attended enough of their receptions over the past few years. He was a short and burly man, probably in his thirties, who quickly stood up as she entered the room, smiled as he offered his hand, and introduced himself as Victor Samoshenko.

'So how can I help you?' Effi asked, more abruptly than she intended.

He reached for a large envelope on the desk behind him. 'This is the screenplay that you've been expecting.'

'Oh. Thank you.' *A Walk into the Future* was stencilled on the cover. 'Is there any reason why it wasn't sent in the usual way?'

'Only one. Please, take a seat. Comrade Tulpanov decided that a personal delivery would give someone—myself—the opportunity to stress how important we feel this film will be, and how important your own involvement will prove in making it a success.'

Effi gave him a sceptical look. 'I'm flattered, of course. But there's no shortage of good actors in Berlin, so I don't quite understand why the Minister thinks I'm indispensable.'

Samoshenko's smile didn't waver. 'I think you underestimate yourself, and your, shall we say, symbolic importance to many Berliners, as both a famous film star and a heroine of the resistance.'

Her acting skills, Effi noticed, were obviously neither here nor there. 'I'm looking forward to reading it,' she said non-committally, picking up the envelope.

'There are also two copies of a contract,' the Russian continued. 'The suggested fee is of course open to negotiation, but we think it's generous.' He paused, while she took a look.

It was probably the most she'd ever been offered for a film, but then Goebbels had been notoriously stingy with actresses who wouldn't sleep with him. 'It is,' she agreed.

'Payable in American dollars,' Samoshenko added, as if that would be the clincher.

'I'll start reading it tonight,' she promised. If only to discover why the film, and her participation, seemed so vital to Tulpanov's Ministry. She started to rise.

'One more matter,' Samoshenko said, as she gathered up her bag.

'Yes?'

'Your adopted daughter, Rosa.'

There was a way in which he accented the 'adopted' that sent a chill through Effi's heart. 'Yes?' she said again, fighting to keep the fear from her voice.

'She has extraordinary talent.'

'She has.' Rosa had been compulsively drawing people and scenes since Effi had inherited her, aged eight, in the past few weeks of the war. One drawing of a Red Army soldier playing with a German child had appeared in a Soviet magazine, and become an almost iconic image of the Soviet liberation. Not in Berlin, of course, where the Soviet-built Tomb of the Unknown Soldier was known as the Tomb of the Unknown Rapist, but almost everywhere else in the civilised world. Stalin's government had even paid her one tranche of royalties.

'A talent that can hardly be nurtured in Berlin today,' Samoshenko suggested. 'In Moscow and Leningrad we have world-famous institutes of art which could really help her development.'

Effi could hardly believe it. 'You're asking us to send an eleven-year-old girl off alone to a foreign country? You must know what she's been through.'

'Yes, of course. And no, not alone. You would be expected to accompany her—we do make films at home, you know. And your husband, too. He's an American journalist, I understand. I'm sure there are many American papers who would welcome a fully accredited Moscow correspondent.'

Effi didn't know what to say. She decided to be diplomatic. 'I appreciate the offer,' she began. 'And I know how wonderful Soviet education is, and the value your country puts on culture. Instinct tells me she's still too young. But I will discuss it with my husband. He's away at the moment, but when he comes back . . .'

'Of course,' Samoshenko interrupted, still smiling. He shook her hand again, and held the door open.

The car was still waiting outside, along with the chauffeur and three impatient colleagues.

'What was that all about?' one of the women asked Effi.

'My daughter,' she said, in a tone guaranteed to deter further questions. As they drove back towards the centre of the city, she went through the conversation again in her head. There had been no threats, so why did she feel so threatened? Was it merely the thought of losing Rosa?

She told herself the whole business was more absurd than menacing. Was it possible that Tulpanov's people didn't know that the Berlin MGB considered John one of their own? How would they feel about the Propaganda Ministry relocating one of their people to Moscow, where the only people he could spy on was them?

No, she told herself, there was no need to worry. They needed John in Berlin, and he needed his wife and daughter with him.

That evening Effi fussed over Rosa more than usual, and received several bemused looks in return. But on the following morning she suffered a serious shock. With another afternoon start at the studio, she spent part of the morning cleaning the flat, and one of the items she tidied away was Rosa's latest drawing book. Looking through it, Effi found several pictures of Rosa's neighbourhood friends, most of them adolescents, three or four years older than her. Many subjects were smoking, which didn't surprise Effi, but there were also bottles in evidence, which she doubted contained lemonade. And then there was a couple kissing, sweetly drawn. And then a girl with small pubescent breasts, sitting astride a naked boy.

'Oh God,' Effi said out loud.

She needed to talk to someone. Not Zarah.

She rang up Thomas, hoping he might be home. He was, and he had a couple of hours to spare before some meeting or other.

'So what's the emergency,' he asked, when she let him in half an hour later.

She showed him the drawing book.

He went through the pictures one by one, shaking his head,

almost in wonder, at the one which had stopped Effi in her tracks. 'Christ, she can draw,' he said.

'That's hardly the point,' she almost snapped.

'No, of course not. I'm sorry. But what can I say? Where did you find this—had she hidden it?'

'On the table.'

'So she doesn't think she's doing anything wrong. She's just drawing what she sees, like she always has.'

'So the point is more what she's seeing.'

'Which comes down to the company she's keeping.'

'I can't keep her locked up.'

'No, of course not. I'm sorry, Effi—I have no answers. Other than talking to her, listening to her. Maybe she needs professional help—I don't know. She's troubled, but with her history it would be strange if she wasn't. And these pictures . . . Well, they're full of innocence. I don't think you should worry too much.'

'I suppose I should talk to her about sex. When did Hanna explain it all to Lotte?'

'I seem to remember it was when she started to menstruate. She started young.'

Effi looked down at the table, shaking her head.

'You could tell Rosa that you'd like to meet her friends, and ask her to bring them back here.'

'How would that help?'

'They'd know that Rosa had adult protection. I'm not saying she needs it, but it couldn't hurt.'

Effi nodded. 'And it would probably be better if John was here too. I wish he'd come home. But thanks, Thomas. I think I panicked a bit when I saw the pictures, but I feel a lot better now.' She got up. 'Why don't you tell me how you are while I make us some tea.'

'Rushed off my feet,' he told her.

'So what happened to the easy life you were promising yourself? When the Russians bought the business you were telling us that all you wanted was a few years' rest.'

'Well, I had a few days off, and just when boredom was setting in an old friend suggested I go into politics.'

'You're loving it, aren't you?'

He grinned. 'A little. In reality, it's not much different—I've still got Americans pulling one way, and Russians the other.'

'How are the family? Is Lotte still working at Radio Berlin?'

'Yes. She finally joined the KPD last week, and she's already a hardliner.'

'I remember when she had pictures of the Führer on her bedroom walls.'

'That's my daughter. She obviously has a knack for being on the wrong side of history.' He smiled. 'But she works hard these days. I'm proud of her.'

'And Hanna?'

'Busy in the garden. She spent the winter planning the biggest vegetable plot in Dahlem, and now's the time to make it happen. If you hadn't called I'd be out there digging.'

'No wonder you hurried over.'

'You'll see it all on Sunday week. If the Russians ever cut the city off we'll all need to take turns guarding the vegetables. Day and night.'

Once Thomas had left, Effi felt relieved enough by their conversation to pick up the screenplay of *A Walk into the Future*. The story, as she already knew, concerned an American Zone-based company's attempted theft of new prosthetic-limb technology from their own subsidiary in the Soviet Zone. The company was interested in making money, the subsidiary in helping those who had lost limbs in the war, and the former was eventually thwarted by two trade-union workers, a widower in the West and a widow in the East, who knew each other from years before, when they worked together in the anti-fascist resistance.

As a story, Effi supposed it was just about feasible, but then so were many of those dreamed up by Goebbels' cinematic minions. The characterisation did nothing to help—even the leads were cardboard cut-outs—and the writing in general lived down to the plot, with both leading characters prone to spout slogans as they turned their hopeful gazes towards the inevitable socialist future. All in all, the script felt as if someone had gone through it ruthlessly, excising any hint of nuance or shades of grey. Even the title was dreadful. Effi wanted no part of it.

Russell visited Father Kozniku's office, which was close to the San Giusto cathedral, late on Friday afternoon. A buxom Italian woman with a wonderful mane of black hair—Artucci's Luciana, presumably—showed him through to the inner sanctum, where the priest himself, a corpulent figure with a bulging red face and almost black eyes, was busy copying figures into a leather-bound ledger.

'I'm here for the Balanchuk papers,' Russell announced, in reply to the look of enquiry. Roman Balanchuk was the name on Palychko's new passport.

'You're new,' Kozniku noted, opening a desk drawer and removing a small sheaf of papers.

Taking the seat that hadn't been offered, Russell reached inside his jacket for the documents Crowell had given him—the passport and fake baptismal certificate—and the wad of Benjamin Franklins.

The priest waved away the baptismal certificate—so much for Draganović's Catholics-only strictures—and didn't even bother to count the hundred-dollar notes. He even looked mildly irked when Russell took time to check the details on the new Colombian visa against those on the American-forged passport. They tallied perfectly.

'The sailing ticket will be waiting in Genoa,' the priest said. 'A pleasure to do business with you,' he finished with, attention already back on his ledger.

Walking back down the hill in search of dinner, Russell found himself wishing that Shchepkin would suddenly appear at his shoulder. There were so few people who shared his utter dismay at what had happened to Europe over the past thirty years.

Russell drank too much that evening, and felt like hell when one of the Marko's daughters woke him the following morning with news that an American soldier had come to see him. The lieutenant in question had scarcely credible news—TRUST, the optimistically acronymed Trieste United States Troops, had run out of jeeps, and Russell would have to reach Udine by other means of transport. There was a military travel pass for him, allowing free passage on all public transport inside Zone A, but once outside the Free Territory, he would have to pay his own way. This information was delivered between disapproving sniffs, as the young man circled Russell's room, examining his belongings like a Kripo officer seeking out evidence of crimes as yet unknown. Only Effi's publicity shot stopped him. 'Your wife?' he asked, as if he could hardly credit it.

'Yes,' Russell admitted. The word still sounded strange, though almost a year had passed since they'd finally got married. They had always said they would wait until love was the only reason, but it had been Rosa's adoption which forced them into it. The love of a child.

The lieutenant stared at the picture once more, probably hoping to find a flaw, and then abruptly made for the door. 'Return the pass to the Miramar HQ as soon as you get back,' was his parting shot.

Russell lifted his battered suitcase on to the bed, and added a change of clothes to the documents in the bottom. He wasn't that sorry about the jeep—he had always loved sitting in trains—but the journey would probably now take most of the day, and he ought to be on his way.

The walk to the station took fifteen minutes, the wait for a train considerably longer. A Venice service eventually carried him up the coast to the Italian border, where the guard demanded payment for an onward ticket to Udine. A change was required at Monfalcone, where a three-hour wait allowed him time to find a reasonable lunch. It was almost three by the time his connection—two ancient coaches behind a rusty tank locomotive—started off up the Isonzo valley, skirting the first of what soon seemed an endless series of First War cemeteries. After a lengthy stop in Gorizia, the train slowly puffed its way northwestward across the southern edge of the Alpine foothills, crossing stream after swollen stream rushing south toward the sea. Once Russell allowed himself to accept the lack of haste, he found himself enjoying the journey—after Trieste and its ludicrous politics, here was the earth reborn again, with all the bright greens of spring.

He had never been to Udine, which was larger than he'd imagined, and seemed, from the back of a cab at least, to be blessed with a wealth of interesting architecture. Another time perhaps.

The Hotel Delle Alpi was impressive, and more luxurious than he'd come to expect when American Intelligence was footing the bill. It and its proprietor, who introduced himself as Boris, and who looked more German than Italian, had survived the war apparently unscathed, a circumstance that Russell always—and, he admitted, often unfairly—considered grounds for suspicion.

Only one room had been booked for himself and Mister Balanchuk, which was much more in line with the usual stingy CIC practice. And it was barely big enough for two, let alone the three which Boris suggested. The rooms on either side were taken, but after only a brief show of annoyance, the proprietor found him two adjoining rooms farther down the corridor. Babysitting a human monster was bad enough, and Russell was damned if he was going to share a bed with him.

The hotel restaurant looked less than inspiring, but it was already growing dark outside, and he supposed he should be there when Palychko arrived. As it happened, the food was exquisite, the wine as good as any he'd drunk since pre-war days. Russell lingered over coffee and brandy, reading with one ear cocked for a vehicle outside, but when the lobby clock chimed eleven he decided to call it a day.

It felt like he'd only just closed his eyes when someone knocked on his door. 'Your friends have arrived,' Boris half-shouted.

Two apparent soldiers were drinking in the bar, one a CIC Major whom Russell recognised from a meeting in Salzburg a year or so earlier, the other Maksym Palychko, who was dressed as a GI corporal. He was shorter than Russell had imagined from the picture, with an unexpectedly appealing smile. The long white scar on the neck seemed the only predictable thing about him.

They all shook hands like civilised people, and the Major—whose name, Russell remembered, was Hanningham—poured Russell a generous measure of Scotch.

'Any problems?' Russell asked, for want of anything better.

'None,' the Major said cheerfully. 'I think everyone manning that border is on our payroll.'

Palychko was looking around the empty bar.

Russell introduced himself in Russian. 'Or would you rather use German?' he added in that language.

'*Deutsch*,' the Ukrainian said shortly. He drained his glass. 'It's been a long day,' he added.

Either Hanningham had no qualms about sharing the bed 'big enough for three' with Palychko, or he was too tired to care, and soon Russell was lying in his own. They met again at breakfast in the wood-panelled dining room with its distant view of the mountains, and after half an hour of Hanningham's overweening arrogance, Russell was beginning to wonder which man was the more objectionable of the two. The mass murderer Palychko just sat admiring the view, offering the occasional friendly smile. Only when the American's jeep had finally shrunk to a dot on the road heading north, did he offer more than a single syllable. 'Where did you spend the war?'

Russell had no desire to tell this man his life story. 'In the States, and then with the US Army in France and Germany, as a war correspondent.' All of which was true enough, if hardly the complete picture. 'How about you?'

'In Poland and Ukraine.'

'Doing what?'

'Fighting communists. And losing.'

'Any regrets?' Russell couldn't help asking.

'You know who I really am, don't you?'

'Yes.'

He offered up that smile again. 'That's more than I do.'

Oh shit, Russell thought, a psychopath with an identity crisis.

It must have shown on his face. 'My father was a priest,' Palychko said, as if by way of explanation. He looked at Russell. 'Were you old enough to fight in the First War?'

'Yes.'

'So you know what men can do to each other.'

'I still don't know why,' Russell said, getting drawn in despite himself.

'Neither do I. That's what I meant—evil is a mystery, even to those who do it. Especially those.'

'That's why we have courts.'

Palychko shook his head. 'Do you really believe after everything you've seen and heard that men are capable of judging their brothers?'

'What's the alternative—universal absolution?'

'Perhaps. I don't know.'

Moving to the lounge when two women arrived to clean the dining room, Russell found an English newspaper from several days earlier. A report from the paper's correspondent in Palestine claimed, with what appeared good authority, that Jewish fighters had massacred nearly all the Arab inhabitants of a village named Deir Yassin. And so it went on, he thought, remembering Shchepkin's list of villages that his current companion had laid to waste. Now even Jews were doing it.

'Do you play chess?' Palychko asked him. He had found the set reserved for the use of guests.

'Badly,' Russell said discouragingly, just as Boris appeared in the doorway.

'I've just had a telephone call,' the hotel proprietor told Russell. 'I'm to tell you that there's been a hold-up, and that your friend won't be here until tomorrow morning. I assume that means you need the rooms for another night?'

Russell sighed. 'I suppose we do.' He explained the delay to Palychko, who seemed neither surprised nor upset.

'So how about a game?' he asked.

'Why not?'

It took the Ukrainian about ten minutes to checkmate him, and the subsequent re-match was shorter still. 'You really do play badly,' Palychko agreed belatedly.

After finishing lunch an hour or so later, Russell was wondering what to do with the afternoon when the Ukrainian suggested a walk. 'I'd like to find a church,' he said, and Russell was still swallowing an unspoken gibe about the other man's need to confess when Palychko admitted that this was indeed his intention. 'I don't think I'll be running into any enemies by accident,' he added, when Russell hesitated.

They found a church on the road heading into the centre, and the first priest they found was willing to take Palychko's confession. Russell briefly wondered how they were going to understand each other, settled for being grateful that he wasn't the listener, and sat in a convenient pew for twenty minutes, wondering whether confessing one's sins really was good for the soul, or was just another way for the church to keep its flock under some sort of control.

When Palychko eventually reappeared, they decided on walking on into town. 'I'd like to try a real Italian coffee,' the Ukrainian told Russell, as they both surveyed the cafés spread around the central piazza. One chosen, they took a table outside, ordered espressos, and stared at the lovely old buildings around them. 'I shall hate America,' Palychko said, almost wistfully.

'Then why are you going?' Russell asked unnecessarily.

Palychko took the question seriously. 'There are too many Europeans who want me dead. Your bosses in Washington actually want me alive, at least until I've told them all that I know. But I shall still hate it.'

Two young boys stopped by their table, hands outstretched, and Russell was still reaching for his pocket when Palychko handed them a small wad of lira. They gave him disbelieving looks, and ran off across the piazza exchanging joyous shrieks.

'How much did you give them?' Russell asked.

Palychko shrugged. 'No idea. After we crossed the border your Major Hanningham said I needed "pocket money", and handed it over. But what do I need it for? You people won't let me starve.'

Back at the hotel, they took to their rooms for naps, then met again for dinner like ordinary travelling acquaintances. Russell kept waiting for the war criminal to emerge from behind the mask, but

Palychko seemed set on being friendly, to Russell, the waiters, the world. Only once did he hint at something else, scanning the room and remarking with a hint of surprise: 'Italians look like Jews, don't they?' I suppose that's why they protected them from the Germans.' Seeing Russell's face, he smiled again. 'I shall have to do better in America, won't I?

They said their goodnights around ten, but Russell needed more than an hour's reading before he dropped off, and his sleep was both fitful and dream-laden. At least the sun was shining when he woke up, and with any luck enough Italian trains were running on Sundays to see him back in Trieste that day.

The first sign that things had gone awry was the lack of response when he knocked on Palychko's door. The second was the door not being locked, the third the sight that greeted him when he stepped inside.

The Ukrainian was laid out naked on his bed, a mass of congealed blood where his genitals had been. These were stuffed in his blood-ringed mouth, where the tongue used to be. This was lying on his stomach.

Which helped explain why Russell hadn't heard anything.

Four Cyrillic letters had been incised in Palychko's forehead—after death, if the lack of smudging was any guide. The language was Ukrainian, but the characters which ended the word were the same in Russian, D and A in English. He would have to look the others up, but JUDA—the Russian for Judas—seemed a pretty good bet. The Jews and the communists hadn't caught up with Palychko, but his old buddies had.

At least the blood was almost dry—the perpetrator or perpetrators would be long gone. They hadn't only known where to find him, but also how to reach his room without sounding an alarm, which suggested careful surveillance and planning. Someone had spilled the beans—could it have been Shchepkin? It was possible, but the Russian had a purely selfish interest in Russell's survival, and he couldn't have known they'd be in separate rooms. Russell could always ask him of course, but he'd never been able to tell when Shchepkin was lying.

The important question was what to do now. An immediate check-out seemed the most appealing prospect, but he knew his American superiors wouldn't commend him for it. On the contrary. They had been using this hotel for several years, and wouldn't want it compromised. More importantly, any sort of police involvement would open a very deep can of worms. He had to get the body out of there, and since he couldn't carry it out into the countryside on his shoulders, he would need help. Boris would have to earn whatever it was the Americans were paying him.

He gave Palychko one last look. If anyone deserved to die like that, this man probably did, but pity welled up nevertheless. Russell stepped out into the corridor, locked the door behind him, and went in search of the hotel proprietor.

Boris, when told the unfortunate news, was surprised, annoyed and alarmed in roughly that order, but he didn't try to walk away from the problem. His face turned white when he saw the body, but a quick retch in the water basin more or less restored him. That would have been his own reaction before the First War, Russell thought. Bodies were supposed to be in one piece.

'Wrap him in his blanket,' Boris said, once he'd recovered, 'I'll get another.' Russell had rolled up Palychko and the bloody sheets by the time the proprietor returned with a second layer and some twine to tie up the ends. 'I could call a staff meeting in the lounge,' Boris suggested. 'Once they're all in there, we could carry him down the back stairs and out to the hotel van without being seen.'

'You're a natural,' Russell told him.

And the plan worked. Fifteen long minutes later, the two of them were manhandling their huge Christmas cracker down the back stairs, out through the empty kitchens, and into the back of the van. 'You wait in the cab,' Boris said. 'I'll tell them the meeting has been cancelled.'

He was back almost instantly, and soon they were on the road heading north.

'Where should we go?' Boris wanted to know.

'You must know the area. Just find us a quiet place, off the main road, where we can dump him.'

'All right.' A few minutes later he turned the van up a narrow side road. 'Are we going to bury him?'

'That sounds like a good idea.'

'But we don't have a spade.'

'Then I guess we can't. Where does this road go?'

'To a farm eventually. There are others off to either side.'

Looking right, Russell could see smoke rising from a distant chimney. 'Just find a place to turn around,' he said. 'And we'll dump him in a ditch.'

Boris did as suggested, but after they'd unwrapped the parcel, rolled the corpse into a stream bed, and covered it with branches torn from a nearby bush, he still seemed unhappy. 'What will the police think when they find him?'

'If they bother to think at all . . . Just another victim of the war, I suppose. Aren't the local partisans still settling scores?'

'He doesn't look Italian.'

'True, but there's nothing on the body to identify it, and no one local will know who it is.'

'What about the blankets and sheets?'

'Call another staff meeting and stick them in the hotel boiler.'

'I suppose . . .'

'Look, if worse came to worst, just say you found him in his room and brought him out here to save the hotel some bad publicity. It's not as if you killed him. All they'll do is slap your wrist.'

'You don't know our police.'

'Maybe. If there's any real trouble, get hold of your American friends. They'll sort it out if they have to. He was their contraband.'

'You're right,' Boris said, as they turned back on to the main road. 'Bastard Americans.'

Russell's second meeting with Bob Crowell was less convivial than the first. Not that Crowell said much—he just sat there looking disappointed. His colleague, a younger man named Tad Youklis with a shaven head and angry blue eyes, did all of the talking, and seemed incapable of mincing his words.

Russell had arrived at the safe house expecting another day of Kuznakov's evasions, but the Russian plant had been spirited away over the weekend, and by now was doubtless lapping up all the wine, women and song that the CIA could deliver. And instead of Dempsey and Farquhar-Smith, he had found Crowell and Youklis lying in wait, demanding a thorough accounting of Palychko's grisly demise.

Russell saw no reason to leave anything out, or otherwise play with the truth, which might have been a mistake.

'What do you call a babysitter whose baby gets tortured and killed?' Youklis asked him sarcastically.

'I don't know—is it a riddle?'

'A fucking moron, that's what.'

'So fire me.'

Youklis gave him a contemptuous look. 'What the hell were you doing sleeping in a separate room?'

'Surviving, as it turned out.'

'Here and now, that doesn't seem like such a great outcome.'

Russell just about kept his temper. 'May I remind you that Bob here told me there was—and I quote—"nothing dangerous" about this job. There was no mention of potential assassins. And while we're at it—how did they know where to find him? Northern Italy's not exactly awash with Ukrainian death squads, so my guess is that one of your people let the cat out of the bag. And probably for the best of reasons, that they didn't enjoy seeing the bastard escape justice.'

'It sounds like you were tempted yourself. And maybe succumbed.'

'I didn't tell anyone,' Russell lied.

'But you're happy enough that he's dead.'

'I don't consider him a great loss to humanity, no.' Unbidden, Russell had a mental picture of Palychko's fingers, poised above the chess board.

'Well, he's a real loss to our cause.'

'You might consider what that says about us.'

Youklis flashed Russell another angry look. 'It says that we do what we have to.'

'Yeah? Well you don't do it very well. And I don't like being blamed for other people's incompetence. Are we done here?'

'Just about. I'm told that our people in Berlin put a high value on your services, but I'm fucked if I can see why.'

'Then send me back there. What do you need me for here now that Kuznakov's gone?'

'You have a job to do in Belgrade, I believe. If you manage that better than you've managed this, then we'll think about it. But I'm not making any promises.'

Russell got to his feet. Another retort came to mind, but why waste any more breath?

* * *

Monday morning in Berlin, and it looked as if spring had been deferred again. A blanket of grey cloud hung just above the rooftops, or, in many cases, the tops still awaiting new roofs. The news was just as depressing: Over the weekend the Soviets had suddenly cut off the Western sectors' milk supply, claiming a sudden shortfall of petrol and labour. The Western authorities were told they were welcome to pick up the milk themselves, but while they scrambled to find the necessary fleet of trucks, several thousand babies were going hungry.

Few believed the Soviet excuses; for most, it was just one more twist in a growing campaign of harassment. The only real question was how long this operation would last, and how far Stalin's cronies were willing to go.

Quite a way, Effi thought, as she waited for Eva Kempka outside the Ku'damm café. If a government was willing to target babies, then who could think themselves safe?

As usual on those rare occasions when she arrived earlier than the person she was meeting, Effi remembered all the times she had kept people waiting, and she resolved to do better in future. It never worked, of course.

She was almost ready to admit defeat when Eva finally arrived, out of breath and full of apologies. With a few drops of rain in the air, they took a table inside, and ordered coffees from a waitress who looked about fourteen. These days nearly everyone in Berlin seemed either too young or too old.

Eva seemed more nervous than she had at the funeral, and kept glancing at the doorway to the street. 'A man came to see me,' she said, as if in explanation.

'Who?' Effi asked. 'What did he want?'

'He never gave me his name, and I was too agitated to ask. He *implied* he was a friend of the family—Sonja's family, I mean. But he didn't actually say so.'

'What did he say?'

'That I was upsetting the family.'

'How? What have you been doing?'

Eva stole another glance at the door. 'Just talking to people, asking questions.'

'Who?'

'Oh, colleagues. I mean, I haven't spoken to the newspapers, or anything like that.'

Effi digested this for a few moments. 'What could you tell the newspapers, Eva? What do you know?'

'Well, nothing much. Nothing definite anyway. But I was with her, a few days before she died.'

'Were you in a relationship?'

Eva smiled sadly. 'Not then. We were for a short time. Last year. Sonja was . . . well, she wasn't really a lesbian. She was fed up with men, and she was willing to give it a try. That's what she told me—almost word for word. And she did, but it didn't feel right. Not to her.'

But it did to you, Effi surmised.

'We stayed friends,' Eva went on, 'and we used to see each other every few weeks, usually somewhere like this, but she couldn't get a babysitter that evening and so she invited me round to her apartment. And that's when I overhead the telephone call. Someone—I don't know who—was trying to get her to do something, and she kept trying to refuse. But whoever it was wouldn't take no for an answer, and eventually she agreed. But I could see she was frightened, and she wouldn't talk about it, which wasn't like her.'

A tear was rolling down Eva's cheek.

'Have you told all this to anyone else?'

'I went to the police, and spoke to a *kriminalinspecktor*. And he wasn't unsympathetic. Women like me usually get very short shrift from men in uniforms—somehow they know—but this one promised to look into it. He warned me not to expect too much, which seemed fair enough. Since I didn't have a name for the caller, or any idea what the call was about, I hadn't really given him anywhere to start.

'That was before the funeral. I went back to see him last Wednesday, and he more or less fobbed me off. He said he'd looked into it, and that there was nothing to suggest foul play. Which might have satisfied me, if he'd seemed like the same man I'd seen earlier. But he wasn't. He was more aggressive and more defensive, if you know what I mean, as if dealing with me was something he resented having to do.'

'As if it made him feel guilty?'

'Perhaps. But maybe I was just imagining it. I mean, he was right the first time—I hadn't given him anything, not really. And I had more or less decided to let it go, when this other man came to see me.'

'A German, right?'

'Well, he wasn't Russian. And he wasn't nasty or anything. But after he'd gone, I felt—I don't know—I felt as if I'd been threatened, even though I hadn't.'

Effi remembered having the same feeling after meeting the man from the Propaganda Department. And though Eva mightn't actually know anything, someone might fear that Sonja had confided in her. But what about? And what could it matter if Sonja had killed herself? Volker Heldt had no doubts about that, and it stretched credulity to imagine him as a creature of the Russians. And even if there was something behind all this—which still seemed far from certain—there seemed no point in pursuing the matter. They couldn't bring Sonja back, and in the unlikely event that they uncovered evidence of a crime, the likeliest sufferers would be themselves.

But how could she convince Eva of that?

'I asked a friend—someone with access to the Russians—to see what he could find out,' Effi said. 'Discreetly, of course. And maybe he'll hear something. But for the moment I really think you should let this go. Think about it, Eva. If you're wrong, and the call you overheard had nothing to do with Sonja's death, then making a fuss *is* going to hurt and anger others who loved her. And maybe that's all the unknown man was trying to tell you. If you're right, and there is something terrible we don't know about, then someone might decide to really shut you up. Either way, you'll be the loser.'

'I know,' Eva said, looking utterly miserable.

'So you'll let it alone.'

'Yes, yes, I will. Thank you for talking to me.'

'It's good to see you.'

'I'm usually better than this. But Effi, you will let me know if your friend finds anything out.'

'Of course,' Effi agreed, with more conviction than she felt. 'But I'm not really expecting him to.'

They exchanged industry small talk for a few minutes, and then went their separate ways.

Walking back to her flat, Effi felt depressed by the conversation. She wasn't convinced that there was anything suspicious about Sonja Strehl's death, but the elements of Eva's story—the threats on the phone, the resentful policeman, the nameless visitor who might or might not be who he said he was—all seemed depressingly characteristic of the current situation.

Earlier that morning Effi had attended a farewell gathering at Charlottenburg Station. Another actor she had known since pre-War days had been offered a part in a Hollywood movie, and had decided to take it. Two years earlier, Effi had heard the same woman scorning those who abandoned Berlin, 'the city where real films are made.' But she, like so many others, had been worn down by the occupiers and their endless machinations against each other. It was a world in which Berliners, high and low, could only function as extras.

Watching the train steam out towards the West, Effi had felt more envious than she expected. In 1945 Russell had persuaded the Soviets to get his whole family out of the city, but even then, with the streets on fire and the Russians raping anything female that moved, she had felt a strange reluctance to leave. She wasn't sure she felt that now.

Effi wasn't looking forward to the conversation, but after supper that evening seemed as good a time as any. 'Before you go to bed,' she told Rosa, once the wireless programme was over, 'we need to have a talk.'

Rosa looked pleased. She had seemed a bit withdrawn since Effi picked her up from Zarah's, and it wasn't the response that Effi expected.

'The other morning, when you were at school, I had a look through your drawing book. There were some I hadn't seen before. Of your friends.'

'What did you think?' Rosa asked, clearly oblivious to the possibility that something might be wrong.

Which was encouraging. 'I think they're wonderful,' Effi said, opening the book. 'But I wanted to ask you about one of them.' She found the drawing in question. 'This one. What are these two doing?'

'You know,' Rosa said with a slight giggle.

'I think I do, but you tell me.'

'They're special friends. Like you and Daddy. They touch each other a lot. Sometimes with their clothes off.'

'And did they ask you to draw them touching each other like that?'

'Oh no. They didn't even know I was there. I found them like that, but they didn't see me.'

'I see. But why did you want to draw them?'

Rosa sighed. 'I don't know. They were excited. And happy. I like drawing happy people.'

Effi felt a growing sense of relief. 'What they were doing,' she said. 'What Daddy and I do sometimes. It's called sex. Or making love. There are lots of words for it.'

'Fucking,' Rosa suggested.

'That's one of them. But the important thing—one of the important things,' Effi corrected herself, 'is that most people like to be alone with each other when they're doing it. It's a private thing, just for the two of them. And they would be angry if someone drew them, or took a photograph. Do you understand?'

Rosa gave her a look. 'I shouldn't draw people fucking without asking them first.'

It seemed a reasonable summation, if not quite the one that Effi had hoped for.

Darkness had fallen when Ströhm emerged from the Wedding U-Bahn station and crossed an eerily empty Muller Strasse. Road transport was still sparse in Berlin, particularly at this time of the day, when most transport was either public or military. At least the U-Bahn and S-Bahn were now running until late in the evening, and one of the latter's trains pulled out of the station above him as he walked eastward along the badly damaged Lindower Strasse.

Harald Gebauer's political office was in the old bankruptcy court building on Nettelbeck Platz, which bore the marks of both Allied bombing and Red Army shellfire, but unlike its neighbours still stood. 'On the second floor,' his old friend had told him on the telephone, somewhat unnecessarily—the ground floor was dark and empty, the sound of several voices coming from above. Ströhm climbed the stairs to find a landing lined with chairs, three of them occupied by people waiting to see Gebauer.

When he put his head around the door to let Harald know he'd arrived, his friend raised ten fingers once, twice and—smiling and shrugging—a third time for luck. Ströhm gave him a grin in return and went back out to a chair. He had known Gebauer as long as he had known anyone—they had gone on KPD youth marches together in the years before the Nazis seized power, and been members of the underground cells centred on the Stettin Station railway yards before and during the war. Since 1945, they had both held relatively important positions—Ströhm in the central railway administration, Gebauer in the yards and on the Wedding District Council.

'You look miserable,' was Harald's greeting forty minutes later, when the last local supplicant had disappeared down the stairs.

'You don't,' Ströhm told him. 'Working every hour God sends must be good for you.'

Gebauer laughed. 'No time to think,' he agreed, 'but let's go and have a drink. I'm afraid I can only spare an hour—I've got paperwork here that has to be finished.' He reached for the coat that was hanging on the back of his door, and fought his way into it. The elbows were in dire need of patching, Ströhm noticed.

Downstairs at the door, they discovered it had started to rain.

'Shit,' Harald said with feeling. 'My shoes leak,' he added in explanation. 'But what the hell.' He led the way across the square and under the railway.

'Are you still living on Liesen?' Ströhm asked.

'I moved into the office. There's an old army camp bed I can use. And it cuts down the journey to work,' he added wryly.

'What happened to your apartment?'

'I let it go. There were so many families living in one room, and there I was living in three—I couldn't justify it. And there were too many memories.'

Gebauer had lost his wife and children in an American bombing raid.

'And, as you so rightly said,' he continued, 'I'm working every hour History sends. What do I need an apartment for?'

Rest, Ströhm thought, but he didn't say it. 'Where are we going?' he asked instead.

'The Northener.'

'It's still open? I thought it had been flattened.'

'It was. But look,' Harald said as they turned a corner, pointing out a yellow light further down the street. 'The wonders of reconstruction.'

It was a different building in all but name, boasting some of the old decorations. But not, Ströhm noticed, the double-faced portrait which had hung on one wall, with Lenin on one side and Hitler on the other. That had presumably been taken by the Gestapo, after the raid that finally closed the bar down. Ströhm had often imagined the moment when they realised that the picture was reversible, and confronted the problem of how to burn one side without harming the other.

In the old days, when most of the clientele were railwaymen, comrades, or both, finding a spot to stand had often been difficult, but tonight's population was no more than twenty. It still made Ströhm feel nostalgic though, and as Gebauer bought their beers, he found himself sifting through mostly fond memories. Life had been simpler in opposition.

Once they were seated he said as much to Gebauer, but his friend didn't want to talk about the past. 'Back then all we did was hide and hope; now the world is at our feet. This is a hard time, I know it is, but it's a wonderful time as well.' He saw the doubt in Ströhm's eyes. 'Yes, yes, but look how well we are doing.'

'We are?' Ströhm asked with a smile.

'I believe so. How many are we—a few hundred, a thousand perhaps? Committed comrades, I mean. And few of us with a proper education—the Depression and the Nazis saw to that. And you remember how it was in 1945—all of us worried that we couldn't do the job, that without the training we'd mess it all up. But we haven't. We improvised, we learnt as we went along, and we've made it work. We had everything against us—even our Allies stealing half our industry—but we've made it work. And this is only the beginning. Anything's possible.'

'You really believe that?'

'Of course.'

'A German socialism.'

'Eventually, yes. Oh it won't happen overnight, but in time—why not?'

His conviction was catching. 'Your job brings you closer to the people,' Ströhm admitted. 'Mine . . . well, it's the worst kind of politics, more about power than people.' He shrugged. 'And then there's the Russians.'

'The Russians are a pain the arse, but if it wasn't for them we wouldn't be here. We'd all be dead, most likely.

'True.' Ströhm laughed. 'It's good to see you.'

'And you.'

They parted half an hour later, Gebauer shuffling wearily back towards his office, Ströhm heading west for the U-Bahn. He didn't have long to wait for a train, and as it thundered through the tunnels he sat in the almost empty carriage reflecting on the evening. He had known quite a few comrades like Harald, who thought personal life was a luxury, who wore leaky shoes and patched-up clothes, and never used an official car when walking was an option. Who were happy to live in material poverty while pursuing a richer life for all.

People like that had always been the heart and soul of the Party, and Ströhm longed to believe that enough of them remained.

In Trieste it had been raining on and off for days, but the supply of defectors had dried up. The general tightening of borders was probably responsible for the shortage of genuine asylum seekers, and as for the fakes, well maybe the Soviets were waiting to see how Kuznakov fared before rolling a successor off the assembly line. Russell's employers didn't seem overly concerned—Dempsey and Farquhar had both taken the opportunity to visit Venice, and the local CIA contingent were busy celebrating their successful purchase of the Italian election. All of which left Russell free to pursue his story.

The business with Palychko had gone some way to confirming his major suspicions. There was always the chance that he was a one-off, but Russell doubted it—there were too many east Europeans with innocent blood on their hands who could help the Americans understand the Soviets. Other questions remained, though. Who was choosing whom to save—the intelligence people in Europe, or the government back home? And did the fact that Draganović had an office in the Vatican mean the Pope himself had sanctioned the Rat Line? Given that the Catholic Church was still apologising for its shoddy performance in the war, a Nazi passport with a Papal signature would certainly win Russell a headline or too.

Such evidence was easier imagined than found. His employers mightn't need him at the moment, but he doubted they'd sanction a week in Rome.

That morning a message from Artucci had been pushed under Russell's door—'same place, same time, FA.' He remembered the place but not the time, which seemed to sum up his sojourn in Trieste. 'Could try harder,' as one schoolmaster had written on his term report several aeons ago.

Eight o'clock rang a vague bell, so Russell allowed ten minutes for the walk, and duly ventured out into the rain. This had grown noticeably heavier since his last outing, beating a heavy tattoo on his umbrella as he splashed his way up the streaming cobbles. Artucci was waiting for him in the small deli-restaurant, alone as before, and apparently wearing the same set of clothes. This time there were no bones on his plate, just a pool of tomato sauce which he was sponging up with a wedge of ciabatta.

He raised the bread in greeting, and summoned the same young woman to pour Russell a drink.

'So what do you have for me?' Russell asked when she was gone. 'Has Signor Kozniku been selling any more documents?'

'He away,' Artucci said. 'Go to family in Verona. For holiday, he says, but Luciana say he runs out the door. Very angry with Americans, but she not know why.'

Russell could guess. Given Kozniku's part in Palychko's intended emigration, certain Ukrainians would be wanting their piece of flesh.

The memory brought a pang to Russell's groin. 'So what *do* you have?' he asked Artucci, shaking his head at the offer of a cigarette.

The Italian lit his own. 'The two Križari I tell you about, the Croats from Osijek. They multiply.' He smiled. 'Is that right word?'

'I don't know. What do you mean?'

'There are four now, and they all move to a house above the city. A house with no one home. An Englishman arranges it all. A man named Seddon. And soon they go to Yugoslavia.'

Russell had met Seddon, and strongly suspected he was employed by MI6. In fact, an MI5 acquaintance had more or less told him so. 'How do you know all this?' he asked Artucci.

'You care?'

'Yes, actually.'

Artucci gave him a resentful glance, as if Russell was deliberately making it difficult for him to play a Man of Mystery. 'There is a man—another Croat—who makes papers for Kozniku. He also make paper for English and Americans, and this week the English ask him to make new paper for Yugoslavia.'

It sounded convincing. 'Do you know when they're crossing the border?' Russell asked. He couldn't see any way to use the information, but you never knew.

'No,' Artucci admitted. 'But why wait when glory calls?'

'Or Goli Otok,' Russell said dryly. Goli Otok, or Naked Island, about a hundred miles south of Trieste, was where Tito had established a prison camp for his growing number of opponents.

Artucci laughed, displaying gold molars which Russell hadn't known were there.

'Can you get me all the names on the new papers?' he asked.

'I think so. How much you pay?' After they'd settled on a price, the Italian pulled the list from his pocket.

At least it had stopped raining when Russell left. He walked back down the narrow streets, between lines of dripping eaves, wondering what benefits the British and Americans thought helping people like that would bring them. Whisking war criminals out of Tito's reach would further stain the West's reputation, and sending their descendants into Yugoslavia was just a waste of lives—the Communist regime there might be vulnerable to Soviet pressure, but not to anything the West and its sordid allies could do. Intelligence services had once seen their job as collecting intelligence, but these days they seemed to be paraphrasing Marx: 'Spooks have hitherto interpreted the world, the point however is to change it.'

And by arming Europe's disaffected and letting them loose on their enemies, they were only changing it for the worst. Russell was sick of the lot of them.

Outside his hostel two of Marko's daughters were playing what looked like a Serbian version of hopscotch on the slippery paving stones. The older of the two, whose name he knew was Sasa, treated him to a big-eyed smile.

Which was something to take from the day.

It was a pleasant spring Sunday in Berlin, and after admiring Hanna's vegetable garden the adults all sat out in the sunshine, sipping the French wine which Bill Carnforth had liberated from the PX stores. Rosa and Lothar were busy exploring the rest of the garden, and Effi found herself remembering Thomas's children at that age, in the last couple of summers before the war. Joachim had died in Russia, but Lotte was only a few feet away, looking now very grown up.

The ten who eventually sat down to eat were likely to share an appreciation of Hanna's cooking, but Effi was wondering how much disagreement the traditional Sunday discussion would unleash. For the moment though, it all seemed fine. Any group containing Major Bill Carnforth and one of the KPD administrators charged with making American lives difficult was likely to be fraught, but, for the moment at least, Ströhm and Zarah's boyfriend were getting on much better than their governments did.

Various aspects of Russian behaviour soon came to dominate the conversation, and Effi was impressed by Carnforth's refusal to join the chorus of condemnation. Others were much less restrained: Thomas with a scathingly funny account of the latest events at City Hall, Annaliese with a heartfelt attack on Soviet interference in the city's hospitals. And Effi soon found herself lamenting the recent

shift by the Soviet cultural authorities, and lampooning the story of
A Walk into the Future.

Ströhm took it all in good spirit, although he regretted the general
tendency to lump the KPD in with the Soviets, as if they were one and
the same. He rhapsodised about his old friend Gebauer, and expressed
his own hope that Germans would get to decide their own future.

It was left to Lotte to defend the Russians. 'What do you expect of
them?' she asked indignantly. 'They lost twice as many people as all
the other countries put together, and they deserve all the reparations
they can take. I know some of their soldiers behaved badly here in
Berlin, but were they any worse than some of our soldiers in the
Soviet Union? They've got the economy moving again in their zone,
and theatres and cinemas open, and their dancers and orchestras
come here to play. And the Americans—I'm sorry, Major—but your
government is so *aggressive*. Everyone knows the Marshall Plan is just
a way of getting their businesses back into eastern Europe. And it *is*
absurd that they and the British and the French have these sectors
inside the Soviet zone. They're like three Trojan horses!'

Effi noticed Thomas smiling and shaking his head.

Bill Carnforth seemed lost for words.

'But cutting off the milk supply?' Zarah asked. 'How could that
be justified?'

'It can't,' Ströhm agreed. 'It was a stupid thing to do. But both
sides make mistakes. I think these mistakes might even be an inevitable consequence of occupying a foreign country.' He turned to
Carnforth. 'And wouldn't your men be happier at home.'

'Sure they would, but how would that work?'

'Get back to the table. Unify the country again. Demilitarise it.
Make it neutral. From what I can see both you and the Russians
have punished all the Germans you're going to punish, so why not
leave us to rebuild our country?'

'It sounds like sense,' Carnforth agreed, 'but then I'm just a soldier.'

'It sounds a bit ingenuous to me,' Thomas said. 'Gerhard, you're a communist—don't you believe that a country has to choose between one socio-economic system and the other? You can't have both free enterprise and state planning, can you? It has to be one or the other—the American way or the Soviet way.'

'I'm not convinced,' Ströhm replied. 'I agree it looks difficult, but just because it's never been done, doesn't mean it never will be. If we could take the best of both systems, and get rid of the worst. A free socialist country—that's what Marx intended.'

'That was his dream,' Thomas agreed. 'And I don't want to demonise the Russians—they have their reasons, like Lotte said.'

'It's all above my head,' Annaliese said equably, 'but I can see what Gerhard's getting at. It just doesn't seem the way things are going.'

'You may be right,' Ströhm admitted, covering her hand with his own. 'I guess we shall see.'

'No more nasty shocks in the offing?' Thomas asked mischievously.

Ströhm smiled. 'I only find out an hour before you do.'

Thomas had the last word. 'Actually, we all seem to be in the same boat. Effi in her studio, Bill and his country, Gerhard and those in his party who don't want to replicate the Soviet experience—we all want to say "thank you, but no" to the Russians and their various offers. And we're all reluctant to do so, for fear of making things worse. It's not a great position to be in.'

Tuesday morning at the Weisensee studio, and the director was confidently predicting that shooting would be complete by the following Monday. Such news usually provoked an end-of-term style euphoria on cast and crew, but not in this case. The on-set atmosphere was unlike any Effi had ever experienced, both regretful and resentful, as if everyone knew that they wouldn't be making more movies like this one. Most people, Effi guessed, had either seen the script of *A Walk into the Future*, or something very like it.

Effi hadn't yet responded to Victor Samoshenko, hoping, against all reasonable expectation, that he might just go away. But he was waiting for her that afternoon, wearing the same grey suit and the same fixed smile. A red enamel badge bearing a golden hammer and sickle shone on his lapel.

Effi tried to let him—and herself—down gently. 'I just don't feel right for the part,' was her opening shot.

He frowned slightly, as if that didn't make sense. 'Surely that's for the writer and director to know,' he said.

'No,' she responded firmly. 'They have their ideas, of course, but the actor has to decide.' And how long would I be considered a serious actor, she thought, if I accepted propagandist rubbish like this? She had played such parts in Goebbels' movies when the alternative was no career at all, but even if that was the choice again, she wouldn't do it twice. She felt bad enough about doing it once.

Samoshenko wasn't done. 'Is there any chance you might reconsider? As a personal favour to Comrade Tulpanov?'

'No, I'm sorry. I have the greatest respect for Comrade Tulpanov—if anyone was responsible for Berlin's cultural re-awakening, it was him. All Berlin is in his debt,' she added, realising as she said it that she actually meant it. But that was then. 'It's not just the part. I need to spend more time with my daughter, and that means I shall only accept work that really engages me.'

Samoshenko's smile was suddenly gone. 'I understand you've accepted a part in a new radio serial at the American Sector radio station.'

'You're misinformed. I've been offered a part, but I haven't decided whether or not to accept it.' Effi decided some annoyance was in order. 'But how did you know about it?'

He shrugged. 'You know what actors are like—nothing is secret for long. And you know what people will say, that you have changed sides.'

'I didn't know there were any sides in film-making.'

He snorted. 'Come now, Miss Koenen, you're a lot more intelligent than that. You must realise how this will look.'

She did. 'If it makes you feel any better, I'll make it very clear to anyone who'll listen that I'm not making a political point, that if I take this part at RIAS, it will be because the hours are fewer and easier, and I'll get to see more of my daughter.'

Samoshenko sighed. 'Comrade Tulpanov will be very disappointed,' he said, adding almost ruefully that he hoped there'd be no regrets, before striding out through the door.

All of which, Effi thought, was little short of ridiculous. Even Goebbels and his minions had taken no for an answer without making a song and dance about it. They wouldn't let you work against them, but working for them hadn't been compulsory. Why did the Russians behave like such idiots?

Samoshenko's car was receding into the distance when she got outside, the battered studio limo waiting by the kerb to take her and her colleagues back to the British sector. The sun was shining for a change, the temperature somewhere up around twenty, and by the time they reached Carmer Strasse, she felt more at peace with the world.

Upstairs she found a letter from Russell, and put it aside to read later. Zarah, Lothar and Rosa had been to the American cartoon cinema, and were still laughing at one of the Tom and Jerry sequences. Effi usually picked Rosa up at Zarah's, and with the children engrossed in a game, took the opportunity of her sister's visit to bring out the offending drawing.

Zarah, rather to Effi's surprise, wasn't shocked. 'You've talked to her?' was all she asked.

'Of course.'

'And was she evasive?'

'Not in the least.'

'Well, then. These aren't normal times.'

'Yes, but given her history . . .'

Zarah wasn't having it. 'We all have things we'd rather forget,' she said pointedly, as if Effi might have forgotten that her sister had been gang-raped for two days by four Red Army soldiers.

'But Rosa was a small child,' Effi protested.

'I wasn't making comparisons,' Zarah insisted. 'But if I was, then people say that children are more resilient.'

Effi let that go—sometimes her sister was less than helpful. 'I'm beginning to wonder whether Berlin's the best place for her,' she mused out loud.

Zarah looked surprised. 'We're more fortunate than most.'

And they were. With Effi's Grade A actor's rations, Russell's income from several sources, and Bill Carnforth's access to US Army bounties, they could hardly be luckier. 'I know,' Effi said, 'but the whole city's on edge. It can't help.'

'No, I suppose not. And . . .' Zarah hesitated, and then smiled. 'I can hardly advise you to stay when I'm thinking of leaving myself.'

'You are? What? Oh! He's asked you to marry him!'

'Last night.'

'Oh Zarah!' Effi said, flinging her arms around her sister. 'That's wonderful.'

'You like him, don't you?'

'Haven't I said so over and over?'

'Yes, yes, you have.'

The penny dropped. 'You'll be moving to America.'

'I suppose so. What could Bill do here? And all his family's back there.'

'All yours is here.'

'There's only you now.' Both their parents had died two years ear-
.lier, within a week of each other. 'And I do find it hard to imagine
you being more than a few minutes away. But what can I do?'

'Nothing. If you love him, go with him. We won't lose touch.'
Something else occurred to Effi. 'But you still haven't got a divorce.'

'Oh Jens will agree—he'll be able to marry his schoolgirl.'

'She's almost as old as I am.'

'Pah!'

'But he won't like losing Lothar. Have you told Lothar, by the
way?'

'Not yet.'

'How do you think he'll react?'

'I don't know. He really likes Bill, and he's crazy about all things
American, but he's always loved his father. God only knows why.'
She shook her head. 'But there's plenty of time. Bill doesn't go home
for another six months.'

Effi gave her another hug. She was happy for her sister, who
seemed, at the second attempt, to have found a man worth having.
But America! Ali Rosenthal, the young Jewish woman whom she'd
lived with during the war, had moved there more than a year ago,
when her husband Fritz had secured a teaching post at a southern
college for negroes, and Effi still missed her. Now Zarah. As sisters
they had always been what John said the English called 'chalk and
cheese,' but from childhood on the bond had been strong. Not seeing each other for six months in 1942 had been painful enough,
and living an ocean apart would be . . . well, impossible was the
word that came to Effi's mind.

After Bill had picked up Zarah and Lothar, she and Rosa played
skat for a while, but Rosa could see that she was distracted. Effi's
usual rule of thumb was to tell her daughter the truth, but in this

case it didn't seem advisable—Rosa, a child with a history of abandonment, was very fond of Zarah.

It was only when the girl was fast asleep that Effi finally opened the letter from John. Written on the previous Tuesday, it was disappointingly short, and said little of what he'd been doing. There were touches of the usual self-deprecating humour—it couldn't have been written by anyone else—but there was something not quite right about it. About him. He wasn't in a good place, Effi thought. He needed to come home. They both needed him to.

Russell stood in the shadows of the covered porch, staring at Kozniku's darkened office. It was a depressingly clear night, stars twinkling in the overhead corridor of sky, an out of sight moon washing the roofs across the street with milky light.

It was almost midnight. In the last quarter-hour two prowling cats had stopped to check him out, offered plaintive meows, before padding away across the cobblestones, but the only signs of human life had been the dousing of bedroom lights.

Earlier that day Russell had visited the office, and told the voluptuous Luciana that he urgently needed to see Signor Kozniku. As he had hoped, she'd told him her boss was still away, and would be for several more days. Russell had looked suitably chagrined, vowed to return, and taken his leave.

Luciana had presumably left at the usual hour, and by this time was probably enjoying a post-coital cigarette with Artucci. Russell had a fleeting mental picture of them, and wished he hadn't.

What was the matter with him?

It had been a bad week. He had spent most of it pursuing leads that went nowhere, asking questions of people who had no answers, no matter how emphatically they claimed they had. He had spent far too many hours sitting in the Piazza del Unità, being shat on by pigeons and watching the wretched little locomotive clank up and down the promenade with its trio of wagons. And he had endured another lengthy briefing from Youklis on his imminent trip to Belgrade. They had someone they wanted him to contact—one of Mihajlović's former favourites, no less—with an eye to recruitment. When Russell had suggested that a man like that would be under surveillance, the CIA man had actually looked surprised, as if something so utterly obvious hadn't occurred to him. He had swiftly recovered himself. The potential gain was worth the potential risk, Youklis had decided out loud, as if the man he was risking was somewhere out of earshot. And when Russell had pointed that out, all he'd received were a smirk and a shrug that translated as 'you're expendable.'

Well, fuck them, he thought. He would go to Belgrade, and maybe—maybe—take a careful look at the man in question, but all other bets were off. And so here he was, loitering outside Kozniku's office with felonious intent, knowing full well that such action would piss the Americans off no end.

It was foolish, and he knew it, but like Shchepkin had said, journalists and spies had the same objectives. So why not use the same sleazy methods, particularly on scum like Kozniku?

He took a deep breath, and hurried across the street. Forcing the front door was out of the question, but there was another entrance off the ginnel which burrowed between Kozniku's building and its neighbour. Here, where the shadows were deepest, he hoped to find a way in.

The door was locked, and seemed more than a match for his shoulder. There were no windows overlooking the passage, so he risked using his flashlight, first on the keyhole and then on the foot of the door. The news was good in both cases—the key was in the lock, and the gap beneath the door looked big enough to take it. He took the folded newspaper from his inside pocket, flattened it out, and slid it through the gap. A gentle prod with the two-inch nail he had brought with him pushed the key out on to the paper, which he carefully drew back out. He couldn't remember which detective novel had introduced him and his school friends to this trick, but in the thirty years since it was the first time he'd performed it.

He unlocked the door, slipped through, and re-locked it from the inside. It was pitch dark within, and after wasting a few seconds hoping his eyes would adjust, he resorted to the flashlight. The door in front of him was, he assumed, the one he'd noticed behind Kozniku's left shoulder during their meeting. This was also locked, but the same trick worked its magic. Kozniku's office was windowless, but there was enough light seeping in through the glass panels of the connecting door for him to see his way. This door wasn't locked, so he walked across Luciana's office to check that the outer one was.

'Okay,' he murmured to himself, stepping back into Kozniku's inner sanctum. He hesitated for a moment over whether or not he should shut the connecting door—leaving it open would give him warning of unexpected arrivals, while shutting it would make it less likely that anyone would notice his use of the flashlight. Close it, he decided—who would turn up at this time of night?

First the desk, he told himself. Then the cabinets. He had no idea what he was looking for, but hoped he would know if he saw it. The man's absence had been too good an opportunity to miss.

Russell tried to leave each drawer as he found it, which wasn't that difficult—Kozniku had everything arranged just so. A sudden burst of laughter in the street gave him a jolt, but also reassured him; the interior wall were clearly thin enough to prevent his being caught in the act.

Two minutes later, he heard more voices—it was like Piccadilly Circus out there. He was just thinking that they seemed surprisingly close when he picked up the sound of a turning key. A few seconds later, the light went on in Luciana's office, and spilled through the windows of the connecting door.

Russell froze. If anyone opened that, at least he'd be standing behind it, but that was the best he could say. For the moment at least, no one in the next room seemed inclined to do so—in fact they seemed more concerned with trying to understand each other. There seemed to be three of them: Luciana, who sounded annoyed to be there, and two males, who sounded annoyed with her. They were all trying to speak English, and mostly failing in the attempt. The men had Balkan accents, and Russell recognised Serbo-Croat when they spoke to each other. Oh great, he thought. He'd spent half that morning listening to a British journalist recount, with wholly reprehensible glee, some of the worst atrocities carried out by the Ustashe. And here he was, at their mercy. Why the hell hadn't he brought his gun with him?

Time to leave, he told himself. And quietly as a mouse. He was just about to make his move toward the back door when the connecting door swung open, and someone seemed to exhale only inches from his head. A switch clicked, flooding the office with light, but before he had time to raise a fist it clicked again, restoring the relative darkness. He heard his own sigh of relief, but by then the men were talking again.

Russell took another deep breath and tiptoed across Kozniku's carpet to the other door. Thanking fate he hadn't locked it, he eased the door wide enough to slip through, and was just congratulating himself on making no noise when the key fell out of the lock, and struck the corridor tiles with a loud ringing sound.

'*Pažnja!*' one male voice exclaimed, and the connecting door crashed open.

Russell's hand was already on the outside door. After almost falling through it, he accelerated down the ginnel, conscious of someone shouting, and reached the entrance just as a silhouette filled it. His momentum threw the man backwards, away from Russell's flailing fist, and into the street. The man's gun clattered away across the wet cobbles, and rebounded from the opposite kerb with a sharp crack.

By this time Russell was ten metres down the street, running for his life. He was just thinking that they wouldn't risk advertising their presence by opening fire, when the first bullet ricocheted down the narrow street, striking sparks on both walls.

He swerved right down a partly-stepped passageway, almost slipping on the wet stone treads, and forced himself to slow his pace just a little. The passageway was longer than he remembered, and another bullet went singing past him just as he gained the street beyond. But no lights went on around him—the neighbourhood was taking as little notice of the odd gunshot as he himself had been doing these past two months.

He heard his pursuer cry out, but didn't stop to find out why. There was silence for several seconds, which suggested he might have fallen, but the footsteps pursuing him soon resumed, albeit further behind. Russell raced down the long and winding street, grateful to its architect for denying the possibility of a direct shot. Another stepped passageway offered itself, and he flung himself down it, still only one slip away from disaster. It opened into a small piazza, where a group of men were sitting out under a café awning, playing cards. He couldn't remember feeling so pleased to see other human beings.

A couple of gaudily made-up women gave him enquiring looks. He smiled, shook his head and hurried on across the piazza, pausing at the top of another street for a quick look back. On the far side of the square a man appeared at the bottom of the steps, one hand held behind his back, and took in the possible audience. One glance in Russell's direction, and he withdrew back up the stairway, feet finally passing from sight.

Russell turned and walked on down toward the distant bay, still breathing heavily, and cursing his own stupidity. If the man had been a better shot, or hadn't slipped on the steps . . . It was all very well risking your life for something worthwhile, but to take such a chance on a childish whim? To get away with a young man's prank, in Trieste or anywhere else, he needed a young man's legs.

Effi had just kissed Rosa goodnight when there was a knock at the apartment door. It was almost ten, which seemed late for a visit, so she raised her voice to ask who it was as she tried to recall where Russell had put their gun.

'You knew me as Liesel,' a woman said clearly.

Effi opened the door, trying to remember someone of that name. Seeing the dark, petite, well-dressed woman in her late thirties who stood on the threshold, her first reaction was almost panicky—had some unknown relation of Rosa come to claim her? But then she recognised the face. Liesel had been one of the Jewish fugitives whom she and Ali had harboured for a night or two while Erik Aslund arranged their escape to Sweden. One of the more self-possessed, Effi remembered, a woman who had known enough to be terrified, but who was damned if she was going to give in to it. Like all the others, she had come and gone without leaving a physical trace, but Effi remembered liking her more than many.

'I'm Lisa now,' the woman said after Effi had invited her in. 'Lisa Sundgren. I live in America, in Minneapolis.'

'My geography's terrible,' Effi said, reaching for the kettle.

'I had no idea where it was either,' Lisa admitted. 'It's in the middle. They call it the Midwest but it's closer to the east coast.'

'So what are you doing here?'

'I came to thank you.'

'You didn't come all this way to do that.'

'Well, no. I've come back for my daughter.'

Effi took out the cups. 'I didn't know you had one.'

'I have two now, but Anna is back home with her father, and my mother-in-law. Uschi was the one I left behind five years ago.' She sighed. 'This is a strange question, but back then, how much did you know about me?'

'Nothing,' Effi said, filling the teapot. 'We were only ever given first names—which for all we knew were false—and instructions on where and when to pass people on. It was safer that way.'

'Well, my name then was Liesel Hausmann. I was from the Sudetenland, which was part of Czechoslovakia until 1938, when the Nazis took over. I'm Jewish of course, but my husband Werner was a Christian, and we were well off. He owned a factory in Reichenberg—the Czechs call it Liberec now—and though the Nazis brought their anti-Jewish laws with them, my husband thought Uschi and I would be safe. And we were for several years, until he interceded on behalf of my brother's family, who had all just been arrested. In case things went badly, he wanted Uschi and me to go off with our maid, whose family lived in a remote mountain village. But I insisted on staying by his side, and Uschi went on her own— she was sixteen by then, and we thought she'd be all right.'

Lisa took the offered cup of tea, and placed it on the table beside her. 'And then my husband was arrested. I heard nothing for several days, and then an old friend from the local police called to tell me that he was dead, that I was about to be arrested, and that I should flee if I could. So I packed a bag and walked to the station and somehow reached Berlin, where we still had friends. And they knew someone who knew someone else, and that's how I ended up staying with you in that house, and finally escaping to Sweden. Which is where I met my second husband. He had a wartime job at the American Embassy in Stockholm, and when he went back I went with him.

'That was four years ago. We got married, and I had another child, but I always intended coming back for Uschi. If my mother-in-law hadn't been ill for most of last year I'd have come over then, despite my husband's objections. He didn't—still doesn't—like the idea of me being over here alone, but he knew he'd have no peace until he agreed.'

'Have you had any news of Uschi?'

'None. Once the war was over, we called the Czechoslovak Embassy in Washington, and they promised to investigate. When weeks went by and we didn't hear anything, we tried again, and they made the same promises. The same thing kept happening, and there was no way we could tell whether they were having a hard time finding her or just fobbing us off. I had no real address, you see, only the name of the village, but even so I can't believe they really tried. And by the time I finally decided that I had to come over myself, the communists had taken over. I'm an American citizen now, and I've been told that no visas are being issued to Westerners in the foreseeable future, so there doesn't seem any way to get in. And as far as I can tell the communists aren't letting anyone out. It seems my only hope of getting Uschi out is to smuggle her across the border.' She smiled. 'And that's my other reason for looking you up.'

'My smuggling credentials? I'm afraid they were only good for a particular time and place.'

'Oh, I know you don't do that sort of thing anymore. I read an article about you in an American paper—that's how I found out who you really were—so I'm not expecting practical help. But I did think you might advise me, or know someone who could. The people I knew here are dead or gone, either to America or Palestine. But with so many families still looking for relatives, there must be people who've learnt how to find them.'

Effi's heart went out to her. She didn't know of anyone, but maybe John would.

She explained that her husband was away, but that she would write and ask him. And maybe Ströhm could help—she would ask him, too.

Lisa thanked her for that and again for Effi's help in the past, and they arranged to meet up once Effi had finished filming. After her visitor had gone, she heard Rosa call her name.

The girl, it seemed, had listened to the whole conversation. 'My mother never left me,' she insisted, as if she feared the opposite.

'No, she didn't,' Effi confirmed. 'And neither did your father. As long as they lived, they would never have done that.'

Stefan Utermann

It was almost one in the morning when Russell was jerked from a doze by the loud and angry rumble of his train on the Sava bridge outside Belgrade. He had left Trieste at seven that morning, looking forward to the three-hundred-mile journey, but a tortoise-like crawl up from the coast had been followed by lengthy waits at Ljubljana and Zagreb, and the long descent of the Sava valley had felt a whole lot longer when the restaurant car inexplicably closed some six hours short of the capital.

As he walked out of the terminus, the sight of a dozen hotels settled the battle between hunger and tiredness. He tried three before he found a conscious night clerk, and happily accepted a key without first checking the room. As far as he could see, no fleas were jumping for joy on the yellow sheets, and the sash window sprang open with only a modest application of brute force. Within a few minutes Russell was fast asleep.

He was woken by the sun streaming in through the curtainless windows, and lay there thanking the stars that nothing had bitten him during the night. He felt like a bath, but one look at the shared facilities down the corridor persuaded him to wait. After getting dressed he made his way down the rickety stairs, paid the exorbitant bill, and ventured out into the city. The sky was mostly blue, the air already warm for that time of the morning. The square in front of the station was busy, and the number of salesmen offering wares seemed high for a communist country. Maybe Tito's Yugoslavia really was different, the way Ströhm kept hoping it was.

On his last and only other visit to Belgrade two years earlier Russell had stayed at the Majestic, which had seemed more than adequate. He thought he remembered the way from the station, but the first landmark he recognised was the Royal Palace, which had been rebuilt since his last visit, though presumably not for royalty. A uniformed man loitering outside gave him a suspicious look, but then provided directions amenably enough.

It looked as if Belgrade was doing better than Berlin when it came to reconstruction—in 1946 every street had seemed full of gaps, but now they were few and far between. And the people seemed younger than they did in Berlin or Trieste, although why that should be he had no idea—among the Allied countries, only the Soviet Union had lost a higher proportion of its population.

He found the Majestic in its small corner square, and happily spent Uncle Sam's money on a suite at the front with a bath. His rooms were clean and almost over-furnished, the water wonderfully hot. After consigning his travelling clothes to the laundry service, he went out in search of breakfast, zigzagging north towards the Marketplatz and a particular café he remembered. It was on the second zig that he realised he was being followed. A man in his thirties, in a grey suit, white shirt and black trilby.

The café was still there, with tables outside for the taking. After sitting there for a minute or so, he casually scanned the square, and found his shadow apparently reading a paper outside another establishment. The coffee, when it came, was surprisingly good, the ham and eggs quite excellent. And the general atmosphere seemed surprisingly relaxed, less gloomy than Berlin, less surreal than Trieste.

After paying his check, he walked on towards the Kalemegdan, whose surrounding gardens offered a pleasant spot for reflection, and found the seat he had sat in two years earlier, in the shadow of the stone citadel, high above the confluence of the Sava and Danube. Then all but one bridge had been down, but another two had since been restored, and, like the two rivers, were busy with traffic.

Then, as now, he had come as a journalist, but this time appearances were more deceptive. These days the Yugoslavs would suspect any visiting pressman of working for an intelligence service, whether full-time or part-time hardly mattered. And since it was the Americans who had persuaded the Yugoslavs to let him in, the latter would assume that Washington employed him in some form or other. Which of course they did.

The Americans, as Youklis had explained at their last convivial rendezvous, wanted to know how things were going between Tito and Stalin. Were they about to fall out, or had they done so already? If and when they did, Youklis and friends presumably had no intention of supporting one group of communists against another. They would just dump as much oil on troubled waters as they could.

All of which was straightforward enough for a journalist of Russell's experience. The American's other request was likely to be more problematic, because Youklis didn't seem to know that much about the man he wanted Russell to contact. Zoran Pograjac had fought with Mihajlović's Četniks and survived—as Mihajlović had not—a post-war charge of collaborating with the Germans. He had apparently kept his head down since, but Russell found it hard to believe that someone with a history like Pograjac's wasn't being watched by the communist authorities.

The Soviets had been more reasonable in their requests. They simply hoped that Russell's American backing would encourage the more anti-Soviet Yugoslavs to open up in private about their future plans. At their meeting in Trieste—convened in a small square beneath an unlikely statue of Aphrodite—Comrade Serov had presented Russell with a list of those they wanted him to interview. All but one were possible traitors to the working class. The exception—Vukašin Nedić—was a friend of the Soviet Union, but he was being closely watched by the Yugoslav authorities. Russell should insist on interviewing Nedić, and if the Yugoslavs tried to refuse, he should say that he could only write his article if given access to all the different points of view. 'They will be keen,' Serov assured him.

When they eventually met, Russell's use of the phrase 'the weather's been unusual today' would tell Nedić that he could be trusted. Russell would then be given an up-to-the-minute estimate of the current situation, and the list that Nedić was compiling of those Yugoslav communists who could still be relied upon to see things from an internationalist perspective.

'Don't you have an Embassy in Belgrade?' Russell had asked the Russian.

'Of course,' Serov had replied. 'But we never interfere in a fraternal party's internal affairs.'

Well, Russell would go and see Nedić if the Yugoslavs let him, hear what he had to say, and make damn sure he didn't get caught with a list of would-be traitors, either by destroying it straight away, or voluntarily handing it in to the authorities. Hearing Shchepkin's disappointed 'tsk' was much less painful than quarrying marble on Naked Island.

Mihajlović's man needed treating with even more circumspection. The Soviets expected to be disappointed—the whole bloody world was against them, and they were used to it—but the Americans took it all as a personal affront. If he wanted to see Berlin anytime soon, he would have to make an effort, or at least give a decent impression. But oh so carefully. If Pograjac wasn't just a CIC fantasy, if he really was a bona fide opponent of the regime, then consorting with him was asking for trouble. Russell could still remember the defendants at the

Moscow show trials falling over themselves to admit contacts with foreign agents. 'Shoot the mad dogs!' had been Prosecutor Vyshinsky's catch phrase.

He glanced across at his shadow, who was gazing out at the river. The man turned his head, as if conscious he was being watched, and when Russell gave him a big smile, managed a wry one in return. A small triumph for humanity.

A young couple walked past deep in conversation, reminding him that he didn't speak the local lingo. A significant handicap in this sort of work. He couldn't even read the damn newspaper—for all he knew, the two parties had resolved all their differences while he was on his train, and Tito and Stalin were busy composing love letters to each other. He needed to talk to someone—there had to be some foreign journalists in Belgrade who spoke one of his languages. In 1946 the Majestic had been full of them.

He walked back there, shadow in tow. The desk clerk spoke enough German to understand his question, and told him that two other journalists were staying at the hotel, one from England and one from France. The former was called Ronald Hitchen, and the clerk thought he worked for *The Times*. Neither the name, nor, later that evening, the face, jogged Russell's memory.

He was sitting in the almost empty hotel bar when a young man with tousled brown hair and a pleasant boyish face came up and introduced himself. 'I'm Hitchen. I hear you've been asking for me.'

'What can I get you?'

'Oh, I'm cultivating an addiction to slivovitz.'

'There are worse things.'

They introduced themselves. Hitchen, it turned out, was also a freelance, but found that people who thought he worked for *The Times* were generally more helpful than people who knew he didn't. He had been in Belgrade for a week, and had already talked to quite a few people. 'I came with a lot of introductions,' he admitted. 'My uncle was part of the British mission to Yugoslavia during the war, and made quite a few friends among Tito's people.'

Gold, Russell thought, I've struck gold. He already had a broad understanding of the differences between Moscow and Belgrade—they arose, like the differences between Moscow and the KPD back home, from a basic unwillingness on Stalin's part to allow the so-called fraternal parties any responsibility for their own affairs. Like the KPD, the Yugoslav Communist Party knew better than Moscow what local conditions required, but it was much better placed to say so. Unlike the KPD, the YCP had largely liberated its own country, and those Red Army units that had passed through Yugoslavia had long since left. If not universally popular, the YCP could, alone in eastern Europe, count on the support of a clear majority. If the Soviets picked a fight with Tito, they wouldn't find it easy.

It had, however, taken them a while to work this out. Russell knew from Shchepkin that late in March the CPSU had sent the YCP an official letter of complaint. According to Moscow, the Yugoslavs had been denigrating the Soviet Union with claims that it was no longer socialist. Which of course was the sort of nonsense you could expect from a party falling well short of genuine Bolshevism.

The YCP had responded on the 13th of April. They were Bolsheviks, and they did love the Soviet Union, but they admitted to loving their own country, too. It had seemed to Shchepkin, and seemed to Russell, a fairly placatory missive, but what neither knew, and what Hitchen now told him, was that Tito was simply keeping things sweet until he pounced on the local fifth column. And that *had* happened while Russell was on his train—the Yugoslav version of the MGB had arrested a slew of Party members who put loyalty to Moscow above loyalty to Tito.

If Nedić had been one of them, Russell thought, then he wouldn't have to worry about the wretched list. But Hitchen didn't recognise the name.

'Are they really spoiling for a fight?' he asked the young journalist. 'It's not just a minor squabble?'

'Oh no. They've really had it with the Russians. First the Red Army raped its way across the country, then the Soviets insisted on setting up joint stock companies to steal them blind, and then they flooded the place with MGB to watch the locals. The last straw was claiming that the Red Army had done all of the heavy fighting, and that Tito and Co only played a minor role in defeating the Germans. Tito wasn't having that. The medals he wears makes you think he'd liberated most of Europe.'

'And they're not afraid that the Red Army will make another visit?'

'A little, perhaps. But I think the Yugoslavs have got it sussed— the Soviets must know it wouldn't be a walkover, and they can't afford a real fight, either politically or militarily. I think they'll just give Tito the boot, and nail down the lid on the other satraps. They're all easy to reach.'

'You're probably right,' Russell conceded. 'I don't suppose the Soviets have commented on the arrests?'

'Not yet. But I expect someone in Moscow's trawling Lenin's speeches for appropriate insults.'

The last remaining scenes of *Anna Hofmann* were shot on Tuesday morning, and lunch turned into a farewell banquet, which lasted most of the afternoon. There was enough alcohol on offer to refloat the *Bismarck*, and the hastily-erected picnic tables literally creaked under mounds of food. DEFA's Soviet supporters were clearly keen to prove that its Hollywood-banked competitors hadn't cornered the market in excessive rewards.

Effi, like almost everyone else, spent the afternoon surreptitiously slipping delicacies into her bag for future family consumption. She was just hiding away a couple of particularly tasty almond biscuits when the Soviet Propaganda Minister loomed in front of her.

'Fraulein Koenen,' Tulpanov greeted her warmly in German. 'They are good, aren't they?' he added with a twinkle.

'I'm taking them home for my daughter,' Effi explained, unabashed.

'Of course. I was sorry to hear that you decided against *A Walk into the Future*.'

'Yes, well . . .'

'I realise that the script was rather crude, compared to some of DEFA's more recent offerings.'

'My feelings exactly.'

'So you haven't turned against DEFA?'

Effi managed to look surprised. 'Of course not.'

'Well, I'm glad to hear that. And it's good to see you looking so, may I say, young?'

Effi smiled. 'I won't complain.'

'Well then. I expect we'll meet again at *The Peacock's Fan* premiere in a few weeks' time. I went to an advanced screening, and I think your performance is really very special.'

'Thank you,' Effi said. She had made that film in the previous autumn, and if she said so herself, she had never been better.

He bowed slightly and moved on.

They really were making an effort, Effi thought. They needed to. The alcohol had livened things up a little, but the gathering still felt more like a wake than anything else. The cast and crew knew they'd made a decent film, but it was hard to celebrate that fact when it looked like being the last, at least for a while. Those who had signed on for *A Walk into the Future* were almost apologetic, stressing their families' need to eat or their hope that DEFA's fall from cinematic grace would be a swiftly passing phase. No one believed the film itself was worth making.

The mood on the ride home to the British sector was a sombre affair, and when Effi waved the others off on Carmer Strasse for the last time, the sense of liberation that usually followed the completion of a movie was noticeably absent. She had made half a dozen films with DEFA over the past two years, all of them entertaining, yet also mature reflections on her country and its recent history. She liked some of her performances better than others, of course, but when it came to the movies, she was proud of them all. Amid all the hardship and horrors of the war's aftermath, something good had been made in Berlin, and knowing it was over was a bitter pill to swallow.

The previous day's Soviet decision to restrict all parcel post between Berlin and the Western zones had provided Gerhard Ströhm with a problem. Since the reason supplied to the angry Allies was the sudden and completely bogus unworthiness of the rolling stock in question, he could hardly leave the stock in plain sight. But what should he do with it? The Berlin sector wasn't so well-endowed with stock that he could afford to hide it away, but if he shifted it into the Soviet zone some bright Red Army spark would send it all east for re-wheeling to the Russian gauge. And then the Soviets would announce that the parcel post was being restored, and where the hell would his trains be?

Relief arrived in the form of a summons from upstairs—Arnold Marohn wanted to see him.

The director lost no time in getting to the point. 'I've been asked to loan you out for the day. You remember Stefan Utermann?'

'Of course. We were both on the Stettin yards committee before the war. He was caught, and sent to Buchenwald.'

'But you've seen him since.'

'Only once or twice, a couple of years ago. He moved out to Rummelsburg when they started the repair works up again.'

'But you'd call him a friend?'

'A comrade.' Which in the 1930s had probably meant more.

'So he might take advice from you?'

Ströhm grimaced. 'On what?'

Marohn sighed. 'He's in dispute with our Soviet allies. The usual issue—one dismantling too many. Just between us, I don't think the Russians have handled the matter that tactfully, but that's the world we live in. And Utermann is being particularly obstinate.'

'Why do the Russians care?' Ströhm wondered out loud. 'Why don't they just ignore him?' The way they usually ignored KPD qualms, he thought to himself.

'Apparently he's made himself very popular with the workforce,' Marohn said. 'And the Party is anxious to avoid any demonstrations of anti-Russian feeling.'

'Of course,' Ströhm said automatically. 'Well, I'll try of course, but it's been a long time.' And Utermann had seemed a different man after Buchenwald—still friendly enough, but wound a lot tighter.

'Just do your best,' Marohn told him. 'And go today.'

'Why the rush?'

'The Russians want it settled.'

'Say no more.'

It wasn't a task he'd have chosen, but it felt good to be out of the office. The white clouds gliding across the bright blue sky made him think of galleons, and one particular book from his American childhood. He wanted children of his own, and he thought Annaliese did too, though they'd never discussed it. But there was plenty of time, and things were bound to improve over the next few years.

The prospect cheered Ströhm, as did the huge red flag in the distance, which fluttered over the Neukölln *rathaus*. It was almost twenty years since he and Utermann had fought all those running battles with the brownshirts on Berliner Strasse and Grenzallee, and in the end it was their flag which had carried the day.

It was gone noon when he reached the Rummelsburg repair shops. Utermann was out of his office, and the worker who pointed Ströhm in the direction of the erecting shop wasn't exactly friendly. Inside, he found two lines of locomotives under repair, and Utermann standing between them, talking to another railwayman. When he saw the suited Ströhm striding towards him, his initial frown turned into a smile, but the frown came back when the pfennig dropped.

'What's a candidate member of the Central Committee doing here? As if I didn't know.'

Ströhm didn't deny the inference. 'But I'm also a friend,' he said, offering his hand. And after only the slightest of hesitations, Utermann took it. 'Where can we talk?' Ströhm asked.

'Outside,' Utermann decided. He led the way to a door at the end, and ushered Ströhm through just as a freight train rumbled by. A stack of pallets outside the stores room provided somewhere to sit. 'You'll get your suit dirty,' Utermann warned him with a grin.

'Least of my worries.' Ströhm sat there for a moment, savouring the sights, sounds and smells of a working railway. This had been his life for more than a decade, and part of him still missed it.

'Feeling nostalgic?' Utermann asked.

'Yes.'

'It was simpler back then.'

'Perhaps.' Ströhm looked at his old friend. 'So, Stefan, tell me what's happened. What's at stake here?'

'What do you know?'

'Not a lot,' Ströhm told him. He wanted the story from

Utermann. 'That you're refusing to accept a dismantling, and have enough support among the workforce to embarrass the Party leadership.'

'That's a fair enough summary, as far as it goes. It's not just one dismantling, though. The Russians took everything last summer, and promised me that was it, that they wouldn't be back. And I sold it to the workforce—that giving them the old works was paying our debt as Germans, and that now we could build a new one as comrades. And we did. We searched the whole bloody Russian zone for the machines we needed, begged, bought, even mounted a couple of robberies. You wouldn't believe how hard everyone worked, what sacrifices they made. I didn't believe it myself. We had everything up and working again in six months.'

'And now they've come back again.'

'Two weeks ago.'

'It happens.'

'Yeah, but they promised me it wouldn't. And when I reminded the Russian bastard of that, he just laughed in my face.'

A suburban train rattled by, forcing a pause in the conversation. Utermann, Ströhm saw, had one fist clenched.

'So you refused?' he said, once the noise of the train had abated.

'I told him to fuck off,' Utermann admitted.

'Ah.'

'The bastard just laughed again. And then he got really nasty. He told me that if I didn't cooperate, the workers here would be given all the details of my *payoks*. He had a list of everything I'd received over the past two years—every last bar of chocolate and tin of ham.' He looked across at Ströhm. 'You must get them, too. And bigger than mine, I would guess.'

'I get them.' Every high- or medium-ranking Party official did, along with government officials, scientists, even poets and artists. All those considered crucial to the building of a socialist Germany. One had been delivered to his apartment earlier that week, delighting Annaliese. He'd come home in the evening to find that she'd given half the stuff away to the old folk who lived in their block. That had pleased him enormously, but he still hated the whole idea. Annaliese had listened, agreed, and told him to let it go. 'What can you do?' she had asked. 'Give it all back? What good would that do?' None at all, as he well knew. He didn't tell her, but it would actually do him harm. Giving them back would be seen as dissent.

'So you know it's not easy to refuse,' Utermann said, as if reading his mind. 'You give some away, and convince yourself you deserve a little pampering after all the years of struggle.'

'Yes.'

'But the workers don't see it that way. They don't see why anyone should be pampered in a socialist society. And they're right. Even the Russian knows it, which is why he thinks I'll swallow the medicine, for everyone's sake. I'll talk the workers around again, do his dirty work for him, and he won't bring up my *payoks*. He'll get his dismantling, the workers will think their interests are still being represented, and I'll get to eat a bar of chocolate twice a month. Everyone's happy.'

Ströhm knew where this was going. 'So you won't change your mind.'

'Enough is enough.'

'I know what you mean. I do, really,' he insisted in response to Utermann's look. 'But it won't help. The dismantling will still go ahead, and you'll get sacked. And the workers will lose a good representative.'

Utermann laughed. 'Fat lot of good I've done them,'

'The Russians won't be here forever.'

'You think not?'

'Nothing lasts forever.

'You really think I should give in?'

'I don't see how refusing helps anybody.'

'Maybe so. I know the arguments for giving in. A situation like this—an individual conscience is neither here nor there. A bourgeois luxury. I know the words. I've been reading them since I was fourteen.'

Ströhm was silent.

'The Russian's are coming back for my answer tomorrow.'

'Save your strength for fights you might win,' Ströhm urged him.

Utermann gave him a wintry smile. 'I might just do that.' As they walked back through the erecting shop he apologised for the way he had greeted him. 'It was good to see you,' he said, as they parted.

In 1946 the Foreign Press Liaison office had been a few blocks south of the Majestic, but according to Hitchen the current version was in a brand-new building on Makedonska Street. Russell breakfasted in the hotel, and then took the short walk, wondering if these days the Yugoslavs were faithfully aping Soviet methods when it came to dealing with the outside world. The fact that the British had given substantial aid to the partisans during their war might have left them feeling grateful, but somehow he doubted it.

He had no trouble finding the right office, but for almost an hour that was the limit of his achievement. The long wait to see someone was unexplained, and of Soviet proportions. His eventual interviewer, far from being apologetic, seemed almost insulted by Russell's temerity in still being there. He was a muscular young man with cold blue eyes, prominent lips and a very flat nose, wearing clothes which he seemed to find too tight—every few seconds he would insert a finger to loosen his collar. A uniform would have suited him better—he looked like he'd been fighting for years, and enjoying it no end. The cigarettes he seemed to be chain-smoking reminded Russell of Artucci's.

No name was offered. He examined Russell's list of desirable inter-viewees, grunting incredulously at some, merely shaking his head at others, then abruptly got up and left the office. Another long wait ensued. Russell was beginning to think he'd been either forgotten or simply abandoned when the man returned with his list. 'Tomorrow,' was the verdict. 'Nine o'clock.'

'Here?'

A grudging nod affirmed as much.

Next morning Russell was back, fully expecting another long wait. But this time he was seen without much delay, and by an official who seemed almost human. Older than yesterday's version, he had warmer eyes, clothes that fitted, and even introduced himself. His name was Popović.

He handed Russell a copy of his own list. Most of the names—including the well-known leaders like Tito, Kardelj, and Djilas—had been neatly crossed out, but three had ticks beside them: Marko Srskić, Jovan Udovicki, and Vukašin Nedić. Srskić and Udovicki were known Tito loyalists and would presumably offer up the cur-rent Party line. But why had they included Nedić?

He soon found out.

'I have taken liberty of arranging times,' Popović told him in very passable English, passing over another sheet of paper. Srskić and Udovicki were both down for that morning, at eleven and twelve respectively, in their offices at Party headquarters. Nedić was at three, at a different address, for which copious directions had been appended.

'That is his home,' Popović pointed out. 'Comrade Nedić has been ill, and remains on leave.'

'Okay,' Russell said, starting to get up.

'There is more,' Popović said hurriedly, causing him to sit down again. 'Comrades Srskić and Udovicki do not speak English, so an interpreter will be supplied for your interviews with them.'

'I also speak German and Russian,' Russell offered.

'They do not,' Popović said firmly. 'But Comrade Nedić does speak English. And Russian, too,' he added, with what might have been the hint of a smile. 'So you won't need an interpreter. But you must supply us with a transcript of your interview, and any articles you wish to file from Belgrade must also be submitted for my approval. Is that clear?'

'Indeed it is,' Russell agreed.

'You are sure?' Popović asked, sounding less than certain for the first time.

'Oh, absolutely,' Russell reassured him. 'Abso-bloody-lutely,' he murmured to himself as he walked back out to the street.

The YCP building was a ten-minute walk away. The interpreter, an attractive young woman wearing military fatigues, was waiting in reception, and she escorted him up to Marko Srskić's third-floor office. The interviews with him and Udovicki proved fairly predictable, and the cynic in Russell wondered if they'd actually been scripted by the same author. On the record, both men affirmed their enormous respect for the first Workers' State, and insisted that Yugoslavia would fulfil every obligation to all their Cominform allies. There had been friction, yes, but that was only to be expected among members of even the happiest family. Off the record—and they were only too happy to be so—both Yugoslav comrades admitted how sick they were of their overbearing mentor, and how ready they were to go it alone, regardless of Soviet threats. It was clear to Russell that both official and unofficial messages were intended for public consumption, the first to tell the world how reasonable they were being, the second to let the Soviets know they wouldn't shrink from conflict.

When he pressed them on how Yugoslav communism might differ from the Soviet model, the lack of any real answer was revealing. Russell was left with the impression that it wasn't so much Soviet methods and policies that were unacceptable, as Soviet insistence that they should be followed. Tito's communists needed to look different, and probably were different in some respects, but they weren't by any stretch of the imagination either pro-Western or anti-communist. If they succeeded in declaring their independence, and somehow fashioning a slightly softer version of communism, both the Soviets and the Americans would have reason to worry.

Neither Youklis nor Serov would be pleased, which had to be good news for humanity.

After lunch at his café in the Marketplatz, Russell took the tram stipulated in Popović's instructions from a stop farther down Jugowitja, and managed to alight at the right corner in the old Turkish Town. As far as he could tell he wasn't being followed, but then they knew where he was going. If there wasn't someone waiting to pick up his trail when he left Nedić's house, he'd be very surprised.

Popović's insistence on a transcript of the forthcoming interview was of course ridiculous—he knew full well that Russell could leave out whatever he chose. So why demand it? Russell could only think of one reason—to provide him and Nedić with a false sense of security. Thus encouraged, they would both blab like lunatics, and someone hidden in a cupboard would write it all down. Or even more likely, the place would be bugged. According to Shchepkin, these days the MGB had a string of science laboratories designing the things, and no doubt they'd passed some on to their Yugoslav disciples in the halcyon days that followed liberation.

Nedić answered the door himself, and he seemed to be alone in the house. He was a stout, balding man in his forties, with a red, drinker's nose and suspicious eyes. His cooperation had been requested, he said in excellent English, and he would answer whatever questions were put to him, although he found it hard to believe that a Yugoslav communist and an American journalist would share enough common ground for any real understanding.

Having said his piece, Nedić led Russell through to a sparsely furnished room at the back. There were landscapes on two of the walls, and a portrait of a young girl on another. Outside the window, ship's masts were visible.

Nedić briefly disappeared, then returned with a bottle and two glasses. After pouring two generous measures, he passed one across and carried his own to an armchair. 'So begin.'

Russell asked him the same questions he'd asked the other two, and got almost identical answers. The difference lay in the intended audience: Srskić and Udovicki had been speaking to the world, while Nedić was addressing his Party enemies. If his house was bugged, he was literally broadcasting his innocence; if it wasn't, he was relying on Russell to spread the news.

When they were finished, Russell walked across to the window. 'It's a wonderful view from here. It must be even better outside.'

Nedić just stood there, waiting for him to go.

'The weather's been really unusual today,' Russell said, hoping it didn't sound as ridiculous as he thought it did.

Nedić's double-take was almost Chaplinesque. 'I suppose it is a good view,' he admitted. 'Come, I'll show you.'

They climbed down the steps to the backyard. Beyond the gate, a single railway line curved along the back of the houses, beyond that, a gentle slope leading down to the river, scattered with trees and the reminders of war. A line of oil barges was heading upstream, presumably from Romania. 'We must be quick,' Russell said. 'I was asked to get your appreciation of the situation, and some sort of list.'

'The first is easy,' Nedić said, looking animated for the first time. 'Tito and his followers have treason in their hearts. They are traitors to the Cominform, and to our own revolution. The comrades in Moscow must act soon, or it will be too late. Tell them there is no hope of a political solution—a show of force is needed to galvanise all those comrades who have fallen for Tito's lies. They will know best what to do, but just moving some troops to the border would bring many comrades to their senses. I am sure of it.'

Russell wasn't, but that was neither here nor there. 'And the list?' he asked, hoping there wouldn't be one.

'I have typed out the names of every member of the Central Committee,' Nedić told him. 'All you have to remember is a number—72731. If a new leadership is deemed necessary, then the seventh, twenty-seventh and thirty-first comrades on the list can be relied upon. As of course can I.'

It was better than Russell expected. But how would he explain a list of YCP Central Committee members?

'It was printed in *Red Star* last year. You copied it out and brought it with you, planning to interview all the comrades that you could.'

'Sounds feasible.'

'The list is inside. But one last thing,' Nedić said, pausing at the back door. 'You must stress what little time is left. We could all be arrested tomorrow, and once we're on Goli Otok, there will be no one left here to invite them back.'

Russell nodded, and stepped back into the house. They had only been outside for a few minutes, but he could almost feel the suspicion seeping from the bugs. He silently accepted Nedić's list, mentally repeated the number, and stepped out through the front door. As he'd expected, there was a man loitering a short way down the street, one who suddenly felt like a walk the moment Russell appeared.

But he wasn't stopped and searched on his way back to the hotel. He spent the rest of the afternoon and early evening transcribing his notes of the interview and writing the article he thought his hosts wanted, a mattress of loyalty on a bed of defiance. That finished, he celebrated with the most luxurious meal he could find, which was neither that good nor that expensive.

The good weather came to an abrupt end while he was eating, rain beating on the windows of the restaurant like someone demanding entrance. No cab appeared to save him a drenching, so he took a hot bath to ward off a cold—an old wives' tale, no doubt, but a pleasant end to a difficult day.

On Thursday, Effi travelled out to Zehlendorf for lunch with Lisa Sundgren. 'I've got nothing for you,' she told the other woman as they entered the hotel dining room. 'My KPD friend said he'd talk to a Czech comrade, but he hasn't had time to meet him yet.'

'Oh that's a pity,' Lisa smiled. 'I'm doing so badly myself, I was hoping you'd come up with a miracle.'

'I'm afraid not.'

'Well let's eat anyway. There's not much choice, but the food's not bad here. Better than I expected.'

'I'm not surprised,' Effi said, scanning the rest of the clientele. Most looked American.

After they had ordered, Lisa described several recent visits to the recently reopened Czechoslovak embassy. 'They've never told me that I can't have a visa. They just say it'll take a long time, longer than they know I've got in Berlin, so there's no point in my even applying. And they're so totally unsympathetic. I've seen three different men there, and all exactly the same—cold, indifferent, almost cruel. One actually told me that many Germans were killed in 1945, so my daughter was probably dead anyway.' Lisa shook her head. 'And she may be, I know that, but . . .'

Their food arrived, limiting conversation for the next few minutes.

'I've met two other women who are looking for their children,' Lisa said eventually. 'One in Poland, one in Moravia. After the Moravian woman had listened to my story, she warned me that the Czech government would be afraid of letting me back in, in case I demanded my first husband's business back, and kicked up a fuss when I was refused. So I went back to the embassy and said I was more than happy to sign away any rights to compensation, that I just wanted my daughter back. And all they said was, "You have no rights to sign away."'

'Bastards,' Effi agreed.

'And if they did suddenly change their minds and gave me a visa, now I wouldn't trust them to let me out again.'

'My KPD friend . . . how did he put it? He thinks the new government's being more Soviet than the Soviets; that they're seeing everyone as a potential enemy at the moment. But he also believes that things will settle down in a few months.'

'I can't wait that long. And I don't think my husband will agree to a second trip. I'm beginning to think—I don't even know if I should be telling you this—but I'm beginning to think that Uschi's only way out is the one I took.'

'But you can't even contact her.'

'I know. But this Moravian woman, she knows people who are willing to carry messages across the border. For money, of course. And she thinks they might also be willing to supply travel permits, and other papers. Forgeries, I suppose. It'll be expensive, but I've already spent a fortune getting here, and to go back empty-handed . . .'

'Be careful,' Effi warned. 'There are thousands of Berliners still looking for lost relatives, and a whole new army of men who see them as a business opportunity. I'm not saying that they're all crooked, but I wouldn't part with any money until I was sure. If they can find Uschi and bring back a message, then they'd be worth paying, but don't start asking after false papers, not yet. I might be able to help with those.'

Buying a newspaper on his way home from work, Ströhm noticed the short piece at the bottom of the front page. The Rummelsburg repair shop workers, after lengthy discussion with Party officials, had reconsidered their opposition to certain new procedures, and re-affirmed their determination to make their workplace a model of socialist enterprise.

At the same meeting time, heartfelt tributes had been paid to Stefan Utermann, veteran of the Party's underground resistance to the Nazis, survivor of Buchenwald and the former manager of the Rummelsburg railway repair shop, who had been killed in a tragic accident the previous evening. The authorities were still trying to piece together the circumstances, but Comrade Utermann had been knocked down and killed by a passing train.

It was still raining in Belgrade next morning, and Russell borrowed a hotel umbrella for the walk to the Foreign Press Liaison office. Comrade Popović took his article away for ten minutes, and then brought it back with a smile. 'Very informative,' he said, without apparent irony. 'But you realise you can't send it from here?'

'Of course not,' Russell agreed. That would imply official approval.

'Are you leaving today?' Popović asked.

'No, tomorrow. I thought I'd have a day off, see the sights.'

Popović looked surprised, and Russell could understand why— Belgrade wasn't the most seductive of cities.

He splashed back to the hotel, and sat with a coffee staring out of the window. A puddle was spreading around a blocked drain; if the rain didn't stop soon the square would turn into a lake.

It was now or never as far as Zoran Pograjac was concerned, and Russell knew he had to make the effort. Youklis might be a piece of shit, but he could make Russell's life a misery. Appeasement was the smart way to go.

Though not at the cost of a Yugoslav prison. Russell knew he needed some insurance.

Back in his room he wrote a short letter on Majestic stationery, which he signed and dated. A two-minute walk brought him to the central Post Office, where a pretty young clerk named Adrijana assured him that it would be delivered next morning.

It wasn't much, but at least it was something.

Back at the hotel, he collected his room key, left his shadow in the lobby, and headed for the back exit which he'd scouted out the previous day, with precisely this eventuality in mind. It took him almost an hour to reach the address Youklis had given him, a crumbling block of flats in an industrial area close to the docks. He spotted no watchers on his first pass, and decided that further loitering would be counterproductive—in this sort of area any stranger was conspicuous.

The outer door was open, the lights inside not working. As far as he could see, there were four flats on each floor, which put Pograjac on the second. Third if your name was Youklis.

He started up the darkened stairwell, which was suffused with the smell of something rotten. If the leaders of the domestic opposition were all living in places like this, Tito had nothing to worry about.

A door opened on the first floor as he went past, and closed almost as quickly, offering the fleetest glimpse of a dark-eyed woman's frightened face. There was no sign of life on the second, and the only numbered door was the one he wanted. He stood there listening for a few seconds, but all he could hear was a distant ship's horn and the sound of his own breathing.

He knocked on the door.

It was opened almost instantly by a middle aged man in working clothes.

'Zoran Pograjac?' Russell asked.

The man nodded and gestured him in with a smile. Russell was barely across the threshold when two more men with guns emerged from adjoining rooms. As he took an instinctive step backwards, he felt another gun in his back.

One of the men in front of him said something in Serbo-Croat, which he assumed meant 'you're under arrest.'

'Is there anything the matter?' Annaliese asked Ströhm, after a supper spent mostly in silence. 'I feel like I'm living with someone who isn't really here.'

'I'm sorry. It's work. I've had a difficult couple of days.'

'Your old friend Stefan.'

He nodded. He couldn't seem to shake it off. The day after seeing Utermann his boss had called him upstairs to congratulate him, which had only made him feel like shit. He kept telling himself that if he wanted an active role in the new socialist Germany he had to accept the occasional setback—omelettes and broken eggs, etc. And if he didn't . . . well, that wasn't an option. What else would he do with his life?

'You said it was settled.'

'It is. Let's talk about something else.

'Okay. Effi dropped in at the hospital today. She said someone told her the weekend trains to Werder were back to normal, and she suggested we take a trip out this Sunday. She says Rosa's hardly ever been out in the country.'

'That sounds like a good idea. Am I invited?'

She gave him a look. 'You're *expected.*'

He smiled, took her in his arms, and kissed her. 'Let's have an early night.'

'All right,' she said, hugging him tighter and resting her head on his shoulder. 'But first I have something to tell you.'

She sounded nervous, he thought, which wasn't like her. He gently pulled back to look her in the eyes.

'I'm pregnant.'

He stared at her, shaking his head with wonder, feeling joy rise up through his chest.

'You look pleased.'

'Oh God, yes.'

'Well, thank God for that!'

'We'll have to get married.'

'We don't have to.'

'Will you marry me?'

Annaliese beamed at Ströhm. 'Of course I will.'

The interrogation started badly. There was no English speaker available, so the UDBA officer—Russell recognised the uniform—put his face a few inches from Russell's and shouted at him in Serbo-Croat. When an English-speaker was found, and Russell was accused of consorting with the enemy, his response—that he could hardly consort with someone who wasn't there—earned him a playful slap in the face which almost knocked him over. Wit, it seemed, was not appreciated.

Russell managed to look suitably cowed by the prospect of more violence—which didn't stretch his acting ability—and things settled down a bit. His interrogator, who introduced himself as Colonel Milanković, was a tall, prematurely grey Serb with an obvious bullet scar on his neck. He made a brief statement, which the interpreter, a much younger man with the scant beginnings of a beard, faithfully conveyed to Russell. His choices it seemed were two: the marble quarry on Naked Island—the good option—or execution as a spy.

'I'm not a spy,' Russell lied.

'What other reason could you have for visiting a known enemy of the state?'

'I didn't know Pograjac was an enemy of the state,' Russell said, choosing his words carefully. 'I knew he was an opponent of the current government, and in my country journalists talk to members of the opposition. And that's why I visited him. To ask him for an interview. As a journalist, not as a spy.'

Colonel Milanković's response seemed much longer than the eventual translation—'we have only your word for that.'

He was then told that his hotel room was being searched, and that questioning would resume once the search team had reported.

'They won't find anything,' Russell insisted. And they wouldn't, unless they had put it there.

He was left to stew in the interview room. The door hadn't been locked, but there was at least one guard outside, and there was nowhere he could run to. He didn't even know where he was, having been brought there in the back of a windowless van. It had only taken about fifteen minutes, so he assumed he was still in Belgrade.

He paced up and down, rehearsing what he should and shouldn't say, wondering how long it would take the Soviets and Americans to realise he'd gone missing, and whether they would or could do anything about it. He still had his insurance, but he wanted to be sure of exactly what he was being accused before revealing his only defence. Proving he wasn't an American spy wouldn't help that much if they thought he was working for Moscow.

His inquisitors returned. Something had been found in his hotel room—the list of Central Committee members.

He used the explanation Nedić had suggested, grateful that he'd resisted the temptation to write the code number down.

'Ah,' Milanković said, with the air of a dog who'd just caught sight of a brand-new bone. Perhaps Mister Russell could recall the five-minute conversation he'd had with Comrade Nedić, behind the comrade's house?

Russell decided not to ask how they knew about that—one slap a day was more than enough. 'We were looking at the river,' he said, trying to sound surprised.

'Why?'

Russell shrugged. 'Why not? It's the Danube. It's famous. I wanted to see it.'

'I don't believe you.'

'Why not? Why would I have a secret conversation with Comrade Nedić? He's a friend of Moscow, isn't he?

'Is he?'

'Well, he has that reputation. As you already know, he said nothing to confirm it.'

'*Inside* the house.'

'Or outside. Are you really accusing me of working for the Soviets?'

Milanković smiled to himself. 'No, Mister Russell, I'm accusing you of working for the Americans. Or perhaps the British. They are both sponsoring campaigns of terror against Yugoslavia, arming and funding former war criminals and sending them across the border on murder missions.'

'I do know that. But I don't work for either of them. I'm a journalist.'

Milanković just looked at him.

'I also know the details of a particular operation, which is either already underway or will be very soon.'

Milanković seemed almost disappointed. 'Comrades you'll now betray in hope of saving your skin.'

Russell shook his head. 'They're no comrades of mine, and I informed your authorities about them before I was arrested.'

'Who? How?'

He explained about the four Križari and their terrorist plans. 'I saw the false papers which a Catholic priest in Trieste had prepared for them, on instructions from American intelligence. The letter I sent to your central bureau contains the names on those papers. Which should make them easy to pick up.'

Now Milanković looked bemused. 'Why didn't you just report this to the police?'

'I'm a journalist, as I keep telling you. I'm supposed to report events, not manipulate them.'

'So why have you? Why would you put the interests of Yugoslavia above those of your own country?

Russell smiled. 'The interests of American intelligence and the interests of America aren't the same thing. And no, I don't have any special affection for Yugoslavia, but I have every reason to loathe the Ustashe. Who doesn't? And I feel ashamed of my government for using such people.' He sounded like he believed it, which was probably because he did.

Milanković was only half convinced. 'So where did you post this letter?'

'In the central post office. A girl named Adrijana sold me the stamp, and I expect she'll remember me.'

'We will talk to her, and wait for the morning delivery. In the meantime, you will have to sleep here. I'm sure a meal can be arranged.'

The food was awful, the cot in his cell as soft as a plank, and if the noises off were any guide his fellow detainees were suffering much more than he was. But he managed a few hours of dream-filled sleep, and felt only slightly less than human when business was resumed.

The letter had apparently arrived, and the UDBA was duly grateful. As for his arrest, well, Mister Russell would surely appreciate that sometimes wrong conclusions were drawn, and that he himself perhaps bore some responsibility for those reached on this occasion.

Russell wasn't about to argue. The way he saw it, they were bound still to be suspicious. He had offered innocent explanations for the missing minutes with Nedić and his visit to Pograjac, and he could doubtless conjure up another for casting off his shadow. But he couldn't disprove their alternative explanations, and with people like these you were guilty until proven innocent. Everything else being equal, he could see himself back in a cell.

But of course it wasn't. He *had* given them four of the hated Križari, they *were* keen to see his article published, and he could tell from Milanković's face that he was about to be released.

Russell risked a question: 'What has happened to Zoran Pograjac?'

He had just been tried, and found guilty of conspiracy against the state.

'Goli Otok for him, then.'

'He wasn't that lucky.'

They met up at Anhalter Station, and joined the waiting crowd on the open platform—the bombed-out roof had still not been replaced. Ströhm's bag contained the rest of the past *payok* parcel, Effi's a bottle of wine which Zarah had passed on from Bill. She had invited them and Lothar, but they were going to a US Army baseball game out in Dahlem. Rosa was carrying her drawing pad and pencils in a satchel over her shoulder, and worrying that the train might be full.

'It's coming from the depot,' Ströhm assured her. 'It'll be empty.'

It was, but didn't take long to fill up. One pregnant woman was left standing, and Effi was about to offer her seat when a Red Army soldier beat her to it, all concern and joviality. This, no doubt unreasonably, made her feel less anxious about taking a trip out into the Soviet zone. None of the people she'd asked had thought there was reason to worry, but there was still a vague sense of placing one's head between the jaws of a playful lion. But at least with Ströhm there, too, they had some good insurance.

The train set off, inching out along the viaduct and through the still-neglected yards. As it slowly gathered a modicum of speed, the gapped streets grew increasingly whole, until, in the farthest suburbs, the legacies of war became almost invisible. And once they were out in open country, it felt like another planet entirely; one where grey was unknown, and the greens of spring shone with a shocking intensity.

It took almost an hour and a half to reach Werder. They emerged from the station into what Effi imagined was Moscow writ small—the square was festooned with posters announcing the Soviet Union's abolition of poverty, unemployment, racism, and everything else that blighted the unfortunate West. A montage of heroes adorned the building opposite the station, and away to the left a group of boys were playing football underneath a giant portrait of Zhukov. All the shops lining one side had been abandoned, although one now housed the local headquarters of the SED, the Socialist Unity Party. Staffed by people like Ströhm, Effi thought, as they walked past it. A lot of people she knew hated and feared the SED, but a party full of Ströhms seemed nothing to be afraid of. Were they misjudging the Party, or did she not know the man?

She looked at Ströhm, who was talking to Rosa. The girl really liked him, which was a good sign. And he seemed happier than usual today.

It didn't take them long to get out of the town, and on to a narrow road that wound between meadows studded with poppies and burrowed through occasional stands of pine, the wide expanse of the Havel glinting not far to the north. The breeze was full of beautiful fragrances, the sky above almost swarming with birds. Everything seemed so alive.

Or almost everything. They passed a Soviet cemetery, red stars on every grave. They had their reasons, Effi thought. And after April's panic they were seeming more reasonable again.

After eating lunch beneath a gnarled tree on the shore of the Havel, Rosa took out her drawing pad, and sat looking across the lake for quite a while before putting pencil to paper. She wasn't used to distances, Effi realised. It crossed her mind that if the Russians laid siege to Berlin's Western sectors, as many feared they would, then she and Rosa could say farewell to days like this.

A gloomy thought. Ströhm was down on the beach, skimming flat stones across the water. 'He looks happy,' Effi thought out loud.

'He's going to be a father,' Annaliese said matter-of-factly.

Effi spun around, let out a cry of joy, and threw her arms around her friend's neck. 'Oh, that's so wonderful!'

'Isn't it?'

She had never seen Annaliese cry before, which considering all they'd been through together, was something of a miracle. 'And you're both really happy about it?' Effi asked, just to be sure.

'Oh yes. The only hard bit was telling Gerd's parents, because I knew they'd be thinking that my child should have been their grandchild, and it would only remind them that Gerd was dead. But they were wonderful. They said how pleased they were for me, and I'm sure they meant it.' Annaliese smiled. 'So I asked them to be godparents, and that made us all cry.' She looked across at the future father. 'I haven't told Gerhard about that bit yet.'

'I don't suppose he believes in God.'

'No, but then neither do I.' Annaliese looked up at the branches rustling in the breeze. 'But sometimes I just believe in . . . I don't know, in all this life. Inside and out. What else is there?'

Sasa

Effi had run into Max Grelling a couple of months earlier, when she and Russell had stopped off at the Honey Trap on Ku'damm for a post-theatre drink. In a beautifully-cut American suit, and with a gorgeous young German blonde on one arm, Grelling had looked the picture of post-war prosperity. Which was hardly surprising. Any member of that shrinking band of Jews still resident in Berlin was entitled to a welter of well-deserved privileges, and a celebrity like Max was entitled to more than most.

He had done more than survive the war in hiding—many had done that—he had been instrumental in helping hundreds of others to escape abroad. An apprentice draughtsman at a Bauhaus design centre before the Nazis rendered such employment illegal, he had taken a long cool look into the future, and taught himself a skill that he knew would be much in demand—forgery. For every ten German Jews now living in exile, Effi reckoned one had an original Grelling framed and hung on a living-room wall. She and Ali had met him on several occasions during the war, picking up a new set of papers when Aslund, for some reason or other, could not. Effi had liked Grelling instantly, and he had taken more than a liking to the much younger Ali. After the war, when Effi had told him of Ali's marriage and emigration, he had looked heartbroken for at least ten seconds.

He had told her and Russell that he was living on Ku'damm,

across from a bombed-out restaurant that they all remembered, and the day after meeting with Lisa, it didn't take Effi long to find his apartment. He seemed pleased to see her, and insisted on making them Turkish coffee, something she loved but hadn't tasted in almost ten years. Considering the ruins visible through his back window, all but one of the rooms were beautifully furnished, the exception being crammed with fully loaded tea chests.

'Are you leaving?' she asked.

'I'm off to Palestine. But not for a few months yet.'

'Okay,' she said, 'a straight question—are you still forging papers?'

'Did the Fuhrer have a foreskin? But I thought you'd gone back to acting.'

'I have. An old friend needs some help.'

'Don't they always? But I have to tell you, my charity work is over. Forgery is my business now. You know the one thing that Jews going to Palestine have in common?'

Effi was tempted to say 'no foreskin,' but that was only the men.

'Nothing, that's what. I plan to arrive a rich man. The rest can have their *kibbutzim*—I'll have a palatial villa halfway up the Via Dolorosa, where I can charge the Christian tourists for a drink of water. That'll teach them to accuse us of murdering Jesus.'

Effi couldn't help laughing.

'So what papers does your friend need?'

'Czechoslovakian documents. Travel permits, exit visas, that sort of thing. We don't have anything to copy yet. Do you have anything like that?'

'I could probably lay my hands on them. How urgent is this?'

'It isn't, not at the moment. But if you can start nosing around, I'll happily give you an advance. In dollars,' she added, taking a small wad out of her bag.

'I'm tempted,' he said, 'but I couldn't take money from you.' He thought for a moment, and then reached out a thumb and finger to snag a couple of bills. 'Okay, maybe a little for expenses.'

It was Monday evening before Russell got home to his hostel in Trieste, only to find he no longer had the same room. Marko, remembering his original request for one at the back, had taken the opportunity of a long-time guest's departure, and Russell's coincidental absence, to shift him and his few possessions. The arrival of a well-to-do fellow-Serb—a former professor of philosophy at Belgrade University, Marko informed Russell with pride— had been purely coincidental.

Russell was too tired to argue. The room turned out to be smaller, but it boasted a small balcony overlooking a sloping overgrown garden and the rising hillside beyond. And it was quieter. He stood there for a few minutes, enjoying the warm night air, glad not to be in Belgrade.

Several men had enquired after him during his time away. 'Suspicious people,' Marko had added, which didn't narrow things down that much when it came to Russell's roster of local acquaintances. They hadn't been English or American, and Marko's rough descriptions didn't match Shchepkin or Artucci. The Croats from Kozniku's office came to mind, but Russell was hoping that they were the men he'd shopped to the Yugo-slavs. Luciana would presumably know, and he was tempted to go straight to her. But that would piss off Artucci, who for all his amateur theatrics was proving surprisingly useful. So it looked as if another tryst at the deli would be required. It sounded like a New York City romance.

The bed seemed lumpier in his new room, but Russell still managed nine hours' sleep. After a bath, he gathered his notes together and ambled down to the San Marco, stopping at one point to sniff the sea and briefly bask in the morning sunshine. Two rolls, two coffees, and he was ready for business.

He had roughed out his newspaper article on the train back from Belgrade, and the report for Youklis would merely be an expanded version of that. It took him an hour or so to write it out, but he felt in no hurry to hand it over, or indeed to see Youklis at all. Instead he ordered another coffee, and carried it outside. On a table nearby two Russian Jews were discussing Friday's end to the British Mandate in Palestine, and how the battle would go thereafter. Towards a Jewish victory, Russell assumed. He wondered where the British would send the newly idle troops. These days the Empire was like a body erupting in boils, so they were probably spoilt for choice.

A shadow crossed his table, and Buzz Dempsey sank into the chair beside him. 'So this is the place where all the artists hang out,' he drawled, shielding his eyes against the glare to look inside the café. 'They don't all look like faggots,' he admitted. 'How's the coffee?'

'They make it weak for the artists,' Russell told him.

'Yeah? Well we haven't got time anyway. Youklis wants to see you.'

'You're delivering his messages now?'

Dempsey looked offended. 'We need you, too. We've got another Russian defector.'

This one, as the American explained on their ride up to the villa, had turned himself in to British border guards the previous evening. He was only a lieutenant, but he seemed intelligent.

But first there was Youklis to deal with. 'Where the hell have you been?' was the shaven-headed CIA man's first question.

'In Belgrade, remember?'

'You've been back almost twenty-four hours.'

'More like twelve. And I've been writing my report,' he added, passing it across.

Youklis read it through slowly, interspersing grunts of contempt with exasperated sighs. 'So Pograjac is out of the game,' he said, looking up and sounding almost surprised.

'One way or another,' Russell agreed. 'He's no use to you any more.'

'Don't you mean "us"?'

'I work for the CIC.'

'We're all in this together, you know.'

'So I'm told. Usually when people use that phrase they actually mean the opposite.'

Youklis ignored that. 'This guy Nedić—why the hell did he give you a list of Yugoslav commies who want to cosy up to the Soviets?'

'Because he thought I was working for the Soviets,' Russell explained patiently.

'And why did he think that?'

'Because I told him so.'

'And where's the list?'

'The Yugoslavs took it. But they don't have the code number, so it won't mean anything to them.'

'And we don't have the list, so the code number's useless.'

'Yeah.'

'You could have made a copy.'

'They would have found it, and that would have made them suspicious. And according to Nedić, it was published in *Red Star* last year, so all you need to do is find the right issue.'

Youklis thought about that for a moment, and decided there wasn't any point. 'I can't see what use we could make of a list like that if we had it. Commies against commies,' he muttered, a hint of wonder in his voice.

In Youklis's world it was Us or Them. Stalin doubtless felt the same.

'You didn't come back with much, did you?' the American concluded.

'On the contrary. You now have a good idea of what's happening between Belgrade and Moscow, and you've found out that you need a replacement for Pograjac.'

'Like I said,' Youklis almost snarled. He rose and stomped out past the arriving Farquhar-Smith, who gave a fine impression of a matador, stepping sharply aside to let the bull pass.

'Idiot,' Russell muttered after the American.

'Don't take it too hard,' Farquhar-Smith reassured him. 'He's just got the hump because his latest bunch of freedom fighters were all arrested the moment they crossed the Yugoslav border. Someone must have leaked the names on their documents.'

For a moment Russell thought he'd been rumbled, but there was only the usual well-bred smugness in the Englishman's expression.

'So let's get going, for Chrissake,' Dempsey drawled from the doorway.

The rest of the working day was devoted to Lieutenant Pyotr Druzhnykov. He was a Russian Jew, and as far as Russell could tell, a genuine defector. He clearly had little love for the Soviet system, but unlike most fake defectors, made no attempt to ingratiate himself by rubbishing it. He had, he said, left no family behind. He had decided Palestine was where he wanted to be, and was willing to buy his passage with whatever information he had that they might find useful. Only a few weeks earlier, this might have caused problems between Dempsey and Farquhar-Smith, but now that the British Mandate was ending they were back on the same page—blithely offering homes to Jews in what was, at best, a still-disputed country.

The only problem with Druzhnykov was that he worked for the Red Army catering corps. As far as Russell could tell, the best they could hope for was a new borscht recipe, but his superiors were more optimistic. 'Strip their lives down to a daily routine, and you'll be surprised what you learn,' Dempsey told Russell once they'd packed up for the day. He was probably quoting from some half-arsed training manual.

With more days like this in prospect, Russell raised the matter of his return to Berlin. 'Youklis promised he'd consider it when I got back from Belgrade.'

'That's between you and him. As far as I'm concerned, we need you here.'

'My wife needs me there.'

Dempsey grunted. 'My wife hasn't seen me for almost two years.'

'How about a week's leave?' Russell asked.

'Not at the moment.'

Russell took a deep breath. 'Okay. I quit.'

'What? You can't.'

As far as Russell could see, the only reason he couldn't was the certainty of MGB retribution, and Dempsey wasn't privy to that. 'I don't see why not,' he said calmly. 'I'm a volunteer, not a conscript.'

Dempsey looked worried for the first time. 'Look, I can't just let you go . . .'

'Okay,' Russell told him, 'this is my last offer. Get my wife and daughter down here . . . no, better still, get them to Venice. For a long weekend. That's not much to ask.'

Dempsey gave him a measured look. 'No promises, but I'll see what I can do.'

Russell held his gaze. 'No promises, but if you get them down here I might agree to stay.'

Later, back at the hostel, he met his old room's usurper. Signor Skerlić, as the hosteller introduced him, was middle-aged, plump, and rather too full of bonhomie to meet Russell's expectations of a philosophy professor, but maybe exile and forced retirement had cheered the man up.

* * *

It was early afternoon when someone knocked on Effi's apartment door. Her first thought was that Lisa had news, her second that the old man downstairs had come to complain about the noise—she had been dancing rather energetically to the band music on her radio.

What she didn't expect was two men in suits, one with an unmistakably Slavic countenance.

His much younger companion looked and spoke German. 'Fraulein Koenen?'

'Yes,' Effi said, rather than confuse them with her married name.

'You will come with us, please.'

She felt suddenly alarmed. 'Why?'

'We need you to answer some questions.'

'About what?'

'You will be told all you need to know at the station.' He reached out a hand for her arm. 'Now, come.'

She shrugged him off, and took a step back, which had the unfortunate consequence of drawing them over the threshold. 'Which station?' she asked. 'And where's your authority? I'm not going anywhere without seeing some identification.'

The German pulled something from his pocket and held it in front of her face. It looked like a police card, but then everyone knew the Berlin police did what the Russians told them. This felt the way she imagined a Soviet abduction would feel, but why on earth would they abduct her? Her husband was working for them, for God's sake.

'I have to use the bathroom before I go anywhere,' she said.

'Go ahead,' the German said, sharing a look with his Russian friend that suggested there wouldn't be trouble.

She locked herself in, turned on the tap in the basin, and quietly opened the airing cupboard. The gun Russell had bought her during a spate of armed robberies two years earlier was on the top shelf, wrapped in an old sweater and hopefully out of Rosa's reach. As Effi reached up, the German shouted out that they didn't have all day.

She took the gun in her hand, wondering if she really would fire it. She didn't know, and there was only one way to find out.

When the German saw the weapon, his jaw almost literally dropped.

She pointed it straight at his chest, and told him she wasn't going anywhere. 'I don't believe you have the authority to arrest me,' she said. 'If I'm wrong, I expect you'll be back.'

The Russian appeared at the German's shoulder, then almost gently pushed him aside. 'Fraulein . . .' he began, stepping towards her.

She depressed the barrel and pulled the trigger, shocking them all with the noise of the blast, and digging a groove in carpet and floor.

Both men had jumped, and the German looked so scared that she half-expected a spreading stain on his trousers. She took aim at the Russian. '*Hier raus,*' she said quietly, gesturing towards the door for the Russian's benefit.

The German looked stunned, but the Russian just shook his head and grinned. He was enjoying her performance.

There were raised voices out in the stairwell now. Any moment now someone would pluck up the courage to put a head around the door.

The Russian gave her a slight bow, and urged his partner out through the doorway, silencing the voices beyond. Once she could hear their feet on the stairs, Effi put her own head outside. 'An accident,' she said to the hovering neighbours, before closing the door to ward off further questions.

She was shaking a little, but considering the circumstances, that seemed appropriate. From the window she watched them cross the street, arguing as they went, then climb aboard an unmarked jeep, which the Russian drove off in characteristic fashion, swerving this way and that like a drunken runner.

Would they be back? What should she do? What would she have done if Rosa had been there?

She supposed she should tell someone. This was the British sector, after all, and one of their offices was only a couple of streets away. She put the gun in her bag, and started walking, half-expecting the jeep to roar up behind her.

It didn't. After listening to her story, the duty-sergeant sternly informed her that Germans weren't allowed private weapons, and that the gun would have to be handed in.

'It's my husband's,' she told him. 'And he's British.' Which was true of his birth, if not his current passport. It didn't seem worth mentioning the fact that the gun was in her bag.

As far as the sergeant was concerned, her marriage to Blighty—what sort of country called itself that?—clearly cast her in a much more sympathetic light. After a long but successful search for the right form, he laboriously took down all the details of 'the incident,' while loudly lamenting how little he could actually do. 'But then it sounds like you did what was needed yourself,' he concluded on a upbeat note.

'But I can't sit there with a shotgun across my knees until the Russians all go home,' she objected.

'No,' he agreed. 'But maybe they've learnt their lesson. I don't think they're used to people fighting back.'

'Maybe.'

'I'm sorry,' he repeated. 'Do you have a telephone?'

'Yes.'

'Well, ring us on this number,'—he passed across a printed card—'if they turn up again. We can be there in ten minutes.'

Which would probably be five too late, she thought, walking on to Rosa's school. Always assuming her would-be abductors allowed her to make the call.

They could stay at Zarah's tonight, and tomorrow she would . . . well, what?

She would try and talk to Tulpanov on the telephone. It would be easier to just turn up at his office, but she wasn't setting foot inside the Soviet sector again until she had some answers. Surely someone had made a mistake. Kidnapping scientists to work in Soviet laboratories made some sort of evil sense, but abducting actors to work on Soviet films? That was ridiculous.

It turned out that Pyotr Druzhnykov actually did have a lot of interesting information to pass on. Russell had never really appreciated the way in which the Red Army lived off the land, much in the manner of a medieval horde. And apparently this hadn't changed when advance turned into occupation—these days eastern Europe's farmers weren't only feeding their conquerors but also filling the millions of parcels which the latter sent back to their families. In fact the whole occupation had become a giant business opportunity for people denied one at home. An anthropologist would have been fascinated.

None of this interested Dempsey or Farquhar-Smith, who were still glued to their grail of battle orders, weapon deliveries and military timetables. Somewhat predictably, stripping Druzhnykov's life down to its daily routine revealed potato supply bottlenecks, not the strength and whereabouts of tank divisions.

The good news, as Russell learned when Dempsey dropped him off on Thursday evening, was that the American had arranged transport for his family—a first flight leaving Tempelhof for Munich at 9 A.M. on Friday week, and a second that afternoon to the old RAF base at Aviano, some forty miles north of Venice. 'You'll have to meet them there,' he told Russell, after handing him all the details. 'Don't say we don't look after you.'

Russell walked back to the hostel feeling better than he had for weeks—even the prospect of meeting Artucci brought a smile to his face. Marko was reading a newspaper behind his desk, his children draped across the stairs as usual. There had been no more suspicious visitors since his return from Belgrade, which might or might not be a good sign—either the bad guys had gone away, or now they knew where he was. The layer of dust on his threshold, which he always took care to step over, was happily devoid of footmarks, and nothing inside had been moved.

He stepped out on to the balcony and savoured the scents from the gardens below, remembering his and Effi's first time in Venice, back in 1934, when they'd only been lovers for six months. One of the happiest weeks of his life.

It would be different now, almost fifteen years later, with Rosa there, too. But they were different, too. And maybe it would be just as wonderful. He could hardly wait.

But tonight, a date with Artucci. He washed, changed, and went out for supper on the Via Nuova before making his way up the hill. The Italian was sitting in his usual seat, the waitress apparently AWOL.

Artucci needed only the merest prompting to relive the evening in question. The Croats had come to Luciana's house—he, alas, had been out on business—and taken her at gunpoint—at gunpoint!—to Kozniku's office. Before disappearing the priest had promised them papers, and the Croats had grown tired of waiting. 'She just hand them over when they hear someone move in next room—a burglar, she think, though robbing priest is bad, even priest like Kozniku. He back, you know. He tell Luciana in Fiume on business, but she not believe.'

'Does he have *any* priestly duties?' Russell wondered out loud.

'The chasing of little boys,' Artucci suggested with a grin. 'They all do this.'

Russell smiled. 'So what happened next? That night, I mean.'

'Oh, the man run down street with Croat chasing. Just for fun, I think. Why they care if Kozniku robbed?'

'But they got their papers?'

'Oh yes. I expect they're in Yugoslavia now, finding new women to make frighten.'

So, Russell thought, either Kozniku hadn't yet heard of the Croats' arrest, or he hadn't shared that news with Luciana. He himself hadn't been recognised, either by her or the Croats. Which was all to the good—his American employers wouldn't have been pleased if he'd messed up their relationship with Draganović.

After digging around inside one cheek with a toothpick, Artucci brought a straggly string of chicken skin out into the light, and examined it carefully before popping it back in his mouth. 'So what other service I do you?'

'Nothing new. Anything to do with Kozniku and his clients, like before?'

'Why you want this?' the Italian asked him earnestly, in the manner of someone keen to solve a riddle.

'I already told you that. For the story I'm writing.'

'Yes, yes. So you say American people have big interest in Nazi and Ustashe who escape to South America. Why they care?'

'Let's just say they didn't fight the war so that people like that could get off scot-free.'

'No? I think they fight because government say they must.'

Russell shrugged. The little bastard had a point.

After seeing Rosa to school the next morning, Effi reluctantly made for her own apartment. Telling Zarah about her visitors would be more trouble than it was worth, and she needed a private conversation, so home it had to be. Walking the last few yards down Carmer

Strasse, one hand gripping the gun in her bag, she felt like a semi-hysterical heroine from a Goebbels melodrama, badly in need of stormtrooper rescue.

But there was no jeep parked outside, and no enemies lurking in the stairwell. The flat was as she'd left it, complete with bullet-scarred carpet.

The telephone worked, which was something of a mercy. Lines within the western sectors had become less erratic of late, but the number of mysterious clicks and breaks during calls to the Soviet sector had seemed to increase. Not this morning, though. Effi had no trouble reaching the DEFA office, nor the number which someone there gave her. It took four calls in all, but she finally had Tulpanov's number.

The great man's secretary was reluctant to connect her, particularly where 'a private matter' was concerned, but eventually she caved in, moved perhaps by feelings of female solidarity.

'Have you changed your mind?' the Russian asked without preamble.

'No,' she admitted. 'I need to talk to you about something else.'

He didn't hang up, which was a start. She went over what had happened the previous afternoon, and asked if there was anything he could do. He wasn't a man to be threatened, so she made no mention of the press—he would think of that himself.

'I'll look into it,' he said, after a few moments' silence. The line went dead.

Effi hung up the earpiece, and wondered what else she could do. Nothing, she decided—if Tulpanov couldn't fix things, then she didn't know who could. Except maybe Russell. If all else failed, she and Rosa would somehow get to Trieste. In John's last letter, he had asked her to consider a visit when the school term ended.

She took up position by the window overlooking the street, and sat there for what seemed like hours, until she felt she could draw it from memory. 'This is silly,' she eventually murmured to herself. She had to do something. Tearing herself away from the window, she tipped an upright chair under the apartment door handle, and settled down on the sofa with the first few storylines for the 'The Islanders' series. They were good, she thought. Not great, but there was definitely scope for something worthwhile.

It was early afternoon when the telephone rang, and she almost pulled it off the wall in her eagerness to answer. 'Effi Koenen?' a male voice asked. It wasn't Tulpanov, but the inflection was Russian.

She didn't know whether to speak or not.

'My name is Shchepkin,' the man said in German. 'I expect John Russell—your husband—has told you about me.'

'He has.'

'I'd like to talk to you. Perhaps we could meet in Savigny Platz, on one of the benches.'

'When?'

'Now.'

'I'm waiting for another call.'

'From Comrade Tulpanov? That's what I wish to see you about. You're in no danger,' he added.

'You're sure of that?'

'I think so.'

She supposed that would have to do. And she was curious to finally meet the man who'd played such a crucial role in their lives over the past ten years.

As she walked towards him ten minutes later, he looked older than she'd imagined, with a rather drawn face and an unusually lean body. Or perhaps it was the white, slightly thinning hair—Effi remembered John had told her that he and Shchepkin were roughly the same age.

He rose with a smile to shake her hand, but the eyes seemed to be in another world. 'So what do you have to tell me?' she asked when they were both seated.

'It was a stupid mistake. The two men coming to your flat, I mean. It won't happen again.'

'That's good to hear,' she said. And it was, but it begged an obvious question: 'What did they think they were doing?'

'I'm not altogether sure,' Shchepkin admitted. 'We're being reorganised, and no one knows what anyone's doing. As far as I can discover, one particular department came across your name in an investigation they're running—something to do with the Sonja Strehl suicide . . .'

'What?'

'They wanted to question you about it.'

'They didn't tell me that. I thought I was being abducted.'

Shchepkin smiled, probably in sympathy, but she didn't take it that way.

'It wasn't a wild assumption,' she went on angrily. 'Several people I know have disappeared over the past year.'

'Yes of course,' Shchepkin agreed. 'If one side doesn't grab them, the other will. It's no excuse, of course, just the way it is. The point is, you have no need to worry. They simply wanted to question you about this actress's death.'

'But I don't know anything about it!'

Shchepkin sighed. 'I will tell them. It has already been made very clear to the Russian officer and his superiors that John Russell is one of our most important assets, and that kidnapping his wife is, as the Americans say, strictly off-limits. Strictly off-limits,' he repeated, savouring the phrase.

'And the German?'

'Ah. One of our recent recruits, I'm afraid. An apprentice of sorts.'

'God help Germany.'

'God help us all,' Shchepkin said wryly. 'Have you heard from Russell lately?'

'I had a letter yesterday. He's still stuck in Trieste.'

'He was in Belgrade last week,' Shchepkin said. 'I saw him a few weeks ago,' he explained. 'We need to get him back to Berlin.'

The 'we' was instructive. And on the walk back home Effi couldn't help wondering what it said about her marriage when the MGB had a more up-to-date location for her husband than she did.

Shchepkin's strange blend of strength and fragility hadn't been what she expected. With all that sadness he appeared to be carrying around, she was amazed he could still muster the energy to pursue his dubious profession.

She had only been back a few minutes when another jeep pulled up outside the house. This one had American markings, and the man walking up to the door was wearing a US lieutenant's uniform. Surely they hadn't come back in disguise?

Effi held the gun behind her back as she answered the door, but there was no mistaking the nationality of the fresh-faced young man standing in front of her. 'Madame Russell?' he asked in a soft drawl, apparently confusing his languages. 'I have some air tickets for you.'

Gerhard Ströhm was lunching with Oscar Laue, a fellow-survivor from the Party's underground organisation in the Stettin yards. Laue was much younger than he was, and had left the railways when the war ended. He was now working at the Party's Economic Planning Institute.

'You seem happier than last time I saw you,' Laue remarked, as they waited for their order to arrive. The restaurant, just off Potsdamerplatz, had only opened the week before, but two of Ströhm's colleagues had already brought back good reports.

'Yes,' Ströhm agreed, just as the food arrived. Several comrades had remarked on his newfound propensity to smile since hearing Annaliese's news.

'Things are about to get better, I think,' Laue continued, mistaking the reason for his companion's cheerful demeanour.

'In what way?' Ströhm asked innocently. The food was more than a match for that served in the Party canteen.

'Well, we're headed for what the Americans call a showdown, aren't we? A sort of Gunfight at the Berlin Corral.'

'And that will improve matters?'

'It will clarify the situation, and that's what's needed. We can't go on like this. The Soviets'—here Laue glanced briefly over his shoulder, just to check that no one was listening—'the Soviets like to see themselves as *in loco parentis*, but they're really the children. I mean, Marx and Engels, Kautsky, Rosa Luxemburg—real thinkers. The Russians have had their moments, of course, but when it comes to sophisticated political thought, they're the children, not us. Children who don't know their own strength sometimes, and need careful handling.'

Like the dismantlers out at the repair shops, Ströhm thought.

'You handled that situation in Rummelsburg very well,' Laue said, reading his mind.

'I wasn't proud of it,' Ströhm admitted.

'Why ever not? From what I heard you averted a crisis. If there's a bear in your house,' Laue said, blithely switching metaphors, 'you don't make him angry. You give him what he wants, and make sure he knows where the door is.'

'And what if he shows no sign of leaving?'

'He will, believe me. We're all comrades, aren't we? Once the Western powers are forced out of Berlin, there'll be no reason for the Russians to stay. That's why I say the coming crisis will clear things up. The children will all go home, and leave us to fulfil our destiny. We Germans invented socialism, and we'll have the last word. Don't you agree?'

Ströhm couldn't help laughing. 'A happy ending, eh?'

By noon on Tuesday even Dempsey was satisfied that Druzhnykov had coughed up all that he possibly could, and the question arose as to what should be done with him. Dempsey and Farquhar-Smith were agreed in believing the Russian unworthy of a $1,500 exit, and inclined instead to dump him at the train station with a one-way ticket to Venice and a few days' worth of expenses in his pocket.

It felt to Russell like they were just throwing the young Russian back in the pool, and he told Dempsey so. He might evade the MGB piranhas, might even find himself a ship to Palestine, but as he spoke only Russian and Yiddish, it seemed a lot more likely that he'd end up in an Italian jail. Wasn't there still a Haganah agent in Trieste, and weren't Dempsey's people in contact with him?

The American reluctantly agreed that they might be, and drove off in his jeep to find out. He returned two hours later with an address. 'You can take him,' he told Russell, 'and if they say no, you can drop him off at the station.'

They all drove back down the hill. As Dempsey threaded the jeep through the narrow streets, Druzhnykov's face seemed to reflect each new sight, alight with curiosity. The American let them out some way from the address, and drove off without even wishing the Russian good luck, but the latter didn't look bothered. He followed Russell, clutching the carpet bag that someone had found for him, and which now contained a single change of underwear and the photograph of his now-dead family, which he'd carried through the war.

The Haganah agent wasn't pleased to see them, although he softened when Russell introduced himself. 'You wrote about us,' the man remembered. 'Many American Jews gave us money after your story. Many farms were bought.'

The Arabs wouldn't thank him, Russell thought. He introduced Druzhnykov, and let them agree to things in Yiddish. The Russian, it turned out, would be the last Jew leaving Europe via this escape line—now that the British had stepped aside, future travellers could take a regular boat.

Russell shook Druzhnykov's hand and wished him well. As he walked back towards the town centre, he had that rarest of recent feelings—that his day had actually been worthwhile.

With no new defectors to engage him, Russell spent most of the following day working on his weekend travel plans. Aviano was on a branch line, one that joined the main line from Udine to Venice, but the two men on duty in the Trieste Station booking office weren't prepared to guarantee any actual trains. One man was sure that the retreating Germans had pulled the bridges down after them, and very much doubted that all had been repaired yet, but his colleague seemed to remember their receiving a letter of notification stating that the line had been re-opened. He couldn't find it though, despite emptying half a dozen drawers. The two men decided that Russell had little choice but to travel to the appropriate junction, where all would be revealed.

It sounded a less-than-reliable way to meet a plane, and the thought of a German woman and child alone on an Italian base rang all sorts of alarm bells. He would have to leave at least half a day early.

Or, it suddenly occurred to him, hire a car. There were such things in Trieste, and surely he could find an owner hungry for dollars. Whatever else he could say about his American employers—whether journalistic or governmental—they paid well.

Thirty-six hours and more than a dozen garages later, he found his vehicle—a maroon and cream Fiat 508 Balilla which had been abandoned on the waterfront two years earlier and brought in by the police. 'They won't let me sell it,' the garage-owner lamented, 'and they won't come and take it away, so I hire it out when I can.'

After driving it up and down the waterfront, Russell decided it would do. After the usual haggle, he drove it carefully up to his hostel, and laboriously turned it around in the small piazza. It was a while since he'd driven.

When he came down from his room an hour or so later, the car's roof had been taken down, and three of Marko's daughters were sitting in it, looking for all the world like passengers awaiting their chauffeur. Which they were. 'Please Mister English, take us for a ride,' the one called Sasa asked him. 'Yes, yes,' her younger siblings chorused.

Some practice wouldn't hurt. After going back in for their father's permission, he drove them all down to the city centre, took the car up one side of the Grand Canal, across the square in front of the cathedral, and back down the other side to the waterfront. The girls were chattering non-stop in Serbo-Croat, and looked like they were enjoying themselves, so he took the coast road to Miramare Castle, turning the car in the space once used by tourist charabancs. It was a beautiful day, the deep-blue sea studded with boats of all types and sizes—warships, liners, freighters, and fishing craft. There were walkers on the beach, which had only just been swept of mines, and several swimmers braving the oily waters and heaven knew what else. Even with the warship, it looked like a world at peace.

Rosa sat by the window, looking down at the snow-covered Alps. The DC-3 seemed to be almost skimming across the peaks, which Effi found both exhilarating and scary. She wondered how Russell had managed to arrange it all, and hoped he hadn't paid too high a price. Over the past ten years, as he'd once admitted, too many deals with various devils had looked worse in retrospect than they did at the time.

She looked at Rosa, still engrossed by the magnificent views. Not for the first time, she wondered if they'd done right by the girl, adopting her as their own. In material terms, Rosa now led a relatively privileged life, and no one else had offered to take her in. But the girl had also become entangled—how could she not?—in the web of political debts and threats that fate had woven around Effi and John.

One evening not so long ago, Effi had shared her misgivings with Zarah, who had given them no shrift at all. 'She's loved. That's the only thing that matters. Particularly if you've been through what she's been through.'

Effi hoped her sister was right. As she reached out a hand to stroke the girl's hair, Rosa turned to face her. 'Lothar told me the Alps are three kilometres high, but the Himalayas are almost three times that.'

'Lothar likes numbers.'

'He's a boy,' Rosa agreed, sounding almost sympathetic. 'Is there snow on the tops all year round?'

'I don't know,' Effi admitted.

'Lothar will,' Rosa prophesised.

'I expect so.'

'Will Papa be there to meet us?'

'He'd better be,' Effi said with a smile.

'But what will we do if he isn't?'

'Whatever we need to. Don't worry about it.'

'Okay,' Rosa agreed, turning back to the view.

Effi leaned back in her seat and closed her eyes. She was looking forward to seeing Russell, and she was also glad to be away from

Berlin. As so often in the past, a 'rest' between jobs was proving more demanding than work. The flat and its cleanliness had been neglected for weeks, all sorts of other matters were crying out for attention, and friends assumed she was permanently available. In the end, Effi had only just managed to get herself packed for the weekend.

She had heard from Lisa Sundgren—good news, or so it seemed. One of the illegal groups Lisa had mentioned had found out where her daughter was—in a small town not too far from Prague—and armed with this information, she was preparing another assault on the indifference of the local Czechoslovak diplomats. Effi hadn't heard from Max Grelling, but maybe his services wouldn't be required.

There was still no contract from RIAS, which might prove a blessing in disguise, because the previous day another, rather startling opportunity had presented itself. She'd almost not answered the knock, but curiosity had gotten the better of her, and with gun firmly clasped behind her back had opened the door to a handsome young American. His German was worse than her English, but as far as she could tell he was there representing the American director Gregory Sinfield, who was currently shooting a film in Berlin. And Sinfield wanted Effi for his next movie, which would commence shooting in Hollywood in approximately three months' time. There was no title as yet, but there was a script for her to read, a script that seemed good, if the first ten pages were anything to go by. She hadn't brought it with her, because she didn't want their weekend spoilt by the possible prospect of another long parting.

Could she cope with that? Could John? Was a Hollywood film, no matter how good, worth the upheaval it would mean for them all?

Effi didn't know, but her excitement at the prospect had certainly pushed other things from her mind. The previous day Eva Kempka had left a message asking Effi to call back, but they'd been airborne before she remembered. Effi hoped it was only a social call, and not some new discovery that Eva had made about Sonja Strehl's unfortunate death.

Russell left Trieste soon after eight A.M., and drove across the bridge connecting Venice to the mainland not much more than two hours later. Having found a place to park the Balilla over the weekend, he took a water taxi down the Grand Canal in search of a hotel. Given the month, he was expecting crowds, but both waterways and streets were emptier than they had been in 1934 when he was there previously, the city seemingly stuck in post-war torpor. After looking at several hotel rooms, with hoteliers almost falling over themselves to offer a bargain, he settled for a three-room suite overlooking the Grand Canal, just south of the Rialto Bridge.

After eating lunch at a restaurant by the water, he walked slowly back to the car, and drove back over the bridge. This had just been opened when he and Effi last visited, and he remembered hoardings hung with photos of the Duce doing the honours. Mussolini had only been dead three years, Russell realised. It seemed a lot longer.

Escaping the city's mainland suburbs, he drove north along mostly empty roads, the mountains drawing ever closer. The Aviano airbase might belong to the Italians, but as far as Russell could see the only planes they possessed were a couple of old trainers from the 1920s. The modern planes parked by the perimeter had USAF markings, and their presence suggested a somewhat less than wholehearted commitment to leave. Then again, compared to buying a national election, a couple of planes didn't seem that much of an intrusion.

Russell watched the DC-3 taxi to a halt some distance from the airbase buildings, then drove towards it across the expanse of tarmac and grass. He got there just as the door was opened to lower the steps, and there was Effi, framed in the doorway like visiting royalty, holding Rosa's hand. Both faces lit up when they saw him, which almost brought a tear to his eye. He'd been away too long.

Rosa ran up to hug him with Effi close behind, and they enfolded each other in a three-way embrace.

No one else had got off.

'Were you the only passengers?' Russell asked.

'We were,' Effi told him. 'Even the pilot was surprised.'

Either the Americans had forgotten the meaning of economy, or he was more important than he realised, Russell thought. Which was worth remembering.

Effi was taking in the air. 'Even the airports smell good down here,' she said. 'And it's so beautifully warm.'

'Is this our car now?' Rosa wanted to know.

'Only for the next few days.'

'But I thought everyone in Venice went everywhere by boat.'

'They do. Well, they walk, too. The car's to get us there and back.' He suggested they all squeeze into the front, but Rosa insisted on sitting in the middle of the back seat, where she had an uninterrupted view of the countryside on either side of the road.

The roads were still virtually empty, and they reached Venice with an hour of daylight to spare. After leaving their bags at the hotel, they took a water taxi down to San Marco, and found that the restaurant behind the basilica which Russell and Effi had patronised on their previous visit was still there. More astonishing, the proprietor recognised them, and insisted on serving them all champagne.

Sailing back up the Grand Canal with a moon rising over the roofs, Russell silently thanked whatever god had brought them there to see it. Once Rosa was in bed, the two of them sat for a while by the open balcony doorway, watching the moon's reflection in the windows across the canal, before finally sharing a look that had them walking hand in hand to their enormous bed. After making love the first time, they lay naked in each other's arms, feeling the warm breeze on their skin, savouring that sense of intimacy that both had sorely missed.

'So tell me your news,' Russell said, after several minutes had passed.

'Where to begin?' she asked rhetorically, before taking him through Thomas's political travails, Ströhm's and Annaliese's impending marriage and parenthood, Lisa Sundgren's arrival in search of her daughter, and the questions Eva Kempka had raised about Sonja Strehl's suicide. And then were the problems the Soviets were causing, both for her and Berlin.

'You have been through it.'

'And that's not all. Two of them turned up at the flat, and tried to take me away for questioning. I thought I was being abducted, so I saw them off with the gun you got me.'

'You what?!?'

'I know, but I was right. Your friend Shchepkin came to see me the next day, and apologised for his countrymen. They wanted to ask me some questions about Sonja Strehl, but now they've been told to leave me alone—you're too important to annoy, apparently.'

'I'm glad to hear it.' He was shocked, but knew he shouldn't be—it wasn't the first time she'd proved she could look after herself. 'So what did you think of Shchepkin?'

'Oh, I don't know. He seemed so wan and sad, but I don't imagine he takes many prisoners.'

'No, probably not.'

'But the really big news,' Effi said, sitting up against the headboard and pulling the sheet across her lower body, 'is Zarah.'

'She's going to marry Bill and live in America,' Russell suggested.

'How did you guess?'

'I saw it coming months ago. I've just been hoping you wouldn't be too upset.'

'Well of course I'm upset! But then I know I mustn't be, because he's just what Zarah needs.'

'He is, isn't he? You know I've got to like your sister, after all those years of just putting up with her.'

'I think she's almost grown fond of you,' Effi said.

He smiled. 'And how's Rosa?'

'You can see for yourself.' She had decided not to tell Russell about the picture just yet—she wanted to see if he noticed anything different about his adopted daughter over the next couple of days. 'But what about you? You seemed to like Trieste for the first few weeks, but lately . . .'

'There's nothing wrong with Trieste. It's the people I deal with.' He described his work as an interpreter, recounted the fun and games in Belgrade, but spared her the details of Palychko's demise.

'But you're writing, too?'

'Oh, yes. But the story I'm on is hardly uplifting.'

'But the fact that you're writing it may be.'

He grinned. 'That's one of the reasons I love you. One of many.'

She slid back down to snuggle up against him. 'Tell me some of the others.'

They spent the weekend roaming the island, only venturing off it once to visit nearby Tocello and its 7th-century cathedral. Otherwise they punctuated gondola rides and rambles through the narrow streets with long rests in coffee shops and restaurants. Their favourite haunt was a café in the Piazza San Marco, where they could simply sit and soak it all in—the beautiful buildings, the music from café phonographs, the square full of people and pigeons. Rosa sat with her sketchpad whenever they gave her the chance, drawing many a compliment from passers-by. But the views that had inspired Canaletto didn't call to her; she drew people against barely realised backgrounds, which could have been anywhere. Or indeed nowhere.

'So how have you found her?' Effi asked Russell on their last night.

He considered. 'More grown-up,' he decided. 'I've only been away for three months, but she seems to have aged more than that. Not physically. Emotionally, I suppose.'

Effi told him about the drawing and her subsequent conversation with Rosa.

His instinct told him there was nothing to worry about, but he trusted hers more. 'Have you stopped her seeing those children?' he asked.

'How can I? She spent three years hidden away with her mother—I can't keep her locked up in the flat. And there's nothing wrong with the children she plays with—I've talked to them—they're just normal kids who don't have the sort of home life that we took for granted. Zarah thinks they're actually more resilient.'

'She might be right,' Russell said. 'I never thought your sister was the brightest spark in the universe, but she's done a great job with Lothar.'

'She has, hasn't she? So you don't think there's any reason to worry?'

He grunted. 'There's always that. But if you hadn't said anything, well, she seems fine to me. And frankly, given her history, I expected a lot more problems than those we've actually had.'

'You never said that before.'

'Why tempt fate?'

'Why indeed? Speaking of which, there's another secret I've been keeping. The day before we left I had a visitor from Hollywood—or to be precise, from a Hollywood company that's making a film in Berlin. The director wants me in his next movie.'

'In Berlin?'

'In Los Angeles.'

'Wow.'

'Yes, wow.'

'Do you want to go?'

'I don't know. Yes for the experience. And yes for Rosa—once I was worried about moving her around too much, but she loved coming here, and getting her out of Berlin would, er—'

'Nip any possible problems in the bud,' Russell cut in.

'Exactly.'

'But?'

'You know the but. I miss you, and the idea of taking off for weeks or even months the moment you come back is . . .'

'Not good,' Russell finished for her. He smiled. 'Maybe the Soviets need a spy in Hollywood. And I'm sure the Americans would like someone on the inside, telling them which actors are secret communists.'

'You're joking.'

'Only a little. Effi, I think you should go. For one film, anyway. It might be good for Rosa—who knows?—but in any case I'm sure she'll love it. And it's too good a chance for you to pass up.'

'I don't know,' Effi said again. 'You know, I actually thought life would get back to normal after the war.'

'You weren't the only one.'

'This film won't happen before September,' she added. 'And I'm not missing Paul's wedding.'

'He would be upset.'

Lying awake an hour or so later, it occurred to Russell that one of his oldest dreams had finally come true—he was sleeping with a Hollywood actress.

* * *

It was raining next morning, which suited their mood, because nobody wanted to leave. They got wet in the water taxi, and then had to dry out the Balilla, because no one had thought to put the roof up. But at least the car was there—Russell had woken up fearing that someone had stolen it, and wondering how he would get them both home.

A gorgeous rainbow appeared as they drove out of the city, and by the time they reached Treviso the sun was draped across the mountains ahead. As they approached the Aviano airbase, Rosa leaned forward and suggested that Russell 'just come home' with them.

'I'd love to,' he told her, 'but I can't. I'll be back soon, though,' he promised, hoping it was true.

'And you have to take the car back,' Rosa remembered.

'Good thing you reminded me.'

They were an hour ahead of schedule, but the DC-3 was already waiting, the pilots anxious to leave at once.

'You two look after each other,' he shouted after Effi and Rosa as they climbed the steps, but he doubted if they heard him over the noise of the engines. They waved once, and disappeared inside, the door slamming shut behind them. Without much more ado, the plane accelerated off down the short runway, rose sharply into the air, and took a long climbing turn towards the mountains. Russell watched it shrink in size and finally disappear, before plunking himself back behind the Balilla's wheel with a heartfelt groan.

Russell arrived back in Trieste early that evening, returned the car to its reluctant owner, and took a tram along the waterfront to the Piazza dell Unità. Feeling less than ravenous, he eschewed the San Marco for once, and opted for one of the Caffè degli Specchi's famous toasted sandwiches. The place seemed more full of couples than usual, but after the weekend he was probably just more conscious of being alone.

Outside a huge orange sun was sinking into the sea. He walked back across the darkening Piazza Cavana, where traditional red lights glowed in half a dozen windows, and sun-tanned British soldiers loitered in groups, noisily drinking beer and sizing up the local whores. Travel back two thousand years in a time machine, Russell thought, and only the details—clothing, drinking receptacles, weapons— would be different. The Roman legion back from Judaea had become the East Staffordshires on their way home from Palestine.

Five minutes later, Russell was climbing the stairs to his room. It wasn't much past eight, but he felt exhausted, and only just summoned the energy to take off his shoes and trousers. The last thing he noticed before sleep overtook him was the moon peeking around his window frame.

It was gone when he woke, the sound of a blast ringing in his ears, a ghostly haze of plaster dust clouding the room.

Silence followed; the silence of the deaf, he realised.

He clambered out of the plaster-strewn bed, reached for his trousers, and pulled them on. The dust was thicker out on the long narrow landing, but was already settling on the threadbare throws which lined the floor. The door to his old room had been blown across the head of the stairs, and through the gap where it had hung he could see a yellow streetlight. The room's outer wall had all but vanished.

And so, he discovered, had the floor. What was left of the bed had fallen into the room below, and the glinting mess at its centre was presumably Skerlić's torso. Daylight would find the rest of him glued to the walls, Russell surmised.

He dimly heard shouting; his ears were beginning to recover. People were trying to get into the room below but something was blocking the door. And now he heard a thin mewling sound coming from directly below him. There was at least one person under the fallen floor.

He hurried downstairs to join those carting debris out into the street, and watched as three of Marko's daughters were carried out. It was the girls he'd taken for the ride only four days before. Two were still breathing, their faces covered in cuts and bruises. Sasa's face, by contrast, was completely untouched, but a falling beam had stove in her chest, and crushed the life from her body.

An ambulance bell was tolling in the distance.

'He said he was a professor,' Marko was half-shouting, half-crying. 'But who blows up professors? He lied to me, he must have done.'

Russell doubted it. The Croats had assumed he was still in his old room, had waited until he returned from Venice, and then detonated their bomb. They hadn't meant to kill any Serbs, but they hadn't much cared if they did.

He had got Sasa killed. He and all the others like him, playing their ridiculous games.

Bearers of light

After taking Rosa to school on Tuesday morning, Effi walked home intent on sorting out her professional life. The first task was to finish reading the Hollywood script, and this took her the rest of the morning.

It had what she considered the usual Hollywood weaknesses—a tendency to sentimentalise, and the habit of assuming that only regular outbreaks of violence would keep the audience interested. But overall she liked it, and a director as good as Gregory Sinfield would doubtless make it better. If she wanted a reason to turn them down, she would have to look elsewhere.

Nothing had come from RIAS, so she called Alfred Henninger on the telephone. He was most apologetic, but had no news. 'I'm sure the series will go ahead,' he said. 'It's just a matter of when.'

Which wasn't very helpful. With three hours to spare before Rosa's return, she walked down to Zoo Station and took a tram to the Elisabeth, hoping that Annaliese would have a few moments to spare. As it turned out, it was her friend's half-day off, and Effi only just caught her leaving for home.

Gerhard had left for Rugen Island and some sort of Party conference, and Annaliese was happy to share a walk along the Landwehrkanal and into the slowly reviving Tiergarten. After one botched effort, the British had finally succeeded in blowing up the huge flak towers that had sullied the landscape for almost seven years, and the park's trees, decimated by bombings and the desperate need for fire-wood, were springing back to life. It seemed to Effi as if the city's lungs were beginning to breathe again.

She asked Annaliese if she had any 'political news,' their code for the rumours and gossip that Ströhm brought home from work.

'None,' she said. 'Either the Russians are biding their time or they've decided the Americans won't be scared into leaving.'

'Which does Gerhard think?'

'That they can't make their minds up. He doesn't believe they have a plan. He thinks they just react to whatever their enemies do. So as long as no one provokes them, they'll be reasonable.'

'Why should the Americans provoke them?'

Annaliese shrugged. 'God only knows. I just wish they'd all go home.'

Russell played the innocent over the next twenty-four hours, as the local police, under the none-too-subtle supervision of the Allied authorities, carried out their investigation. Two visits from Dempsey kept him informed of their progress in concoct-ing a politically acceptable narrative. The bomb had apparently been planted by 'remnants of the Ustashe,' as part of an ongoing cycle of revenge attacks that went back at least to the war and probably a thousand years further. If Skerlić hadn't been a phi-losopher in this life, Russell thought sourly, he would surely be one in the next.

'He must have been a spy,' the hosteller kept saying, loading the three-letter word with enough contempt to sink one of the cruisers out in the harbour. One of the surviving daughters had lost an eye, the other had two badly broken legs, but they would both live. The building, on closer inspection, was less badly damaged than might have been expected. Russell's old room needed reconstruction, but those around it hadn't been that badly damaged. None of the guests had had to leave.

On Wednesday afternoon, a car came to take Russell up to the villa, where Youklis and Dempsey were both waiting on the pine-scented terrace. 'It was Croat *Križari*,' Youklis told him. 'And they were definitely after you. Would you like to tell us why?'

Anticipating the question hadn't provided Russell with a satisfactory answer. He couldn't admit to shopping Croat 'freedom fighters' or writing an exposé of the Rat Line without bringing the wrath of his American employers down on his head. 'Beats me,' he said, with all the insouciance he could muster. 'All I can think is that it must have been the fucking Ukrainians—either friends of Palychko who think I sold him out, or enemies angry that I tried to help him.'

'It was Croats,' Youklis insisted. Dempsey was saying nothing, just looking disappointed, as if Russell had let their side down by becoming a target.

'What have I done to offend *them*?'

'That's what we want you to tell us,' Youklis persisted.

Russell shrugged. 'I can't. Unless I've trodden on some toes without realising it. I have talked to victims of the Ustashe . . .'

'Why, for God's sake?'

'The same reason we held the Nuremberg Trials, so that war crimes won't be forgotten. I'm a journalist, remember?'

'So you keep telling me. I don't suppose you've been playing around with a woman named Luciana Fratelli?'

'What? Who's she?'

'Monsignor Kozniku's secretary.'

'Her? No, not my type. Why do you ask?'

'Her body was found floating in the docks on Sunday evening. And Dempsey here had the mad idea that her boyfriend discovered the two of you were playing around behind his back, and decided to kill you both.'

'Brilliant theory,' Russell noted sarcastically. 'She's an Italian, not a Croat.'

'She works for a Croat organisation,' Dempsey insisted.

'And I've only ever met her once,' Russell went on, ignoring him. 'When I collected Palychko's papers.' He guessed that the Croats, seeking the betrayer of their comrades, and knowing that she had access to the names, had tortured the truth out of her. He didn't ask Youklis what state the body was in.

'Right,' Youklis was saying. 'And there's no other Croat woman you've been fucking, no Croats you owe money to?'

'No and no. Maybe they really were after the Serb.'

'Not according to our informants.' Youklis sighed with apparent frustration. 'But whatever you've done to piss them off—and I don't for a goddamned minute think you've told us all you know—you've made yourself a target. And we can't carry on babysitting you until they get bored and go home.'

'I wasn't aware that you had been.'

'You know what I mean. You're no use to us here anymore. We're sending you back to Berlin.'

'Well, I won't object.'

'I didn't think so. But on your way home, there's a job that needs doing.'

His punishment, Russell thought, or was he just being paranoid? 'Where this time?'

'Prague.'

'And what's the job?'

'You'll be briefed in Vienna.' Youklis extracted a sheet of paper and an envelope from his briefcase. 'That man at that address, he's expecting you sometime tomorrow. Your ticket's in the envelope.'

Russell's first thought was that he would miss Sasa's funeral, after promising her parents he'd be there. His second was that denying him even that modicum of atonement was strangely fitting. Killers shouldn't turn up at a victim's funeral.

Youklis, bizarrely, was holding out a hand in farewell. Russell shook it, marvelling at the hypocrisy. The American disliked and distrusted him, and had cheerfully risked Russell's life in Belgrade without a moment's compunction, but no one could fault his manners.

After Dempsey had dropped Russell off downtown, he started for home intending to pack, and then realised he couldn't cope with any more of Marko's grief at this particular moment. Instead, he ate a final dinner at his favourite restaurant, and then sat out in the Piazza dell Unità, watching the sunset until the darkness was almost complete. Walking back up the hill he stopped at a public telephone to ring Artucci's two contact numbers, but no one answered at either. The Italian was long gone, Russell guessed—either communing with the fishes, or halfway to Sicily.

He approached the ravaged hostel with caution, but no one was lurking in the piazza's shadows with murderous intent. Two of Sasa's younger siblings were sitting on the stairs, their bodies listless, their faces full of dull resentment. As well they might be, he thought, shutting the door to his room, but taking the faces in with him. He should be glad to be alive, he thought, but that feeling was beyond him.

Wednesday morning brought rain and a letter from Eva Kempka. Effi had twice tried to call her on the previous day, but each time the phone had kept ringing. That and a line in the letter—'I know it's ridiculous, but I think I'm being watched'—convinced her a visit to Kreuzberg was in order.

Eva lived opposite an infants' school, just around the corner

from Russell's pre-war home on Neuenburger Strasse. Block resi-
dents had been forbidden to open their windows when the heat-
ing was on, and sometimes Russell's top-floor flat had grown so
hot that they'd stretched out naked on his bed with a pair of borrowed film-set fans blowing right at them. The *portierfrau* Frau
Heidegger had always called her John's 'fiancée,' and assuming
she'd survived the war, would doubtless be pleased to hear of
their marriage.

Eva's flat was on the second floor. There was no response to Effi's
first knock, nor to a louder second. The view through the keyhole
was limited, and offered no clues to the tenant's whereabouts. After
finding that everyone else was out on that floor, she went down to
the basement in search of the *portierfrau*.

The woman in question was around fifty, unusually fat for post-
war Berlin, and disinclined to be helpful, particularly when she
found out who Effi was looking for. 'Frau Kempka has been arrested,'
she stated, almost triumphantly.

'What for?' Effi asked.

'I don't exactly know, but I'm sure we could both make a good
guess. Your kind can hardly . . .'

'My kind?'

'You know what I mean. It's still illegal, you know, despite everything that's happened.'

If the woman hadn't been so fat, Effi thought, she'd be one of
those people painting 88 on high walls and bridges—88 for HH or
Heil Hitler. 'I am not a lesbian,' she told the *portierfrau*, adding a
note of indignation for effect.

'Oh. Well I'm sure I've seen you before.'

On the silver screen or a wanted poster, Effi wondered. 'Not here,'
she said.

'So what did you want with Frau Kempka?'

'I'm a work colleague,' Effi improvised. 'She hasn't turned up, and her boss wants to know why.'

'Oh, I see.'

'So when was she arrested?'

'They came on Sunday afternoon. About four, I think.'

'Were they German or Russian?'

'They weren't in uniform. The one who spoke was German, but the other one could have been Russian. He had that flat face they have.'

'Did Eva, er, Frau Kempka resist?

'Oh, she kicked up a right fuss, screaming her head off as they put her in the car.'

'But no one tried to help her?'

'Well, it was the police, and anyway, no one around here likes her kind.'

'I understand. Look, if she comes back could you ask her to telephone Effi?'

'Oh, I doubt she'll be back. Like I said, it is still illegal.'

'But if she does?'

The woman was staring at her. 'You're Effi Koenen, aren't you? I remember you in *Mother*. And what was that other one? *More Than Brothers*. Wonderful films. They knew how to make them before the war. Not like the moody nonsense they put out today. Would you give me your autograph?'

Without waiting for an answer she ducked back inside for something to sign.

Effi stood there, thinking that now the woman would call her if Eva did return. Fame did have its compensations.

There was a long wait while their first-class carriages were shunted aboard the ferry for the short ride to Rugen Island. As he watched others travellers stream past his window on foot, Gerhard Ströhm couldn't help noticing the resentful looks aimed his way, and the reason offered for his and his comrades' special treatment—that they would be able to work on the journey—suddenly seemed a lot less convincing.

He had never been to Rugen Island, and neither, he imagined, had most of the others. In pre-Nazi days only the bourgeoisie had been able to afford weekends or weeks away in the expensive hotels, and after 1933 eager groups of *Hitlerjugend* and *Bund Deutscher Mädel* had pretty much monopolised the island's woods and beaches. The only people working there had been those shipped in to service others.

It was as beautiful as Effi had said it was, Ströhm thought, as a conference-centre car carried him and three other delegates the last few kilometres to the converted hotel. The local Party had suggested a new holiday camp for city workers and their families, but had been overruled by Berlin. Too many echoes of 'Strength Through Joy,' one official had told him; the Party needed a conference centre away from the capital, where its leading officials could escape the stresses of their daily work, and plan for the people's future.

It didn't look as if any expense had been spared. Ströhm's room was probably the nicest he'd ever had, with its own tiny bathroom, large soft bed, neat modern desk and leather-backed chairs. The terrace below his window was a few steps up from the beach, the grey-blue Baltic beyond, stretching to a sharp horizon.

The main conference hall, as he soon discovered, was even more impressive, a slight stage overlooking rows of comfortable chairs beneath gabled wooden rafters. It all felt so new, so modern, so clean.

The first session that afternoon was devoted to administrative procedures, and the importance of standardisation in a socialist economy.

Ströhm found nothing to argue with in either the initial presentation or the various remarks from the floor. Of course they had to be efficient. Who would argue otherwise? Afterwards, as they all trooped off to the dining room, he found himself hoping that future sessions would offer rather more in the way of controversy.

The food, when it arrived, was something of a shock. For one thing there was so much of it, for another everything tasted so incredibly good. Scanning the room, Ströhm could see that others were just as surprised. Some agreeably so, as if they could hardly believe their luck, although others had dubious looks on their faces. Ströhm could imagine the chain of thought: the initial uneasiness turning into self-doubt, and then to a sort of wry resignation—'I won't help anyone else by leaving it on the plate.'

Or in the bottle. Ströhm knew very little about wine, but had no doubt that this was the best he had tasted. It was so smooth, so velvety. So rich.

After dinner, he joined one of the groups in the lounge. The conversation quickly settled on their pasts, and after a few minutes Ströhm realised why—that was where they had to go to find their justification. They had all worked hard, often for many years, with precious little reward. Many had suffered, losing friends and family, spending years in Nazi prisons or camps. Even those in exile had hardly slept on beds of roses. After all those years of sacrifice surely a little pampering wasn't so inappropriate.

With his head full of wine, Ströhm was inclined to give them all the benefit of the doubt, and eventually a drunken chorusing of the 'Internationale' sent them all off to their beds with a glow in their hearts.

The journey to Vienna was as long and irksome as Russell expected it to be. It took him over three hours to reach Udine, where a further two-hour wait was promised. He resisted the temptation to drop in on Boris the hotelier for a chat about dismembered corpses and their disposal, settling instead for a second breakfast at the surprisingly well-stocked station buffet. The train for the Austrian border eventually arrived, and chugged slowly up into the mountains, eventually passing Pontebba, where he'd run into Albert Wiesner almost three years earlier, while researching the Jewish escape line to Palestine. Albert was probably commanding a brigade by now.

The border formalities took less time than Russell expected, as did the wait for his connection in Villach. He'd taken this train in the opposite direction at the end of 1945, and been uplifted by nature's handiwork after too many months of living with man's. The sunlit mountains looked much the same today, but he felt like a different person, and the views were only that.

At Semmering, where the British Zone ended and the Russian Zone began, the walk from train to train was the same, and the Austrian capital, at first sight, looked little repaired from 1945. Taking a taxi from the Südbahnhof to the address in the American sector which Youklis had given him, the only real signs that thirty months had passed were the overgrown buddleias running riot in the ruins.

The address was in Josefstadt, an innocent-looking four-storey house on Florianigasse. His contact Sam Winterman had a top-floor office at the back of the building, with windows looking out on a plain brick wall. Winterman himself was tall and muscular, with a face that first looked handsome, but soon seemed merely wooden. He spoke with the sort of faint Southern accent that Russell associated, probably wrongly, with Virginia. His eyes were brown, and as dead as Youklis's blue. 'John Russell,' Winterman muttered, for no apparent reason.

So far, so familiar, Russell thought, but a shock was in store.

'Ah, good,' Winterman said as the door behind Russell opened. 'I think you two have met.'

They had indeed. It was Giminich—formerly Obersturmbann-nführer Giminich of the SS Security Police, the *Sicherheitsdienst*—whom Russell had last seen in Prague, towards the end of 1941. And Giminich wasn't in handcuffs, chains, or some other appropriate form of restraint. In fact, he looked as pleased with this new world as he had with that previous one. He was older, of course, and the blond hair was no longer swept back in imitation of the great god Heydrich, but the smile was still every bit as smug.

'Herr Russell,' Giminich said, offering his hand.

'You've got be joking.'

Giminich was unperturbed. 'I understand,' he said, in such a way that he seemed to be apologising for Russell's lack of manners.

'Let's not beat about the bush,' Winterman said. 'We all know that you two were enemies once, but that war is over now. And Volker here is a key player in our Czechoslovak game plan.'

Volker? Russell thought. During their last encounter in Prague, 'Volker' had casually ordered the shooting of ten hostages. The reason for their both being in the Czech capital had been Giminich's command of an elaborate SD sting operation against Admiral Canaris's Abwehr, for which Russell had then been working.

'What do you know about Masaryk's death?' Winterman was asking.

'Father or son?' Russell asked, just to be difficult.

'Jan Masaryk, the son,' Winterman patiently explained. 'He was Czech Foreign Minister until someone threw him out the window of his official residence. He was the only non-communist with a popu-lar following in the government, so they got rid of him, and told the world he'd committed suicide.'

'Maybe he did,' Russell suggested, although he didn't believe it for a minute. 'There wasn't much of a future for him in a communist Czechoslovakia.'

'He was killed,' Winterman insisted, 'and some of Volker's people in Prague have been gathering the evidence. Three affidavits signed by men who were in the building at the time, or saw the crime scene straight afterwards. We need you to bring them out.'

More *déjà vu*, Russell thought. 'Wouldn't it be simpler to forge them?' he asked.

Giminich smiled at that, but Winterman seemed faintly outraged. 'These men have risked their lives for these documents,' he said sternly.

'You mean you've risked their lives.'

Winterman wouldn't rise to the bait. 'We're not holding a gun to anyone's head. These men are Czech patriots—they want the Russians and their commie stooges out.'

Russell felt like pointing out that the Czech communists had won post-war elections fair and square, but debating democratic values with men who had just bought an election in Italy seemed a waste of energy.

'You're writing a story on Czech popular culture for our magazine,' Winterman went on.

'Your magazine?'

'We've just started one. It's called *The Lampadary*—do you know what that means?'

'A bearer of light?'

'That's what we are. We've arranged for you to interview a filmmaker, a poet, and a conductor. All have leftist views, and the commie authorities are only too happy to have you talk to them—it'll be great propaganda for them.'

'And at some point during your stay,' Giminich interjected, 'you'll be contacted by one of our people, and given the arrangements for collecting the affidavits.'

Russell nodded. In each of his last three trips to Prague, his life had hung by a thread, and this visit seemed set to continue the pattern. 'And if at any point I smell a rat, then I just walk away?'

'There's no reason to think that any of my people in Prague have been turned,' Giminich said.

'But if it looks as if they have?' Russell asked Winterman.

'Well it obviously won't help us to have the documents seized and you arrested, ' Winterman conceded.

'That's all I wanted to hear.'

'I'm not done. We won't get anywhere being over-cautious. This is important stuff, worth a few risks.'

'Why?' Russell wasn't to know. 'I mean, why is it so important? How will these affidavits help? I wasn't joking when I said you might as well forge them, because the Soviets will certainly claim that you've done so, whether you have or not.'

Winterman smiled for the first time. 'I can see where your reputation comes from,' he told Russell.

'For being perceptive?'

'For being a pain in the arse. Now you have your instructions—Volker will fill you in on the details. We've found you a bed at the American Press Club—you know where that is?'

Russell nodded.

'You're travelling tomorrow, staying the weekend, coming back on Monday. With the affidavits. Right?'

'I'll do my humble best.'

Winterman wished him gone with a gesture, and went back to the file on his desk. Giminich ushered Russell down the corridor to a smaller office with the same brick view. The framed photograph of Patton on the wall was probably reversible, Russell thought. But who was on the back—Heydrich or Hitler?

'Ironic, us meeting again like this,' Giminich observed.

'Ironic?'

'Once we were enemies, and now we are on the same side,' Giminich explained.

'That's tragedy, not irony,' Russell told him. 'Now give me the boring details—who, where, when. The usual preposterous password.'

The German's eyes narrowed for a second, but the smile was soon back in place. The man had learned to control his temper on his journey from Nazi to American buddy. He had probably needed to.

Walking back towards the Press Club half an hour later, Russell found himself passing one of Vienna's more famous hotels, and went in to ask whether, by some miraculous chance, the old telephone connection between Vienna and Berlin was operational again.

'If you pick the right place,' the desk clerk told him mysteriously. The lines were still officially out of use, but private calls could be arranged for a price.

Half an hour later Russell was ensconced in what felt like a large cupboard somewhere deep in the bowels of the Central Exchange, twenty dollars lighter, and standing on a carpet of cigarette stubs. Someone was doing good business.

The telephone looked as if it had only just been screwed to the wall, but dialling their Berlin number elicited a ringing tone.

Rosa answered.

'Rosa, it's me, Papa.' Russell still felt strange using that name, but she had settled on it, and Effi had told him not to discourage her.

'Are you in Trieste? I didn't know you could phone from there.'

'I'm in Vienna. I should be home in a few days. Maybe Wednesday.'

'Oh good. Do you want to tell Mama?'

'Yes, sweetheart.'

He could hear them talking, then Effi came on. 'In a few days?'

'Yes, thank God.'

'What changed their minds?'

'Oh, this and that.' He didn't want to tell her about the bombing over the phone. 'I'm off to Prague tomorrow, and I wanted you know that. I don't really think there's anything to worry about, but just in case. If by any chance I do disappear, then Shchepkin will eventually come looking. Tell him where I went, and he'll ride to my rescue. Okay?'

'Not really, but I'm used to it by now. I don't suppose you'll have time to look up Lisa's daughter?'

'I don't know. Do you have an address?'

'I'll get it.'

He could hear them talking again, hear something drop. His home, he thought. He would soon be back there.

'I just found it in the rubbish,' Effi said. 'She's in Kolin.'

'I remembered that.'

'Seventeen Karlova Street.'

Russell wrote it down. 'If I get the chance,' he promised. 'Is everything okay with you two?'

'We're fine. The sun was even shining today.'

'I'll see you next week. I love you.'

'And I love you, too. I can't wait.'

Which had to be worth more than twenty dollars, he thought. Twenty million perhaps.

His good mood lasted most of the evening, and it wasn't until he was lying in bed at the press club that an unfortunate thought occurred to him. He was assuming that the Americans had forgiven Giminich his crimes in exchange for his anti-communist contacts in Prague, but what if the Austrian had kept his new allies in ignorance of some misdeeds? He might be worried that Russell would betray him. Giminich might even be worried enough to sabotage his own mission, and get Russell himself locked away.

His first stop in Prague, Russell decided, would be the Soviet Embassy; he needed one of those 'Get Out of Jail Free' cards that he'd mentioned to Shchepkin. When it came to the Czechoslovak police, he would just have to trust that these days they were playing by Soviet rules.

At the Rugen Island conference centre, the morning's topic was 'Material Incentives: For and Against.' It was, Ströhm thought, in many ways the crucial issue. Workers were accustomed to working for money, and deciding how hard or enthusiastically they would work according to how much they were paid, so the Party couldn't hope to do away with material incentives in the short run. But if socialism was the goal, then a start had to be made in weaning the workers away from this way of thinking—seeds had to be sown. The question was how.

No satisfactory answers emerged, but the discussion itself was fruitful, perhaps even hopeful. Which was more than could be said for the afternoon session on 'Central Planning and the Political Process.' This seminar made Ströhm profoundly uneasy; the subheading could have been 'Managing the People.' All in their own interest, of course. The Party always knew best, after all. It had the information, the statistics—it knew what was actually possible and what was reckless utopianism. The latter was an enduring curse—offering what couldn't be delivered would, in the long run, lead to mass unhappiness and unrest.

The responsibility for such decisions could only be borne by the Party. An over-reliance on democratic procedures would open the door to a bourgeois resurgence, with all that that implied. The workers would again be seduced by the one big lie, that the free-for-all was fair to all, when in fact it was just a lottery, and a heavily rigged one at that.

No, they couldn't go down that route. The Party would consult of course—no worker's voice would go unheard—but since it alone spoke for all, it had to have the final say. There would have to be safeguards against abuses of power, but the power itself could not be questioned. Not yet.

It was a delicate balance that had to be struck and, not surprisingly, there was some disagreement as to how that should be accomplished, with some delegates arguing for more openness inside the Party, others less inclined to see the need. Ströhm was in the former camp, and might have argued his case a trifle too forcibly, for that evening, after another sumptuous dinner, he was publicly taken to task by Hans Gerstein, one of the two Central Committee members who were attending the conference.

'You people who spent the war at home,' Gerstein began. 'All very heroic, no doubt, but hardly a learning experience. While you were hiding from the Gestapo, those of us lucky enough to be in Moscow were learning how to run a country. Yet here you all are, looking down your noses at us!'

He was more than a little drunk, but Ströhm could see he meant it. 'Surely we can talk openly among ourselves?'

'A naive point of view, Comrade Ströhm. Any divisions weaken us. Unity is everything. We must accentuate what unites us, not what divides us.'

'If we don't talk things through in an open manner, how can we be sure we have reached the right decisions?'

Gerstein snorted. 'Are you no longer a Marxist-Leninist? The Party is the agency of history—its decisions have to be right.'

Ströhm refused to be cowed. 'I expect the Yugoslav Party leaders are saying much the same thing.'

Gerstein's face turned an angry red. 'It takes more than a few adventurers to forge a true communist party. What have these comrades ever done but kill honest German soldiers?'

* * *

Soon after six on Saturday evening a DEFA limousine arrived to take
Effi and Thomas across town for the premiere of *The Peacock's Fan*.
With Russell away, Effi had been resigned to the lack of an escort,
but when Thomas let slip that Hanna was away visiting her parents,
she had successfully inveigled him into the role.

On the ride he seemed quieter than usual, and it suddenly occurred
to her that he might be nervous about entering the Soviet sector.

He laughed at the suggestion. 'God, no. The day I'm frightened to
go anywhere in my own city is the day I'll leave. What gave you that
idea?'

'You haven't said a word since we left.'

'Oh, I suppose I haven't. I'm sorry. Just wretched politics—I'm
beginning to regret ever standing for election.'

'Do you want to talk about it?'

'Why spoil the evening?' He smiled. 'You look fantastic, by
the way.'

'Thank you,' she said, looking down at the low-cut burgundy
dress. She had taken a lot of trouble, and for one particular reason—
Tulpanov had said he would be there tonight. If she knew him, and
she thought she did, then he was one who might be swayed by other
things than reason.

Since Tuesday, barely an hour had gone by without her picturing
Eva Kempka in a prison cell. But what could she actually do? She
had telephoned everyone she could think of who might know Eva,
but nobody had heard anything. She had called the police in all
four sectors, and made a physical nuisance of herself at the three
Western sector HQs. The only reason she hadn't made her presence
felt in the Soviet sector was a realisation that she wouldn't help Eva
by sharing her fate.

Tulpanov was the only high-ranking Soviet official with whom she was on speaking terms, and somehow or other she would make him listen. As she and Thomas were shown to their seats, she looked around for the Russian, but the rows at the front, the usual preserve of Soviet officials and guests, were still largely empty.

Surveying the scene, she had to admit that the cinema looked the part. It had been one of Berlin's seediest in the 1930s, and the last time she'd walked down Neu König Strasse it hadn't been much more than a shell. But the Russians had restored whatever grandeur it had once possessed, and added some more of their own besides. They might have given up on making better films than the Americans, but they could still out-do them when it came to glitter and pomp.

But where was the master showman? Effi was beginning to worry that Tulpanov wasn't coming, when he suddenly appeared, striding down the aisle amidst a coterie of uniforms. As he took his seat in the front row the lights submissively dimmed.

Effi hadn't yet seen a final cut, and the film was even better than she'd thought it would be. Watching its subtle interplay of ideas and emotions against an all too believable historical backdrop, she wondered what the officials three rows down were thinking. Could they not see the difference—the enormous difference—between this and *A Walk into the Future*?

When the credits rolled, Thomas turned and gave her a smile. 'That was excellent,' he said, like someone whose heart and mind had just been fed.

'And how was I?' Effi asked.

'Oh, you're always good.'

Tulpanov and coterie were already filing out to the lobby for the presentations. 'Thomas,' Effi said in a whisper. 'I may be about to cause a bit of a stir. You might want to head straight for the limousine and wait for me there.'

Thomas shook his head. 'What will you be making a stir about?'

'That woman I told you about—the one who knew Sonja Strehl and thinks there was something suspicious about her death. Now she's disappeared, and I'm going to ask Tulpanov if he knows anything about it.'

'And why would I want to miss that?'

'Thomas!'

'They could hardly like me less than they do already, and they're not going to start arresting people tonight, not after they've put on a show like this. But what exactly do you have in mind?'

'I don't know really. I was going to play it by ear.'

'Okay, but in my experience the only way to talk to the Soviets is one-on-one, preferably with no one else in earshot. If you try and show them up in public they either get abusive or turn into hedgehogs—they certainly don't listen.'

Which did sound sensible, Effi thought. And when the time came, and Tulpanov was standing in front of her, happily admiring her cleavage, she spoke accordingly. 'Comrade, I need to talk to you again on a matter of some urgency. After you have finished here, in the manager's office perhaps.'

He looked slightly nonplussed. 'I thought we had sorted this out. I have another appointment.'

'It's either you or the newspapers,' she told him.

That focused him. 'Very well,' he said, his voice suddenly colder.

Half an hour later, she found him and another Russian waiting for her in the office. The latter was hovering at Tulpanov's shoulder like a teacher intent on keeping close watch on a potentially unruly pupil.

'I wanted a private conversation,' she said.

He shrugged. 'That will not be possible.'

'All right. Did you know that the makeup artist on the film you just watched was kidnapped last weekend from her flat in the American sector?'

'No, I didn't.'

'Well she was. By two men who said they were policeman. One was German, the other probably Russian. From the description someone gave me they sound very much like the two who tried to arrest me. And I can find no record of her being taken to any police station in Berlin, in any sector. I will take the matter to the press, but because I respect you and all you have done for the arts in this city, I wanted to speak to you first, and see if you can shed any light on my friend's disappearance.'

He said nothing for a few moments, as if carefully gauging his response. 'We do not kidnap makeup artists,' he said eventually. 'Why on earth would we?

'She was a friend of Sonja Strehl, and she's been making enquiries into Sonja's death—she doesn't believe it was suicide, and the people she was harassing may have decided that giving her a scare would shut her up.'

While Tulpanov considered this, the other Soviet official just stared at Effi. He wasn't looking at a woman, she thought, just at a piece of meat.

'I will look into this,' Tulpanov said, with obvious reluctance. 'In the meantime, I strongly advise you not to repeat these anti-Soviet accusations in public. And especially not to the Western press. As tonight's film showed, you have done wonderful work for us—for DEFA, I mean—and I would hate to see such a mutually beneficial relationship come to an end. Let me look into it, before you do anything which can't be undone.'

It was all she was going to get. She wanted to explode with anger, but that wouldn't help Eva, so she thanked him for talking to her, and promised to hold fire until she heard from him again.

Tulpanov took her hand and kissed it. 'I hope we shall meet again,' he said, the stiffly spoken words starkly at odds with an almost fatherly look of warning. He would have made a good actor, she thought.

'Any success?' Thomas asked, once they were in the limousine.

'Not really. He promised to investigate, but I got the feeling that he doesn't have that sort of clout anymore, if he ever did. The man who was leaning over him on the other hand . . .'

'MGB?'

'I suppose so. Thomas, what else can I do?'

'When's John back?'

'Sometime this week.'

'His Soviet friends might be able to help.'

'They might,' Effi agreed, with more hope than conviction.

The final session of Ströhm's conference was concerned with Culture and Sport, two subjects which would normally have interested him. This time though, he gave them a miss, and went for a walk on the beach. A couple teaching their infant son to swim reminded him of his own impending fatherhood, and brought a smile to his face. At first he had wanted a boy, but over the past few days the idea of a daughter had become more appealing.

Cilly had been on his mind lately; Cilly, the first love of his life. The Gestapo might have hurled her to her death from a fourth-floor window, but she still lived on in his memory, and, through the influence she retained over him, still played her part in the world. Ströhm wondered what she would think of their Party now, and how she would judge his own increasing uncertainty. She wouldn't want him to walk away, to give up—that much he knew. But neither would she want him to lose touch with those gut feelings which had anchored their shared beliefs—the hatred of injustice, of a system in which the pleasures of the few were bought with the pain of the many.

Somewhere in all of this was a line he couldn't cross without betraying her, without betraying himself. He still wasn't yet clear where that line was, but he now had no doubt it existed. My Party, right or wrong, was no longer an option.

Russell's train pulled into Prague's Wilson Station—named after the US president who had sponsored Czechoslovak independence—soon after three on Friday afternoon. The Nazis had called it something else during the war, but he couldn't remember what.

Both here and at the border crossing, the number of men in uniform had tripled since his last visit, and considering the swastikas hanging everywhere back then, that was some achievement. So far icy politeness was the worst he had suffered, but there was plenty of time. And it wasn't the ones in uniform, he reminded himself, who constituted the real enemy. The *Státni bezpečnost*, or StB, had built itself a fearsome reputation when the post-war coalition was still in charge, and now that the communists were ruling alone, the gutter was presumably the limit.

It was a cool spring afternoon, the sun flitting between clouds. He walked across to Wenceslas Square, then down the wide Václavske Náměstí to the Europa Hotel, already aware of being followed. When he'd stayed there in 1939 the desk clerk had been a male fan of Kafka's; now it was a stick-thin woman who looked like she'd just eaten a lemon. But she agreed to his renewing his acquaintance with his old room, which overlooked the boulevard from the third floor. He had survived his previous stay there, which might be a good omen. With any luck he'd be in Berlin by Wednesday, back where at least a few people loved him.

After a bath he dressed and went back down in the lift, intent on seeking out a restaurant he remembered, but was accosted halfway across the lobby by a smartly dressed woman in her twenties, with short black hair and a catlike face.

'John Russell?' she asked, though he didn't imagine she had any doubt. 'My name is Petra Klíma, from the Ministry of Culture. Could we talk for a few minutes?' She gestured towards a couple of armchairs in the farthest corner of the lobby.

'Of course,' Russell said equably. Her English was excellent.

'I know you have your schedule,' she said, once they were seated, 'and nothing has changed in the arrangements which the Ministry agreed with your magazine *The Lampadary*, so you have no reason to worry.' She smiled. 'Which is good.'

'It is,' Russell agreed, wondering exactly where this was going.

'If there are any problems, or if you have any special needs, then call me on this number.' She passed across a hand-cut piece of cardboard on which some figures had been scrawled.

'Thank you.'

'That is all I need to say. But for my own curiosity, I wonder if I could ask you a question about your magazine. The name—what does it mean?'

'In the old Greek church a lampadary carried a flaming taper to light the way for his patriarch,' Russell explained. This had been included in his CIA briefing sheet, along with other information about the Agency's newly created—and paradoxically long-standing—arts journal.

'I see,' Klíma said. 'Whose idea was that—the owner's?'

Which was seamless enough for a Hollywood script, Russell thought. '*The Lampadary* doesn't have one,' he told her, following his own. 'It's owned by a cooperative—a group of Americans who believe that art transcends politics, and can act as a unifying force.'

'But how can art not be political?' she wanted to know.

'Mozart? Van Gogh?'

Klíma looked doubtful. She probably thought that despair at the condition of the Dutch proletariat had taken Vincent out to the wheat field. 'Perhaps music and painting,' she reluctantly conceded, 'but poetry, literature?'

'"When a talk about trees is a crime, because it implies silence about so many horrors,"' Russell quoted Brecht.

'Yes, yes. That is what I mean.'

'Well, these are the sort of questions I want to explore in my interviews,' Russell told her. 'How artists use their individual talents in the service of the community,' he added glibly. 'That's what *The Lampadary* is all about.'

'I shall look forward to reading it,' she said, getting to her feet.

Which was more than he would, Russell thought, as he walked through the Old City in search of his restaurant. He found a building he thought he recognised, but the boards nailed across the ground-floor frontage offered no clue to its former use, and he had to settle for another establishment, a few metres farther along. This, like his hotel, seemed strangely empty, but it couldn't be the menu to blame—Prague had suffered relatively little in the war, and if the dishes on offer at this restaurant were any guide, the economic situation was a lot better here than it was in Berlin or Vienna.

After eating, he ambled back to his hotel. The streets were subdued, as if Sunday had come a day early, and even with the window open, it was quiet enough for an early night.

He was up too early for a hotel breakfast, but a café was open just down the street. His first interview—with a female poet he'd never heard of—was scheduled for eleven A.M. at the Charles University, which he reckoned gave him enough time to visit the Soviet Embassy. A tram carried him north across the Štefánika Bridge, and a short walk down Pod Kastany brought him to the Embassy gates.

The preceding ten years—and Shchepkin's patient tutoring over the past three—had vastly honed his skills when it came to dealing with Soviet officialdom, and he emerged only fifteen minutes later with the local MGB emergency number for Soviet agents in distress. After his tram dropped him at the eastern end of the Charles Bridge, he walked across the river and up the hill, arriving at the university with ten minutes to spare.

The poet, a woman in her fifties, was a delight. A lifelong communist with an apparently bottomless faith in human possibility, she had met and befriended several of the current government at university in the years following the First War. She cheerfully admitted that a few might succumb to megalomania, but insisted the others would sort them out. This, as she said with a laugh, wasn't Poland; this was a country with a long industrial history, and a politically conscious working class to prove it. As for the arts, there might be some temporary limits, but the eventual flowering would be more than worth it.

The conductor, whom he interviewed that afternoon in a well-appointed Old City apartment, was pleasant enough but far less interesting. His recent adherence to the Party, Russell quickly realised, had less to do with ideology than Soviet sponsorship of his chosen field. While the Nazis had belittled Smetana and Dvorak, the Soviets had presided over the post-war resurrection of these two Czechs in particular and classical music in general. The way this conductor talked, one could be forgiven for thinking that Stalin had personally driven a van-load of surplus violins all the way from Moscow.

Which, Russell supposed, was the point. Since classical music was, to most intents and purposes, politically neutral, the Soviets could pick up cultural brownie points from promoting it. And for people like this conductor, the future was set fair—as long as he kept any non-musical opinions to himself, he could expect a secure and privileged life. Russell didn't like the man or his Habsburg furniture very much, but that was neither here nor there.

Walking back to the Europa, he wondered what Winterman and Co would do with these interviews. Just print them verbatim, he supposed. It would be good propaganda for the Soviets in the short run; but the CIA would be playing a long game, establishing the magazine's reputation for political impartiality, so that when they eventually stuck in the knife, it would be that much more effective.

Sitting down to another excellent meal, Russell wondered how much easier his life would have been if he'd just done what he was told. Why hadn't he? What had made him the pain in the arse that Winterman and others thought him? His father had been conventional to a fault, his mother more rebellious in spirit, although not when it really mattered. The First War had confirmed Russell's belief that the status quo was a kind of freewheeling murderous cock-up that only served the rich, but he'd felt that since he was about fourteen. A born communist, except that when the time came, he had rejected the comrades as well.

What did it matter? He was who he was, approaching fifty with the same basic anger, a disgust that seemed to be deepening, and a lack of answers that was almost comical. The only trick, he suspected, was to look for love in the margins, but even they seemed narrower by the year.

Back in his room, he was preparing for bed when the softest of knocks sounded on his door.

A man was outside, middle-aged, with luxuriant iron-grey hair which flopped across his forehead. He was wearing what looked like two halves of different suits and a white shirt smeared with egg stains. He also had a finger raised to his lips.

Russell let the man in, and followed him into the bathroom. Once the tap was running, his visitor curtly offered the agreed password— 'spring is beautiful in Prague'—and introduced himself as Karel. He didn't, however, have affidavits stuffed in his pockets. 'They wouldn't be safe in your room, and these days foreigners are often stopped and searched on the street, so we must hand them to you at the final moment. When do you leave?'

'At six o'clock on Monday, from Wilson Station. The evening train to Vienna.'

'Okay. You know where the National Museum is?'

'Yes.'

'There are two entrances, one at the top of the boulevard and a second on the far side, in the gardens. Get to the first at around three thirty P.M., check your suitcase as if you're intent on touring the exhibits until it's time to go to the station, then shake your shadow and leave by the back entrance. From that door you can see the end of Římská Street, and there is a small café, with a dark-red awning, about fifty metres down. There's no name outside, but should you need to ask, locals know it as the Galuška Café. Be there by five, and order a coffee. Within a few minutes a departing customer will offer you a newspaper that they've finished with, and the affidavits will be inside. Once you have them, go back to the museum, pick up your suitcase and shadow, and walk to the station. Understood?'

'Understood.'

'Good. And good luck.' He gave Russell a reassuring pat on the shoulder, and headed for the outer door.

Russell reached to turn off the tap, then remembered he hadn't yet brushed his teeth. 'Some more cloak-and-dagger to look forward to,' he told his reflection in the mirror.

Sunday morning was sunny, warm, and ideal for sightseeing, but Russell reluctantly decided that Lisa's daughter Uschi had a prior claim on his time. Over breakfast he thought the matter through, and decided that there was no cause for subterfuge. The communist government had not, as far as he knew, introduced any new restrictions on the movements of foreigners, so a morning trip out to Kolin shouldn't set any legal tripwires twanging. And unless the Czech Embassy in Berlin was keeping its business to itself, the authorities here in Prague would already know that Lisa Sundgren, the former Liesel Hausmann, was trying to track down her daughter Uschi. What could be more natural than her asking him to look up the girl while he was in the vicinity?

There seemed no reason why Uschi should suffer from the attention. The Czech authorities already knew who her parents were, and she couldn't help the fact that her father had been a wealthy industrialist.

So he would go to Kolin that morning, and take his shadow along for the ride, because shaking him off would indeed look suspicious, and make him harder to ditch on Monday, when he really was doing something illicit.

His latest shadow—the third so far—was lurking in the lobby, as yet unaware of the journey in store. The Kolin trains went from Masaryk Station, which in the past he had always used on his trips to and from Berlin—it was here Giminich's goons had intercepted him seven years earlier. The Nazis had called it the Hibernerbahnhof, but the original name had been restored in 1945. As he walked in through the gabled glass front of the terminus Russell wondered if the new government would change it again, now that it served as a reminder of the son's suspicious demise.

There was a train to Kolin in twenty-five minutes. He bought a return ticket and took a seat on the concourse. His shadow, who had followed him into the booking office, and doubtless enquired as to where he was going, now strode across to one of the public phone booths, and peered out at Russell before dialling a number. After brief conversation, he re-emerged and took a seat of his own. Head Office had apparently sanctioned their jaunt to Kolin.

The forty-mile journey took almost two hours, the train squeaking to a halt at every conceivable platform, and a few other places beside. The booking office clerk at Kolin had never heard of Karlova Street, but one of the waiting passengers had—it was out on the other side of town, a fifteen-minute walk away. Once through the centre, he should follow the smell of the brewery.

His shadow had walked straight through to the forecourt, for reasons that now became clear—he'd been met by a local colleague in a Skoda Popular. They and their car now settled into Russell's wake, purring along behind him at walking pace as he headed across town. Once through the centre, a group of boys playing football gave him further directions to Karlova Street, and soon he was walking down a line of workers' cottages, looking for Number 17.

A woman in her fifties or sixties answered his knock.

'Uschi Hausmann?' he asked, knowing it couldn't be her.

She shut the door without a word, but gently enough to suggest she might be back.

A young man re-opened it. There was an enamel red star in his jacket lapel, and he didn't look particularly friendly, but to Russell's relief he spoke passable Russian. 'What's your business with Uschi?' he asked aggressively.

Russell explained that he had a message from her mother.

'What message? Her mother abandoned her.'

'The message is for her.'

He thought about that for a few seconds, then stepped aside for Russell to enter. A girl of about twenty was waiting in the front room, looking anxious. Her wavy blonde hair framed a strikingly beautiful face. She spoke German of course, but insisted on translating everything for the young man, whom she introduced as Ladislav. 'I thought my mother was dead,' was the first thing she said after Russell had explained his reason for being there. 'Where has she been all these years?'

Russell explained as best he could.

'So she's in Berlin. Why didn't she come herself?'

'The authorities won't give her a visa. You may not know it, but your government in Prague has been restricting travel in and out of the country over the past few months.'

The boy bristled at that. 'It's the Western governments who have been making things difficult. They send many spies—everyone knows it.'

'Whoever's to blame,' Russell told Uschi, 'your mother can't get to you. So she is hoping that you can come to her. I'm sure the government wouldn't stand in the way of a family reunion,' he added, more for the young man's benefit than because he really believed it.

Ladislav was shaking his head. 'This is out of the question. We are getting married in a few weeks.'

'Ah. I understand. Would you like to write to your mother?' he asked Uschi. 'I could take a letter back with me.'

She looked uncertain.

'Ladislav said that you think she abandoned you,' Russell said. 'I have to tell you that she believes she saved you from the Gestapo by sending you off to the mountains, and that when they came for her, she had no choice but to run. That if she hadn't abandoned you, you would be an orphan.'

'It's been so long.'

'America is a long way away, and she had a baby to look after. You have a little sister.'

She said something to Ladislav in Czech, which Russell guessed was a plea for permission. When he nodded, she turned back to

Russell, and said she would write the letter. Would he like some tea while he waited?

Now that the main matter was decided, Ladislav seemed to relax, and the two of them spent the next twenty minutes discussing Czechoslovakia's future. The lad obviously cared for his country, fellow citizens and soon-to-be wife, but Russell wouldn't have entered him in a political perspicacity contest. He kept his own fears for Czechoslovakia to himself, and hoped that in this one instance he would be proved wrong.

Eventually Uschi emerged, her letter written and sealed. 'I hope my mother understands,' she told Russell. 'That I'm grown-up now, and my place is here. I've included a photograph of Ladislav and me, so that she'll know.'

'I'm sure she'll be happy that you're happy,' Russell told her. 'And I'm sure she'll write back, now that she knows exactly where you are. And later, when things are a bit more settled, maybe she can visit you or you can visit her.'

'America is a long way away,' Ladislav insisted, but Russell could see the young man was drawn by the prospect. As he turned to leave, he remembered the Skoda outside. 'I was followed when I came here,' he told them, 'and I expect they'll follow me back again. But later, someone will want to ask you what we talked about. I just thought I'd warn you, so it's not a surprise.'

Walking back to the station, the car twenty metres behind him, he thought about Lisa Sundgren. He'd never met her of course, but they shared one terrible thing—both had been forced to choose between leaving a child and almost certain death. He had never really hesitated, because both were forms of abandonment, and the former at least held hope of eventual reunion, but he was still acutely aware of what havoc his sudden departure had wreaked on Paul's psyche.

And now, just like his own son, Lisa's long-lost daughter was getting married, setting the distance between them in stone. From this point forth the best either could hope for were letters full of news and strangers' names, pictures of grandchildren, and once-in-a-blue-moon visits.

The Soviet response to Effi's challenge—or at least its first instalment—arrived on Monday morning. The top-grade ration card given to first-rank artists was being withdrawn, on the grounds that she was no longer actively pursuing her career in Berlin. Her rejection of the DEFA script proved as much.

This was annoying, but hardly shattering. With Russell's multiple employers and Zarah's American connection their extended family wasn't short on privilege, economic or otherwise.

The second instalment, which appeared at Effi's door that afternoon, was of another order altogether. The official from City Hall looked meek enough, but the message he brought was potentially devastating. Irregularities had been discovered in their adoption of Rosa, which was now to be reviewed. There were doubts as to whether sufficient diligence had been exerted in the search for Rosa's real father, doubts as to whether a former star of the National Socialist film industry could be considered a suitable parent.

Effi treated the official with what seemed appropriate disdain, but dissolved into tears the moment the door closed behind him. It was all absurd, but what did right or reason have to do with it? They were playing their games to win, and they didn't care how.

The film director Jaromír Císař was short and wiry, with longish black hair and busy eyes. His Smichov apartment had a distinctly Bohemian air, which wasn't that common in Gottwald's Bohemia. Shelves and tables were crowded with exotic *objets d'art*, walls plastered with film stills. Some of the latter were doubtless from Císař's own films, but others Russell recognised—the dentist's chair scene from *Horse Feathers*, Dietrich wreathed in smoke on the *Shanghai Express*, Arletty and a love-sick Jean-Louis Barrault in *Les Enfants du Paradis*.

Císař was talkative enough, but Russell had the sense of someone calibrating his answers quite carefully. He was, he said, convinced that good films could be made in the current political climate, but the way he said it made you wonder whether they would be. 'Let me put it this way—everyone knows that in capitalist countries commercial pressures distort the artistic process. Well, we have to admit it, so do political pressures in the new socialist countries. In both environments, artists have to make compromises that they don't really want to make. And in both environments it's possible to . . . I am looking for the right verb here, and the one that comes to mind is "smuggle"—so, it's possible to smuggle good work past the distorters.'

'So socialism offers no advantage to the artist?'

'Oh, I didn't say that. Under capitalism, the freedom to create is spurious, because it so rarely transcends the individual. Under socialism, the artist is invited, encouraged, to use his creativity for the society as a whole. Which means that in the more popular forms—like cinema—we can offer something more than shallow entertainment. There is a deeper purpose at work.'

The more Císař talked, the more Russell wished he'd actually seen one of the man's films. He remembered Effi being complimentary about one of them, and said as much to the director.

'You are married to Effi Koenen! She is one my favourite German actors—some of her recent work with DEFA—well, it's been superb. She always had a face made for the camera, but these days . . . Look,' Císař said, leaping up and striding across to the wall of pictures, 'here she is in *The Man I Shall Kill*.'

And there she was, playing Greta Larstein. It wasn't a still that Russell had seen before, and it felt strange finding it there, on a Prague apartment wall.

'She doesn't speak Czech by any chance?'

'No.'

'Well, maybe I will work in Berlin one day,' he said, still looking at the photo. 'What a face she has!' He closed his eyes, as if picturing her in front of his camera.

As they said goodbye at the door, Císař twice insisted that Russell pass on his respect and admiration for Effi's recent work, and he loudly lamented the fact that any flowers he sent her would be dead before they reached Berlin.

Russell walked down to the river, pleased that someone Effi admired liked her so much in return. In the 1930s she had often seemed too good for the roles she was asked to play, but over the past few years most of the parts had given her talents full rein. At least one good thing had come out of their unfortunate Russian connections, he thought, as he walked out across the Legii Bridge. The Charles was divided by Střelecký Island at this point, and down to his left he could see the site of his first contact with the Resistance in the last month of peace, a bench now occupied by two old women. One day he would like to arrive in Prague with no clandestine meetings in prospect. Some hope.

Feeling hungry, Russell walked into the first decent-looking restaurant he found on Národní. Anticipating a likely dearth of edible fare on his evening train, he ordered three courses and a bottle of expensive Moravian wine. The American taxpayers would have to fork up, which served them right for employing Winterman.

It was three P.M. by the time he got back to the Europa, which made packing and checking out a hurried affair, but the local clocks were only just striking the half-hour when he passed through the

National Museum's front entrance, the usual distance ahead of his StB shadow. After handing his suitcase in at the cloakroom, he leisurely sauntered on into the first gallery, abruptly changing pace the moment he was out of sight. His tail, having lost him, would have no choice but to stay with his luggage.

He found the back entrance without much trouble, lingered a while to make sure he had thrown off the shadow, then started down Římská. He could already see the dark-red awning, a splash of colour in the grey stone street. Or perhaps, the thought crossed his mind, a red rag to a bull.

At least this *treff*, as the Soviets called such meetings, was in a public place. If the UDBA officers had shot him dead at Pograjac's lonely Belgrade apartment, the rest of the world would have been none the wiser.

Only two of the tables were occupied, one by a middle-aged man in a suit, the other by a young woman in a blue summer dress. Both had folded newspapers in front of them.

As instructed, Russell ordered a cup of Viennese coffee. He still felt full from lunch, and one sip was sufficient to deter any more.

A shadow crossed his table, and the girl was standing over him, holding out the paper and saying something in Czech. The stress in her voice was palpable, but then she didn't have an MGB help number.

'*Dekuji*,' he said with a smile, using up most of his Czech vocabulary.

She nodded abruptly and walked out through the open door.

He carefully opened the paper, making sure that anything falling out would land in his lap. An envelope did.

Knowing it was out of sight, he let it lie there while making a show of refolding the paper and examining its front page. He only recognised a few of the words, but the picture featured a smiling Klement Gottwald, surrounded by eager young children. After a few moments he held the paper up as if he was reading the bottom half, and slickly moved the envelope from lap to inside pocket.

It was time he got back to the museum. After digging out some coins for the tip, he headed for the street.

They were waiting on the pavement, two to the left and two to the right. He didn't resist, but they insisted on frog-marching him to the paddy wagon and almost throwing him into the back. It was only when the door clanged shut that he realised the girl was there with him, tears already glistening on her cheeks. When he responded to her rapid-fire Czech with a shrug of incomprehension, she began to sob, and he took her in his arms.

The drive took fewer than five minutes, and they were separated on arrival in the cobbled courtyard. Russell was led down a flight of worn stone steps, past several cells of Thirty Years War vintage, and propelled through the empty door of the very last one. As he turned to protest, a fist rammed into his stomach, doubling him up and exposing the back of his neck to some sort of truncheon. This put him on his knees for a split second, before one boot tipped him over, and another took the wind from his chest. He was still laboriously trying to curl himself up when he heard the cell door slam.

After lying there for a few minutes, he painfully manoeuvred himself into a sitting position, up against the wall. He had no memory of their being taken, but watch, wallet and affidavits were gone. So too was his 'Get Out of Jail Free' card, the local MGB's telephone number. He had taken the precaution of memorising it, but the recent assault had apparently scrambled his memory.

It was at least two hours before they came back for him. This time there was no violence, just more stone steps and cold efficiency. He reckoned the room he ended up in was on the third floor, but the lack of a window meant he couldn't be sure. This lack was comforting, though—the Czechs were famous for their defenestrations.

The latest interrogator shared traits with several of his predecessors—a uniform pressed within an inch of its life, a fussy way with his hands, and a smugness quotient of around 200 percent. This one's name was Colonel Hanzelka, and the only remaining question was whether or not he was also a sadist.

At least he spoke German. Russell wasted no time announcing his attachment to the MGB.

Hanzelka looked incredulous.

'Telephone their Embassy,' Russell told him. 'Better still, call the number which is in the wallet your men took. It's a direct line to the local MGB.'

The Colonel gave him one more look, then turned to a subordinate. Russell didn't understand their interchange, but the subordinate's subsequent exit boded well.

'If you work for the MGB, why are you part of an American plot against this country?' Hanzelka asked icily.

'I don't think the Soviets would thank me for telling you.'

'The Soviets are our allies, not our masters, and this is not the Soviet Union. You would be well advised to remember that.'

Russell nodded. 'As long as you're happy keeping Moscow's secrets, I'm happy to explain.'

That brought doubt to Hanzelka's eyes, but he overrode it. 'Please do.'

'The Americans think I work for them. Occasionally I'm ordered to do something which strengthens their illusion.'

'You are a double-agent?' The Czech sounded surprised, though God only knew why.

'Of course,' Russell told him.

'Well, well.'

The subordinate returned, and another exchange took place in Czech.

'Comrade Rusikov is on his way,' Hanzelka told Russell, who tried not to look too relieved. 'Since we're on the same side,' the Colonel, was saying, 'you might as well tell me what you know about this operation.'

'It looks like you know it all already.'

'Most of it,' Hanzelka conceded.

'I was asked to collect some signed affidavits. Statements from people who witnessed Jan Masaryk's murder.'

Hanzelka was smiling.

'Fakes, I presume.'

'How could they not be when Masaryk jumped?'

'They were bait,' Russell suggested.

'Of course.'

They had probably rolled up half of Giminich's organisation, Russell thought. Which felt strangely satisfying until he remembered the girl in the blue dress.

'So, who was in charge of this operation?' Hanzelka asked.

'An Austrian named Volker Giminich.'

'On his own?'

Russell was reluctant to name Winterman, who as far as he knew wasn't a mass murderer. But neither did he want the Soviets to find out that he was keeping things from them. He opted for partial disclosure: 'An American was in nominal charge, of course, but Giminich is running the show.'

'He likes to do that,' Hanzelka allowed.

'You know him?'

'He was based here during the war—one of Heydrich's more zealous disciples.'

Russell wondered whether to reveal his own previous acquaintance with Giminich, and decided against it. His earlier visits to Czechoslovakia seemed like a can of worms best left unopened—he

had no idea what had happened to the Czechs he had been involved
with in 1939 and 1941, or whose side they might now be on. 'The
Americans have some strange allies,' was all he said.

'"Strange" is not the word I would use to describe Volker
Giminich.'

'You know him better than I do,' Russell said, realising it must be
true. This Czech had a personal score to settle.

Rusikov's arrival spared him the details. The MGB officer gave
Hanzelka a warm handshake, and Russell something more perfunc-
tory. For the next few minutes the conversation was conducted in
Czech.

'You will take the affidavits to Vienna as planned,' Rusikov told
Russell eventually.

He looked suitably surprised.

'They won't stand close scrutiny,' Rusikov explained. 'If the Americans publish them, we will have no trouble proving they are forgeries. People will assume one of two things, that the Americans forged
them themselves, or that they were duped by their own supporters
here in Prague.'

'Okay, I'll take them.'

'You realise that Giminich must not know that any of his people
have been arrested,' Rusikov went on. 'Some have already been
turned, and we hope to entice him close to the border—so a snatch
squad can bring him back here for trial.'

'I understand,' Russell said. And he did. Put Giminich in a Prague
courtroom, and the new Czech authorities would be able to draw
damning connections between Nazi war crimes, American spies, and
the regime's current domestic opponents. A real political bonanza.

The Soviets were so much better at this stuff than the Americans.
If they had a cause worth fighting for they'd be damn near
invincible.

'You can still catch the night train,' Hanzelka was telling him. 'The lieutenant here'—he indicated the young man who had just arrived with Russell's suitcase—'will take you to the station and make the arrangements.'

As they emerged on to Bartolomejská, where a car was waiting, Russell glanced back at the building. It seemed utterly anonymous; the grey walls and shuttered windows were a highly effective mask. Somewhere in the basement the girl in the blue dress would still be crying.

The lieutenant said nothing on their drive, but proved singularly efficient when it came to securing him a private sleeping compartment. Russell had concluded that he only spoke Czech, but at the carriage door the young man wished him 'a safe journey, Comrade,' before striding almost jauntily back down the platform.

The train set off on time, its large locomotive convulsively blowing off steam. There was, Russell discovered, no restaurant or bar on board, so he spent the next fifteen minutes by an open window, enjoying the warm air on his face, gazing out at the dark countryside. Dark in more ways than one, he thought. He wouldn't come this way again in a hurry.

Considering the terrible state of the track, sleep came quite easily, and when he finally woke they weren't much more than an hour from Vienna. It was still only seven A.M. when he finished his breakfast in the Nordbahnhof buffet, so he took a taxi to Josefstadt, and sat enjoying the morning sunshine in a small park not far from the house on Florianigasse. He resisted the temptation to read the affidavits—if and when they blew up in Winterman's face, he wanted the man to remember that the envelope had been sealed.

He knocked on the CIA's door at nine A.M., and was surprised to find both Winterman and Giminich already at work. They were excited by the affidavits, and appreciative of his efforts, which at least made a change. They asked very few questions—their operation had gone according to plan, which was only to be expected. And no, there was nothing to detain him further. With the help of the duty officer downstairs he should be back in Berlin by evening.

As it turned out, that day's flights were already full, but Russell was happy to spend another day in Vienna—his Rat Line story needed a few hours' work, and it would be safer to send it on from there—Berlin's channels of communication were less reliable and much less discreet. At the American Press Club he commandeered a typewriter, and spent most of the rest of the day turning his notes into a series of three articles that would, he hoped, embarrass the hell out of any institution with a moral compass. Whether the State Department and Vatican qualified as such was another matter.

After sending it all off to Solly Bernstein in London, Russell walked around to the Press Club. There he found an abandoned London *Times*, in which he learnt that the Nationalists had won the previous week's election in South Africa. From earlier reports he knew that these were people who believed in keeping the country's races apart, and *apartheid* was apparently the name of their creed, the Afrikaans for 'separate development.' This was post-war progress, he thought—from Aryans murdering Jews to Aryans merely enslaving Negroes. And all in three short years!

After dinner in a local restaurant he walked over to the Central Exchange and purchased another illicit telephone call to Berlin. 'I'll be back tomorrow,' he told Effi. 'The flight from Frankfurt should reach Tempelhof around four, give or take an hour or so.'

Effi's 'thank God' was a little too heartfelt.

'What's happened?'

'Nothing. Not yet, anyway. Someone turned up at the door and suggested that Rosa's adoption might not be legal.'

'Who? When?'

'Yesterday. He said he was from City Hall, and he probably was, but the Russians must be behind it. Thinking it over, I feel sure they're just trying it on, but at the time I felt almost hysterical.'

'I can see why.'

'Well, I'm glad you'll be back tomorrow. I'll come to the airport.'

She sounded calm enough, but Russell could hear the tension in her tone. Next morning, as his military flight droned its way across Bavaria, he found himself willing the pilot to step on the gas, as if some inner voice was warning him that their time was finally running out.

Merzhanov

Berlin from the air was more of a shock than Russell expected—either three months away had blunted his memory, or he'd just grown accustomed to cities that didn't look like some fantastic giant had repeatedly hit them with an outsize hammer. There were signs of rebuilding, but they still seemed far too few for the time that had passed. One thing was certain—if the Führer suddenly emerged from hiding, he would recognise the place.

Effi was waiting at the terminal doors, lovely as ever, eyes full of worry. Before taking the U-Bahn home they went for a walk in nearby Viktoria Park, where in pre-war days they'd often enjoyed the panoramic view from the top of the Kreuzberg. This time they eschewed the climb, circling the base of the hill as they discussed the latest Soviet behaviour.

'You and Shchepkin can fix this, can't you?' Effi half-asked, half-pleaded.

Russell shrugged. 'I hope so. I just don't understand what anyone thinks they could gain from threatening us like this. It doesn't make sense. And until it does, it's hard to know what we should do about it. But I can't believe they want to take Rosa away from us—they're just trying to scare you. We just don't know why.'

'According to Shchepkin the two men who tried to take me for questioning were investigating Sonja Strehl's death, but back in April the police were telling everyone that no investigation was needed. It must all have something to do with Sonja's death—I can't believe the Soviets are that upset about losing my services.'

'They should be,' Russell suggested gallantly, 'but they probably aren't. Shchepkin will be able to find out.'

'I hope so. This feels worse than waiting for the Gestapo to turn up.'

Russell pulled her to him. 'They won't take Rosa away from us,' he promised.

'I'll kill anyone who tries,' she vowed.

'We'll do it together. Now, I have some bad news for your friend Lisa.'

Effi looked up. 'Uschi's not dead, is she?'

'Far from it. She's getting married in a couple of months. To a young Party zealot.'

'And she isn't the slightest bit interested in escaping to America,' Effi guessed.

'Precisely.' Russell explained what had happened, and how the girl had thought herself abandoned. 'I've got a letter for Lisa, and a picture of the happy couple.'

'Oh dear.' Effi looked at her watch. 'It's time we went to pick up Rosa. I'll go and see Lisa tomorrow.'

As they walked back to the U-Bahn she told him that Zarah was cooking him a 'welcome home' meal, and that Thomas had been invited.

'Just Thomas?'

'Hanna's still at her parents, and Lotte's got a new boyfriend, another young zealot by all accounts. Thomas told her he was pleased with her romance. When she asked why, he told her the family needed all the political insurance it could get.'

'Annaliese?'

'She's fine, positively glowing, as they say. But worried about Gerhard. She says he keeps muttering under his breath.'

Russell sighed. 'He's too honest for Ulbricht's KPD. Have the Russians been acting up?'

'Nothing serious.'

After collecting an excited Rosa, they dropped off Russell's suitcase at the flat and continued on to Fasanen Strasse. Zarah was already cooking, and Thomas arrived not long after. It felt like a real homecoming to Russell, and the joy of seeing his family again was only slightly marred by the absence of his son, and the fear that soon they might all be scattered again. Catching Zarah alone in the kitchen, he offered congratulations for her and Bill's engagement.

'I'm sure Effi could get work in America,' Zarah said, clearly unaware that some was already on offer. 'And you know you could,' she added, conveniently forgetting the devil's bargain that held him in Berlin.

The thought of returning to America was far from unappealing, Russell thought later, although Zarah's prospective hometown in Iowa was probably not the most obvious fit for Effi or himself.

He had another 'welcome home' the following morning at the Berlin Operations Base HQ in Zehlendorf. It wasn't as warm or fulsome as the one on Fasanen Strasse, but still a big improvement on his usual reception in the villa above Trieste. His old Berlin boss Scott Dallin was long gone, and the current incumbent, Brent Johannsen, was less annoying than most of the Americans Russell had met in the Intelligence business. He looked as Scandinavian as his name suggested— tall, blond, and almost insultingly handsome. Johannsen was quick on the uptake, impressively thorough, but rather too narrow-minded. He was ruthless enough when he had to be, but unlike some he didn't seem to enjoy it.

Johannsen was in a talkative mood that morning. 'This is top secret,' he confided, with the air of someone who didn't give a hoot how many people knew. 'There was a high-level meeting yesterday in the British Sector—we really are going to bring in a currency reform.'

'I don't suppose the Russians were invited.'

'No way. This reform's coming, and soon. Before the month is out.'

'Here in Berlin?'

'Maybe, maybe not.'

Russell shook his head. 'That's not good enough. Whoever controls the currency runs the economy, and whoever controls the economy runs the country. If Washington leaves Berlin out, then they're handing it to the Russians.'

Johannsen just shrugged. 'That's above my pay-grade. All I know is there's no such thing as a secret meeting in Berlin, and the Russians will be fully briefed on this one. Which means trouble for us. They'll want to get their retaliation in first.'

'Probably,' Russell agreed. He was wondering if this might be how the Americans meant to abandon Berlin, but he couldn't really believe it to be true. That would be like admitting they'd finally lost the peace. Could they do that? If they could, then he really should send Effi and Rosa away.

'When's your next meeting with Ilych?' Johannsen was asking. Ilych was Shchepkin's codename.

'We meet on Fridays.'

'Well, see what you can get out of him. In the meantime, we're fresh out of defectors, but seriously short-staffed. Martin Bronson's on compassionate leave, and I'd like you to run Claptrap until he comes back.'

'Fine,' Russell agreed. After Trieste, BOB's long-standing surveillance of VD-stricken Soviet officers would be refreshingly straightforward.

* * *

After reading her daughter's letter, Lisa Sundgren stared blankly out at the busy Ku'damm, a solitary tear running down each cheek. Angrily wiping these away, she picked up the photograph and scanned it again, as if she might have missed something crucial. 'I hardly recognise her,' she said eventually.

'It's been a long time,' Effi said.

'I know, but what can I *do*?' Lisa almost pleaded.

Go home, Effi thought, but that seemed too brutal an answer. 'You have another daughter,' she offered gently. This one is lost to you, she thought.

'I know that, of course I do. But I can't just walk away from Uschi, forget she exists. I can't.'

'It needn't be forever. John thinks the situation will improve over the next few months, and then travel in and out will get easier.'

'I can't wait that long.'

'I know,' Effi said. She found herself remembering John's stories of Irish children who'd emigrated to America in the past century, exchanged letters for decades, but never actually seen their parents again. Heartbreaking.

'So what can I do?' Lisa repeated, defeat in her tone.

'Sometimes there's nothing you can do. And John did say she seemed very happy.'

Lisa seemed almost to wince. 'Well, that's something. Everything really.' She turned her gaze to the street again, where an over-crowded tram was passing. 'There's nothing worse than losing a child,' she added, sounding almost surprised.

They parted with promises to keep in touch, but Effi doubted they would. When she got home there was a hand-posted letter from Max Grelling waiting for her on the mat. He had samples of the documents she'd asked for, and now only needed a photograph of Uschi.

After lunch Russell took the U-Bahn south to Steglitz, where Operation Claptrap was based. A year into the peace, BOB had stumbled across a biddable Polish doctor, set him up in his own VD clinic, and supplied him with enough precious penicillin to actually cure his patients. He didn't need to advertise—catching VD was a court martial offence in the Red Army, and once word spread that relief was on offer in the privacy of the American sector, Russians of all ranks came flocking.

A fluent Russian-speaker, Doctor Kaluzny was given a camera for photographing any documents carelessly left in pockets or bags, and guidance in which questions he should casually ask the patients. He then filled in forms which his control—in this case, Russell—scoured for anything useful.

Reading the latest batch in a nearby bar, Russell found nothing of interest—just a stream of young men with identical physical symptoms, and the sort of complaints which life in any army tended to provoke. The prospect of a court martial certainly scared them, but mostly they were there because they were terrified their girlfriends at home would find out. When it came to military secrets, the best most could manage was the name of their sergeant.

When they were both in Berlin, Russell and Shchepkin usually met at the same time and place. Bad practice in theory, but since both sides knew of their meetings any attempt at subterfuge seemed gratuitous. So later that morning Russell made his usual trek to the northeastern corner of the Tiergarten, where the open black market had flourished in the immediate post-war years, and where a panoramic sweep of the eyes could take in the gutted

Reichstag, a deforested park and the Soviet monument to the Unknown Rapist.

It was a warm day, and Shchepkin was wearing a lightweight charcoal suit and open white shirt. It was the first time Russell had seen him in daylight for more than three months, and the Russian looked a lot more drawn than he remembered.

'A lovely day,' was Shchepkin's opening remark.

'For some. Your people have been hounding Effi again.'

Shchepkin didn't look surprised. 'What has happened?'

Russell went through the sequence of events—Effi's appeal to Tulpanov, the withdrawal of her Leading Actor ration card, the threatened review of Rosa's adoption.

Shchepkin listened without interrupting, occasionally shaking his head. 'I doubt there's anything I can do,' he said. 'But I wouldn't worry about your daughter—that sounds like an empty threat to me. I can't see them bringing up your wife's career in Nazi films when they've just been saluting her in ours; and as for the father— you have evidence of his death?'

'Several affidavits.'

'Well, then. The important thing is for Effi to keep away from Eva Kempka and the whole Sonja Strehl business. It's clear to me that someone important wants something kept quiet.'

'So it wasn't a suicide?'

'I don't know, and I'm happy to remain in ignorance. Tell Effi she's playing with fire.'

'I'll try.'

'Succeed. Now, we have a more pressing problem to deal with. Schneider wants more from you.'

'More what? Personal hygiene advice?' From their only meeting, Russell had deduced an aversion to water, soap, or both.

Shchepkin gave him an exasperated look. 'This man is a danger to us.'

'I thought you outranked him.'

'I do, but the friends he's been cultivating out-rank me. And the last meeting I attended, several supported his point of view.'

'Which is what exactly?'

'A more aggressive approach.'

'But what does that actually mean?'

'I don't know, and I doubt that he does either. He's restless. And he doesn't think we're making any progress.'

'I've only just got back. And I thought it was agreed that I was a long-term investment, that I'd need several years to gain enough trust from the Americans to make myself really useful.'

'According to Schneider, it *has* been several years, and that far from trusting you more, the Americans are losing faith in you.'

'Where does he get that from?'

'I don't know. Have you done anything to annoy them lately?'

'Nothing special.'

Shchepkin sighed. 'Well, we need to boost your reputation, before one side or other decides to abandon their long-term investment.'

'And cash me in?'

'And cash us in.'

'Point taken. So, how do we make the Americans love me more?'

'I'll see what I can get out of my GRU contact,' Shchepkin said. 'If he knows the names of any upcoming fake defectors, then you can give them up. Which will remind the Americans of how useful you are, without upsetting Tikhomirov and Schneider.'

'Okay.'

'But we also need to give my bastards something to crow about— the names of some American agents in our zone would do. But not ex-Nazis—it has to be people they might actually care about.'

'But I . . .'

'Yes, you would be condemning them to death. Or Wismut if they're lucky.'

'Where the hell is Wismut?'

'It's not a place; it's our uranium mining stock company in Saxony. Look, John, this is a war we're fighting, and all these people are soldiers. There are no innocents in our business—one way or another, they all chose to get involved. Like I did. Like you did. Remember that.'

'Oh, I do, believe me.' Shchepkin rarely called him by his first name, and when he did it was always for emphasis.

'Good. I shall expect the names next week. Is there anything else?' The Russian seemed unusually eager to get going.

'Yes,' Russell remembered. 'Johannsen wants to know what your people are planning for Berlin. We assume you know about the currency reform.'

'Of course. And I think our response is still being discussed. One thing I do know is that our people will soon be leaving the Kommandatura.'

'For good?' If the Soviets abandoned the Four-Power Council, that would mean the end of joint decision-making in Berlin.

Shchepkin shrugged. 'Who knows? If the Allies agree to exempt Berlin, then perhaps we'll return.'

'And if they don't?'

'A shut-down, most likely.'

'Meaning?'

'No road or rail transport, in or out.'

'A siege.'

'More or less.'

Russell considered the implications. How would the Western sectors feed themselves? Where would they get the fuel for heat and electricity from? You couldn't bring coal in by air. It was hard to see what the Western Allies could do, but surely they wouldn't just throw in the towel? And if they tried to break the siege by force, then another war would erupt. He said as much.

'It's possible,' Shchepkin agreed.

'But what about the atomic bomb?'

'Maybe Stalin knows something we don't.'

'A Soviet bomb.'

'Why not?'

Why not indeed? There was nothing backward about Soviet scientists, and they'd had a lot of help from German colleagues and sympathetic spies, himself among them. It was buying his family's safety with German atomic papers that had placed Russell at the MGB's mercy, because if the bargain was ever disclosed, the Americans would probably arrest him for treason.

And the Russians had the uranium—as Shchepkin had just said, there were important mines in their German zone. If a point was reached where the atomic arsenals cancelled each other out, the Red Army could then presumably roll right over the Western armies.

Except the Russians really had been ripping up the railways in eastern Germany. Which made no sense at all if they intended marching westward. Their willingness to fight another war had to be a bluff. But would the Americans have the sense to call it? Or the balls? Russell guessed they would soon find out.

Was this why no one seemed eager to reconstruct the city? he asked himself, casting his eye across the still-serrated skyline. Why bother if another battle was coming?

BOB's HQ in Berlin was an innocent-looking mansion on Föhrenweg, a quiet, leafy Dahlem street not five minutes walk from Thomas's and Hanna's. There were more floors underground than above, and the starkly lit interrogation suite on the second floor of the basement reminded Russell of a ship deck below the waterline.

There were two defectors to process that Friday afternoon. Both had presented themselves at American barracks on the previous afternoon, one in Schönfeld, the other in Neukölln; but as neither had yet arrived from the military holding cells where they'd spent the night, Russell and his colleague John Eustis spent most of the morning chatting, sweating, and twiddling their thumbs.

Eustis was from Providence, Rhode Island. He had been with CIC for almost four years, and had no compunction in telling all and sundry that the work was beginning to bore him. Which didn't surprise Russell. Eustis was clever but lazy, and his only real interest in other human beings was what half of them had under their skirts. He was nominally in charge, but usually he allowed Russell to just get on with it—the interrogations took so much longer if every last question and answer was translated. This suited Russell in more ways than one—the job was done quicker, and it was easier for him to pick and choose which pieces of intelligence he passed on, and which little nuggets he squirrelled away.

Their first Russian arrived soon after eleven A.M., loudly complaining that he hadn't had breakfast. Once this had been provided and eaten it was almost lunch time, and by mid-afternoon, Eustis was beginning to glance at his watch. The second Russian would be waiting a few doors down, and this one seemed incapable of answering the simplest question without setting the scene like a novelist with verbal diarrhoea. He was a long-serving Major in an artillery unit—he had apparently fought his way from the Polish border to Moscow and back again—and would doubtless prove a mine of basic information on the Red Army and its workings, should anyone have the patience to hear him out. By the time several hours had passed, Russell and Eustis were fully agreed that Army Intelligence should be given the chance.

'Why don't we leave the second guy till tomorrow?' Eustis suggested, once the first Russian had been taken away. 'I've got a hot date tonight, and preparation is everything.'

Russell laughed. 'A fraulein?'

'No, no. I've been there. Sweet but short—not much in it for us, other than the obvious. No, this is an American girl—a general's daughter, spending the summer with Daddy. She's gorgeous, and he's rich, and I hope to God she's willing.'

'It's only four P.M.,' Russell said, checking his watch. 'Let's see the guy at least—maybe we can just move him on, and then you'll have tomorrow free to show her the city. Johannsen'll be pissed off if he sees us sneaking off this early.'

Eustis threw up a weary arm in surrender. 'Okay, let's see the bastard.'

His name was Konstantin Merzhanov, and he said he was twenty-five years old. With blond hair, blue eyes, and clean-cut features, he could easily have passed for a young American. He described himself as a technician, which seemed boring enough until he mentioned his place of work—the MGB HQ at Karlshorst—and the nature of his expertise, which was cinematic.

Russell was just about to translate these facts for Eustis, when Merzhanov dropped his bombshell. 'I am in possession of a film,' the Russian said carefully. 'A film in which the Minister in charge of the MGB kills a young German woman.'

'The Minister?'

'Beria. You know who he is?'

Even Eustis's ears pricked up at that. 'Did he say Beria?'

'Yes,' Russell said, rapidly thinking on his feet. The Russian mightn't be saying what Russell thought he was saying, but if he was . . . 'He says he's the devil himself,' he told Eustis, before turning back to Merzhanov. 'We'll talk about your film later,' he told the Russian. 'For now, we need your history and personal details, your reasons for wishing to defect.'

Merzhanov gave Russell a doubtful look, but shrugged his acceptance, and over the next hour he answered questions with a precision his predecessor in the chair had so sadly lacked. Russell dutifully translated most of the answers, omitting only the Russian's references to his time at film school in Moscow, which had been cut short by the German attack in 1941.

At five o'clock Eustis suggested they call it a day, and Russell offered to finish up on his own. 'A small fish,' he assured the American. 'I won't need much longer.'

Once the door had closed behind his colleague, Russell wasted no time. 'We can talk about your film now,' he said. 'You said it shows Lavrenti Beria killing a German girl. Really killing her, right? This is not a work of fiction?'

'No, no, this is real.'

'Okay. So where, when, why?'

'The film was shot at a house just outside Berlin, the one where important visitors stay. Beria came to Berlin in February, and he stayed there for several days. During that time he entertained several girls.'

'And he was being filmed?' Russell found this hard to believe.

'He didn't know it. All the rooms have hidden cameras, and of course this one should never have been turned on—it was a mistake. But I watched it, and I saw him kill one of the girls. And I knew what I had. This would be great propaganda for the West, yes?'

'I should think it would,' Russell said drily. 'Where is it now?'

'My girlfriend Janica has it.'

'And where is she?'

'In Prague. She's a Czech.' He took a dog-eared photograph from his jacket pocket and passed it across. The 'girl' looked about thirty, but she wasn't unattractive, and there was definite intelligence in the gaze she offered the camera. 'I met her when we liberated the city,' Merzhanov went on. 'She was being attacked by some of my comrades, and I managed to rescue her. We've been in love ever since.' The Russian's eyes were shining, Russell noticed, and when the young man offered a long list of the girl's qualities and charms he didn't interrupt.

'But why does she have the film?' he quietly asked, once the panegyric was over.

Merzhanov gave him an almost triumphant look. 'Because I didn't feel safe keeping it here in Berlin, and because bringing her out will be your only way to get hold of it.'

'That's your price?'

'We don't want *money*,' Merzhanov insisted, as if he wouldn't soil his hands on the stuff. 'But you must take us somewhere safe—once the film is made public, they will realise that I must have taken it, and they will try to hunt us down.'

They all said that, Russell thought, but in this case it would be true. The Rat Line came to mind. If he could get them to Draganović's man outside Salzburg, they would be on their way to safety. Theirs, and his. 'So how do we contact Janica?' he asked. 'What's her surname?'

'You don't need to know that. She will be waiting on the Masaryk Station concourse at five P.M. on Wednesday the sixteenth. With the film. And you people will bring her out to the West.'

It sounded simple, and maybe it was. It occurred to Russell that a film was easier to get across a border than a woman, and that after she'd handed it over, he could simply leave her there. She would be in no position to call the police.

Then again, in the heat of the moment she mightn't stop to consider her own best interests. And even if she did, Merzhanov would clearly be more than upset, which might prove just as damaging. If the film was to have any value to Russell and Shchepkin, then it had to remain their secret, and the best way of ensuring that was to keep its suppliers happy.

Merzhanov seemed blissfully unaware of the possible flaw in his scheme; but Russell already suspected that Janica had thought the whole thing up, and that she might well have a back-up plan. Well, she wouldn't need one. A deal was a deal, and Russell would bring her out. Or probably die trying.

'We must keep this absolutely between us,' Russell told the Russian. 'I will tell my boss of course, but no one else. As I'm sure you know, the MGB has spies in this sector—in this building, most likely—and if word of all this gets out, your life won't be worth a kopek. So you mustn't mention Beria or the film to anyone. Understood?'

'Yes,' Merzhanov said, with only the slightest hint of doubt.

'It's for your own safety,' Russell insisted. BOB's other Russian-speaker, Don Stafford, wasn't due back until the following Friday, so Merzhanov's chance of spilling the beans was minimal, but the need for secrecy was hard to exaggerate. 'And I'll need to borrow the photograph,' Russell said. 'For new papers,' he added, when Merzhanov expressed reluctance. The Russian handed it over with the sort of reverence a Biblical scholar might have shown for a first edition of the Sermon on the Mount.

Once Merzhanov had been taken away to new accommodation on the floor below—a cell in all but name, but a comfortable one for all that—Russell just sat there for several minutes, wondering at what had just—apparently—fallen into his lap. This was it, the thing that Shchepkin had named in London's Russell Square more than three years earlier. He could still hear him say it: 'Something on them that trumps everything else; a secret so damaging that we could buy our safety with silence.'

Well, only Stalin throttling a nun would trump what Merzhanov's film allegedly showed.

But it wouldn't be easy. Russell had to collect Janica and the film, and then get the lovebirds out of Europe, all without raising any suspicions among his American colleagues. And then he and Shchepkin had to make their deal with Beria, the psychopath in charge of the world's largest plain-clothes army. In return for their keeping silent about what was on the film, he would need to promise no Soviet disclosure of Russell's role in securing the German atomic papers for Moscow, allow them both to retire from Soviet service, and allow Shchepkin's wife and daughter to leave for the West.

Put that way, it sounded like a pipedream.

But try as he did, Russell could see no logical flaw in the plan. Executing it was another matter, though. How the hell would they contact Beria—c/o the Lyubyanka? He hoped Shchepkin would know.

There was no instant way of getting hold of his Russian partner. Russell could and did arrange an emergency meeting with a phone call, but the place and time were already pre-set. The former was chosen at the end of each regular meeting, the latter always noon on the following day, which gave him eighteen hours to wait.

He didn't say anything to Effi that evening—he didn't want to raise her hopes—but once she'd fallen asleep in his arms, he allowed himself the luxury of some daydreaming. If he could escape the Soviet embrace, then the American one would be easier to shrug off. He could be a real journalist again, not in Berlin perhaps, but in England or America. Effi already had one offer from Hollywood, and he was sure she'd find work in either country. It would be so good to live near Paul again, and he didn't think Rosa would really miss Berlin.

'And with one bound he was free,' he thought.

Or one spool of film.

Masaryk Station.

On Saturday morning Russell pleaded work as his excuse for abandoning Effi and Rosa, who'd planned a family walk in the Grunewald. After seeing them off, he started out for the Funkturm, the spot he'd chosen for the emergency *treff* with Shchepkin. He was almost an hour early, which gave him ample time to dwell on the memories the structure evoked. The radio tower—Berlin's smaller version of the Eiffel—had been badly damaged in the final weeks of the war, with one leg severed and the restaurant burnt out, and was still closed to the public. But in pre-war times, when Paul was living with his mother and stepfather, this had always been his first destination of choice, and the two of them had spent countless Saturdays together staring out across the city from the observation platform.

Shchepkin was also early, as if he'd somehow got wind that something important had happened. Natty was the word, Russell thought, as he watched the Russian walk towards him. Effi had been reminded of a theatre director she once worked for, and Russell could just imagine Shchepkin among Berlin's pre-Nazi avant-garde.

As they circled the tower together Russell went through everything that Merzhanov had told him. By the time he'd finished describing the plot of the film, the Russian's pinched expression was as bleak as he'd ever seen it. 'Is this all possible?' he asked Shchepkin. 'Do you know about this house outside the city?'

'Yes, it exists.'

'And could Beria have been there?'

'He was here around that time although I can't remember the exact dates. And there have been rumours over the years. I never respected the man, but they weren't the sort of rumours that anyone who cared for the Party could bring himself to believe. That he had young girls abducted off the street in Moscow and taken to his dacha—that sort of thing. Something like this would be worse, much worse.'

'The film might be a fake,' Russell offered.

Shchepkin shook his head. 'We'll know when we see it, but somehow it all rings true.' He fell silent for a few moments. 'So you intend to collect the woman from Prague, reunite her with her lover, and send them both off to South America, yes?'

'Yes.'

'I can see two major problems.'

'Only two?'

'At first sight. One, you'll need papers to get her out of Czechoslovakia. I may be able to help with those, but it's far from certain. Two, you have to persuade your Mister Johannsen that Merzhanov deserves such special treatment. What has he done to deserve it?'

'I'm working on that,' Russell said, somewhat less than truthfully. The problem had occurred to him, but so far he'd chosen to ignore it.

'I think I can help there,' Shchepkin told him. 'I'll meet you tomorrow with something special. I don't know what exactly, but something that'll make Merzhanov seem worth the extra effort. You'll have to be the ventriloquist.'

'That should work,' Russell agreed, mentally rehearsing the process. 'I am his only channel of communication until our other Russian speaker gets back. And I'll just have to move Merzhanov south before he does.'

'Yes,' Shchepkin said thoughtfully, as if something had just occurred to him. Then he allowed himself a wry smile. 'If the Americans find out about the film, and realise that you've chosen not to tell them, that will be the end—you must realise that. At best they will sack you. At worst, I don't know. Either way, your use to us will be over. You and I, we will both be loose ends that need cutting off.'

He was right, Russell thought, but what choice did they have? He didn't want to grow old checking Doctor Kaluzny's patient reports, doing odd jobs for men like Youklis and his Russian equivalents. How many Sasas would there be in that future?

He smiled at the gloomy Russian. 'So let's make sure we don't fuck it up.'

The next morning, Russell went back to the Föhrenweg basement for a two-hour session with Merzhanov. He had nothing new to ask the Russian, but he needed to establish a time in which the information Shchepkin was providing could actually have been divulged. For the most part they chatted about their time as soldiers—Merzhanov was interested in Russell's experiences in the First War, and he was still shocked by what he'd witnessed himself during the Red Army's four-year war against the Germans. The Russian also talked more about Janica, with a fondness Russell found unusually touching. He found himself hoping that the Czech girl was worthy of such devotion.

By midday Russell was in the Potsdamer Strasse café Shchepkin had specified for the hand-over. This time there was no conversation, just the usual rolled newspaper casually left, which Russell scanned and took with him. On a Tiergarten bench half an hour later he read through the papers inside, which contained a complete breakdown of the new KI organisation in Berlin, complete with names, ranks and personal habits which might expose the officers involved to successful blackmail. As a bonus, Shchepkin had included the names of two MGB agents employed by the American Zone administration in Frankfurt.

It was more than enough to warrant two exit visas. Now all he had to do was convince Eustis that he was hearing it all from Merzhanov.

* * *

With Russell still absent on duty, Effi and Rosa went over to
Dahlem without him. Hanna had just arrived back from her parents' farm in the American Zone, and Lotte had her new boyfriend
Karl on display—a serious young man who seemed painfully inhibited by the various members of her extended family: the American
major, the British journalist, the notorious actress, even the famous
young artist, who drew him with a star-struck look on his face.

Annaliese arrived late and without Ströhm, who was also spending
the Sunday at work. Ströhm had sent a message to Russell hoping they
could meet for a drink sometime in the next few days.

Late in the afternoon, all the guests shared a tram to Ku'damm,
and then went their separate ways. It had been a good day, Effi
decided, as she and Rosa climbed their stairs. Thomas seemed reju-
venated by politics, and her worries about Rosa seemed less substantial than they had. Thinking back over the long conversation at table,
Effi could hardly remember an optimistic statement, but it didn't
seem to matter—whatever the world might throw at them all, somehow love and friendship made life worth living.

She found Russell scribbling away at the table, surrounded by
sheets of Cyrillic script. 'This has to be done tonight,' he said apologetically after embracing them both. 'I need it for the morning.'

'But what is it?' Rosa asked.

'I can't tell you that. It's top-secret.'

'But something to do with the Russians?'

'You've guessed it.'

'Let him work,' Effi told her. 'We'll find something to do in the
other room.'

It was several hours before Russell had finished re-casting Shchepkin's information as an imaginary interview with Merzhanov, and by

then Rosa was fast asleep. It was time, he decided, to tell Effi what was happening. After sitting her down on the sofa, he went through the story, omitting nothing. 'And before I go to Prague,' he concluded, 'I want you and Rosa on a train to Frankfurt.'

She ignored that. 'You're going back to Prague,' she said incredulously. 'Just the name gives me the shivers. Every time you've been there something terrible has almost happened—sometimes it actually has. You were shot there! Only last week you were beaten up in one of their jails.'

'They let me go when they found out I worked for the Soviets.'

'Can't Shchepkin do that part? Isn't Czechoslovakia one of their countries now?'

'I don't think it works like that. And I dread to think what Janica would do if a Russian approached her at Masaryk Station.'

'How will you get her across the border?'

'I haven't decided yet. As my daughter maybe. Shchepkin's looking into papers, and if he can't help, I'll have to see Max.'

Her eyes lit up. 'How old is Janica?'

'She looks about thirty. Why?'

'Because I asked Max to forge some papers for Lisa Sundgren's daughter. She's only twenty-one, but I can probably take a few years off Janica.'

'Wait a minute . . .'

'No, this is fate. I'm coming with you.'

'Oh no.'

'Oh yes, and I'll tell you why. Where's the best place to hide a reel of film?'

'In a projection booth?'

'Almost. Among other films. You told Jaromír Císař how much I liked his work, and he said he'd like to work with me. Well, I can go and see him, and tell him in person that I'm interested in working with him. And I can take some audition reels with me—DEFA were always good about giving us copies of the rushes. And we can hide your film among them.'

It did sound almost perfect, but . . .

'And if it looks like I'm choosing the Czech version of DEFA over the Americans, the Soviets will be overjoyed,' Effi went on excitedly. 'Which should stop them thinking about Rosa.'

'But what about Rosa?' Russell asked, hoping to bring her back to earth. 'If both of us end up in a Czech prison . . .'

'We won't. Didn't you just remind me that they let you go because you work for the Soviets?'

'Yes, but . . .'

'I know what you're saying,' Effi conceded quickly. 'Of course I do. And I also know that if worst came to worst, Zarah would be as loving a mother as I would. But it won't. I won't let it.'

At ten o'clock on Monday morning, Effi presented herself at Max Grelling's Ku'damm apartment. He was in his dressing gown, and the bed through the doorway still seemed occupied, but he smiled when he saw her, and urged her into the well-stocked kitchen, where coffee was loudly percolating.

'Would you like a cup?'

'I wouldn't say no.'

Grelling took the pot from the stove, and lined up a couple of cups. 'Do you need the papers after all?'

'Yes, but for a different woman. I have her photograph here. It's not in very good shape, I'm afraid.'

Grelling passed her a cup, and examined the picture. 'Can't you give up rescuing people?' he asked.

'Apparently not.' The coffee was wonderful.

'Well, this one doesn't look twenty-one,' he said.

'Could you change the birth date?'

He shook his head. 'Not without leaving a mark. It would pass a normal scrutiny, but I think you'd be better changing the woman's appearance. Anyone who checks photographs on a regular basis knows that very few people look just like their picture, and they're much more likely to accept a discrepancy there than they are in the writing.'

'You're the expert,' Effi told him. 'But I am in rather a hurry.'

'Of course. Who is this woman?'

'She's a Czech. And she's not Jewish, if that's what you're wondering.'

'Ah. But for you . . . Will Wednesday do?

'That would be perfect. And can I insult you by offering payment?'

'Insult away.'

Russell read a newspaper on the tram journey out to Föhrenweg. The Soviets had indeed abandoned the Kommandatura, but only after the American representative Colonel Howley had flounced out. Since Shchepkin had known about the Soviet decision two days earlier, Russell could only assume that Howley had been stupid enough to hand the Soviets a propaganda victory on a plate. Elsewhere in the paper there were rumours that the Arabs were considering a ceasefire in their war with the infant Israel. If they thought time was on their side, they had another think coming, Russell thought. Now that the Brits had got out of the way, the Jews would only get stronger.

It was also reported that Eduard Benes had resigned as President of Czechoslovakia on grounds of ill health. He might be sick for all Russell knew, but his departure still felt like the end of an all-too-short era, one in which people still believed that social democrats and communists could work together. If they couldn't do it in Prague, then they couldn't do it anywhere. Now it would be a fight to the death.

At the BOB HQ Russell found a yawning John Eustis in the canteen, and laid the fictional report in front of him. After skimming his way through the first few pages, Eustis suddenly pulled up short, and went back to the beginning. 'Have you told Johannsen?' was the first thing he asked after reading it properly.

'I thought we'd get it all wrapped up and tied with a ribbon,' Russell told him. 'Get ourselves some brownie points.'

'They wouldn't hurt. I expect my new girl's father is checking me out as we speak.'

'Well then, let's get Merzhanov back up.'

The hours that followed—around eighteen of them spread over two and a half days—were some of the most exhausting Russell had ever endured. Having turned Shchepkin's breakdown of the MGB operation in Karlshorst into a series of individual profiles, he now had to cope with Eustis's supplementary questions, a process which demanded almost instant creativity. In the time that Merzhanov took to answer Russell's mostly footling questions—ones which bore no relation to those that Eustis thought were being translated for him—he had to think up answers for Eustis, mixing fiction with a few odd facts that he had wisely withheld from the written report. So Eustis would ask about one Russian's apparent ascendancy over another, Russell would translate this as a question about Merzhanov's army training, and then turn the Russian's description of a Soviet boot camp into a probable consequence of the recent Soviet intelligence reorganisations, which he knew about from Shchepkin's endless complaints.

Eustis never suspected a thing—he was, thank God, so used to their way of working together—but Merzhanov became increasingly baffled by the Americans' apparently bottomless appetite for irrelevant details of his earlier life, and clearly puzzled by some of the unfamiliar Russian names which cropped up in Russell's English translations. By Wednesday morning Russell was silently praying for his colleague to run out of questions.

He did so soon after eleven A.M., which gave them the rest of the morning to polish their report, before presenting it to Johannsen early that afternoon. Their boss was sparing in his praise—why hadn't they told him straight away about the MGB plants in Frankfurt?—but Russell suspected he was more pleased than he let on. The three of them were all CIC veterans, and Johannsen would make damn sure their new CIA bosses were aware of that fact.

That however was the end of the good news. When Russell asked permission to move Merzhanov on, he was told 'not yet'—Johannsen thought the Frankfurt base would want to ask some questions of their own once they heard about the plants. As for sending Merzhanov and 'his wife' down the Rat Line, BOB simply couldn't afford it—the quarterly budget had all been spent. And if all that wasn't enough, Johannsen let slip that Don Stafford, the base's other Russian speaker, was already back in Berlin.

'But not working this week?' Russell said, barely managing to keep the anxiety out of his voice.

'Oh he's working. He's on Claptrap and the cleaners for the next few days.'

By the time he met Shchepkin, Russell's panic had subsided. Before leaving the Föhrenweg building he had heard from Johannsen that Frankfurt would be on the line next morning, and that once their questions had been answered Merzhanov would be allowed to leave Berlin. Which left Stafford and the money as the next hurdles to overcome. Since Stafford was out in Steglitz dealing with Claptrap he shouldn't present any immediate problem, but the lack of money certainly did. Russell and Effi didn't have $3,000, and he very much doubted whether Thomas did either.

'I thought you told me that only some people paid for this Croat's services,' Shchepkin said, once the problem had been broached.

'Only Catholics travel free,' Russell told him. 'And they're mostly fellow Croats or OUN Ukrainians like Palychko.'

'Couldn't you pass Merzhanov and his girlfriend off as Ukrainians?'

Russell beamed at Shchepkin. 'Why not? I could even have him tattooed.'

He got back home to find that the Czech Embassy had welcomed Effi with open arms. 'They could hardly believe it when I told them I wanted to visit Císař, with a view to working with him—one official gave me a heartfelt speech about how few foreigners appreciated Czech culture, and another wittered on about how international socialism moves in mysterious ways. Or something like that. Anyway, you just have to go in and sign something, and you can pick up both our visas.'

'Your friend Lisa should have been so lucky.'

'Don't. When I saw her off this morning she looked like death.'

'Well I don't know about international socialism, but something must move in mysterious ways—if she hadn't come to see you we'd never have got the papers in time for next Wednesday.'

Next morning, Russell entered the building on Föhrenweg with some trepidation. Had some evil genie persuaded Johannsen to change his mind and switch Russell's duties with Stafford's? But there was only Eustis in the room below, and when the telephone call came through from Frankfurt it was Russell doing the interpreting. The man at the other end seemed barely interested in what Merzhanov knew—the two plants had been arrested, and doubtless offered a much more immediate source of intelligence. Once he had elicited a few extra nuggets of fictional information the Frankfurt agent was happy to flaunt his laurels. 'You people should leave this stuff to the professionals,' he said in parting, only slightly in jest.

Russell went up to Johannsen's office. 'So can I move him now?'

'Where to? I told you—we're out of money.'

'I'll take him down to Salzburg, pass him and his wife off as Ukrainians.'

Johannsen smiled, but shook his head. 'I need you here.'

'Why? You've got Stafford back now.'

Johannsen did a double-take. 'I assumed you knew. He was found dead outside his billet last night. Someone after a few cigarettes, it looks like.'

'Shit.' Russell took a deep breath. He wanted to ask for details, but didn't trust his voice. 'Look,' he said, 'I'm sorry about that, but Merzhanov's given us a lot, and he'll be just as dead if we don't get him out of the city. And I promised him safety, or he wouldn't have given us anything. I'll only be gone for the weekend.'

Johannsen sighed. 'Oh, all right. But be here Monday morning.'

'I will.' Russell got up to leave, and only stopped himself when halfway through the door. He had to know. 'Was Stafford single?'

'A wife and two children,' Johannsen told him. 'I'll be writing the letter this evening.'

Gerhard Ströhm sat at his desk, feeling disinclined to begin his day's work. He had always been a conscientious worker, and still completed each task with exemplary efficiency, but the symposium on Rugen Island had stripped the process of any remaining joy. Annaliese had noticed the change on his return, and since that day he had tried to be cheerful at home, a far from impossible task now that the swell of her belly offered growing proof of their child-to-be. But at work he made less of an effort, despite the looks from his fellow-workers. He was in an ideological sulk, and no matter how often he resolved to shake himself out of it, somehow it persisted.

The nature of his current work did nothing to help. Everyone at the office knew the crisis was upon them—it was their job to make it tangible—but the starting gun had still not been fired. Breaking the rail link between Berlin and the Western zones wasn't exactly difficult as all it required was a red signal at either end of the tracks that traversed the Soviet zone. But if Stalin had really decided on such a drastic step, he hadn't yet told his German comrades.

Merely slowing things down was more complicated, particularly if you wanted to pretend that the slow-down wasn't deliberate, and even more so if you weren't sure what you wanted the other side to believe. And the Soviets kept changing their minds, first insisting that 'technical difficulties' be blamed for interruptions in the rail service, then claiming that they'd limited interzonal traffic in order to protect the local economy from the contagion of Western currency reform. And while one moment stressing that such measures were temporary, at others they strongly implied that only a change in Western behaviour could guarantee a restoration of the status quo. It sometimes seemed as if the Soviets were playing with the Western allies, but Ströhm had the sneaking suspicion that they were simply incapable of reaching a decision.

In the meantime, the harassment went on. Passenger trains now left from Friedrichstrasse, whose short platforms dictated the removal of four coaches. Single freight wagons were rejected for minor mistakes in their labelling, causing whole trains to be shunted aside. Crews were ordered to present their personal belongings for inspection, which might only take a few minutes, but the stoppages soon began to add up.

Ströhm was tired of it all. He had always thought that the

Western powers' foothold in Berlin made it harder for the Soviets to let go, but now he was beginning to wonder—perhaps it was only the Western presence which prevented the Russians from tightening their grip. Either way, he wanted to know. 'If there has to be a showdown,' he told one colleague over lunch, 'then let's have it now. And Moscow should be open about it. Tell the Western Allies that they're stopping all traffic to Berlin, and tell them what they can do to get it started again. The British and Americans started all this with their currency reform, and they can end it by coming back to the table and agreeing to a four-power solution. I would understand that. More to the point, the people of Berlin would understand it. But "technical difficulties"? No one believes this nonsense. They just think we're liars.'

His colleague gave him a pitying look. 'This is a difficult time,' he agreed, and changed the subject.

Back at his desk, Ströhm went through the press release he had written that morning, explaining the sudden rash of mechanical defects in the wagon fleet. He sighed, and resisted the temptation to crumple up the piece of paper. He had nothing against deception—for much of his life his survival had rested on his ability to deceive his enemies. But was that what he was doing now? He seemed to spend most of his time deceiving the people he supposedly served.

After dropping Rosa off at school on Friday morning, Effi and Russell walked to the Czechoslovak Embassy on Rauch Strasse. She was met by smiles, he by frowns, but both their travel permits had been approved. Císař was looking forward to discussing a future collaboration with Effi, and happy to answer her husband's follow-up questions. The new Ministry of Culture had booked them into a hotel not far from the director's home.

With their new papers safely stowed away in Russell's pocket, the two of them walked down to Tauentzien Strasse, where Effi had shopping to do. The pavements were crowded for ten in the morning, particularly given the dearth of goods on display in store windows, but Effi wasn't surprised. 'Zarah said it was like this on Wednesday,' she said. 'With all the rumours of currency reform, everyone's spending what money they have while it's still worth something.'

As if to prove her point, a woman walked by with an exceptionally ugly table lamp under each arm.

'I guess we're the lucky ones,' Russell said. The Americans had always paid him in dollars, and Thomas had helped Effi shift some of her earnings into Swiss francs. Whatever transpired over the next few weeks, they would be all right. At least in terms of money.

The theatrical shop wasn't overwhelmed with customers—bulk-buying makeup supplies as a hedge against inflation had obviously not caught on. Effi went in to replenish her personal stocks, which she hadn't used since the war. Then she'd been ageing her own appearance; making Janica look younger would be more of a challenge.

Russell waited outside, watching other shoppers walk by. The procession of faces—most agitated or shut down, very few smiling—got him thinking about the city and its recent history. In the 1920s, when he had come here to live, there had been few places in the world more exciting, either politically or culturally. Then the Nazis had re-cast it as the capital of their swelling boil of an empire, and their enemies had reduced it to rubble. For three years the politics and culture had grown interesting once more, but there was no doubt in Russell's mind that the shutters were coming back down. So what now, division or Soviet takeover? Which sort of prison would it be?

Back at the flat, he barely had time to pack a small bag before kissing Effi goodbye and setting out for Föhrenweg. Merzhanov and the ordered jeep were waiting for him, the former looking smart in American civvies. The Russian wore a wary expression on his face during their chauffeur-driven journey to Tempelhof, as if he couldn't quite believe his luck.

Their plane was waiting in a distant corner of the airfield, one of many DC-3s parked around the perimeter. Russell's accreditation saw them straight on board, where seven other passengers were already waiting. They all looked German, but none seemed disposed to exchange any form of eye contact, let alone smile or converse. Merzhanov's face was now sporting an idiot grin, which only faded as they roared down the runway.

The flight to Rhein-Main took a little under two hours, the wait for their connection to Munich a little over. Another jeep was waiting in the Bavarian capital, and by five o'clock they were crossing the border between the American zones of Germany and Austria. At CIC HQ in Salzburg, Russell found an old acquaintance waiting— he had crossed paths with Major Rick Sewell on several occasions, and as far as he knew he had caused no lasting offence.

'Johannsen let us know you were coming,' Sewell said, as he looked Merzhanov over. 'Sing a good song, did he?'

'Oh yes,' Russell agreed. The American had put on weight since their last meeting, the buttons of his tunic straining to contain his new belly.

'Well, let's get him tucked up in bed. I'll drive 'em,' Sewell told the young corporal who'd collected them from Munich.

'Yes, sir.'

Sewell, as Russell now remembered, thought jeeps cornered best on two wheels. He hung on grimly as they wove their way through the early evening traffic, occasionally glancing over his shoulder to check that Merzhanov was still with them. Soon they were out of the city, and jolting along the hilly road which led to the farm the CIC used as a safe house. Russell had been there the previous year, after Sewell's boss, in dire need of an interpreter, had virtually press-ganged him into helping out.

Behind him, the Russian was staring at the mountains filling the southern horizon the way someone raised in a desert might gaze at an ocean. At that moment he looked the picture of inno-cence, not the lust-sick deserter and traitor which most of his erstwhile comrades would think him. But what did that matter? As long as he kept his mouth shut. And the film lived up to its billing.

The safe house had a permanent staff of six—two housekeepers and four armed guards on twelve-hour shifts. Merzhanov was intro-duced to those on duty, shown his private sleeping quarters, and offered dinner. The man looked profoundly pleased with life, Russell thought as he left, like someone who had taken a difficult decision and been thoroughly vindicated. Or would be, once Janica was shar-ing the bed. Before leaving, Russell had taken Merzhanov aside and forcibly reminded him not to mention the film.

Sewell was chatty on the ride back into town, but Russell wasn't feeling sociable. 'I was up at five A.M.,' he lied glibly, when the Amer-ican suggested a bar. 'I can hardly keep my eyes open.'

'Then I'll take you to your hotel. Maybe tomorrow.'

'If I'm still here,' Russell promised, knowing perfectly well he wouldn't be. 'I assume Father Cecelja is still in Alt Aussee?'

'He is. I guess you'll need a jeep in the morning.'

'Yeah, please.'

'I'll put your name down at the pool. You remember where it is.'

'I do.'

'Okay, then. Sleep well.'

Well, the man couldn't have been more accommodating, Russell thought, as he wearily climbed the hotel stairs. And he was likeable enough. So why had he given him the bum's rush?

An hour or so later, alone in the hotel bar, he asked himself the question again. The answer, he decided, was simple enough—he'd just had enough of men in uniforms.

Alt Aussee was about forty miles to the east, a small village nestling beside an eponymous lake, in the shadow of a stark plateau. The hour's drive was stunningly beautiful, almost ironically so given the ugliness of the person at the other end.

Father Vilim Cecelja was Draganović's man in Austria. He was an Ustashe from way back—he had even taken the ritual oath, complete with daggers, candles, crucifixes, and all the other clichés, which allowed him to use the revered title of a 'Sworn Ustashe.' After the Nazis invaded Yugoslavia he had served as senior military chaplain to the Ustashe militia, officially blessed Pavelić and his odious regime, and he had done nothing to suggest he disagreed with their genocidal goals. In 1944, sensing the game was up, Cecelja had moved to Vienna and founded a new branch of the Croatian Red Cross, which hitherto served as a cover for his work in aiding escapers from Allied justice. In April 1945 he had moved again, this time to Alt Aussee. With Red Cross credentials, new American papers, and Draganović's support, he had opened the Rat Lines for business.

The local CIC had proved more resolute than the US Army, and six months later Cecelja had been arrested. Eighteen months of imprisonment followed, but no charges were brought by the Americans, and Yugoslav requests for his extradition were eventually refused. In April 1947 the US Government finally decided that the priest did have crimes to answer for, but by then it was too late—he had already been released. With increasing numbers of Soviet defectors to shift, the CIC had decided that the Rat Line could be useful in more ways than one, and put Cecelja back in business.

Russell would have preferred not to use him, but there wasn't much choice where fugitive escapes to the sun were concerned. The real question was how to get the priest's help without paying for it, at least in monetary form. Russell was more than willing to promise the Earth on the CIC's behalf—one more burning bridge behind him seemed neither here nor there.

The priest was around forty, and looked more Irish than Croatian. He was Russell's height, with dark hair showing hints of grey. He wasn't wearing a robe or dog-collar, and no church abutted his two-storey house. Like Father Kozniku, clearly he had placed God on the back-burner.

He expressed no surprise at receiving a visitor from the CIC, although he insisted on seeing Russell's accreditation.

'We have a favour to ask,' Russell began, once they were seated in the large lounge overlooking the lake, and an Austrian youth had brought them both coffees. 'Two Ukrainian Catholics, a man and a woman, whom the Soviets are pursuing.'

Cecelja paused in the act of transferring sugar from bowl to cup. 'I presume you know the fees.'

'A favour we shall reciprocate,' Russell went on. 'But not, in this case, with cash. Our funds have been frozen,' he explained. 'Temporarily, we hope.'

Cecelja found that amusing. 'The mighty United States war machine can't put its hands on three thousand dollars?'

'I'm sure the war machine could, but not our little part of it.'

'So what are you offering us?'

'We're offering you a free pass. A statement to the effect that the accusations of collaboration raised against you have been officially dismissed. And all previous statements to the contrary expunged from our official records. Put the two together, and any future application for a US visa will be a formality.'

Cecelja looked interested, but didn't reply right away.

'This situation won't last for ever,' Russell told the priest.

'Which situation is that?'

'The one in which Uncle Sam is so desperate for help from people like you that it's willing to forgive and forget.'

'Ah, that sounds like a threat.'

'You could see it as a choice. On the one hand, securing your own future safety and helping two good Catholics escape from the communists. On the other . . .'

Cecelja steepled his fingers. 'Put that way, the choice does seem rather obvious.'

'I would say so,' Russell agreed. And it was—sending the two down the Rat Line wouldn't cost Cecelja anything, but the promised paper might prove priceless. Even if it failed to materialise, he wouldn't be out of pocket.

'So when can I expect these "good Catholics"?'

'I'll be dropping them off next Thursday.'

'Along with the document you promised?'

'Of course.'

'Then . . .' The priest rose and offered his hand, which Russell duly accepted. Over the past few years he had met several men with copious blood on their hands, and all they had shared was a certain coldness. Cecelja didn't even have that. Without a knowledge of his deeds, there was literally nothing to set him apart.

Russell drove back to Salzburg with the window open, revelling in the freshness of the wind. He had forgotten to arrange a meeting with Sewell, but despite its being Saturday, he found him in his CIC office.

'I can't believe you persuaded the good Father to take them free of charge,' Sewell said, as they drove across town to the Photo and Document lab. 'You must have got him on a really good day.'

At the lab, Russell placed his order with the CIC's resident forger—new passports, travel documents, transit passes, extra IDs, and baptismal certificates for two. The American didn't want to start work without photos, but eventually agreed that they could be affixed near the end of the process. Russell came away feeling positive: success with Cecelja, success with the documents—it seemed like his luck was in.

And there was one more piece of good fortune to enjoy. Before he took to the road again, Sewell suggested calling the local airbase, and sure enough, a transport was leaving for Frankfurt in less than an hour. He was on a roll.

It didn't last. The flight was smooth enough, but the sky over Rhein-Main was humming with traffic, and the queue to land took almost as long. The reason, as he discovered on reaching the offices, was a general alert. While Russell had been travelling south on Friday, the Soviets had been shutting the Berlin rail link down, and American reliance on their air links had risen accordingly, tripling their flights in and out of the city.

It was dawn on Sunday before Russell had a seat on one, and seven in the morning before he stepped blearily down on to the tarmac at Tempelhof. Reaching home to find Effi and Rosa at breakfast, he grabbed a fork and took turns stealing scrambled eggs off their plates.

'Did it all go all right?' Effi asked, when Rosa left them for a few moments.

'Better than I hoped. How's Rosa?'

'She's worried about us both going away. She doesn't actually say so, and I do keep reminding her that we'll only be gone for two or three nights, but I know she is.'

'Mmm. Well, let's make sure we have a good day today.'

'We're going to Zarah's for lunch. And Bill will probably be there.'

'Well, that'll be good.'

'Oh, and Ströhm rang for you. He sounded disappointed when I told him you were away, and that Monday we were both going off again.'

'He must be feeling the pressure,' Russell said.

'The baby or the Russians?'

'He can't wait for the baby. It'll be the Russians. Stuck between the devil and the deep red sea.'

'The devil being Comrade Ulbricht.'

'Or the Americans. He's spoilt for choice.'

Effi dismissed it all with a wave of the hand. 'Anyway, I'm packed. And these,' she said, pointing them out, 'are my audition reels.' There were four of them, each in small round cans of roughly similar size.

'I hope Merzhanov's isn't a lot bigger,' Russell observed. 'It'll stand out if it is.'

Effi shook her head. 'We can empty one of these and rewind the new film on to it,' she said.

Russell gave her an admiring look. 'You should have been the secret agent, and I should have been the beauty.'

Bill Carnforth was at Zarah's when they arrived, peeling potatoes in a rather fetching apron. His news was more sobering—having allowed a resumption of rail traffic between Berlin and the Western zones, the Soviets had turned their attention to the only road link, and closed its bridge over the Elbe, ostensibly for repairs. 'They're just messing with us,' Carnforth said. 'And they're gonna keep on doing it until we throw up our hands in despair and head back home.'

'And you should have seen it on Ku'damm yesterday,' Zarah interjected. 'Thousands of people spending their money like they couldn't wait to get rid of it. If they don't reform the currency soon, we'll be back to barter.'

'And if they do,' Russell mused, 'then God only knows how the Soviets will react.'

'But what could they do?' Zarah wanted to know. 'Money is money.'

'I think they're doing it already, honey,' her fiancé observed.

'You mean blocking the autobahn?'

'And the railway.'

'But you won't let them cut us off,' Zarah insisted, as if he was the one who would make the decision.

'I wish I was certain of that,' he said, placing another peeled potato in the saucepan. 'Me and General Clay would give them a fight, but it won't be our call. The politicians will have to decide.'

'They'll stand up to the Russians eventually,' Zarah said confidently. 'But it still doesn't seem like a very good time to go waltzing off to Prague,' she told Effi. 'Couldn't you wait a few weeks?'

'It's all arranged,' Effi told her. A year ago she would have filled Zarah in on what was actually happening, but since Carnforth had appeared on the scene she and Russell had opted not to burden her sister with a possible conflict of loyalties. 'And I do want to see Císař,' she added. 'You liked that film of his you saw.'

'Did I? What was it?'

'*Beloved Morning*.'

'Oh yes, that was good. So you're back on Wednesday or Thursday?'

'I think so,' Effi told her.

'Can we meet you at the station?' Rosa asked.

'No, sweetheart. We don't know which train we'll be on, and it might be very late.'

The girl looked crestfallen. 'Will you wake me when you get back?'

'Of course we will.'

That afternoon they all went to see a Fred Astaire and Ginger Rogers musical at a recently re-opened local cinema, and half-danced their way back to Zarah's flat. There was an undamaged double staircase fronting one of the bombsites on Kant Strasse, and this provided Effi and Russell with the opportunity to recreate one particular scene. Their attempt seemed more than creditable to Russell, and he failed to see why their audience found it so amusing.

Back at Carmer Strasse that evening, Rosa did a drawing of the two of them whirling each other around in the street. Examining it over her shoulder, Russell felt close to tears.

Janica

It was chaos at Anhalter Station on Tuesday morning. Overnight the Soviets had decreed that any Berliners wanting a ticket to the Western Zones could only buy it at Friedrichstrasse Station, and every available railway employee at Anhalter was surrounded by people haplessly protesting the inconvenience. But it was much more than that, Russell realised. As Friedrichstrasse Station was in the Soviet zone, the Russians had effectively awarded themselves a veto over who might leave the city.

It didn't affect him and Effi for now. They weren't leaving Stalin's new empire, and they already had their train tickets. Their route was the usual one via Dresden, which Russell had taken in March 1939 with the German naval plans concealed in a false-bottomed suitcase. He still sometimes wondered how he'd managed not to soil himself during that particular border inspection. On that occasion he'd had a publicity shot of Effi to divert the guards; now he had the real thing.

It was a bright summer morning, and soon they were rolling through a healthy-looking countryside, the fields of flourishing crops only blighted by the occasional hulk of a burnt-out tank. These were all German, and Russell guessed that they had been left beside the line deliberately, as a visible reminder of who had won the war.

Their train made reasonable time by post-war standards, but it still took three hours to reach Dresden, which had the dubious distinction of looking even worse than Berlin. Russell shared the opinion, widely-held among Germans, that the air attack on Dresden in February 1945 had been a war crime, and he saw no reason to stop there—as far as he was concerned all those responsible for the Allied bombing of civilian targets should have ended up in the Nuremberg dock.

He had once said as much to an RAF wing-commander.

'Those were brave men!' the man had barked out in response.

'I'm sure a lot of them were,' Russell had replied. 'And so were a lot of the Germans who committed war crimes in Russia.'

The RAF man had looked as if he wanted to hit him, but had just about managed to restrain himself.

Why were people so stupid? Did they really think bravery always went hand in hand with virtue?

As their train sat in Dresden platform, Russell told Effi about the exchange.

She smiled at him. 'After two thousand years of this,' she said, waving a hand at the partly-cleared ruins beyond the tracks, 'you'd think men would step aside and give women a chance. But I don't see it happening.'

'Touché,' Russell observed.

Forty minutes later they reached the border, and climbed out to take their walk through the inspection shed. The two of them were almost waved through, as Russell had assumed they would be—people entering Czechoslovakia at the state's invitation were unlikely to be searched. Most of the people travelling in the opposite direction, however, weren't so lucky. The Czechoslovak natives presumably all had permission to leave, but it looked as if each and every one of them was being subjected to a rigorous search. By contrast, the only obvious foreigners—two Germans and a Russian—were barely inspected at all.

As they walked forward to their waiting train, Effi drew what seemed the logical conclusion. 'I think I should come back alone.'

'I don't think . . .'

'I'll be fine. They were only searching Czechs, and as long as I don't have you standing behind me, making me nervous . . . and we did talk about you and Janica going on to Vienna.'

'And you pointed out that the train toilet was the logical place to put on the makeup. If she goes with me there won't be an opportunity, unless we find some way of sneaking her into our hotel.'

'That would be crazy,' Effi said. 'She'll have to do without the makeup. She's only twenty-nine, for heaven's sake—I looked the same at twenty-nine as I did at twenty-one. And there's another thing. After what we saw this morning it looks like Berlin will get harder to leave. If we take Janica back there, we may not be able to get her out again.' .

It was a good point, but hardly relevant to Russell's main concern. 'I don't want you bearing all the risk,' he said.

'Well, you're going to have to get used to it. Don't you see? It makes so much more sense not to put all our eggs in one basket. If you and Janica go on to Vienna, and for some dreadful reason she's stopped at the border, then at least we'll still have the film.'

'And a very disappointed Merzhanov,' Russell pointed out. But he would face that problem if and when it arose. He hated the thought of Effi carrying the film out alone, but he could see she was right. 'Okay,' he said. 'But I'm not happy about it.'

'You will be when it works.'

The Czechoslovak railways seemed in worst shape than the German, and it was early evening before their train entered the outskirts of the capital. As they rumbled into Wilson Station, Russell remembered Karel hustling him into the bathroom. 'When we get to our hotel room, be careful what you say,' he advised Effi. 'It'll probably be bugged.'

'Will there be hidden cameras to film our love-making?'

'God only knows.'

They barely had their feet on the platform before a familiar face turned up. 'This is Petra Klíma,' Russell said, introducing her to Effi. 'Ministry of Culture,' he added.

'I loved your film,' Klíma told Effi, as if she'd only made the one.

There was a car waiting outside, along with a young male chauffeur. He quickly stamped out his cigarette when he saw them approaching, then opened a door with studied insolence, as if regretting the show of deference. Once Effi and Russell were in the back, Klíma joined him in the front.

Their hotel was supposedly close to Císař's apartment, and the drive to Smichov took about twenty minutes. En route they passed the sites of several lacunae in Russell's espionage career, but given Klíma's probable fluency in German he forbore from pointing them out to Effi. It looked as though their time in Prague would be highly supervised, which might be a problem when it came to meeting Janica.

The hotel was on Zborovska, one block west of the Charles River. It didn't look much from the outside, but their suite was large and well-furnished. Once Klíma had left them to get settled in, they left the tap running noisily in the wash-basin and sat either end of a brimming hot bath, discussing their plan for the next two days. They were still there when Klíma started banging on the outer door, intent on escorting them down to dinner.

While Effi was dressing, Russell told the Czech woman that their travel plans had changed, that while he still planned on travelling on to Vienna, Effi would be going straight back to Berlin. Could Klíma check the Vienna trains on Wednesday, and arrange the appropriate permit?

She didn't foresee any problem.

There were no other guests in the dining room, which seemed a trifle strange, and Klíma's explanation—that people ate late in Prague—bore no relation to Russell's experience. She didn't sit with them, claiming she'd already eaten, but sat alone at a table near the door, as if on sentry duty. Her German, they'd discovered, was as good as her English.

The food and wine were both excellent, but the thought of microphones close by inhibited conversation. After coffee, when Russell announced that they were going to take a romantic stroll by the river, the Czech woman said she would join them.

'How are we going to get rid of her?' Effi asked Russell, once back in their bathroom with the tap full on.

Russell had already come up with an answer. 'After lunch tomorrow, you'll say how you've never been here before . . .'

'I haven't.'

' . . . And ask to see some sights. I'll say I'm coming, too, and then I'll drop out at the last moment. I'll say I'm tired, and am coming back here for a snooze.'

'You *are* fifty next year.'

'Thanks for reminding me. I still have some youthful vigour, you know.'

'Remember the cameras!'

'They'll be in the bedroom.'

The appointment with Jaromír Císař was at ten the next morning. He was clearly overjoyed to meet Effi, kissing her several times on both cheeks and cupping her face in his hands to study it more thoroughly. Russell would have slapped him, but she took it all in her stride. Bloody thespians, he thought, echoing a character in a movie whose name he couldn't remember.

'What a lucky man!' was all Císař said to him, but even that was

four words more than Klíma received. She just hovered in the background, smiling an uncertain smile.

One of the apartment's two bedrooms had been converted into a
projection room, with four seats facing a plain white wall. Císař had
already seen two of the sampled films, so they watched the rushes
from Effi's performances in the other two. The director sat with a
rapt look on his face, expressing his appreciation of a particular look,
gesture, or spoken line by patting Effi's hand with his own.

'I already have a project in mind for us,' he told Effi when they
emerged. 'An adaption of a book by one of our best young writers,
which our Culture Minister has publicly praised, so there should be
no problems from that direction.' He shot Klíma a glance, and
received an angry one back.

'What's it about?' Effi asked.

'It's about who we are. Czechoslovaks, that is, but also human
beings. The central character, which you would play, is a Sudeten
German mother. People assume that all Sudeten Germans were eager
to join the Reich in 1938, but they weren't. This woman's family
opposes the Nazis, and she loses a son as a result. And seven years
later, she loses another one, when the Czechs take out their frustra-
tions on all the Germans they can lay their hands on. And through it
all, she refuses to grow bitter—she's convinced that people are people, no matter which group they think they belong to. When she
finds out that her daughter is having a love affair with the son of one
of the Czech vigilantes—a nod to Romeo and Juliet, of course—she
moves heaven and Earth to save the girl from the wrath of her own
third son. That's a very crude summary, but you get the idea. When
I've finished the adaption'—he nodded towards the desk, where a
pile of pages and an overfull ashtray flanked his typewriter—'I shall
send you a copy.'

Their leave-taking was extended by another long examination of

Effi's face from various angles, but eventually Císař let them go. The Skoda was waiting outside, the driver smoking another cigarette, which he took his time stubbing out. 'Hollywood suddenly seems less appealing,' Effi remarked once they were seated.

'I don't suppose Mickey Mouse has heard of the Sudetenland,' Russell added flippantly.

'You know what I mean.'

'Yes, of course. But they do make good movies in Hollywood. Just not the sort that he makes.'

The car was on the move.

'Where are we going?' Russell asked.

'To lunch,' Klíma told him.

The restaurant was only a few minutes away, and a table had been reserved in the garden, which overlooked the Charles and offered a panoramic view of Malá Strana and its looming castle. This time Klíma did eat with them, and Russell set out to disarm the young woman with questions about her family. It half-worked, but no matter how many times he offered the bottle of wine, she refused to take a refill. She was, he decided, depressingly single-minded.

He asked if she'd remembered his train ticket. 'Yes,' she said, digging in her handbag, 'I forgot to give it to you.' The hand emerged with an envelope. 'Here it is. The Vienna express leaves Wilson Station at 10 A.M.—that's half an hour after Fraulein Koenen's train to Berlin.'

Russell pocketed the envelope and thanked her, glad that his train was departing after Effi's. After his recent experiences in Prague he hadn't fancied leaving her on the platform.

'So what shall we do this afternoon?' Klíma asked, like a mother inviting suggestions from the children. 'Now that your business is done, some sightseeing perhaps. Prague is a very beautiful city.'

'I've been here many times,' Russell told her, 'and I think I'd rather have a lie-down at the hotel. But I'm sure Effi would like to see some sights.'

'I'd love to,' Effi agreed enthusiastically.

Klíma looked flustered for a moment. 'But how would you find your hotel?' she asked, adding with more than a hint of suspicion that she hadn't thought he spoke the language.

'I wouldn't,' Russell replied cheerfully. 'But you can hail me a cab and tell the driver where to take me.'

She looked relieved at that. 'Yes, why not?' she said thoughtfully. 'But first I must, how do you say it in English? Powder my nose.'

It took her a long time, long enough to ensure that someone would be waiting when he got back to the Slovan.

When she returned they all walked out to the pavement, and a cab was duly waved down. Klíma gave the driver his instructions, which included an awful lot more than the name of their hotel, if the cabbie's face was any guide. Russell gave Effi a parting kiss, wished both women an enjoyable afternoon, and climbed into the front seat.

'And you have a good rest,' Effi said sympathetically.

As Russell had hoped, his driver headed for the Legii Bridge. There were traffic lights at the far end, and his 50-50 chance came good—they were red. He slid the $10 note into the other man's pocket with one hand, opened the nearside door with the other, and deftly stepped on to the road. '*Cigaretten*,' Russell said, miming a smoke and raising a hand in farewell. The cabbie sat there stupidly for a few seconds, until the rising chorus of horns behind forced him to let in the clutch.

Russell walked in the opposite direction, and ducked through the doorway of the first suitable sanctuary, which turned out to be a junk store piled high with old furniture. He didn't think the cabbie would come looking for him, but those the man reported to probably would. Russell skulked inside the store for at least ten minutes, searching through a tray of second-hand earrings, swapping smiles with the bewildered proprietor, and keeping a watch on the street.

Eventually he ventured out. The tram route was two blocks north, so he hurried in that direction, keeping as much as he could to the shadows. Once aboard a northbound car, he consulted his watch. He had almost three hours to kill before his *treff* with Janica, and he didn't want to spend them out in the open. A bar seemed a good bet, and after changing trams and re-crossing the river he found one in the Old Town backstreets, about a ten-minute walk from Masaryk Station. With only an incomprehensible Czech newspaper to read, he worked his way through two beers and a compensatory cup of strong black coffee, before finally setting out on the final lap. The first thing he did on reaching the station was find the public toilets, and relieve the pressure on his bladder.

Back on the concourse, he sought out an ill-lit corner and began his vigil. It somehow seemed fitting that his future should hang on a meeting here, in a station whose name reeked of failure. Both father and son had sought the humanist middle ground between rampant capitalism and communism, and both had failed. They had not been alone—the entire European left, himself included, had sought in vain for a socialism that worked—but Jan Masaryk's tragic end, thrown from a window by communist thugs, seemed like the final straw.

Masaryk Station, the end of the line.

It was getting busier by the minute, as people who worked in the centre of town took their trains home to the suburbs. Which was perhaps why Janica had chosen that time of day. If so, it was a smart move.

The clock above the platform barrier was showing two minutes past, but so far he hadn't seen the face in the photograph. But it was then that he noticed her, sitting on a bench on the other side of the concourse. As he did so, she threw him an irritated glance and nodded slightly. She'd probably been there for a while.

He ambled over and sat down beside her. 'Janica, how good to see you,' he said softly in German. Merzhanov had claimed she spoke it quite well, or at least much better than he did. 'Have you been visiting your mother?' Russell asked, completing the password which the Russian had given him.

'No, she moved to Brno,' Janica answered, which according to Merzhanov was actually true. She was a slightly plump, full-breasted woman, with dark shoulder-length hair, an attractive mouth, and surprisingly steely eyes. Her ensemble of white blouse, black skirt, and two-inch heels nicely avoided the twin pitfalls of too conspicuous and too anonymous. Another smart move.

And she looked younger than her photograph, which was a definite bonus, now that they wouldn't be making her up.

'Let's walk,' Russell suggested, getting to his feet.

She followed suit, taking his arm, and only asked where they were going as they emerged on to the street.

Russell steered them across before answering. 'To Wilson Station to buy you a ticket,' he said. 'In my pocket there are papers with your picture in the name of Ruza Zdeněc,' he told her, remembering how Effi had considered it a good omen that Grelling had chosen the Czech equivalent of Rosa. 'Do you have the film with you?'

'It's in my bag. And it stays there until we cross the border.'

'That won't be possible,' Russell said. 'My wife will be taking the film to Berlin, and I shall be taking you to Salzburg, and Merzhanov. It will be safer for us all that way. My wife is less likely to be searched at the German border than you are, and if they stop you at the Austrian border you'll be better off without the film. A lot better off.

You'd only get five years for trying to leave the country without permission, but if you're caught with this film the Russians will shoot you.' Though exaggerating for the Czech woman's sake, he still felt a shiver of apprehension for Effi.

Janica was silent for a while, mulling over what he had said. Eventually she asked the inevitable question—'Why should I trust you?'

'I can't answer that.' He had thought about confiding Effi's plan to hide the film among others, but the StB might get that information out of her before Effi reached the border. 'Except to say this,' he went on, 'why would we get you false papers and buy you a railway ticket if we meant to betray you?'

'I haven't seen these papers yet.'

The street they were on was empty. 'Take them now,' he said, extracting the envelope from his pocket. 'Put it in your bag,' he advised her. 'The papers are there, and the money you'll need for the ticket to Vienna. You can see for yourself in the station toilet.'

They walked across the park that fronted Wilson Station and in through the main entrance. Russell waited while she went off to examine the contents of the envelope, and on her return he led the way to the station buffet. There was an empty table in one corner.

'I will trust you,' she told him, when he came back with two coffees. 'I have no other choice. Do you want the film now?'

'Not yet,' he decided, looking around. 'You must get your ticket now. Tomorrow morning, the ten A.M. train to Vienna. You will probably need to show the papers, and if anyone asks you why you're going, say you have a Russian boyfriend there. If you leave your bag with me, I'll take the film first chance I get.'

She nodded, left it open on the floor between them, and strode calmly out of the buffet. Glancing down after a decent interval, he could see the reel of film. It wasn't in a box, and would fit nicely in his jacket side pocket. A minute or so later, when no one seemed to be looking, he reached down a hand and worked the transfer.

Looking up again, he half-expected to see a posse of StB thugs lunging towards him, but there was only the same bunch of customers, enjoying their coffee and cakes.

She was back in ten minutes, bearing a ticket with a seat in Coach 4.

'I'm in Three,' he told her, showing his own. 'But it'll be safer for you if we don't make contact again until the train reaches Vienna. As a foreigner, I'll be watched.'

'I understand,' she said, closing up her bag.

'Where are you going now?' he asked.

'Home,' she said, without volunteering a location.

'Very well then, I'll say goodbye.'

She smiled slightly, the first time she'd done so, kissed him lightly on the cheek and walked off towards the exit.

A cool one, he thought. It was only then that he realised she'd never even mentioned Merzhanov.

But that was the Russian's problem. Russell's was the film now burning a hole in his jacket pocket. As he headed south towards Wenceslas Square he wondered what the StB would do with the reel if they ever got hold of it. Meekly hand it over to the Soviets or melt it away in a furnace? No one was safe with a secret like this.

He crossed Wenceslas Square and began cutting through the back streets in the general direction of the river. This seemed safer than taking the major thoroughfares, until the two Czech cops spotted him emerging from a New Town alley. As they strode towards him, he barely resisted the urge to turn and run.

One of the cops asked him something in Czech.

'*Nechápu*,' he said. I don't understand.

One cop reached out a friendly arm, clearly intent on taking him in charge.

'Hotel Slovan,' Russell said desperately. 'Smichov.'

'Ah,' the first cop said. He put a hand on Russell's shoulder, pointed him down the street, and indicated that he should turn right at the end.

'*Děkuji*,' Russell almost gushed, as a rivulet of sweat ran down his back.

Both cops insisted on shaking his hand, and he could feel their eyes on his back as he hurried off in the suggested direction. He was getting too old for this sort of thing.

At that moment he was passing a post office, and the thought of putting the film in the post—and sparing Effi this sort of grief— caused him to slacken his pace. But it was no good. Given the current levels of official paranoia, there seemed an excellent chance that the Czech authorities were checking any remotely suspicious package bound for foreign parts. The film's interception would certainly end all their hopes, and would most likely prove the start of a nightmare, since the StB and their MGB allies would have the address they needed to track down the intended recipient. No, the only safe way to dispose of the damn thing was to write Stalin's name on the parcel.

Or just drop it in the river, he thought, as he walked across the Legii Bridge. But he knew he wouldn't do it. He told himself to stop imagining the worst, and concentrate instead on averting it.

The immediate problem was Klíma, who by now would know he'd gone AWOL. What was his explanation?

'I changed my mind,' he told her a few minutes later, when they met in the Slovan lobby. 'I guessed you would walk across the Charles Bridge, so I walked up this side of the river and waited, but you never appeared.'

'You waited all this time?'

He laughed. 'Oh no, after an hour or so, I went and found a bar. Your beer is excellent.'

She looked torn between incredulity and the knowledge that he was a foreign guest she shouldn't offend without being sure.

Seeking to tip the balance, Russell reached into his pocket and brought out the pair of earrings he'd bought at the antique shop. 'These are for you. A token of our appreciation for all your help.'

She looked at them. 'Thank you, but . . .'

'I'm hungry,' Russell interrupted her. 'Are we eating here again?'

During dinner, Russell set out to allay any remaining suspicions Klíma might have, and only realised he was overdoing it when Effi gave him a kick under the table. Back in their bathroom with the taps full on, Effi couldn't decide which of the audition films she should sacrifice for a reel.

'The film that made the smallest splash,' Russell suggested. 'In case the guards feel like a showing.'

'Surely they won't have a projector at the border post,' Effi objected.

'They will at their local cinema. It's just a matter of improving the odds,' he explained. 'If by some chance, they choose to check one out, they're more likely to pick one they've heard of.'

'I suppose that makes sense,' Effi agreed.

If there was a hidden camera in their bedroom they couldn't spot it. Which didn't mean it wasn't there. Russell left the film in his jacket pocket until all their lights were out, and they lay there in the dark waiting for a decent interval to elapse. He wondered if Beria had checked for a camera, or merely assumed it wasn't running. How could he have made such a stupid mistake? Overweening arrogance, most likely. People with that much power often ended up thinking that nothing could touch them.

After ten minutes had passed, Russell removed the film from his jacket, and they both crept into the bathroom, where the thinnest of lights was seeping in through the transom window. Effi had already removed the film from one of her reels, and now took on the job of replacing it. The lack of light made things difficult, and it took her an age to fix the end of the strip.

Once Merzhanov's film was finally wound and boxed she sat on the toilet seat for a minute or more, regaining her composure and wondering what to do with the roll she'd taken off.

'Put it back on Janica's reel,' Russell whispered, after turning on the tap. 'I'll take it with me.'

'Okay,' she agreed.

The thought crossed his mind that at least he'd have a souvenir of her, a thought that kept him staring at the ceiling long after she'd slipped into sleep. She had once told him that when she first started working for the resistance worry and fear had often kept her awake, but after one very real scare everything had suddenly changed, and sleep had come easily again. Somehow her mind had learned to shut itself down.

Next morning, though, she did seem tense.

'What do I say if they do find it?' she asked him in the bathroom.

'You're an actor,' he told her. 'A very good one. Be shocked. You know nothing about this film; you have no idea how it came to be on that reel. Someone must have taken yours off, and put this one on, with an eye to stealing it back in Berlin. You're outraged. So much so, that you'll help the police find out who it was. They can follow you home and catch the man who comes for it.'

'They won't believe me,' Effi said.

'Maybe not, but it's worth a shot. And believe me, most men are distracted by gorgeous women.'

'I do believe you, but you're forgetting that I'm forty-two.'

'And still gorgeous.'

'I'm glad you think so. And I suppose I should be grateful it won't be the Gestapo.'

'Yes.' He decided to let her keep whatever illusions she might have about the greater kindliness of the MGB.

'And what about you?' she asked.

'I'll be safe as houses. I might be on the same train as Janica, but if she's stopped at the border I'll just keep walking.'

'She might denounce you.'

'I doubt it. She seems pretty level-headed, and there's no way she could involve me without telling the whole story, and that would make things worse for her. No, she'll hope that Merzhanov refuses to budge without her, and that we'll be forced into another attempt at getting her out.'

'Would we?'

'I doubt it,' Russell admitted. 'How could we?'

On the way to the station Russell noticed that Klíma was wearing her new earrings. She seemed less on edge than usual, probably relieved at the prospect of seeing them off. Their driver was surly as ever though, snarling at any tram or bus that dared to block the Skoda's path.

After Effi's train had steamed out, Klíma insisted on waiting with him, even though her successor was already on the job, hiding behind a newspaper some five metres down the platform. This man followed Russell on to the train and took a seat in the same coach, around ten rows farther back. Which was all to the good, Russell supposed—for once in his clandestine life he had nothing to hide, and the more they watched him, the less likely they would notice Janica.

He had watched her arrive on the platform with some relief. She had seen him, too, but there'd been no batted eyelids or faltering steps. If he didn't know better, he'd have said that she was the professional.

Which was a disturbing thought. Not for the first time, he found himself wondering if the whole business was a gigantic set-up, with a purpose that eluded him. For all they actually knew, the film was blank. Or a record of Stalin, thumbs in ears, derisively waggling his fingers at the camera.

But he couldn't really believe it. Merzhanov had convinced him from the start, and Janica had said nothing to make him suspicious.

Beyond the window, mist draped the meadows and shrouded the trees. The sun would probably soon break through, but it was already hot in the carriage, and even with the toplights open, the air was oppressively close. Russell took off his jacket, and tried not to worry about Effi.

Assuming she didn't run into trouble, and he successfully shipped the other two off, what did they need to do next? Did they have to send Beria a copy of the film, or would merely describing its contents be enough? How else could they have known about the events in question? From the other woman, of course, assuming she survived. But hearsay wouldn't be enough. They had to provide proof of the film's existence—a presentation copy was the only way. And now he came to think of it, several copies might make all the difference— if they hid them in different countries, Beria would have a hell of a job tracking them down. And even if he did, he could never be certain he had them all.

But they couldn't make copies themselves, and whoever did so would need to be in on the secret. Effi might know someone from her work whom she could trust with something like this. A political innocent would be best; someone who'd never heard of Beria, and who wouldn't recognise him.

Outside the train, the sun was busy dispersing the mist, and conjuring pinpoints of light from the dew-sodden fields. Russell decided he would visit the buffet car, partly for the exercise and partly for a drink, but mostly because he wanted to check on Janica. With his StB shadow a few steps behind him, all he could see on the way forward was the back of her head, but when he returned half an hour later they swapped innocent glances. She looked like she hadn't a care in the world, but then she wasn't married to Effi.

Effi's train was about ten minutes away from the German border when the man reappeared. He was about fifty, she guessed; he was smartly dressed and looked more like a Czech than a German. Early in the journey he had walked slowly past the compartment, given her a lingering look, and moved on out of sight. Now he repeated the process, this time with the faintest of smiles.

It all brought back the war. All those hours, days, weeks she'd spent permanently on edge, waiting for the knock on the door, the tap on the shoulder, the car pulling up in the street outside. She'd thought that life was over, but here it was again. How did John stand it, year after year?

They had to leave, get as far away as they could. Russell had always believed the Soviets would punish a desertion, that either they'd tell the Americans how he'd bought his family's freedom with atomic secrets, and so bring a treason charge down on his head, or they'd simply kill him, along with heaven knew how many other members of the family. He could be right—he usually was when it came to expecting the worst—but just this once he might be wrong. Maybe it was time to call their bluff. From a great distance, if that proved possible. Effi knew Stalin had sent someone all the way to Mexico to kill Trotsky, but Russell, much as she loved him, was a much smaller fry. And if they were going to live in fear, they might as well do it in Hollywood.

The train was slowing down. Effi reached up for the overnight bag in the luggage rack, and pulled it down beside her. She couldn't think of any reason why they should question the four reels of film. Her papers were in order; she was travelling first class courtesy of a communist Culture Ministry; these same four reels had been in the bag when she entered the country two days ago. And she would top it all off with a winning smile, she reminded herself. John had insisted on one of those.

She stepped down on to the cinder path and joined the stream of passengers heading toward the inspection hall. It was only as she passed through the doorway that she realised who was behind her—the man from the corridor.

Her heart skipped a beat, but he did nothing more threatening than stand there in the queue. The urge to turn and challenge him was strong, but she knew she mustn't. If he was StB, then what would she gain? If he wasn't, then what was the point? She would merely be making herself conspicuous.

So she kept her face forward, aware of his breathing, aware of his feet on the move each time the queue shuffled forwards, until an official in front of her commanded all her attention.

He went through her papers, asked to place her bag on the table, and began to empty its contents. After opening one can and exposing its reel, he repeated the process with the other three, and asked her something in Czech.

She shrugged her incomprehension and offered up the winning smile, but the official was already walking away, having signalled by hand that she should stay where she was. Behind her, she could feel the queue sighing with impatience.

The official was back almost instantly, a German-speaking colleague in tow. He extracted one film from its tin. 'What are these?' he asked her.

'They're audition reels,' she told him. 'I'm an actress. I've been to

visit one of your directors—a man named Jaromír Císař. He's thinking of casting me in one of his films, and he wanted to see examples
of my work.'

The official had never heard of Císař.

'It was all arranged by your Ministry of Culture. They will confirm what I say.'

The man looked at the film in his hand, said something in Czech
to his colleague, and strode off again.

A third official returned with him, and took his turn staring at the
films.

'The names of the films are on the boxes,' Effi volunteered. 'Each
one contains a few scenes, which I use for audition purposes.'

The man looked at her, then back at the films. 'You will have to
leave these with us,' he finally said in German. 'Once they have been
examined, we will send them on to Berlin.'

Neither Effi nor Russell had foreseen this eventuality—they had
both been too busy worrying that she would be held. 'But I need
them,' Effi protested. 'I have an appointment to show them in the
morning,' she lied.

'I'm sorry,' the man said. 'But we have only your word for it that
you're an actress.'

'But that's ridiculous . . .'

A voice behind her started speaking in Czech. It was the man
who'd been watching her on the train.

I'm done for, she thought.

'This gentleman says he can vouch for you being an actress,' the
third official told her.

She turned to face him.

'And of course I've heard of Jaromír Císař,' he added in German.

'Thank you,' she said, but he was speaking to the Czech official again.

'I suggested he telephone the Ministry of Culture,' he eventually told her, 'but he doesn't want to hold the train up. So he says you can take your films.'

'Oh thank you so much.' She turned back to the official. '*Děkuji*,' she said, with a second flash of the winning smile. Resisting the impulse to shovel her possessions back into the overnight bag, she carefully restored them one at a time, before striding out through the exit door.

In the German building a hundred metres farther down the track, each official had his own Russian shadow. Here, too, her baggage was searched, the boxes opened, but this time her explanation had official backing. Comrade Tulpanov had sanctioned her trip, she told the German official, and he should refer any queries to Berlin.

He started to tell his shadow, but was cut short. Presumably the Russian had understood her German, because his hand now waved her through.

She walked back out into the sunshine, and on towards the waiting train.

It left about ten minutes later, and not long after that her saviour appeared in the compartment doorway. 'Is everything all right?' he asked.

'Yes. And thank you again.'

'Could I buy you a drink?'

It seemed churlish to refuse, and perhaps unwise—she still harboured a faint suspicion that he'd saved her for purposes of his own.

But it turned out he was just a cineaste and fan, a decent Czech man with a wife and two children who had seen her recent films and admired them. He had recognised her soon after they left Prague, but had been too shy to approach her.

Russell's train reached the Austrian border soon after two. As the train slowed down he wondered whether he should pass through border inspection ahead of Janica, and put himself clear of any subsequent fall-out, or stay behind her in the queue, and know for certain how she had fared.

It all proved academic. As he could soon see through his window, a spanking new border post was under construction on the site of the old, and the inspectors emerging from a grounded old carriage were clearly intent on boarding the train. They started at the back, and took around twenty minutes to reach Russell's carriage. His documents were scrutinised with great care, his bag rifled through, but he had the feeling their hearts weren't in it—in the new Czechoslovakia a foreigner leaving was a problem solved.

They would look a lot closer at Janica.

After they'd passed through into her coach, he nervously waited for sounds of trouble, his eyes fixed on the corridor connection ahead, in case she erupted through it. 'I've never seen this woman before,' he murmured to himself in rehearsal. Would they believe him? They couldn't prove otherwise, but would that worry them?

Each minute that passed with no sign of alarm left him feeling a little more confident, and then, mercy of mercies, he saw the two officials and their military minder walking back across the tracks towards their temporary office. Without a woman in tow.

Almost immediately, the train clanked into motion, and within seconds it was rumbling across the small river that marked the border. They were out of Czechoslovakia, and into Austria's Soviet Zone, which should be a good deal safer. The Russians were too busy trying to stop their own fleeing nationals to worry overmuch about one Czech woman. And few Soviet officials would know a dud Czechoslovak ID from a genuine one.

Russell even managed an hour or so's sleep as the train chugged on towards Vienna. It was a minute to five when they crossed the Danube, two minutes past when the train wheezed to a grateful halt in the roofless Nordbahnhof. He found Janica waiting for him on the platform, suitcase in hand. 'Take my arm,' he said.

There were uniforms at the barrier, but either they were waiting for someone specific, or only had a watching brief. No tickets or papers were being inspected, and no one approached them as they calmly walked through to the forecourt, where a line of taxis was waiting. Theirs had seen better days, and its driver looked about eighty. 'Stephansplatz,' Russell told him, deeming it wise to seek sanctuary in the international sector.

'You have dollars?' the driver asked, without starting the cab. He was probably used to passengers arriving from Prague without convertible currency.

'I have dollars,' Russell admitted.

The driver smiled and let in the clutch. Soon they were passing the Riesenrad Ferris wheel and heading down Prater Strasse towards the Danube Canal bridge. As they crossed the latter, Russell felt a huge sense of relief—for the moment, at least, they were beyond the reach of the Soviets. As if to reinforce that feeling, an international patrol drove past in a jeep, the Russian sat beside the French driver, the Anglo-Americans perched in the back.

Janica, he saw, was staring wide-eyed at the Viennese ruins. 'But the war's been over for years,' she said.

He told her she should see Berlin.

They were almost at Stephansplatz when Russell remembered the hotel on Johannesgasse that he'd stayed in three years earlier, and redirected the driver. It was still standing, and offered more in the way of discretion than the American Press Club. She looked it over with ill-concealed distaste. 'Is there nothing better?' she asked.

'It's only for a few hours,' Russell promised.

He told the desk clerk the same and got a predictable leer in return. 'There's only one bed,' Janica complained when she saw their room.

'It's all yours,' Russell told her. 'I'm off to see about our train to Salzburg.'

'Tonight?'

'If possible. Aren't you in a hurry to see Merzhanov?'

'Yes, of course.'

'Okay. I'll be back as soon as I can. Don't go out.'

'Where would I go? I haven't any money.'

He left her curled up on the bed, probably hoping for a more prosperous future. Outside, his first port of call was the Central Exchange, and the familiar room with the long-distance connection. Effi's train had been due an hour before his, so by this time she should be home.

The phone in the Carmer Strasse flat rang for a long time, and he was beginning to hope she'd gone straight on to Zarah's when at last she picked up. 'Who is this?' the familiar voice asked.

The sense of relief was strong enough to take his breath away. 'It's me. You didn't have any trouble then?'

'Not too much. Only a mild panic. Everything all right at your end?'

'So far.'

'Do you still think you might be back tomorrow?'

'Tomorrow or Saturday. Was Rosa pleased to see you?'

'Very. I think she was really worried.'

'Tell her I miss her.'

'All right.'

He hung up, and just sat there for several moments, smiling into space.

The CIC offices were a few blocks west in the American sector, or had been the previous year. Russell walked to the house in question, hoping that the local CIA hadn't got around to absorbing their local rivals, the way they had in Berlin, but hadn't in Trieste. His luck was in—the Viennese CIC was still parading its own independence, and the duty officer that evening was a man he'd dealt with before. Russell explained about Janica, and their need to reach Salzburg. Could the two of them take the Mozart train that night?

'Not a chance,' Jack Dearlove told him cheerfully. 'You know it's Americans Only, and these days the Russians check *everybody*. This girl of yours will need American papers and a new wardrobe, and that will take several days to arrange. Even with them, you'll spend the whole trip praying that no one starts asking her questions in English.'

'Shit,' Russell muttered.

'But no worries, eh,' Dearlove said with a grin. 'The Russians get tough; we get airborne. There's a morning shuttle from Salzburg now, leaves there at eight, here at ten. In the morning take a cab out to Meissner Park—that's where the airstrip is. I'll let them know you're coming.'

Russell thanked him profusely, and walked back towards the city centre. This was the way things were going, he thought—intelligence people flying where and when they wanted, while ordinary joes formed orderly queues at frontier posts. Well, he might as well enjoy it while he could—if everything went according to plan, he'd soon be a civilian himself.

Janica looked like she'd been dozing when he got back, but perked up at the promise of a meal. It was a hot summer evening, and they ate at an outdoor restaurant in the Stadtpark, where she batted away his queries concerning her family history, and plied him with questions about life in America. She ate surprisingly sparely, but drank several glasses of wine, and seemed somewhat unsteady walking back. In the hotel lobby, she looked almost scornful when Russell paused at the reception desk to rent a second room.

They shared breakfast at a nearby café, and a cab out to Meissner Park. 'I've never been on an aeroplane,' she admitted, as they drove across the grass to what looked like a makeshift control tower. She sounded more curious than nervous.

The usual DC-3 touched down about ten minutes later. This was the last trip, the pilot told them. Now that the Russian blockade of Berlin had begun, their squadron was being sent north. His luck was holding, Russell thought, but the German capital's might have run out. He asked the pilot for specifics, but came up empty. 'They've locked it up tight,' he said. 'On the ground, that is; they can't block-ade the fucking sky.'

Russell wasn't so sure, but he hoped the man was right. Consider-ing their situation, this didn't seem like the best of times to be trapped.

The flight to the Salzburg airbase took just under an hour, the wait for a jeep almost as long, and it was one o'clock before they reached the farm. When he saw her, Merzhanov face's lit up with joy. She was more restrained, but there was real affection there, Russell decided. Maybe he'd misjudged her.

'Can we have some time alone?' Merzhanov asked.

'I'm afraid not,' Russell told him, feeling mean but not really car-ing—they'd have weeks at sea to cuddle each other. 'We have to leave straight away.'

Merzhanov's small bag was already packed, and the two of them followed him out to the jeep. Sitting together in the back, they whispered endearments for most of the ninety-minute ride, leaving Russell to take a mental wander through the minefield of the next few weeks. With the Allied air forces now providing the only ways in and out of Berlin, Russell's idea of hiding copies of the film in various countries seemed likely to be a non-starter. If the Brits or Americans got their hands on one, then Beria's crime—or a suit-ably edited version thereof—would end up on Pathé News, and Russell and Shchepkin would have lost their bargaining card.

A kilometre short of Alt Aussee, Russell pulled the jeep over to the side of the road and turned to face the lovebirds. 'As I told Konstantin last time I saw him—these people believe you are Catholics. That's why they're willing to help you. I wish we'd had time to give you a crash course in Catholicism, but we didn't. If a problem arises, Konstantin will have to say that he had no chance to practise his religion in the Soviet Union—which would be true enough—and so he only knows what little his grandmother told him. But you *feel* like a Catholic,' Russell told the Russian, 'and you're hungry to learn more. And if anyone questions you, Janica, just say you're planning to convert as soon as you can.'

'All right.'

'Okay. Now, Konstantin, what do you know about the Ukrainian nationalist groups?'

'They're all murderous bastards.'

Russell smiled. 'Well, forget that for a while. They're popular murderous bastards with the people who are taking you south. You don't have to claim you were in the OUN, or anything like that, but if the subject comes up, be tactful. Make up a history which they'll like.' He looked at them both.

'Where are we going?' Janica asked him abruptly.

'America. South America to begin with, I expect.'

'But we want to live in the USA.'

'I know. And I'm sure you'll get there eventually.'

'We will need money,' she insisted.

'I have five hundred dollars for you,' Russell said, reaching into his pocket.

'Is that all?' Merzhanov said, more surprised than angry. He had apparently forgotten his earlier disdain for the stuff.

'I'm afraid so.' Johannsen had only provided $200; Russell and Effi had supplied the rest. 'It'll go a long way if you're careful,' he added.

'And we have each other,' Merzhanov rallied, putting an arm around Janica's shoulder.

'Of course,' she agreed, managing to return his smile.

'You should be at sea within a week,' Russell told them. 'One last thing. The MGB aren't looking for you now, and I presume you'd like to keep it that way. So *don't*, whatever you do, tell anyone about the film.'

'We understand,' Merzhanov said.

'Yes, of course,' Janica said, a little sulkily.

'If they find out you took it, they'll kill you both,' Russell reiterated, just to make sure they fully understood.

'Yes, yes,' Janica said. 'We know. We say nothing.'

Mordechai's advice

After returning the previous evening, Effi had dropped in on Zarah to let her know she was back. She hadn't stayed long, but as she was leaving her sister had presented Effi with a rare gift—around a hundred grams of Jamaican Blue Mountain coffee, part of Bill's winnings from a poker match with some Brits. Now, having taken Rosa to school, she made herself a cup, and curled up on the sofa to savour every last sip.

The tins containing the film reels were stacked on the mantelpiece, Merzhanov's among them. 'Hiding something in plain view,' Russell called it, and she hoped he wasn't being too clever. Maybe she was missing the point, but a film tin seemed a good place to look for a film.

Looking at the boxes started her thinking about how they were going to view the one in question. They could take Merzhanov's film to one of the studios she'd worked at over the years and persuade a technician to let them watch it—minor celebrity status could move such minor mountains—but ensuring privacy would probably prove more difficult. The technician would want to work the projector; would, in fact, be the only one there who knew how. And even if he could be bribed into setting things up and leaving them to it, they could hardly lock themselves inside a screening room without raising all sorts of questions. No, it wouldn't do. They would have to hang a white sheet on the wall the way Císař had, and somehow get hold of their own projector.

But from where? Resisting the temptation to make another coffee, Effi sketched out a list of possible sources and started making calls. None of her first respondents had one, but most had suggestions as to where one might be found, and an hour or more into her search she finally struck gold. There was a company in Wedding that hired out projectors—there was, it seemed, a booming trade in private showings of pornographic shorts. The Russians and French were particularly enamoured, her informant told her; the Brits and Americans much more prudish.

After ringing the shop, and hearing that it did have the appropriate equipment for hire, Effi took the U-Bahn to Muller Strasse and walked the short distance to the address she'd been given. The sign above the window was for a butcher, but once inside the premises the only flesh on display was human. Someone had been enlarging stills from pornographic movies. A sales pitch, Effi realised, both legal and enticing—the scraps of cloth being worn in the photos were doubtless removed in the films.

Inside, a youth of around twenty was surrounded by film equipment of various types and vintage. He seemed ill at ease, a state Effi attributed to an unfamiliarity with real women. Knowing she badly needed his help, she set out to reassure him, presenting herself as a potent combination of motherly concern and female hopelessness in the face of machinery. After modestly admitting that she had made some films herself—'several years ago now,' she added wistfully—she took one of her audition reels out of her bag. 'I want to show some films like this to a few friends at home,' she said innocently. 'Do you have the right projector? And if you do, could you teach me how to work it?'

He did and he could. They went through the process twice together, Effi coyly stopping the film each time the opening frames appeared on the wall, and trying not to notice how keen he seemed to sniff her hair. Once certain she knew how to work the projector, she paid a week's hire, and left him to box it up. Outside on Muller Strasse the wait for a cab seemed endless, but when one eventually came the youth carefully placed it on the seat beside her, and raised a hand in nervous farewell.

Back at Carmer Strasse a neighbour helped her carry it in, and when Rosa came home from school, they watched one of the audition reels together. Every now and then the girl would turn her eyes from the screen Effi to the one who sat beside her, just to check they were one and the same.

Around six, they walked over to Zarah's. Lothar and Bill Carnforth was there already, and after dinner the five of them played skat. They had the radio playing low in the background, and they almost missed the transition from soothing music to worrying news: The Allies had announced a currency reform. From midnight on the following Sunday the old Reichsmark would no longer be legal tender. Initially, at least, the change would only apply to the British, French, and American zones, and not to their sectors in Berlin; but Bill was convinced it was only a matter of time.

And so, apparently, were the Soviets. Each time the news was repeated, it came with fresh hints of a Russian response, and at midnight it was finally made official—all rail and road passenger traffic between Berlin and the Western zones had been summarily halted. By this time Rosa was fast asleep, whereas Effi, like hundreds of thousands of other Berliners, was much more awake than she wanted to be, staring blankly at the radio, waiting for someone to say something hopeful.

Russell picked up the news at Rhein-Main on Saturday morning. He had known something was up from the moment he arrived at the sprawling airbase as both people and planes seemed to be charging around like headless chickens. At one spot on the edge of the tarmac a surreal pile of passenger seats had accumulated, torn out, he later realised, to make more room for supplies.

Did the Western Allies really think they could sustain their Berlin sectors by air? They might be able to fly in enough food, but how would Berliners cook it? How would they heat their homes? The Soviets only had to cut off the fuel supplies to the power stations, and that would be that. And if, as seemed increasingly likely, they really meant business this time, then that was exactly what they would do. How could the Allies fight them? With coal planes?

That morning they seemed reluctant to increase Berlin's population by even one—Russell needed a phone call from BOB to secure him passage in the belly of a C-47, jammed between sacks of flour and potatoes. And if the physical discomfort was bad, the stress of listening to the two young pilots imagine Soviet fighters behind every approaching cloud was even worse. After listening to that for an hour, Russell was almost wishing that the Russians would shoot them down.

He got back to Carmer Strasse early that afternoon. Effi and Rosa returned from the park a little bit later, and while Rosa was using the toilet he asked Effi if she'd watched the film. 'No,' she told him, 'I was waiting for you.'

He felt strangely reluctant to watch it himself, more because it felt like another burnt bridge than because of its probable content. 'Let's both wait for Shchepkin,' he suggested. 'Before I left, we arranged a meet for tomorrow—I can bring him straight back here. If Zarah can take Rosa, that is.'

'We were all going to see *The Wizard of Oz*,' Effi said wistfully. 'I suppose I'll have to feel unwell.'

That evening the three of them went in search of a slap-up dinner on Ku'damm. There were many others doing the same, either drawn out by the sense of gathering crisis or simply intent on spending their Reichsmarks while they could. The authorities still held that the currency reform didn't apply to the city, but few Berliners were confident of things remaining that way, and already some restaurateurs were only accepting payment in dollars. Small rows were breaking out up and down the boulevard, with would-be customers insisting that their money was still legal tender, and proprietors just as certain that it wouldn't be for very much longer.

Russell's dollars secured them a table in a recently re-opened bistro, long renowned for its pfifferling mushrooms. Though now supplied by an entrepreneurial Red Army unit, they were still delicious. Sitting, eating, chatting—the evening passed more than pleasantly. A last chance to breathe easily, Russell thought, because the minute Beria knew they had the film everything would change, for better or for worse.

Rosa was smiling at him. He could see how happy his daughter was that they were all together again, and for a moment he felt almost overwhelmed by the enormity of the risk they were taking. With evenings like this still possible, how could he say that the old life couldn't be sustained?

But it couldn't, he knew it couldn't. Sooner or later a juggler dropped a ball, and Russell's arms felt more tired by the week. Life was a risky business, and one needed wisdom about choosing which risks to take. And this opportunity did seem to offer a huge reward— to all of them—at a relatively low risk. In the end, it was a miracle that any one of them had survived the war, let alone all three. Maybe fate had them under its wing, he thought.

The Tiergarten almost looked like its old Sunday self the next morning, at least insofar as the people walking there were concerned. The trees might still be saplings, the open spaces pocked with craters, but hundreds of families were strolling across the re-sown grass, enjoying the warm sunshine.

As he waited for Shchepkin, Russell wondered whether to mention Don Stafford. Did he want to know whether the Russian had arranged Stafford's death? The answer, of course, was yes, if he hadn't, and no, if he had. But if Shchepkin had, Russell knew he would never admit it, and so eliciting a denial would serve no purpose. Russell knew he would just have to live with fearing the worst.

The Russian looked worse than he had the previous week. Maybe it was the brightness of the light, but his lips seemed almost purple, his cheeks tinged with grey. He seemed in good enough spirits, though, and eagerly asked about the film.

'We've got it,' Russell told him.

'And?'

'You're invited to the premiere.'

'You haven't looked at it yet. So when?'

'Now, if you're not too busy.'

Shchepkin assured him that he wasn't.

They took a tram from the park entrance to the Zoo Station, and walked on towards Carmer Strasse.

In the flat, Effi had the projector all set up. The first thing that became apparent was the quality of the film—Soviet technology in this field had clearly come on apace. The light was poor, and parts of the room seemed pools of shadow, but the human occupants were clearly recognisable. If the man in the dressing gown wasn't Beria, then it was his double.

'Oh my God, it's Sonja Strehl,' Effi said, as one of the two women's faces turned towards the camera. 'When did you say this was filmed?' she asked Russell.

'In February, according to Merzhanov.'

'But she didn't die until the end of the March.'

'No. Do you know the other woman?' Russell asked.

'No, but she can't be more than sixteen.'

'Does Beria have a reputation for liking them young?' Russell asked Shchepkin.

'So it's said,' the Russian replied tersely.

The women were undressing, presumably at Beria's command. There was certainly nothing in their faces that suggested pleasure or excitement. Watching, Russell felt ashamed of the stir in his groin.

Effi wanted to run, or at least to close her eyes, but she forced herself to keep watching. Sonja's lips were moving, but Beria's eyes were on the girl, and as he moved forward to grab her by the wrist his penis sprang out of his robe.

Things happened fast after that: Sonja flung aside, the girl's run to the door, a gun in Beria's hand. As he circled the kneeling, shaking girl like a cat tormenting a petrified mouse, Effi finally did close her eyes, and when Russell's 'oh shit' forced them open again, the girl was a crumpled heap in the background, and Beria was walking towards Sonja, pushing her across the edge of the bed and taking her from behind. After pulling out, he held her face down with his knee as he carefully emptied the gun, then turned her over and forced it into her grip.

'Fingerprints,' Russell murmured.

Using a handkerchief, Beria carefully retrieved the gun, and after retying his dressing gown and smoothing back his hair in front of the mirror, he knocked on the door and was swiftly let out. Once he was gone, Sonja groped her way across the carpet to cradle the dead girl's head in her arms, shoulders shaking with grief for what felt like several minutes, before the film abruptly cut off.

The three of them exchanged stunned looks. It was all they had hoped for, Effi thought bitterly.

'Who was she?' Russell murmured.

'Someone at the funeral said Sonja had a younger sister,' Effi remembered. 'Who couldn't come because she was in Leningrad. She's at the Kirov Ballet School.'

'Or not,' Russell said. 'What's the betting that was her?'

Effi didn't want to believe it. 'But why would Sonja keep silent? She must have been scared out of her wits, but once she decided to kill herself, why not leave a note?'

'Shame,' Russell suggested.

'Shame for what?' Effi retorted angrily. 'You saw it all. There was nothing she could have done to save her sister. Or herself.'

'We know that, but maybe she didn't.'

'Beria came back to Berlin at the end of March,' Shchepkin said. 'My guess is she couldn't face the prospect of another meeting.'

Effi was still not satisfied. 'That would explain why she killed herself when she did, but not why she didn't leave a note.'

'She wanted to save her children,' Shchepkin said simply.

Effi stared at him. She was, Russell thought, suddenly seeing the Russian for who and what he was.

'I know,' Shchepkin told her. He looked like death, Russell thought.

Effi just sighed.

'We can't bring Sonja or her sister back,' Russell said. 'And they may never get justice if we use this film to blackmail Beria. But the living have to take precedence, even when it's only ourselves.'

Effi smiled at that. 'I suppose so.'

'So how are we going to approach your boss?' Russell asked the Russian.

'I'll take it to him. But first we need copies—two, I think, one for me and one for you. Do you know where we could have them made?'

'I could ask people I know in the industry,' Effi said, 'but if someone gives me a name I'll have no way of knowing how trust-worthy the person is.'

Russell shook his head. 'A professional job is out of the question. Copying something like this must be illegal, for a start. If we knew what equipment we needed, maybe we could borrow it. Even buy it, as a last resort.'

Effi had a realisation. 'The people I got the projector from make most of their money from hiring out sex films. They'd need copies of their best earners, and they can't be getting them from the studios. Not openly, anyway.'

'You think they're making their own?'

'Or know someone with the right equipment who doesn't ask questions. I'll visit Muller Strasse in the morning.'

'We both will,' Russell decided. He turned to Shchepkin. 'And once we have them, you'll what? Knock on the bastard's door?'

'Why not? He doesn't live in the Kremlin. He has a mansion on Kachalova Street, out near the Zoo.'

'How appropriate.'

'I shall tell him we have the original, and what we want in exchange for keeping it hidden—that he will allow my wife and daughter to join me here in Berlin, promise to keep silent about your work for the Soviet Union, and guarantee that no retributive action be taken against members of your family. I'll need a list,' Shchepkin added.

Russell wasn't sure about that, as giving Beria a list of who he cared about felt like asking for trouble. But then again . . . 'The man's not going to like being threatened,' was all he said.

'Of course not,' Shchepkin agreed. 'But he won't let that get in his way. He needs what we're offering; he doesn't need what we want in return. Why should he refuse?'

Spite, Russell thought, but Shchepkin knew the man better than he did. 'In the long run? Can we trust him? Come to that, will he trust us?'

'Trust doesn't come into it. He has nothing to gain by coming after us, and everything to lose. And why would we release the film as long as he leaves us alone?'

'You're assuming everyone will act reasonably.'

'Well, you and I will. And Beria may be a psychopath, but he's not irrational.'

'Is that good news or bad?'

'For us, good,' Shchepkin said, getting to his feet. 'You must call me on the usual number the moment you have copies.'

'And then you'll head off to Moscow?'

'Not directly. Provided you agree, I shall take the original some-where else first. I think I know how to put it beyond even Beria's reach.'

'Do we need to know where?'

'On the contrary. And I won't want to know where you've hidden the other copy. To be brutally frank, our lives may depend on Beria being unable to discover both hiding places from either one of us.' He didn't use the word, but the prospect of torture hung in the air.

'Makes sense,' Russell agreed.

As Shchepkin turned to leave, Effi had a last question for him. 'After what we've just seen, doesn't the prospect of knocking on that man's door and making him extremely angry frighten you?'

The Russian thought about it. 'Yes and no,' he said eventually. 'But I've already had that conversation with John. I think he'll grind his teeth and accept our terms. If I'm wrong, and I'm dragged off to a cell, he'll also come after you. It won't stop the film seeing the light of day, of course, but I'm sure he'd want to take you down with him.'

That evening, Rosa wanted to see another of Effi's audition films. As they watched it in the darkened room, Russell kept seeing the naked women entwined on the carpet, the one who was dead and the one who wasn't, but might as well have been.

The shop on Muller Strasse was closed when they reached it the following morning, so the two of them set up a vigil in a café window across the street. Almost an hour went by, and they were beginning to give up hope, when the youth who had served Effi on her previous visit ambled into view on the opposite pavement, and inserted his key in the oversized padlock.

As they walked across the wide thoroughfare, Russell agreed that Effi should do the talking. And, if necessary, the charming.

The youth smiled when he saw her, and then made a valiant effort to hide his disappointment when he realised she wasn't alone. 'Is the projector outside?' he asked.

'No, I still have it at home. It's fine. Look,' Effi said, 'you were very helpful the other day, and I was wondering . . . Well, given your line of business, I imagine you need more than one copy of your films?'

'Yes,' he said cautiously.

'You see, my film—I'd like to make some copies of it. For directors I know. You understand?'

'Yes, yes. I could do that for you.'

'Do you make the copies yourself? You don't use a professional setup?'

'Nothing so grand. And yes, I make them myself. We . . . I . . . simply set up a camera alongside the projector, and film the film so to speak. On a white wall, of course.'

'And that makes good copies?' Russell asked with a disarming smile.

'Good enough,' the youth said. 'They're not *quite* as sharp, but you don't lose much.'

'Where do you do it?' Effi asked.

'In the basement.'

'Ah. The reason I ask is that I don't want any strangers to see what's on the film, and so would it be possible for you to set up the equipment in the way that you said, show us how to operate it, and then leave us to make the copies ourselves?'

'That's not . . .'

'We'd pay you well,' Russell interjected.

'How well?'

After five minutes of haggling they agreed on a price. 'I should have let you go in alone,' Russell admitted once they'd left. 'He knows how to deal with men.'

That evening they returned with the film, and followed the youth down a flight of stone steps to a whitewashed basement. The equipment was already set up. 'It's simple,' their tutor explained, after pocketing the wad of dollars. 'You just switch them both on, here and here. Adjust the focus with this if you need to, but you probably won't. How long is it?' he asked, as he threaded the film on to the sprockets.

'Only twenty minutes or so,' Effi told him.

'Well after you've made the first copy, have a look at it. If there's a problem, I'll be upstairs. If not, make the second.'

They did as he told them. Neither wanted to see the film again, but occasional glances were enough to assure them that it was running to speed. Once the first copy had been made, Effi transferred it to the projector, and played the first couple of minutes. It wasn't as crisp as the original, but in Russell's opinion was good enough.

The second copy took them another half an hour, and when they finally emerged onto the pavement, darkness was falling. As they waited on the U-Bahn platform Effi asked him where they would hide theirs.

'I haven't a clue,' he told her. 'Anywhere but Hanna's vegetable patch, I suppose.' That was where he'd buried the atomic research papers in 1945.

'I suppose that *would* be the first place the Russians would look.'

After they emerged from the Zoo Station entrance, Russell stopped at a public telephone and rang the number in the Soviet sector which he used to contact Shchepkin. After the usual coded exchange, he hung up secure in the knowledge that a meeting was arranged for noon the next day.

'So we've lit the fuse,' Effi said, as they walked underneath the railway bridge on Hardenberg Strasse.

'I guess we have.' Thinking over Shchepkin's warning, that a vengeful Beria might very well come after them, he decided that their one gun mightn't be enough.

At noon the next day Russell waited for Shchepkin at the eastern end of the Tiergarten. It was the Russian's favourite meeting place— like most of his compatriots he seemed to enjoy staring at the ruined Reichstag—but Russell found the whole setting profoundly depressing. He remembered the park when it was a lovely place for a stroll, and the parliament wasn't packed with Nazis.

Sitting on their usual bench, he wondered how Shchepkin would cover his tracks when he took the original film 'beyond Beria's reach.' Did the Russian have easy access to some office out in Karlshorst where the MGB manufactured false papers? Shchepkin's position in that organisation was a complete mystery to Russell. He knew the Russian had been imprisoned for several months—maybe more— towards the end of the war, but he had never really found out why. All Shchepkin had said to him was that he'd ended up on the wrong side in some inter-party dispute, and been rehabilitated, at least in part, because of his suitability as Russell's control. But he obviously had other duties to perform, and other agents to supervise, so presumably someone in the Kremlin must like him.

Trusting Shchepkin was rather like stepping out into a river of unknown depth. And yet he did.

The list the Russian had asked for—of those whose untimely death would trigger the film's release—was in Russell's inside pocket. It hadn't been easy to compile. Some names were obvious—Effi and Rosa, Zarah and Lothar, Thomas, Hanna and Lotte—but others were not. He hesitated before dragging Paul and Marisa into things, but the MGB knew he had a son, and would have no trouble finding him. At Effi's insistence he included Bill Carnforth, although God only knew what the American would think if he knew his name had ended up on Beria's desk. He wondered what Zarah had told her fiancé about his own past dealings with the Soviets. Not much, he suspected—her fears for Effi would keep her silent.

And there Russell had drawn the line. If Beria was still desperate to inflict punishment, he would have to settle for friends or very distant relations, and he would have to find them himself.

Shchepkin was walking towards him, white hair glinting in the sunlight. There was nothing distinctive about his appearance, Russell thought, nothing to indicate his nationality or line of work. He looked as much like a French businessman or German professor as he did a Soviet agent.

After taking possession of the reels in their brown paper parcel, Shchepkin seemed reluctant to leave.

'So what's the latest from Karlshorst?' Russell asked.

'You know about Sokolovsky's letter.'

'I think everyone in Berlin does.'

'Well, today our man at the Control Council will be willing to discuss a compromise. And this afternoon, our man at the City

Council will announce the introduction of a new Soviet currency for all of Berlin.'

'Keep them guessing, eh?'

'Something like that.'

'It won't work. The Allies will just extend their currency to Berlin.'

'Probably. And then the shutters will fall.'

'And after that?'

Shchepkin shrugged. 'By then, you and I may be past caring.' He got wearily to his feet. 'I won't reach Moscow before Friday, so you have a few more carefree days. After that, watch out.'

'We will.'

'Have you hidden yours away?'

'Not yet.'

'Do it, but not too deep. It won't be there long.'

'Why not?'

Shchepkin smiled. 'I'll tell you that when I get back. Early next week, I hope.'

'Good luck.'

The Russian nodded, and strolled off towards the Brandenburg Gate, leaving Russell to walk back across the park. He hadn't yet hidden their copy of the film because he couldn't decide where to hide it. There was no place of concealment in their small flat which would escape a thorough search, and leaving it in a station left-luggage locker would simply transfer the problem. In the old days he would have sent the ticket to himself at a *poste restante*, but with Berlin's immediate future so uncertain—and the Soviets already wreaking havoc with the postal services—that course also seemed much too risky.

Burial was the obvious alternative, but where could he bury the damn thing? There was only an overlooked courtyard at Carmer

Strasse, and, as Russell had said to Effi the previous evening, he could hardly return to the scene of his earlier excavations in Thomas's garden. Which only left the Grunewald. That evening, he thought. A long walk through the trees.

Carrying a spade was clearly not on, so he spent most of the afternoon trawling the local shops in vain for a digging implement he could carry under his jacket. In the end he settled for one of their serving spoons, on the dubious grounds that it was better than nothing.

After dinner with Effi and Rosa, he caught a 76 tram on Ku'damm, rode it to the end of the line, and then walked down Königs Allee to the old Hundekehle restaurant, where he and Paul had often shared a Saturday ice cream. Beyond it, the forest stretched several miles to the west, and several more to the north and the south. A haystack for his needle.

There were an annoying number of people on the paths, out enjoying the evening sunshine. And as he discovered a few minutes later, there was a surprisingly large band of optimists casting their flies out into the Grunewald See. He turned off into the trees on his right, and soon found the clearing where they'd often picnicked more than ten years before. While the children had played their games, he, Ilsa, Thomas and Hanna had sat and drunk wine and ridiculed the Nazis. Who had had the last laugh? he wondered.

There was no one there now, only dappled grass and branches swaying in the breeze. Russell walked around the edge of the clearing, looking for a suitable place. It couldn't be too obvious, but he had to be able to find it again.

One tree with spreading overground roots seemed to be a good bet, and for several minutes he sat with his back to the trunk, listening and watching for the sounds of humans nearby. On such a lovely summer evening it was hard to believe that the city beyond the forest was under virtual siege.

When he was certain as he could be that no loving couple was likely to rise out of the nearby long grass, he went to work with his spoon, carefully scooping the earth out from between two roots. The soil was looser than he expected, and it didn't take him long to excavate a foot-deep well for the tin. After laying it flat on the bottom, he re-filled the hole, and did what he could to disguise the fact that one had been dug. The sun had sunk behind the trees, and it was hard to see his handiwork, but he was fairly confident that no one would find the tin by accident.

For all that, he felt reluctant to leave. He couldn't shake the thought that he might have been watched, that someone had seen him bury something, and was only waiting out there in the dark for the chance to dig it up. He knew it was crazy, but there it was. And as he sat there, Russell remembered Mordechai Kohn, the death camp escapee he had interviewed a year or so after the war. Mordechai's survival tip was to imagine how things might pan out, like a novelist unfolding a plot in his mind, and then take what steps seemed appropriate to help himself and hinder his enemy. 'A simple example,' he told Russell, 'you imagine people coming to arrest you. What will you do when they knock on your door? Well, the first thing you do is head for a back window. And if it's already open, that will save you precious seconds. So you go and open the window now, *before* they knock on your door.'

Sitting against the tree in the rapidly-darkening forest, Russell tried to follow the young Jew's advice. He imagined what might happen, and what he could do about it. One thing came to mind.

It became apparent next morning that their days of waiting were also likely to decide the fate of the city. The morning papers bore out Shchepkin's predictions of the previous day, and later that morning an RIAS news reporter announced that General Clay had rejected '*in toto* Soviet claims to the city of Berlin.' This was followed up midafternoon by the much-anticipated news that the Western currency reform would be extended to include Berlin. Details would be broadcast at eight that evening.

Like most of the city's inhabitants, Russell, Effi, and Rosa tuned in to hear them. From midnight on Friday, the old Reichsmarks could be exchanged for new Deutschmarks, on a one-to-one basis for the first sixty, and at a rapidly declining rate thereafter.

'The shops will be packed for the next two days,' Effi said.

'Those that are open.'

The three of them went down to Ku'damm to see what was happening, and found the pavements jammed with people trying to spend their Reichsmarks on goods or extravagant dining. But most of the shops had shut early, and several restaurants had already altered their menus, offering only food that would spoil, and hoarding the rest until the change had been made.

'Have we got any bills to pay?' Russell asked Effi on the way home. 'Because now's the time to pay them.'

Next morning they woke to a steady drizzle, and the news that the Soviets had closed the road and railways between the Western Zones and Berlin. Some people, though, were already fighting back. KPD demonstrators had been thwarted the previous evening when they'd tried to break up a City Assembly meeting, and the latter had then decided by a large majority to allow competition between the new Western currency and its Soviet counterpart.

Another hour, and RIAS was reporting sporadic power failures in all three Western sectors of the city. Asked to explain these interruptions in the electricity supply, a Soviet spokesmen claimed serious 'technical difficulties' were affecting one of the generating stations in their sector.

Soon after that, Thomas phoned. There was going to be a mass meeting at the Hertha stadium that afternoon—Russell was welcome to a lift if he wanted to come. He did. An hour or so later, when Thomas arrived at the door, the American garrison commander Frank Howley was spitting defiance on the wireless. After promising Berliners that the American people wouldn't let them starve, he warned the Soviets not to trespass in his sector. 'We are ready for you—and if the day comes, believe me, many a comrade will go across the golden Volga.'

'The Chinese curse,' Thomas said, as they both walked down to the car, 'to live in interesting times.'

To Russell's surprise, the Plumpe stadium was packed to capacity, something it had never quite managed in all his and Paul's years of watching Hertha. It had been a day of ominous portents, but the mood among the crowd was unmistakably upbeat. Hardship might be in prospect, but so was real change, and after the past five years that was a deal that most Berliners were more than willing to make. As Ernst Reuter, the main speaker, explained: It was about systems, not money—while the latter could conceivably be integrated, the former could not. The choice was between a Soviet Berlin and a divided Berlin—there was no third option.

Russell knew he was right, but still felt saddened at the thought of his home being sundered in two.

For Thomas, though, the glass was half-full. 'Bastards have been running our Berlin for fifteen years. Better to get half of it back than none.'

Gerhard Ströhm couldn't remember a morning when he'd felt less inclined to go to work. He had arrived home the previous evening to a long tirade from Annaliese about conditions at the hospital; the electricity supply cuts, which everyone was quite rightly blaming on the Soviets, had necessitated a reduction in surgery hours. What sort of people, she raged, used the sick as a weapon to blackmail their enemies?

Ströhm had had no answer for her then, and walking to work had none for himself. He still found it hard to believe that the Soviets intended starving the city into submission, still hoped that it was all a big bluff in extremely bad taste. As if to remind him of what was at stake, yet another American C-47 roared in across the rooftops a few streets behind him on its approach to Tempelhof. If it was a bluff, it looked as if the Allies were preparing to call it.

He didn't think the morning could get any worse, but he was wrong. A note calling him upstairs was waiting on his desk, and Ströhm knew he was in trouble when Marohn mentioned 'the business' at Rummelsburg. 'You did well there,' his boss told him. 'So now that a similar problem has arisen again, well, the people upstairs are hoping you can repeat the trick.'

Ströhm didn't like the suggestion that he'd 'tricked' the workers at the railway repair shops—and, by implication, had 'tricked' Utermann into taking his own life—but he let it go. Worse seemed likely to follow, and Marohn was only the messenger, and so Ströhm simply nodded his acquiescence, and waited for the explanation.

The 'similar problem' had arisen in Aue, a small town in Saxony. Railways workers there were refusing to load ore from Wismut's uranium mines, and the Soviet authorities were hoping that their German comrades could straighten the situation out. If not, they would have to take 'administrative measures.'

'Why are the workers refusing?' Ströhm asked.

'You'll have to ask Manfred Pieck—he's the local union leader.'

'No relation to Wilhelm, I assume.' Wilhelm Pieck was second only to Ulbricht in the KPD hierarchy.

'No, but he is a Party veteran. Joined in 1926. He ran the underground in Chemnitz during the war.'

Another Utermann, Ströhm thought, his heart sinking at the prospect.

'I've arranged a car for you,' Marohn was saying, as if that might make the job palatable. 'With a chauffeur, of course.'

'I can drive myself,' Ströhm retorted. 'But why don't I just take a train? If I arrive like visiting royalty no one'll listen to me.'

'The Soviets will, and that's the point. They'll only treat you as an equal if you look like one.'

Ströhm knew when he was beaten. 'All right. But I will drive myself.'

Which was easier said than done, of course. He had learned to drive at university almost twenty years earlier, but had hardly been behind a steering wheel since. People said you never forgot, but his first few miles in the shiny Horch 851 were a painful lesson in remembering. The watching faces on the pavement, he noticed, seemed universally contemptuous, though whether of his driving or his privileged status he couldn't be sure.

According to Marohn, the autobahn would 'whisk' him all the way to Chemnitz, but his boss obviously hadn't been down it recently. There were pot holes everywhere, and huge cracks in the concrete hosting columns of swaying weeds. On the bright side, it was virtually empty, and after a while Ströhm began to enjoy himself, slaloming south across the crumbling surface. He loved trains, and the chance they gave you to sit by the window and watch the world go by; but there was something just as liberating about sitting alone in a car, controlling your own direction and speed. An illusion of independence perhaps, but an intoxicating one nonetheless.

Soon after six P.M. Ströhm reached Chemnitz, where Marohn had suggested he spend the night. He found the local Party office easily enough, and was given a room reserved for official guests in the nearby hotel. The owner was too sycophantic for words, but both dinner and room were more than adequate. After eating he went upstairs, and read until his eyelids began to droop. As he drifted into sleep, he wondered what the next day would bring, what challenge to his conscience awaited him in Aue.

Russell woke with a start on Saturday morning, not knowing where he was. He'd been walking down a snow-covered street, with shadows lurking in every doorway, but here was Effi making gentle snuffling noises in her sleep.

Shchepkin should be in Moscow, he thought. He would probably be seeing Beria that day. Russell didn't need to imagine the rage on the Georgian's face when he heard what Shchepkin had to tell him—he'd seen it in the film.

From now until Tuesday, these were the dangerous days. Shchepkin would tell Beria that if he wasn't back in Berlin by then, Russell would make his copy available to the Americans. And as Shchepkin had said, the sensible thing for Beria to do was accept the deal on offer, and for him to get used to the idea that at least one other recording of him committing murder was hidden out of reach. But would Beria be able to do this? Or would he hold on to Shchepkin, and gamble on scooping Russell up by Tuesday? In that case Beria would assume that once everyone was safely ensconced in the Lyubyanka, eliciting the location of the films would not present too great a problem. And in this he was certainly right.

Russell slipped out of bed, walked across to the window, and lifted the edge of the curtain. Since he wasn't expecting to see anything, the car standing by the opposite kerb a little way down the street came as something of a shock. Especially as there didn't appear to be anyone in it.

Were they already in the house, coming up the stairs?

He walked quickly through to the other room, checked that the bolts were drawn on the apartment door, and put his ear to the wood. If there was anyone out there, they were very quiet.

He went back to take another look at the car, only to find it was gone. A false alarm, he thought, but as someone wise once said, a false alarm was only a real one waiting to happen.

He woke Effi. 'You know we talked about going away for the weekend? Well, I think we should.'

'Why, what's happened?'

'Nothing yet. But it's the safe thing to do.'

'Okay, but where?'

'You remember that hotel on Havelsee we stayed at, back when we were young?'

'The one we never left. The bed we never left.'

'That one.'

'I can't imagine it's still there.'

'The bed or the hotel?'

'The hotel.'

'It is. I called them yesterday, and they said they had some rooms. As long as we paid in dollars.'

'Okay, so when do we leave?'

'The sooner the better.'

Effi went in to wake Rosa, and found her getting dressed. 'Sweetheart, we're all going away for the weekend.'

Rosa's face lit up. 'Where to?'

'The Havelsee. There's a hotel we know. So pack up your drawing stuff and a book to read.'

She went back to Russell. 'We have to tell Zarah. And Thomas.'

'Tell them what?'

'I don't know. Something. If Beria's people do come looking for us, the first places they'll try when they draw a blank here are Zarah's and Thomas's. We have to give them some kind of warning.'

'You're right,' Russell agreed reluctantly. 'But don't scare the life out of Zarah, or we'll never get away.'

'So what do I tell her? It's okay to worry, but not too much?'

Russell grinned. 'Just tell her that there's probably nothing to worry about, but to keep her eyes open, just in case. And tell her not to let any strangers into the flat.'

They made the calls. Zarah, as predicted, was upset, and angry at Effi for making her so. Thomas was his usual stoic self: 'If I understand you right, you're not going to tell me where you're going, and you don't want me to tell anyone else.'

Fifteen minutes later they were carrying their bags down the stairs. If they'd forgotten something crucial, at least it wasn't the gun that Russell had bought in Wedding the previous day, as that was in his pocket.

The street outside was blissfully empty, the walk to the station free of alarms, false or otherwise. But Rosa knew there was something up. 'This feels like an adventure,' she said as they climbed the stairs to the platform.

Aue was an hour's drive southwest from Chemnitz, but Ströhm had only been going ten minutes when the first checkpoint appeared. There were no signs to say so, but he was clearly passing into territory the Soviets considered their own. After his credentials had been examined with almost painful thoroughness, he was given explicit instructions on where to report in Aue, and strongly warned against leaving his present road for any reason at all. As he drove on through the pleasant Saxon hills, the Erzegebirge looming on the southern horizon, Ströhm wondered what terrible secrets might lurk down the various turnings.

Aue sat in the mouth of a valley, a much smaller town than Chemnitz, but with more sense of bustle. At the Soviet Military Administration office on the town's main street, the MGB officer that Marohn had mentioned—a Major Abakumov—was waiting for him. The Russian greeted him politely enough, but he was clearly impatient.

'So what exactly is the problem?' Ströhm asked.

'You do not know?!'

'Not the details, no,' Ströhm said calmly.

'The problem is that your railwaymen have been making difficulties. And they are now threatening a strike!'

'Why?'

'They say that working with uranium is too dangerous, that some men have developed serious illnesses because of their proximity to the ore.'

'Are they right?'

Abakumov shrugged. 'Such work is not pleasant, of course it isn't. But needs must. The Soviet Union needs this uranium, for reasons that I'm sure you know. And we won't tolerate this sabotage.'

'What would you like me to do?'

'Put a stop to it. How you do it is your concern, but feel free to tell the comrades that if they won't listen to you, they'll have to listen to me. If we have to arrest every last one of them, and draft in replacements, then we will.'

They were, Ströhm realised, determined to get the uranium.

'The chief troublemaker is a man named Pieck,' Abakumov was saying. 'Do you know him?'

'Only by reputation. He was a resistance leader in this area.'

Abakumov wasn't impressed. 'That war is over. It's time he realised that another struggle—one every bit as crucial—is now underway. We have one hundred-thousand workers in this area, all busy taking uranium from the ground, and we won't have their efforts brought to nothing by a few cowardly railwaymen.'

Ströhm ignored the insult. 'If you tell me where to find Pieck, I'll go and talk to him now.'

'Down by the station. The union offices are in the yard.'

Ströhm considered leaving his car outside the Russian HQ—if it didn't impress them, it would certainly alienate Pieck—but what was the point in pretending? He was the Man from Berlin, come to scold them back into line.

Manfred Pieck was alone in his office. He was a man of around Ströhm's own age, with a shock of dark brown hair and watchful grey eyes behind small spectacles. He listened patiently to Ströhm's explanation of his presence, merely sighing with obvious frustration at a couple of points. 'I saw you drive up,' he said eventually. 'If you'll take us both out, I can show you what's going on.'

'All right.'

Once they were in the car, Pieck ran a hand along the leather dashboard. 'Very nice,' he said.

'My boss in Berlin thought it might impress the Russians.'

'You should have come in a tank.'

Pieck directed him through the town, and on to a small road which wound up a wooded hillside. After about ten minutes they suddenly emerged above another valley, and Pieck asked him to stop. At the bottom of the slope a small town straddled a fast-running stream, and in the fields further down hundreds of tents had been pitched on either side of a single railway line. 'There's a mine a little way up the valley,' Pieck told him. 'You can't see it from here, but that's where the miners live,' he added, pointing at the tents. 'Men and women.'

'Are they locals?'

'Not many of them. There were some volunteers to begin with, but that supply soon dried up. Most are prisoners of one sort or another—POWs brought back from Russia, youths from all over the Zone whom the Russians claim were Nazi werewolves. I tell you, with all the ones they've captured, it's a miracle the Nazis lost.'

'Did any of these people have any mining experience?'

'Hardly a one. With predictable results. This year, in the Aue district, we've had more than two thousand deaths.'

'Two thousand!'

'I think that's why they call Aue the "Gate of Tears,"' Pieck said drily. 'But accidents are only part of it. The working conditions are appalling—there's not enough food, no sanitation, and that's before you get to the problem of radiation. These people spend half their days either knee-deep in radioactive sludge or breathing in the dust. Do you know what radiation does to the body?'

'I'm not a scientist.'

'Neither am I, but I've talked to people at Chemnitz University. And I've seen the results with my own eyes—the skin lesions, the infections, all sorts of symptoms which can't be explained any other way. The doctors around here are out of their depth, and they know it. The local hospitals are all full up, but the Soviets won't let them move any patients on to other districts.'

Ströhm thought for a moment. 'All of which is terrible,' he said eventually. 'But none of these people are your responsibility.'

Pieck gave him a look. 'Strictly speaking, that's true. So let's drive on down, and I'll show you what my men are doing.'

Just above the town the railway line ended in a pair of sidings. Between these, there was a narrow gauge line which came down from the mine. One trainload had just arrived, and a large crowd of railwaymen were shovelling ore from one group of wagons to the other in a dense cloud of yellowish dust. They all had cloth masks tied across their faces, but they might just as well have hung charms around their necks.

'They're working,' Ströhm said stupidly.

'For the moment. There were a few walk-outs at different sites last week, but we got everyone back, and then called meetings. The vote for a strike was almost unanimous.'

'When?'

'Monday.'

'And what do you expect the Russians to do?'

'Arrest the leaders. At the very least. Beyond that . . .' Pieck shrugged. 'You get to a point where that doesn't matter.'

Ströhm knew the script, knew what he was supposed to say. But if he hadn't yet reached Pieck's point, he knew it wasn't that far away. Those were workers filling their lungs with poison, at the strident behest of the one and only workers' state, his and Pieck's guiding star for all their adult lives. Workers that they were supposed to represent. Pieck was doing exactly that, and so who the hell was he speaking for?

'I understand,' was all Ströhm said. 'I've been sent to tell you that the bigger picture's all that matters, that the Russians will get their uranium one way or another, that all in all you might as well save your strength for battles you can win. Okay? If you'd like a well-honed excuse to change your mind and take the easy way out, there's no shortage. There never is. And as a gesture of the people's appreciation the leadership will probably give you a fucking car.'

Pieck looked at him, a smile creasing his mouth. 'They gave it to you?'

'God no, this is just a loan. But if you call off the strike . . .'

'Not a chance.'

'I'm glad to hear it. I never liked cars.'

They parted almost friends, but Ströhm's sense of well-being was fleeting. After dropping in on Abakumov, and ingenuously reporting that he'd done all he could, he continued on towards Chemnitz. It was early evening by the time he arrived, but the thought of driving home to Annaliese seemed infinitely preferable to hours spent shuffling doubts in a hotel room.

It wasn't much better alone with his thoughts on the empty autobahn. Somewhere between Dresden and Lübben Ströhm became aware of tears streaming down his cheeks, and pulled the car on to the hard shoulder. The last time he'd cried like this he'd been twelve years old, and both his parents had just died in a Californian road accident. And that was the clue, he realised. That was the last time he'd felt such a crushing sense of loss.

Out at Wannsee the weather was poor, and Russell, Effi and Rosa spent most of Saturday cooped up in the hotel. Between venturing out for meals and one shower-drenched walk along the lakeshore, they read and listened to the wireless. The post-Goebbels range of music was something to be welcomed, although the lack of news reports was surprising; someone had apparently decided that Berliners already had a surfeit, and so had sent all the journalists home for the weekend. Effi utilised an hour of big band music to teach Rosa some basic dance steps, and with Hollywood in mind Russell gave the two of them a lesson in American English. 'You're *so* cute,' they told each other, before collapsing in a fit of giggles.

The sun came out on Sunday morning, and they took to the water in a rented boat. Every few minutes an American plane would roar above their heads as it headed into Tempelhof, while a few miles to the north British planes were flying in and out of their airbase at Gatow. When Rosa asked why, Russell did his best to explain the situation, and saw its essential craziness reflected in her expression. He sometimes thought they should be more open with her about their own problems, but how did you tell an eleven-year-old that Daddy's Russian friend might at that very moment be enduring torture at the hands of his Moscow employers?

That evening they were eating outside when another sharp and violent shower erupted, beating a thunderous tattoo on the roof of the covered terrace and drawing a pulsating curtain of rain across the world beyond. Sitting there, Effi felt like she was taking part in a scene from a film, and that if only the director would shout 'cut,' someone would then switch the rain machine off.

Sacrificial wolf

Monday morning Ströhm took Annaliese to work in the car. They had used it twice the previous day, once to visit her former boyfriend's parents out in Spandau, and once for a ride around the city. Ströhm had felt a little uneasy, but they had paid for the petrol, and—as Annaliese said—what use was a parked car? As the better driver, she had done most of the driving, and this had given him ample opportunity to notice the facial reactions of the people they passed. Some had looked envious, some resentful, a few had simply smiled. It *was* a beautiful vehicle, after all.

Ströhm was behind the wheel that morning. 'I could get used to this,' she said, as they passed a crowded tram stop.

'I'm sure we'll have one eventually,' he told her. 'I expect every family will.'

She made a face. 'I forgot to tell you—last week at the hospital one of the ambulance drivers told me about this, er, this painting, it's on a wall in Link Strasse—you know where that is?'

'It's one of the streets off Potsdamerplatz.'

'Yes. It's in the American zone, but only a few hundred metres from the Russian, which I guess is why they chose it.'

'Who? What is it?'

'You must have played Monopoly?'

'Of course.'

'Well, someone has painted the board on the wall of a

bombed-out house. It's big. It must have taken him all night. Or her, I suppose.'

'What for?'

'Ah, there's a twist. But I won't spoil the surprise. You should drive past it on your way to work. Today, before the Russians get permission from the Americans to wipe it away.'

After dropping her at the hospital entrance, Ströhm did as she suggested. The giant monopoly board was too large to miss and exquisitely detailed, but for a moment he couldn't see the point. And then he did—the three most expensive properties had new names. Unter den Linden had become Wall Strasse, where the KPD Central Committee had its headquarters, and Grunewald had turned into Bernicke, where the same institution had its luxurious rest home. Insel Schwanenwerder, the most expensive square of all, now bore the name Seehof, where the Party had just opened an even more exclusive resort for the use of Senior Members of the Central Secretariat.

Ströhm stared up at the wall, awed by the sheer amount of effort that he, she or they had put into making this oh-so-simple statement, knowing only too well that its life would be measured, at best, in days. He was indeed surprised to find it still there—if the higherups knew about it, a squad of cadres would have been sent to expunge it over the weekend, American permission or not. But surely some Party members must have seen it. A delicious possibility crossed Ströhm's mind, that those comrades who had seen the painting had failed to report its existence. And that could only be because they felt the same way he did, that he wasn't alone, with his doubts and sense of loss.

If Ströhm had had a camera, he'd have taken a picture, and sent it to the *Neue Zeitung*. Maybe someone already had.

He was still smiling when he reached his office, and found that

Marohn had asked for him. He went upstairs expecting criticism of his conduct in Aue, but his boss had other things on his mind. Did Ströhm know that General Sokolovsky, the head of the Soviet Military Administration, had written a letter to his Allied counterparts more or less claiming Soviet control over the whole of the city?

Ströhm said he hadn't. 'Has there been a reply?'

'Not yet,' Marohn conceded, 'but maybe the Western allies really will leave. Then we can get back to running a railway.' He was clearly in a good mood—'at least you tried' was all he said about the trip to Aue. The only time Ströhm felt disapproval was when he said he'd brought back the Horch.

'No, you must keep it,' Marohn told him.

'But I don't need a car,' Ströhm protested.

'It's not a matter of need; it's a token of respect for the position you hold. All cadres above a certain level are to be allocated personal vehicles, and refusing to accept one will be interpreted as dissent. Understood?'

Ströhm nodded.

On his way home he picked up a paper, but there was no news from Aue. The Soviets would keep this one quiet, he thought.

Annaliese knew him well enough not to be over-delighted with the car, simply noting that after the baby was born, they could take him or her out to the country. Ströhm just grunted—on the way home from work he'd been wondering how to get rid of it, but all he'd come up with was hiding the damn thing away in a garage and throwing out the key.

As he got off the train at Zoo Station, Russell wondered whether he should make an effort to disguise himself. Some workingman's clothes perhaps, or a pair of spectacles. But he hadn't, and it was too late now. He pulled his hat down another centimetre and walked on towards Carmer Strasse.

Reaching the end five minutes later, he saw a couple of pedestrians and several parked cars, but neither of the former were loitering and all of the latter looked familiar. As he neared their building one of the neighbours emerged, saw him, and raised a hand in greeting before walking off in the other direction. If Beria's men were lurking in the stairwell, they were well-concealed.

The stairwell was empty. He listened outside their door for a few moments, then rapped on it. No one answered, which seemed a good sign until he put himself in their position. Why would they?

He had tried to leave the new gun with Effi, but she had insisted he take it. 'If they're after us,' she had said, 'then they'll be waiting for you.'

Well, were they? Russell took out the gun, turned the key, and pushed the door all the way open. There were no Russians on the sofa, and none in the bath. Everything looked exactly as they'd left it.

It was half-past two P.M.; he had half an hour to wait. He spent it by the window, eyes on the street and ears cocked for feet on the stairs. After an hour he reluctantly accepted that Shchepkin wasn't going to ring, then belatedly checked that the phone was working. It was.

He locked the flat back up, and showed the same caution departing that he had on arrival. At a bank on Hardenberg Strasse he joined the queue for changing currency and eventually took possession of sixty new Deutschmarks. After walking back to Zoo Station, he spent the half-hour waiting in the buffet for the Wannsee train, and reading the local British newspaper. All the good news was on the front page—two days earlier, Foreign Secretary Bevin had told the world the British wouldn't leave Berlin 'under any circumstances.' The Americans had not yet given any such assurance, but that didn't worry Russell. The steady stream of C-47s skimming the Wilmersdorf skyline seemed a lot more compelling than any words.

Ströhm had been anticipating the radio programme for most of the day. The Hungarian Arthur Koestler had been a member of the Party in the 1930s, and Ströhm had a vague memory of seeing him at a KPD meeting in the pre-Hitler years. He had worked for the Comintern in France, and as a journalist in Spain, before disillusionment caught up with him, and caused him to write the novel which RIAS had dramatized for that evening's broadcast, *Darkness at Noon*.

Ströhm had heard a lot about the book, but was still unprepared for the impact it had on him. He already knew it concerned a fictional Bolshevik named Rubashov, whom Stalin had turned on and imprisoned. The man's philosophising proved fairly predictable—it was more his memories that undid Ströhm. Little Loewy, the Party secretary who hanged himself, was Rubashov's Stefan Utermann. In *Darkness at Noon*, the Bolshevik Rubashov journeyed from Moscow to Antwerp, and ordered Loewy to sacrifice comrades and conscience for the greater good of the Soviet Union. He had travelled the much shorter distance from Hallesches Ufer to Rummelsburg, and done exactly the same.

Ströhm thought of Harald Gebauer up in Wedding, as he often did at such moments. That usually reassured him, but not this time. Harald's criticism of the Party was implicit, because it came from the heart, and he would probably pass unnoticed for longer than those more cerebrally-gifted comrades whose critiques were spoken or written. But eventually someone would notice, and be all the angrier when they realised how long it had taken. And then someone else would discover that Ströhm had known the man for years, and might be prevailed on to show him the error of his ways. The error of believing in mankind.

The play was still underway, but Ströhm was caught by this glimpse into his future: Gerhard Ströhm, closer of doors, firer of metaphorical bullets. Confiscator of dreams.

Once Rosa had fallen asleep, Russell and Effi discussed how long they could afford to wait for Shchepkin. They had agreed to give him until Tuesday, but how much longer than that? There was no easy answer. The moment they made the film public, their bargaining power would be finished, but so, they hoped, would be Beria's career. At that point the MGB chief would have nothing to lose, but, unless Josef Stalin was completely impervious to world opinion, he and his country did. But would Uncle Joe act quickly enough, and kill Beria before a vengeful Beria succeeded in killing them? Even if Stalin did move promptly, the chances were still good that Russell's role in the atomic business—not to mention his concealing of the film from his CIC bosses—would reach the light of day. Broadcasting proof of Beria's infamy might bring justice for Sonja, her sister, and all the other women the man had probably raped or killed, and it might even lead to a diminishing of Soviet cruelty at home and abroad, but it wouldn't do much for Russell and Effi.

Waiting, though, would get riskier by the day. If Shchepkin was in the Lyubyanka, then literally hundreds of MGB agents would be scouring Berlin for them and their copy of the film.

'A few more days,' Effi suggested. 'Until Thursday. We can take it to the Americans on Friday morning.'

'I'm not so sure,' Russell argued. 'I wish we'd made more copies. I'd feel a lot happier if we had a dozen to distribute. Then we'd know it couldn't be suppressed.'

'Why would the Americans suppress it?'

'Think about it. If we can blackmail Beria with it, then so can they.'

Annaliese was on nights that week, and Ströhm was alone when the phone rang late that evening. It was Uli Trenkel from the office, and he sounded more than a little drunk.

'Have you heard?' he asked excitedly.

'Heard what?'

'The Yugoslavs. They've been kicked out of the Cominform.'

'What?!'

'I've seen tomorrow's *Telegraf*. The headline reads "Tito breaks with Stalin; Tito accused of Trotskyism."'

'But that . . .' Ströhm was lost for words.

'Absurd. Isn't it? But there's nothing we can do.' Trenkel prattled on, until Ströhm abruptly ended the call for both their sakes. He poured himself a glass of *payok* whisky and went to stand by the open window. It was a chilly night, the sky full of stars.

So that was it, he thought. He had always imagined their first years in power as years of trial and error, the way they had been in Russia. An experimental journey, in which they all learnt from their mistakes. But now he knew different. There would be none of that in Germany, or anywhere else in eastern Europe. Wherever the Soviets were in control, their journey was being re-run. And if they hadn't learnt from their mistakes, then those condemned to repeat them wouldn't be allowed to either.

'To the comrades in Belgrade,' Ströhm murmured, raising his glass to the star-filled sky.

It was raining again on Tuesday morning. Russell had anticipated another solo trip into town, but Effi and Rosa, having exhausted the possibilities of all those things they'd brought to entertain themselves, refused to live in exile any longer. 'We'll go to Zarah's,' Effi told him. 'And if Shchepkin rings with good news then we can just walk home.'

'And if he doesn't?'

'I don't know. Let's worry about that when it happens.'

Russell wasn't convinced, but there was no changing her mind. After they got off the train he accompanied them to the end of Zarah's street, and then approached Carmer Strasse with the same caution, and the same result, as before.

Only this time the telephone rang, and it was Shchepkin who spoke when Russell picked up. 'Remember your daughter's namesake?' he asked. 'Where we remembered her? Five o'clock.'

The line clicked off.

No mention of success, but maybe Russell was supposed to infer that from the Russian's survival. The only other explanation he could think of was that Shchepkin had shrunk from confronting Beria, and that they were all back to square one.

He would know soon enough.

A café on Ku'damm offered refuge for an hour or so, and then Russell started working his way westwards through the streets north of the elevated Stadtbahn. Shchepkin hadn't stressed the importance of not being followed, but he hadn't needed to, as finding the two of them together in one place would now be the stuff of Beria's dreams. Russell was already convinced that no one was shadowing him, but he used the Elisabeth Hospital to make sure, using the main entrance and then leaving by a back service door which Annaliese had shown him and Effi the previous year. The street outside ended by the Landwehrkanal.

Reaching it, he sat down on a convenient bench. The waterway was devoid of traffic, a victim no doubt of the Soviet blockade, and

despite the early evening sun, walkers were almost as sparse. The
towpaths on either side of the canal had always been a favourite spot
for exercising Berlin's dogs, but the latter's population had hardly
begun to recover from the ravages of the war.

The city's cats had fared slightly better, and one mangy specimen
emerged from a nearby bombsite and rubbed itself against his legs,
meowing piteously.

The spot where Rosa Luxemburg's corpse had been fished from
the water was a few hundred metres to his right, close to the bridge
that carried Potsdamer Strasse over the canal. It was at least two years
since he and Shchepkin had last met there, and Russell idly wondered how differently the Russian Revolution might have developed
had she survived the Spartacus Rising. No other figure in European
Marxism had possessed the moral and intellectual stature that might
have given Lenin pause.

It was a minute to five. He rose from the seat and walked on, the
cat following for a few metres, before abruptly giving up on him,
and scampering off across the cobbles.

Shchepkin was waiting on a bench near the bridge, his white hair
hidden under his hat. It occurred to Russell that they were only a
stone's throw from the Soviet sector. 'Well?' he asked, sitting down.

'He accepted our terms,' Shchepkin said calmly, with only a hint
of a smile.

As Russell let his breath out, he realised how much he'd expected
the worst.

'Irina and Tasha are in a hotel on König Strasse,' the Russian went
on. 'Tomorrow morning the three of us will hand ourselves over to
the Americans. I shall tell them that the Soviets finally realised that
you and I were working against them, offer myself as a defector, and
demand asylum for my wife and daughter as the price of telling
them all that I know. You will tell the Americans that since the

Soviets have finally rumbled us, your usefulness has to be over, and you're submitting your resignation. And once you've convinced them that you won't reveal any of their secrets, they'll have to let you go.'

'It sounds good,' Russell said. In fact the sense of relief was so overpowering that he began to doubt it. Had Beria really caved in so completely? Were they safe again? Was he finally off the hook?

Searching for a flaw, he found one. And with sinking heart wondered how they—and particularly Shchepkin—could have missed it. 'Look, as things stand he kills one of us and the other releases the film. But if he captures us both at the same moment, then neither of us will know what's happened until it's too late. Okay, we have him for now, but in the long run, surely it won't be beyond him to coordinate two kidnappings. No matter where we go, we'll be looking over our shoulders.'

Shchepkin smiled briefly. 'There's one thing you don't know,' he said. 'There is no long run for me. I shall be dead in a few weeks.'

'What?'

'The doctors tell me my heart is giving out. Broken, perhaps,' Shchepkin added with a wry smile.

Russell felt a mixture of emotions, of which sadness was the strongest.

'But I've put the film beyond their reach, and I shall be in American custody. I will tell them Beria wants me dead—not why, of course—and they will protect me as long as I keep telling them things. And believe me, I will talk and talk.'

His pauses for breath, Russell realised, were not for dramatic purposes.

'Beria will have no reason to threaten you, because he believed me when I told him that you don't know where I've hidden it.'

'I hope so.'

'One more thing. The moment I'm safe with the Americans, you must destroy your copy of the film. It kept me alive in Moscow, but after tomorrow it will serve no purpose. On the contrary, if Beria's enemies ever learned of its existence . . .'

'His enemies?'

'The Americans, the GRU, he even has enemies in the Politburo. If any of them found out about the film, and forced you to reveal its location; or if someone stumbled across it by accident in its hiding place, then Beria would consider we had broken our side of the bargain, and God only knows what he'd do. So better to get rid of it. My copy is enough to keep you safe.'

'I'll see that it's destroyed. But your wife and daughter—do they know you're dying?'

'I think Irina guesses, but she hasn't said anything.'

'How will they survive in the West without you?'

'I don't know. They will have no money, but at least they'll be safe. Natasha is a bright girl.'

'I know, I've met her.'

'So you have. Of course, if you can help them in any way I would appreciate it.'

'I'll do my best.'

'I don't think they'll miss me,' Shchepkin said, surprising Russell. Personal emotions didn't usually come up in their conversations. 'These past few days I've realised—we're strangers to each other. I feel like I'm standing outside their house and watching them through the window. I love them, of course, but more in memory than anything else. And love should be more than an echo.' He glanced at Russell. 'But now I'm getting morbid, and you and I have work to do. For three years now we've been feeding the Americans a diet of truths, half-truths, and outright lies, and now they'll expect to be told which is which. Unless we intend to be completely honest with them—which I, for one, do not—there are some comrades, for example, whom I won't betray—then we need to agree on our version of events.'

'That could take a week,' Russell observed.

'I told Irina I'd be back in three hours.'

For the next two, as the sun slowly sank towards the distant rooftops, and the American planes droned across the sky beyond the canal, they trawled their joint career, discussing those American and Soviet agents they had betrayed and those they had not, agreeing which names they would offer up and which they wouldn't, going over which nuggets of information they could happily divulge and which would be safer to keep to themselves. As a rough guiding principle, they agreed to protect those on either side who actually believed in their cause, and give up those who were only interested in advancing their careers.

Russell's brain was spinning by the time they finished. 'I'll never remember it all,' he said.

'Neither will they,' Shchepkin said reassuringly. 'I had an old teacher, back in the twenties,' he went on, almost dreamily. 'He was about sixty, and he'd faced interrogations in a dozen countries. When we found ourselves in that situation, he told us, we should make our inquisitors feel like they were looking in an honest mirror, seeing both the good and the bad in themselves. And once we'd managed that, we should try and offer them some sort of absolution. He said we'd be surprised how grateful they would be, and how much getting them to question themselves reduced their ability to question others.'

'You don't have a manuscript stashed away somewhere, do you? *"Tips for Political Prisoners: A Bolshevik Handbook."'*

Shchepkin's eyes twinkled. 'Unfortunately not.'

A tram was crossing the bridge to their left as they both stood up.

'I doubt we'll meet again,' the Russian said, offering his hand.

Russell took it. 'I won't forget your wife and daughter,' was all he could find to say. Or you, he thought, as Shchepkin walked slowly off in the direction of the Soviet sector.

When Russell got to Zarah's, she and her American fiancé were having a loud argument in the kitchen.

'It's nothing serious,' Effi told him. 'And quite wonderful in a way—I don't think she ever shouted at Jens.'

Russell put his hands on her shoulders. 'Speaking of wonderful, it seems we're in the clear.'

Her eyes lit up. 'Really?'

'According to Shchepkin.' He sighed. 'Who's dying, by the way.'

'What's wrong with him?'

'He wasn't specific. Some sort of heart disease apparently.'

'I'm sorry.'

'Yes, me too. But he's got his wife and daughter out, and he thinks we're all safe.'

'And you think so too?'

'Well, he's never been wrong about anything before.' Apart from the system he'd devoted his life to, Russell thought, but didn't say.

'So we can go home?'

He considered suggesting they stay for the night, but the argument in the kitchen showed no sign of abating. 'I don't see why not,' he said.

Told they were leaving, Zarah emerged. 'Rosa's half asleep,' she said, 'why don't you leave her here, and I'll take them both to school in the morning?'

Rosa, though, was keen to go home. 'Why are they fighting?' she asked once they were outside.

'People do,' Effi told her. 'It doesn't mean they don't love each other.'

'I know that.'

They walked most of the way in silence, the two adults digesting what seemed their new-found liberation. They were turning on to Carmer Strasse when Effi wondered out loud how the Americans would react.

'Oh, I expect they'll give me a hard time for a few weeks,' Russell told her. 'But they'll let me go eventually.'

'And in the meantime, I can decide between *The Islanders* and Hollywood,' Effi said. 'Assuming we can still get out of Berlin.'

'Can't you do both?'

'Maybe. And you know, I really would like to do a movie with Císař. Not right away, but when I can think about Prague without shivering.'

There were several cars parked close to their building, but Russell recognised them all, and the stairwell was reassuringly empty. It was only after he'd closed the apartment door behind them that the two young men emerged from the bedroom. One had fair hair and a typical Slavic countenance, the other Asian eyes and slightly bowed legs. Both were gripping Tokarev pistols with business-like silencers.

One held them at gunpoint while the other patted them down, and then ordered them on to the sofa while his comrade searched Rosa and Effi's bags. A grunt of minor triumph accompanied his discovery of the newly-purchased handgun.

Russell was noticing signs of a search. Things had been moved and then put back, but not quite in the same position. They'd been looking for the film.

'Do these two speak Russian?' the obvious Russian man asked him, waving his gun in Effi and Rosa's general direction.

Russell could see no point in lying. 'No,' he said.

This seemed to please his interrogator. 'Well, where is it?' he asked.

'Where's what?'

The man smiled. 'If you waste our time you'll only make it harder on yourself and your family. We know you have it, and if you won't tell us where it is, we shall take you all to our sector and question you until you do. And once we have you over there, I can't see what reason we'd have for ever bringing you back.'

Listening, Russell knew he had no choice. His first thought when the two men appeared had been that Shchepkin had badly misread his boss, but this Russian's repeated use of 'it' suggested otherwise. If these men believed there was only one copy, then they hadn't come from Beria. GRU most likely, Soviet Military Intelligence. But how had they found out about the film? There was one obvious candidate. 'How is Merzhanov?' Russell asked.

'He's dead.'

'And the woman who was with him?'

'The same. You admit, then, that they gave you the film?'

'Yes.'

'Where is it?'

'If I tell you, what's to stop you killing us, too?'

'If you give us the film, why would we do that?'

He was almost certainly lying, but as Russell had noticed in a similar situation three years earlier, hope really did spring eternal. And sometimes with reason.

The Russian added a real stick to his dubious carrot: 'But if you don't tell us where it is, I shall hurt your wife or daughter. And if that doesn't convince you, then I shall kill one of them.'

As Russell looked at Effi and Rosa, it felt like ice was forming in his brain. 'I buried it in the forest,' he told the Russian.

'Which one?'

'The Grunewald,' he said, noting the flicker in Effi's eyes as she caught the word.

'We will go there at once. My comrade will stay with the woman and girl as a guarantee of your behaviour.'

'Can I explain that to them?'

'Tell them to do as he says.'

Russell explained the situation to Effi, trying not to scare Rosa any more than she already was. There was no point in telling Effi to take any chance that arose—she would know that already—and for all he knew one of the Russians understood German.

Effi squeezed his hand and gave him an unconvincing smile. The thought that he might never see her again seemed utterly ridiculous.

As he and the Russian walked down the stairs, Russell tried to think through the implications. The GRU wanted the tape to use against Beria, but they wouldn't want the world to know about it—only the West would gain from that. This was both good news and bad news. Good because the Americans would remain in the dark; bad because any Westerners who knew about the film would need to be silenced.

The bad news seemed to render the good news redundant.

The car, a Maybach SW42, was around the corner. 'You drive,' the Russian said.

It wasn't a car he'd driven before, but after grinding his way down to Ku'damm, he finally got the hang of the gear stick. The boulevard was busy, and when a red light held them halfway down, he thought about leaning his head out of the window, and telling the world he was being abducted. What would the Russian do—shoot him?

He probably would. And then shove the body on to the street and drive off. There would be plenty of witnesses, but none would lift a finger to help Russell, any more than they had in the '30s, when the brownshirts had picked on some hapless Jew.

And what was the point of fighting back now? Effi and Rosa should be safe until the Russians had the film in their hands. It was better to wait, and take the chance he'd planned for.

He drove on, half-blinded by the setting sun, crossing the Ringbahn by Halensee Station, and following the winding Königs Allee to the Grunewald's eastern perimeter. Private vehicles weren't permitted beyond the lightless Hundekehle Restaurant, but Russell drove on down the access road. There seemed little chance of their being challenged at this hour, and he had reasons of his own for not wanting too long a walk after he had dug up the film.

They only passed one couple, who gave them a dirty look but kept on walking. The twosome had taken them for *warmer brüder*, Russell thought, men who were out for an illegal fuck in the forest.

A minute or so later he brought the car to a halt. As far as he could tell in the fading light, they'd reached the nearest point on the road to where he'd buried the film.

They both got out.

'How far is it?' the Russian asked.

'A few minutes. No more.'

They started walking, Russell showing the way. Under the eaves it was darker still, but he found the clearing without any problem. 'It's over here,' he said, walking towards the tree.

'Where?'

'Here,' Russell told him, sinking to his knees. This was the moment he feared, when the Russian might order him aside and do the digging himself.

He didn't.

Russell took his time scooping out the still-loose earth with his hands, and just as his questing fingers made contact with metal, the Russian leaned over his shoulder to see what was happening.

'You're in my light,' Russell told him.

'Well, hurry up,' the Russian said, stepping back a pace.

Uttering a short and very silent prayer that interment hadn't disabled the gun, Russell curved his hand around the grip, inserted one finger ahead of the trigger, and jerking it free of its temporary grave, opened fire at point-blank range.

The crack echoed through the forest, scattering loudly cawing birds up into the night sky.

The Russian was still moving, whimpering softly. The eyes looking up at Russell were those of a small boy.

He raised the gun, steeled his heart, and fired again.

When the door closed behind Russell and his escort, Effi's first impulse was to have a good weep. But Rosa had beaten her to it— Effi's daughter was sobbing in eerie silence, the way her real mother had taught her, when they lived in a Christian friend's garden shed, and the Gestapo's main hobby was seeking out hidden Jews.

She took the girl in her arms and tried to hide the hatred she felt for their Russian guard. After drawing the curtains he had sat down opposite them, lit a cigarette, and held them in his gaze. His narrow eyes made Effi think of Mongols, and cruelty, but so far at least he'd shown no sign of murdering them.

Effi told herself there was no reason for despair, not yet anyway. When Russell had told her about his brainstorm—the death-camp escapee's advice and the gun he'd buried with the film—she'd thought it all a touch absurd, but it might well save their lives. It would be almost dark by the time they reached the Grunewald, which would surely improve his chances. She had to believe he'd come back.

What would happen when he did? What would he do? Just knock on the door and shoot this staring Russian when he opened it?

But she didn't think the Russian would be so obliging. Either he and his partner would have a signature knock, like she and Ali had had in the war; or he'd wait to hear the other man's voice.

And if he didn't hear it, then what? He would probably assume it was a friend or a neighbour who had knocked, and send her to answer it. And he would hold on to Rosa just in case. If Russell just burst in shooting, the girl might be killed in the crossfire.

But Russell would already have worked all that out, Effi knew. The reason he'd taken the death-camp escapee's advice to heart so readily was that it chimed so well with his own way of doing things.

So, what would he do? And how could she help them all survive it?

It had taken Ströhm until late afternoon to get his hands on the full text of the Cominform Resolution, and after leaving work he stopped at a bar on Potsdamer Strasse to read the whole thing through. His sense of outrage increased as he did so. The Yugoslavs were accused of 'left deviationism' one moment, and then 'supporting capitalist elements'—a rightist deviation—the next. The Yugoslavs were criticised for their 'hostile attitude to the Soviet Union,' when everyone knew they had bent over backwards in praise of Stalin; and for creating a 'military bureaucratic system,' which was too ironic to be true. Ströhm didn't see how anyone could believe such rubbish. But all the East European parties, including his own, had put their signatures to the Resolution and its principal demand, that the current Yugoslav leadership either change course or face instant removal.

Ströhm ordered another beer and read the Resolution through again, seeking even the faintest echo of the movement he had joined and served. There was none. It was the work of bullies looking after their own.

He was tempted to get really drunk, but told himself not to be so pathetic. Ströhm knew he needed to be strong, to look the truth in the face without anger or self-pity. He needed to talk to someone.

His first thought was Trenkel, whom he knew shared much the same doubts, but what was the point of talking to a mirror? John Russell would be better, Ströhm decided. Russell had left the Party a long time ago, but he understood why others had stayed.

Ströhm walked out to the wretched car, glad for once that he didn't have to walk, and clambered in behind the wheel. He felt sober enough to drive.

Ten minutes later he pulled up outside the building on Carmer Strasse. Darkness was beginning to fall, and he wondered if it was too late for a visit—he should have called them first. But the living-room curtains were rimmed with light, suggesting they hadn't yet gone to bed. And it wasn't that often that a friend mislaid his purpose in life. They would make allowances.

He ascended the stairs and knocked on the door to their apartment.

No one came to answer.

Ströhm heard nothing when he put his ear to the door, but perhaps they were in the other room. After some hesitation he tried again.

This time there were footsteps.

The door half-opened, revealing Effi. He was still smiling apologetically when she said, 'I'm sorry, Kurt, but I can't talk to you now,' and firmly closed it in his face.

He stared at the door. Kurt? Had she been drinking too?

Ströhm raised his hand to knock again, then let it fall. After standing there for a few moments, he walked downstairs and climbed back into his car. Something was wrong, he thought. But what?

As he turned to look up at the flat, a curtain twitched. Someone was making sure he went.

He obliged whomever it was, driving down to Steinplatz and

around the triangular block, pulling over on Kant Strasse where he couldn't be seen from the flat. Lighting a cigarette, he wondered whether to call the police.

Ku'damm was still busy as Russell drove back towards Carmer Strasse. He'd been running through options since leaving the Grunewald, but still hadn't found one that seemed at all promising. The moment he stepped through the apartment door without his escort he would be putting the others' lives at risk. The other Russian might just open fire, with God only knew what results; but if the guard's gun was already at Rosa or Effi's head, he'd have no need to gamble. The threat would force Russell to drop his gun, and they could all be shot with impunity.

But sooner or later he had to go through that door. He needed a diversion of some sort, but short of shouting 'fire' and hoping for the best, he couldn't think of one.

Driving around Savigny Platz he wondered where he should stop. Since it no longer mattered who saw the car, the Russian inside would expect him to leave it out front, but he didn't want to advertise his return until he knew what he meant to do. He couldn't leave it too long—that would make the Russian nervous—but he had to have some sort of plan.

There was a Horch 851 in the old spot, another Soviet favourite. Had the man in the flat been joined by colleagues? And, if so, what chance did he have of saving Effi and Rosa?

As Russell eased past the other car, he saw there was someone behind the wheel.

It was Gerhard Ströhm, staring straight back at him.

What was he doing there? Russell wondered, as he pulled the Maybach over. Surely Ströhm couldn't be with the Russians.

He watched Ströhm get out of his car, walk forward, open the passenger door to Russell's car, and plunk himself down in the adjacent seat.

'I've just been up to your flat,' Ströhm said.

Russell's heart missed a beat. 'And?'

'Effi opened the door, called me Kurt, and shut it again.' He looked enquiringly at Russell.

'Ah.' He had to tell Ströhm something, but what? The truth? Russell had always liked the man—they'd become good friends over the last couple of years—but Ströhm was still a high-ranking KPD functionary, part of the new establishment.

Russell decided he would say that he and Effi had just had a row, and she was in a bad mood.

He turned to Ströhm, opened his mouth, and then closed it again. To hell with it, he thought. This man had gone way out on a limb for him in 1941, and again in 1945. If he couldn't trust Ströhm, then what was the point?

'When Effi opened the door to you,' Russell told him, 'there was a Russian in the other room holding Rosa at gunpoint.'

Ströhm blinked. 'Why?'

'There were two of them waiting in the flat when we got back a couple of hours ago. They want something from me. This,' he added, pulling the tin box out from under his seat. 'It's a reel of film. I'd buried it in the Grunewald, and the other Russian drove me out to dig it up.'

'What's on it?'

'You don't want to know.' He doubted that Ströhm would be brushed off so easily, but his friend had an even more pertinent question.

'Where's the other Russian?'

'In the boot.'

Ströhm almost burst out laughing. It wasn't the slightest bit funny of course, but he'd been harbouring homicidal thoughts about the Soviets for most of the day. 'MGB, I presume?'

'GRU, I think, actually. But right now it doesn't seem to matter that much.'

'No. Well, the obvious thing to do is call the police.'

Ströhm sounded as unconvinced by that idea as Russell was.

'There are problems with that idea.'

'The man in the boot.'

'Apart from him, unfortunately. Look, Gerhard, with that bastard holding Effi and Rosa I don't have time to explain what this is all about. I do know that the police would worry a lot more about the consequences of killing a Russian official than they would about Effi and Rosa's safety.'

'I do have some influence.'

'I know, but anything like that would take an age, and Ivan up there is already wondering why his buddy and I are taking so long. Help me think up some sort of diversion.'

'Use me.'

'What?'

'I'll go up there and force my way in. He's not going to shoot a candidate member of the KPD Central Committee.'

'They planned to kill us all once they had the film. I'm sure he'd apologise profusely after killing you, but that would be the only difference.'

'He won't shoot me out of hand,' Ströhm insisted. 'Not if he thinks I'm there on Party business. He'll wait for his partner before taking a decision like that.'

'I'm not convinced.'

'What else do you have?'

Russell tapped his fingers on either side of the steering wheel. 'Nothing,' he admitted.

'Well, then.'

'What's your reason for turning up?'

'The last time I talked to Effi, she was being pressured by the Soviet culture people. I could be an emissary from Tulpanov.'

Russell had a sudden inspiration. 'No,' he said, 'I have a better idea. One that should save Rosa.'

* * *

Up in the flat, the Russian was still staring at Effi and Rosa through his veil of cigarette smoke. His partner had been gone for almost two hours now, but he didn't seem concerned. Rosa had stopped crying, and was simply hugging her mother as tightly as she could, her blonde head pressed against Effi's chest.

When the knock sounded on the door, the guard gestured Effi to answer it, and moved himself behind the sofa, his gun at Rosa's neck.

As Effi opened the door, Ströhm breezily forced his way past her, talking in Russian. 'Comrade,' he said, 'I know you're in there.'

The Russian's gun was pointing straight at him, and for a moment Ströhm thought he would shoot. 'Our kommissariats have reached a mutual decision,' he added quickly.

'What kommissariat? Who are you?'

'I'm sorry. My name is Ströhm. KPD Central Committee. And K-5 of course, though it doesn't say that on my papers. May I?' He reached in a hand before the Russian could say no, and brought out his Party accreditations.

The Russian studied the papers without moving his aim. 'So this is who you are. What are you doing here?'

'I'm here for the girl.'

'The girl?'

'You do know who she is?'

The Russian looked blank.

'This is the girl who drew the famous picture of the Red Army soldier on Bismarck Strasse. You must know it.'

'Of course.'

'Well your culture people have plans for her. And your department has agreed that she be spared.'

'We were told no witnesses.'

'She'll be in Moscow, so that won't matter.' He reached into his pocket for cigarettes, and offered one to the Russian. 'I thought there were two of you.'

'My partner will be back soon. He will decide about the girl.'

Rosa was staring at Ströhm as if he'd gone mad, and he suddenly realised that she might use his name. He leaned forward and ruffled her hair. 'Pretend you don't know me,' he said in German. 'I told her she has nothing to fear,' he told the Russian in his language.

'We shall see.'

'You said your colleague wouldn't be long,' Ströhm said, checking his watch. In two minutes Russell would be at the door. With the Russian happy to wait in silence, he counted out sixty seconds, then abruptly strode across the room, winking at Effi once his back was turned to the enemy. He peeled back the edge of a curtain, and looked out.

'They're here,' he said over the Russian's angry insistence that he come away from the window. 'Let me take the girl in the other room,' Ströhm pleaded. 'If she sees you kill them she'll be harder to handle.'

'All right,' the Russian agreed. For all his sangfroid, he was obviously relieved that his partner was back.

Ströhm took Rosa by the hand, gave her a reassuring smile, and ushered her through the bedroom door. 'Stay in there,' he said gently, and shut it behind her.

It was almost too late. Turning back to the room, he heard the key click in the apartment door, and as the Russian reached, almost casually, for Effi's arm, Ströhm bundled into her back. They were both still falling when the silenced gun coughed, and the sound of their bodies hitting the floor found an echo a few seconds later.

The Russian was seated on the floor, his back against the sofa, his legs splayed out in front of him, a bullet hole in his chest. He wheezed, grimaced, and somehow seemed to settle, like a puppet whose strings had been dropped.

Effi got to her feet, took one look at the dead Russian, and went through to the bedroom to comfort Rosa.

'What are you going to do with him?' Ströhm asked Russell after a few moments' silence. 'Him and his partner.'

Russell put down the pistol and ran a hand through his hair. 'While you were doing your K-5 impression I was wondering exactly that, and I did come up with one idea. I have no right to ask you this—you've done more than enough already—but . . .'

'How can I help?'

'Well, I need to dump them somewhere in their car. It has to look like an accident, or we'll be getting more visits like this one. If you bring your car along, you can give me a lift back.'

'Okay, but won't the bullets be a giveaway?'

'They'll have to come out.'

Ströhm went to the window to look at the street. 'When do you think we should leave?'

'The sooner the better. The place I have in mind is up in the British sector, and they don't do night patrols anymore. But let me tell Effi what we're doing.'

'Give me the keys and I'll bring the Russians' car around,' Ströhm offered.

In the other room Effi sat on the bed, Rosa's head on her shoulder.

'It's all over, sweetheart,' Russell said, leaning over to kiss the child on the forehead. 'He can't hurt you and Effi now.'

'Is he dead?' she whispered.

'He is. It was him or us, I'm afraid.'

'I'm glad,' Rosa said.

'What about the body?' Effi asked.

'Gerhard and I will take it away. Are you okay?'

'Yes, I suppose so. Be careful.'

'Aren't I always?'

One thing about their building, as Russell and Effi knew from previous complaints, was that they were always the last ones to bed. The two men carried the corpse down through the silent stairwell, and once Ströhm had signalled the all-clear, Russell dragged it out to the street. Fitting another body into the boot wasn't easy, but between them they managed somehow. There was always the chance that someone had seen their struggle from a window, but the street lighting was poor, and Berliners weren't as conscientious about reporting wrong-doing as they had been at one time. Either they'd seen too much of it, or their trust in authority was at a very low ebb. Both, most likely.

'Where are we going?' Ströhm asked.

Russell told him.

'Okay. I'll get my car and follow you.'

'If I didn't know better,' Russell said wryly, 'I'd say you were almost enjoying yourself.'

'I might be now,' Ströhm admitted, 'but I wouldn't want to go through those ten minutes again.' As he walked to the Party car, he asked himself why he had actually risked his life. Several reasons came to mind—too much alcohol, his fury with the Russians, loyalty to a friend. But what mattered now was that he'd got away with it.

Ströhm started up the Horch, and drove it around the corner into Carmer Strasse, where Russell was just walking out to the Maybach with bottle in hand.

They started off, and within a few minutes were heading northwest up a mostly empty Berliner Strasse. Occasionally another car would pass in the other direction, but they saw no British patrols. The Western Allies would all be keen to save petrol, Ströhm thought, now that they couldn't bring anymore in.

Up ahead, Russell was looking for flaws in his hastily conceived plan. If a proper investigation was held—and he hoped the British authorities would make that as difficult as possible for the Soviets—then it had to look like the two GRU men had been on their way home with the film when one of two things had happened—either Beria's men had got to them, or they'd had a terrible accident. And since he couldn't think of any way to fake the former, it had to be the latter. Complete with flames. Two burnt bodies and one burnt film.

The boys in the boot had even supplied the accelerant—the spare of can of petrol in the back was probably standard issue for GRU murder squads.

It took twenty minutes to reach the bridge across the choked canal. The long gap in the parapet, which he'd noticed several months earlier, was, like most of Berlin, awaiting repair. Even the string of warning flags had blown away. It was, as Russell had thought at the time, an accident waiting to happen.

He stopped and got out. There were lights in the distance in both directions, but the immediate area was lit by the moon, revealing an industrial wasteland of hulk-filled docks, burnt-out factories, and sidings strewn with splintered wagons.

Ströhm joined him, and they pulled the corpses out on to the bridge. 'Now for the difficult bit,' Russell murmured, getting down on his haunches and taking out his pocket knife. In the First War they'd used to say that dead men didn't bleed, but digging out the bullets was a messy business, and the smell of innards did evoke the trenches with a vengeance. When he was done, he walked back twenty metres and dropped the three bullets in the stagnant water below.

There was still no sign of other traffic. After lifting the Russians into the front seats, and jamming their Tokarev pistols into their pockets, Russell doused them and the film with petrol, then fashioned a Molotov cocktail using the bottle and handkerchief he'd brought along for that purpose.

There was no need to push the car—just removing the handbrake and turning the wheel would suffice. In the event, the car gathered speed faster than Russell expected, and he barely had time to light the cocktail and thrust it through the open window. The blaze was instant, the two bodies silhouetted in flame as the car toppled over the edge and out of sight. A split-second later it hit the concrete towpath with a crash that was probably heard in Karlshorst, and a curtain of flame soared upwards, like an all-too-effective beacon.

'Let's get out of here,' Russell said, unnecessarily.

They spent several minutes in fear of approaching lights, but once Ströhm had pulled them off the main highway and into the Westend back streets both men felt a lot safer.

'Thank you,' Russell said. The two words seemed hardly enough, but he couldn't remember meaning them more.

'You're welcome,' Ströhm said lightly.

'What chance in a thousand brought you around tonight?' Russell asked him.

Ströhm laughed. 'Believe it not, I wanted to talk about the Yugoslavs.'

'What about them?'

'Haven't you heard? The Soviets are throwing them out of the

Cominform for having minds of their own. It's over,' he added after a moment.

'What is?'

Ströhm ignored that. 'What made you leave the Party?' he asked.

So that was it, Russell thought. 'You know I can't remember any particular thing—it was a lot of things, all adding up. One day I just knew that I wanted out. That the reasons I'd had for joining no longer made any sense to me.'

Ströhm thought about that for a minute or so. 'They say Brecht's coming back,' he said eventually, as if the poet's blessing might make all the difference.

'"Hatred, even of meanness, contorts the features,"' Russell quoted.

'Always?'

'I don't know. I do know that socialism's dead in the water, for our lifetime at least. The Yanks and Stalin—they've got each other now, perfect scapegoats for anything that goes wrong in their own empires. The Yanks prattle on about freedom and free enterprise, the Soviets about welfare and full employment, and neither will admit that they lack what the other has. They'll both spend a fortune on weapons and come down like a ton of bricks on anyone who makes trouble on their own patch.' Russell grunted. 'You know what happened? The Nazis made everyone look good for a few years, but now they're gone, and we're back with crap meets crap.'

Ströhm shook his head, but more in sadness than disagreement. 'Only a year ago, I would have pitied you for your cynicism.'

'And now?'

'It fits the facts. But I haven't given up on socialism—not quite yet.'

'I may have given up on politics,' Russell said, 'but I don't think I have on justice. Though what that means in practice . . . well, I guess I'll have to find out.' He turned to Ströhm. 'When we ran into each other this evening, and I told you about the film and the dead Russian in the boot, why didn't you just walk away, like any sensible human being?'

'You still haven't told me what's on this precious film.'

'And I'm not going to. There are some things you're safer not knowing.'

'All right. But one day?'

'One day,' Russell agreed. The day they put Beria into the ground, or someone drove a stake through the bastard's heart. 'What will you do?' he asked, changing the subject.

'God knows. Work for a change, of course, and get kicked out of the Party? Hold my nose and join the SPD? I can't learn Serbo-Croat and run off to Belgrade—I have a child coming. Which reminds me: Annaliese must not hear about tonight. From you or Effi.'

'If you say so. But after all the adventures she and Effi had, I think she'd understand.'

'Oh, so do I, but that doesn't mean she'd forgive me. And she'd probably be right.'

Russell didn't argue. They drove on through the moonlit streets, seeing no other vehicle until they reached Bismarck Strasse.

'Drop me a few blocks away,' Russell said. 'You don't want this car seen on Carmer Strasse again.'

A few minutes later he was watching the Horch recede, Ströhm's arm held aloft in farewell. After wiping his gore-stained hands on a convenient tuft of grass, Russell started for home. He felt tired to the bone, but strangely buoyant considering the past few hours. Would it all work? It just might, he supposed.

Some Soviet forensic genius might find bullet holes in the charred flesh, or some unforeseen proof that it hadn't been an accident. The GRU bosses might wonder why Russell was still alive, and why their men had shown such mercy. Would they try and correct this oversight? Perhaps, but probably not—with the film gone, what would be the point?

There was no sure and certain way out, no Gordian knot that Russell could cut. He would have to live with the knowledge that assassination by the GRU was a life-threatening possibility, like cancer and falling masonry. To be actively avoided, but not at the cost of all else.

He walked on through the dark and silent streets. Beria would be in bed at this hour, if he wasn't out trawling Moscow for young girls. After his tête-à-tête with Shchepkin the bastard would be perching a little less easily on his blood-stained throne, which was something. He would certainly be more careful when it came to hidden cameras.

It occurred to Russell that if the GRU did succeed in killing them all, then the film's release and Beria's subsequent fall from power would posthumously offer some slight compensation.

It was almost three in the morning. In a few more hours Shchepkin would be knocking at the Americans' door, and not long after that Johannsen would ring with the terrible news that Russell's cover was comprehensively blown.

It would doubtless take several weeks of boring questions, but then he would be free of them all.

His strange career in the shadows, which Shchepkin had launched more than ten years before in that shabby Danzig hotel room, would finally be over. They might eventually kill him, but they would never recruit him again.

And in September his son was getting married. His son, who'd survived the Eastern Front, and now seemed as sane as anyone could be, who'd entered that madhouse with a functioning heart and a soul. And if he and Effi had anything to do with it, Rosa too would come into her own.

Russell turned into Carmer Strasse, where the only light showing was theirs.

'It's me,' he said softly, as he opened the door.

'So it is,' Effi said, taking him into her arms.

Historical addendum

The Soviet siege of Berlin's three Western sectors, and the airlift which frustrated it, lasted until May 1949. By the end of that year the country as a whole was formally divided into two states, the Western-backed Federal Republic (West Germany) and the Soviet-backed Democratic Republic (East Germany). Berlin was also divided in two, the Soviet sector becoming the capital of East Germany, the Western sectors a West German enclave. Movement between the two halves of the city was restricted but possible.

East Germany was doomed from the beginning by the behaviour of its Soviet sponsors, particularly that of their soldiers in the months straddling the end of the war. Only a party of saints could have sold the German people on communism in such a context, and the KPD was far from that. Those leaders returning from exile had long since interiorised the Soviet model, and they quickly sidelined comrades like my Gerhard Ströhm who had other ideas of how a socialist state might develop. Bertolt Brecht did finally return in 1951, and spent his last five years outwardly supporting the new regime and inwardly lamenting its tyrannical nature.

After a brief and brutally suppressed uprising in June 1953, East Germany settled into being one of the hardest of the hard-line regimes in the Soviet Bloc. This encouraged emigration and flight, particularly of those educated and skilled people the regime could least afford to lose. The most porous border was that between West and East Berlin, and the only way to close it proved to be a wall. One was duly erected in August 1961, and stood for the next twenty-nine years as a potent symbol of Soviet communism's moral and political bankruptcy.

It was finally torn down in the aftermath of the Soviet Union's collapse, and in the brief interregnum which followed socialist opponents of the East German regime debated the possibility of establishing something new in their country, a system which was neither capitalist nor Soviet communist, but an authentic German socialism which drew on the best of both systems. Like the 'Ströhms' of 1945–48, they saw their hopes denied.

Series acknowledgments

I would like to thank my publishers—Ben Yarde-Buller at Old Street in the UK, Katie Herman and Juliet Grames at Soho Press in the US—for their faith, support and general hard work over the last seven years. The series wouldn't have happened without them, and the same could certainly be said of my agent Charlie Viney, who helped me convert a very different original idea into a series that was both commercial and rewarding to write. I also owe a great deal to David Reynolds, who not only edited most of the books, but shared in their gestation process during many long walks through the Surrey countryside.

Many others have unwittingly contributed to the series. Among the numerous books I have used for research, I would like to mention two in particular. Jan Valtin's *Out of the Night* and Victor Serge's *Memoirs of a Revolutionary* are autobiographical accounts of communists, and both offer vivid, highly readable, evocations of the struggles the two men were engaged in. The idea of communism is discredited now—the Soviet version deservedly so—but understanding what motivated so many idealistic and intelligent people to fight for it is essential if twentieth-century history is to make any sort of sense. When it comes to fiction, no one nailed ideological intrigue like Eric Ambler, and in recent years Alan Furst has proved a worthy successor.

As far as Berlin is concerned, I am indebted to the many authors who lived and wrote there in the 1930s and 1940s, and to all the various archivists who continue to preserve (these days mainly on the net) photographs and maps of how it was back then. It may no longer be possible to visit the city that Russell and Effi lived in, but the archivists' work makes it so much easier to imagine.

Lastly, I must acknowledge the contribution of my wife, Nancy, as sounding board, critic and inspiration. She and Effi differ in many ways, but I couldn't have imagined Effi without her.

David Downing, November 2012

Continue reading for a sneak preview of

JACK OF SPIES

The Blue Dragon

—◆—

At the foot of the hill, Tsingtau's Government House stood alone on a slight mound, its gabled upper-floor windows and elegant corner tower looking out across the rest of the town. Substantial German houses with red-tiled roofs peppered the slope leading down to the Pacific beach and pier; beyond them the even grander buildings of the commercial district fronted the bay and its harbors. Away to the right, the native township of Taipautau offered little in the way of variety—the houses were smaller, perhaps a bit closer together, but more European than classically Chinese. In less than two decades, the Germans had come, organized, and recast this tiny piece of Asia in their own image. Give them half a chance, Jack McColl mused, and they would do the same for the rest of the world.

He remembered the Welsh mining engineer leaning over the *Moldavia*'s rail in mid–Indian Ocean and spoiling a beautiful day with tales of the atrocities the Germans had committed in South-West Africa over the last few years. At least a hundred thousand Africans had perished. Many of the native men had died in battle; most of the remainder, along with the women and children, had been driven into the desert, where some thoughtful German had already poisoned the water holes. A few lucky ones had ended up in concentration camps, where a doctor named Fischer had used them for a series of involuntary medical experiments. Children had been injected with smallpox, typhus, tuberculosis.

The white man's burden, as conceived in Berlin.

McColl had passed two descending Germans on his way up the hill, but the well-kept viewing area had been empty, and there was no sign of other sightseers below. To the east the hills rose into a jagged horizon, and the earthworks surrounding the 28-centimeter guns on Bismarck Hill were barely visible against the mountains beyond. Some magnification would have helped, but an Englishman training binoculars on foreign defenses was likely to arouse suspicion, and from what he'd seen so far, the guns were where the Admiralty had thought they would be. There was some building work going on near the battery that covered Auguste-Victoria Bay, but not on a scale that seemed significant. He might risk a closer look early one morning, when the army was still drilling.

The East Asia Squadron was where it had been the day before—*Scharnhorst* and *Emden* sharing the long jetty, *Gneisenau* and *Nürnberg* anchored in the bay beyond. *Leipzig* had been gone a week now—to the Marianas, if his Chinese informer was correct. Several coalers were lined up farther out, and one was unloading by the onshore wharves, sending occasional clouds of black dust up into the clear, cold air.

These ships were the reason for his brief visit, these ships and what they might do if war broke out. Their presence was no secret, of course—the local British consul probably played golf with the admiral in command. The same consul could have kept the Admiralty informed about Tsingtau's defenses and done his best to pump his German counterpart for military secrets, but of course he hadn't. Such work was considered ungentlemanly by the fools who ran the Foreign Office and staffed its embassies—not that long ago a British military attaché had refused to tell his employers in London what he'd witnessed at his host country's military maneuvers, on the grounds that he'd be breaking a confidence.

It was left to part-time spies to do the dirty work. Over the last few years, McColl—and, he presumed, other British businessmen who traveled the world—had been approached and asked to ferret out those secrets the empire's enemies wanted kept. The man who employed them on this part-time basis was an old naval officer named Cumming, who worked from an office in Whitehall and answered, at least in theory, to the Admiralty and its political masters.

When it came to Tsingtau, the secret that mattered most was what orders the East Asia Squadron had for the day that a European war broke out. Any hard evidence as to their intentions, as Cumming had told McColl on their farewell stroll down the Embankment, would be "really appreciated."

His insistence on how vital all this was to the empire's continued well-being had been somewhat undermined by his allocation of a paltry three hundred pounds for global expenses, but the trip as a whole had been slightly more lucrative than McColl had expected. The luxury Maia automobile that he was hawking around the world—the one now back in Shanghai, he hoped, with his brother Jed and colleague Mac—had caught the fancy of several rulers hungry for initiation into the seductive world of motorized speed, and the resultant orders had at least paid the trio's traveling bills.

This was gratifying, but probably more of a swan song than a sign of things to come. The automobile business was not what it had been even two years before, not for the small independents—nowadays you needed capital, and lots of it. Spying, on the other hand, seemed an occupation with a promising future. Over the last few years, even the British had realized the need for an espionage service, and once the men holding the purse strings finally got past the shame of it all, they would realize that only a truly professional body would do. One that paid a commensurate salary.

A war would probably help, but until Europe's governments were stupid enough to start one, McColl would have to make do with piecework. Before McColl's departure from England the previous autumn, Cumming had taken note of his planned itinerary and returned with a list of "little jobs" that McColl could do in the various ports of call—a wealthy renegade to assess in Cairo, a fellow Brit to investigate in Bombay, the Germans here in Tsingtau. Their next stop with the Maia was San Francisco, where a ragtag bunch of Indian exiles were apparently planning the empire's demise.

A lot of it seemed pretty inconsequential to McColl. There were no doubt plenty of would-be picadors intent on goading the imperial bull, but it didn't seem noticeably weaker. And where was the matador to finish it off? The Kaiser probably practiced sword strokes in his bedroom mirror, but it would be a long time before Germany acquired the necessary global reach.

He lit a German cigarette and stared out across the town. The sun was dropping toward the distant horizon, the harbor lighthouse glowing brighter by the minute. The lines of lamps in the warship rigging reminded him of Christmas trees.

He would be back in Shanghai for the Chinese New Year, he realized.

Caitlin Hanley, the young American woman he'd met in Peking, was probably there already.

The sun was an orange orb, almost touching the distant hills. He ground out the cigarette and started back down the uneven path while he could still see his way. Two hopeful coolies were waiting with their rickshaws at the bottom, but he waved them both away and walked briskly down Bismarckstrasse toward the beach. There were lights burning in the British consulate, but no other sign of life within.

His hotel was at the western end of the waterfront, beyond the deserted pleasure pier. The desk clerk still had his hair in a pigtail—an increasingly rare sight in Shanghai but common enough in Tsingtau, where German rule offered little encouragement to China's zealous modernizers. The room key changed hands with the usual bow and blank expression, and McColl climbed the stairs to his second-floor room overlooking the ocean.

A quick check revealed that someone had been though his possessions, which was only to be expected—Tsingtau might be a popular summer destination with all sorts of foreigners, but an Englishman turning up in January was bound to provoke some suspicion. Whoever it was had found nothing to undermine his oft-repeated story, that he was here in China on business and seeing as much of the country as money and time would allow.

He went back downstairs to the restaurant. Most of the clientele were German businessmen in stiff collars and spats, either eager to grab their slice of China or boasting of claims already staked. There were also a handful of officers, including one in a uniform McColl didn't recognize. He was enthusiastically outlining plans for establishing an aviation unit in Tsingtau when he noticed McColl's arrival and abruptly stopped to ask the man beside him something.

"Don't worry, Pluschow, he doesn't speak German," was the audible answer, which allowed the exposition to continue.

Since his arrival in Tsingtau, McColl had taken pains to stress his sad lack of linguistic skills, and this was not the first time the lie had worked to his advantage. Apparently absorbed in his month-old *Times,* he listened with interest to the aviation enthusiast. He couldn't see much strategic relevance in the news—what could a few German planes hope to achieve so far from home?—but the

Japanese might well be interested. And any little nugget of intelligence should be worth a few of Cumming's precious pounds.

The conversation took a less interesting tack, and eventually the party broke up. McColl sipped his Russian tea and idly wondered where he would dine later that evening. He glanced through the paper for the umpteenth time and reminded himself that he needed fresh reading for the Pacific crossing. There was a small shop he knew on Shanghai's Nanking Road where novels jettisoned by foreigners mysteriously ended up.

More people came in—two older Germans in naval uniform, who ignored him, and a stout married couple, who returned his smile of acknowledgment with almost risible Prussian hauteur.

He was getting up to leave when Rainer von Schön appeared. McColl had met the young German soon after arriving in Tsingtau—they were both staying at this hotel—and taken an instant liking to him. The fact that von Schön spoke near-perfect English made conversation easy, and the man himself was likable and intelligent. A water engineer by trade, he had admitted to a bout of homesickness and delved into his wallet for an explanatory photo of his pretty wife and daughter.

That evening he had an English edition of William Le Queux's *Invasion of 1910* under his arm.

"What do you think of it?" McColl asked him once the waiter had taken the German's order.

"Well, several things. It's so badly written, for one. The plot's ridiculous, and the tone is hysterical."

"But otherwise you like it?"

Von Schön smiled. "It is strangely entertaining. And the fact that so many English people bought it makes it fascinating to a German. And a little scary, I have to say."

"Don't you have any ranters in Germany?"

Von Schön leaned slightly forward, a mischievous expression on his face. "With the Kaiser at the helm, we don't need them."

McColl laughed. "So what have you been doing today?"

"Finishing up, actually. I'll be leaving in a couple of days."

"Homeward bound?"

"Eventually. I have work in Tokyo first. But after that . . ."

"Well, if I don't see you before you go, have a safe journey."

"You, too." Von Schön drained the last of his schnapps and got to his feet. "And now I have someone I need to see."

Once the German was gone, McColl consulted his watch. It was time he visited the Blue Dragon, before the evening rush began. He left a generous tip, recovered his winter coat from the downstairs cloakroom, and walked out to the waiting line of rickshaws. The temperature had already dropped appreciably, and he was hugging himself as the coolie turned left onto the well-lit Friedrichstrasse and started up the hill. The shops were closed by this time, the restaurants readying themselves for their evening trade. The architecture, the faces, the cooking smells, all were European—apart from his coolie, the only Chinese person in sight was a man collecting horse dung.

It was quiet, too—so quiet that the sudden blast of a locomotive whistle from the nearby railway station made him jump.

The coolie reached the brow of the low hill and started down the opposite slope into Taipautau. The township was almost as neat and widely spaced as the German districts, and in the cold air even the smells seemed more muted than they had in Shanghai. They were halfway down Shantung Strasse before McColl could hear the beginnings of evening revelry in the sailors' bars at the bottom.

The Blue Dragon was open for business but not yet really awake. The usual old man sat beneath the candlelit lanterns on the rickety veranda, beside the screened-off entrance. He grinned when he recognized McColl and cheerfully spat on the floor to his right, adding one more glistening glob to an impressive mosaic.

McColl was barely through the doorway when an old woman hurried down the hall toward him. "This way, please!" she insisted in pidgin German. "All type girls!"

"I'm here to see Hsu Ch'ing-lan," he told her in Mandarin, but she just looked blank. "Hsu Ch'ing-lan," he repeated.

The name seemed to percolate. She gestured for him to follow and led him through to the reception area, where "all type girls" were waiting in an assortment of tawdry traditional costumes on long red-velvet sofas. Some were barely out of puberty, others close to menopause. One seemed amazingly large for a Chinese woman, causing McColl to wonder whether she'd been fattened up to satisfy some particular Prussian yearning.

The old woman led him down the corridor beyond, put her head around the final door, and told Madame that a *laowai* wanted to see her. Assent forthcoming, she ushered McColl inside.

Hsu Ch'ing-lan was sitting at her desk, apparently doing her accounts. Some kind of incense was burning in a large dragon holder beyond, sending up coils of smoke.

"Herr McColl," she said with an ironic smile. "Please. Take a seat."

She was wearing the usual dress, blue silk embroidered in silver and gold, ankle-length but slit to the hip. Her hair was piled up in curls, secured by what looked like an ornamental chopstick. She was in her thirties, he guessed, and much more desirable than any of the girls in reception. When they'd first met, she'd told him that she was a retired prostitute, as if that were a major achievement. It probably was.

He had chosen this brothel for two reasons. It offered a two-tier service—those girls in reception who catered to ordinary sailors and the occasional NCO, and another, more exclusive, group who did house calls at officers' clubs and businessmen's hotels. The latter were no younger, no more beautiful, and no more sexually inventive than the former, but as Jane Austen might have put it, they offered more in the way of accomplishments. They sang, they danced, they made a ritual out of making tea. They provided, in Ch'ing-lan's vivid phrase, "local-color fuck."

She was his second reason for choosing the place. She came from Shanghai and, unlike any other madam in Tsingtau, spoke the Chinese dialect that McColl knew best.

She pulled a bell cord, ordered tea from the small girl who came running, and asked him, rather surprisingly, what he knew of the latest political developments.

"In China?" he asked.

She looked at him as if he were mad. "What could matter here?" she asked.

"Sun Yat-sen could win and start modernizing the country," he suggested. "Or Yuan Shih-kai could become the new emperor and keep the country locked in the past."

"Pah. You foreign devils have decided we must modernize, so Yuan cannot win. And you control our trade, so Sun could win only as your puppet."

"Yuan bought one of my cars."

"He thinks it will make him look modern, but it won't. It doesn't matter what he or Sun does. In today's China everything depends on what the foreign devils do. Is there going to be a war between you? And if there is, what will happen here in Tsingtau?"

"If there's a war, the Japanese will take over. The Germans might dig themselves in—who knows? If they do, the town will be shelled. If I were you, I'd take the boat back home to Shanghai before the fighting starts."

"Mmm." Her eyes wandered around the room, as if she were deciding what to take with her.

The tea arrived and was poured.

"So what do you have for me?" McColl asked.

"Not very much, I'm afraid." The East Asia Squadron was going to sea at the end of February, for a six-week cruise. The *Scharnhorst* had a new vice captain, and there'd been a serious accident on the *Emden*—several sailors had been killed in an explosion. The recent gunnery trials had been won by the *Gneisenau,* but all five ships had shown a marked improvement, and the Kaiser had sent a congratulatory telegram to Vice Admiral von Spee. And a new officer had arrived from Germany to set up a unit of flying machines.

"I know about him," McColl said.

"He likes to be spanked," Ch'ing-lan revealed.

McColl wondered out loud whether verbal abuse might sting the Germans into indiscretions. Maybe the girls could deride their German clients, make fun of their puny fleet. What hope did they have against the mighty Royal Navy?

As she noted this down, a swelling sequence of ecstatic moans resounded through the building. Ch'ing-lan shook her head. "I'll have to talk to her," she said. "The others do the same because they think their tips will be smaller if they don't, and after a while none of us can hear ourselves think. It's ridiculous."

McColl laughed.

"But I do have some good news for you. I have a new girl, a cousin from Shanghai. She speaks a little English, and now she's learning a little German—she knows that a lot of the men like someone they can talk to."

"That sounds promising."

"And more expensive."

"Of course—I have no problem paying good money for good information." He thought for a moment. "She could be worried that her officer might be killed in a war. The British are so much more powerful, yes? She could ask for reassurance, ask him how he thinks his fleet can win."

She nodded.

"And the flying-machine man. I'd like to know how many machines, what type, and how he intends to use them. Between spanks, of course."

She nodded again. "Is that all?"

"I think so. I'll come back on Friday, yes?"

"Okay. You want girl tonight? Half price?"

He hesitated and saw Caitlin Hanley's face in his mind's eye. "No, not tonight." He smiled at her. "You're still retired, right?"

"You couldn't afford me."

"Probably not." He gave her a bow, shut the door after him, and walked back down the corridor. Bedsprings were squeaking behind several curtained doorways, and several girls seemed intent on winning the prize for most voluble pleasure. Out on the veranda, the old man gave him a leer and added another splash of phlegm to his iridescent patchwork.

It was enough to put a man off his dinner.

The following day was as clear and cold as its predecessor. McColl rose early and took breakfast in the almost empty hotel restaurant, conscious that half a dozen Chinese waiters were hovering at his beck and call. Once outside, he made straight for the beach. A westerly wind was picking up, and he could smell the brewery the Germans had built beyond the town. The ocean was studded with whitecaps.

As he'd calculated, the tide was out, and he walked briskly along the hard sand toward the promontory guarding the entrance to the bay. The field-artillery barracks he'd noticed on the map were set quite a distance back from the shore and, as he had hoped, only the roofs and tower were visible from the beach. He was soon beyond them, threading his way down a narrowing beach between headland and ocean.

Another half a mile and he found his path barred by a barbed-wire fence. It ran down slope and beach and some twenty yards out into the water, to what was probably the low-tide mark. He had first seen barbed wire corralling Boer women and children in South Africa, and finding it stretched across a Chinese beach was somewhat depressing, if rather predictable. There was no EINTRITT VER-BOTEN sign, but there didn't really need to be. Only an idiot would think the fence was there to pen sheep.

McColl decided to be one. A quick look about him failed to detect any possible witnesses, so he took off his shoes and socks, rolled up his trousers, and waded out and around the end of the fence. The water was deeper and colder than he had expected. After drying his feet as best he could with a handkerchief, he wrung out his trouser bottoms, inserted his sand-encrusted feet into the dry footwear, and ventured on down the forbidden beach. I went paddling in the Yellow Sea, he thought. Something to tell his grandchildren, should he ever have any.

As he approached the end of the headland, the stern of a passenger ship loomed into view. It had obviously just left the harbor and was already turning southward, probably bound for Shanghai. McColl found himself wishing he were on it, rather than seeking out German guns with a pair of cold, wet trousers clinging to his thighs. He'd already earned the pittance that Cumming was paying him. What did the man expect from a brief visit like this one? A serious spying mission to Tsingtau would need a lot more time—and a lot better cover—than McColl had at his disposal. Cumming's favorite agent, Sidney Reilly, had lived in Port Arthur for several months before he succeeded in stealing the Russian harbor-defense plans.

McColl stopped and scrutinized the view to his right. The guns were up there somewhere, and this looked as good a spot as any to clamber up the slope. If he ran into officialdom, he would play the lost tourist, afraid of being cut off by the incoming tide.

Five minutes later he reached the crest and got a shock. The gun emplacements were up there all right, just as the Admiralty had thought they would be, but so were watching eyes. McColl was still scrambling up onto the plateau when the first shout sounded, and it didn't take him long to work out that dropping back out of sight was unlikely to win him anything more than a bullet in the spine. They'd seen him, and that was that.

Two soldiers in pickelhaube helmets were running across the grass. He walked toward them, mind working furiously. The lost-tourist act already seemed redundant—an Englishman this close to German guns was surely too much of a coincidence. But what was the alternative?

One of their guns went off, and for a single dreadful moment he thought they were shooting at him. But it quickly became obvious that one of them had pulled his trigger by accident. Seizing what seemed like an opportunity, McColl lengthened his stride, shook his fist, and angrily asked in German what the hell they thought they were doing.

"No civilians are allowed up here," the older of the soldiers insisted. He looked a little shamefaced but had not lowered his rifle. "Who are you? Where have you come from?"

"My name is Pluschow," McColl told him impulsively. There were two thousand soldiers in the garrison, and it seemed unlikely that these two would have run into the aviation enthusiast. "Lieutenant Pluschow," he added, taking a guess at the man's rank. "I am sorry— I did not realize I had strayed onto army territory. But I can't believe your orders are to shoot first and ask questions later."

"That was an accident," the younger man blurted out. He couldn't have been much more than eighteen.

"And no harm done," his partner insisted. "But you still haven't explained what you're doing here."

"I'm surveying the area. Tsingtau needs an aerodrome, and I'm getting a feeling for the local air currents." He reached for his packet of cigarettes and held it out to the soldiers.

There was a moment of hesitation before the older one extended a hand and took one. His partner happily followed his lead.

"If I need to come up here again, I will get permission from army command," McColl promised. "Now, is there a supply road back to town?"

There was, and they were happy to show him where it started, on the other side of the emplacements. Walking past the latter, he took in the ferroconcrete installations, heavy steel cupolas, and lift-mounted searchlights. And the guns were new-looking 28-centimeter pieces, not the old 15-centimeter cannons on the Admiralty list. "Our base seems well protected," he said appreciatively.

He thanked the soldiers, promised he wouldn't mention the accidental discharge, and left them happily puffing on his cigarettes. He managed to cover a hundred yards or so before the urge to burst out laughing overcame him. Moments like that made life worth living.

Fifteen minutes later he was skirting the wall of the barracks and entering the town. In the square in front of the station, a bunch of coolies were huddled over some sort of game, their rickshaws lined up in waiting for the next train. McColl walked the few blocks to Friedrichstrasse and wondered what to do with the rest of the day. Tsingtau in winter was worth a couple of days, and he'd been there for more than a week. Like an idiot he'd forgotten to bring any reading, and the two bookshops on Friedrichstrasse had nothing in

English. A German book on his bedside table would rather give the game away.

It occurred to him that the British consulate might have books to lend, and indeed they did. Just the one—a copy of *Great Expectations* some careless English tourist had left on the beach the previous summer. But the consul was out playing golf, and the English-speaking Chinese girl left in charge of His Majesty's business was unwilling to let the salt-stained volume out of the building without his say-so. It took McColl fifteen minutes and no small measure of charm to change her mind. And all this, he thought bitterly, for a book he already knew the ending to.

Still, Pip's early travails kept him entertained for the rest of the morning and half the afternoon. He then ambled around the German and Chinese towns before dropping anchor in the bar of the Sailors' Home down by the harbor. Through the window he could see the huge gray ships straining at their chains in the restless water.

What would this fleet do if war were declared? It could hardly stay put, not with England's ally Japan so close at hand, with ships that outmatched and outnumbered the Germans'. No, if the East Asia Squadron weren't already at sea when war broke out, then it soon would be. But sailing in which direction? For its home half the world away? If this was the intention, then whichever direction it took—west via the Cape of Good Hope or east around Cape Horn—there would be ten thousand miles and more to sail, with uncertain coal supplies and the knowledge that the whole British fleet would be waiting at the end of its journey, barring its passage across the North Sea. And what would be the point? More than five cruisers would be needed to tip the balance in home waters.

If McColl were in charge, he knew what he'd do. He'd send the five ships off in five directions, set them loose on the seven oceans to mess with British trade. That, he knew, was the Admiralty's nightmare. Each German ship could keep a British squadron busy for months, maybe even years, and that *might* tip the balance closer to home.

Whether or not the Imperial Navy had such suicide missions in mind, neither he nor the Admiralty knew, and he doubted whether any of his current drinking companions did either. He bought beers for a couple of new arrivals, traded toasts in pidgin English to Kaiser and King, and eavesdropped on the conversations swirling around him. But no secrets were divulged, unless Franz's fear that he had the French disease counted as such. Most of the seamen had their minds on home, on babies yet unseen, on wives and lovers sorely missed. No one mentioned the dread possibility that none of them would ever see Germany again.

McColl stayed until the sun was almost down, then walked back through the town as the lamplighters went about their business. Guessing that von Schön had not yet departed, he looked in on the hotel bar and found the young German sharing a circle of armchairs with several fellow-countrymen. Seeing McColl, von Schön smiled and gestured him over. "Please, join us," he said in English, "we need your point of view."

He introduced McColl to the others, explaining in German that the Englishman was also a businessman. They raised their hands in greeting.

"What are you all talking about?" McColl asked von Schön.

"Whether a war will benefit Germany," the other replied.

"And what's the general opinion?"

"I don't think there is one. I'll try to translate for you."

McColl sat back, careful to keep a look of noncomprehension on his face. One middle-aged man with a bristling mustache was making the argument that only a war could open the world to German business.

"If we win," another man added dryly.

"Of course, but we haven't lost one yet, and our chances must be good, even against England."

Several heads were nodding as von Schön translated this with an apologetic smile, but one of the younger Germans was shaking his head. "Why take the risk," he asked, "when we only have to wait a few years? The biggest and fastest-growing economies are ours and America's, and the rules of trade will change to reflect that fact. It's inevitable. The barriers will come down, including those around the British Empire, and their businesses will struggle to survive. In fact, if anyone needs a war, it's the British. It's the only way they could halt their decline." He turned to von Schön. "Ask your English friend what he thinks. Would British businessmen favor a war with Germany?"

Von Schön explained what the man had said and repeated his question.

McColl smiled at them all. "I don't think so. For one thing, most businessmen have sons, and they don't want to lose them. For another, it's only the biggest companies that make most of their profits abroad and that benefit most from the empire. If the rules change, they'll find some way to survive—big companies always do." He paused. "But let me ask you something. After all, it's governments that declare war, not businessmen. How much notice do the Kaiser and his ministers take of what German businessmen think?"

It seemed like a good question, if the wry response to von Schön's translation was anything to go by. "This is the problem," one youngish German responded. "The old Kaiser understood how to rule. Like your Queen Victoria," he added, looking at McColl. "A symbol, yes? And an important one, but above politics. It didn't matter what his opinions were. But this Kaiser . . . We Germans have the best welfare system, the best schools. We have given the world Beethoven and Bach and Goethe and so much else. Our businesses are successful all over the world. We have much to be proud of, much to look forward to, but none of that interests this Kaiser. He grew up playing soldiers, and he can't seem to stop. In any other country, this would not matter a great deal, but because of our history and our place at the heart of Europe the army has always occupied a powerful position. I agree with Hans that we can get what we want without war, but when the crucial moment comes—as we all know it will—I think the Kaiser and his government will follow the army's lead, not listen to people like us."

It was a sadly convincing analysis, McColl thought, and as von Schön translated the gist of it, he listened to the others muttering their broad agreement. These German businessmen had no desire for war, but they realized that their opinions counted for little with their rulers. The one named Hans might be right in thinking that Britain was in decline, but only in an abstract, relative sense. And while it might be in a few traders' interests to fight a war of imperial preservation, it wasn't in anyone else's. As far as most British businessmen were concerned, peace was delivering the goods. McColl himself was thirty-two years old, and he'd been born into a world without automobiles or flying machines, phonographs or telephones, the wireless or moving pictures. Everything was changing so fast, and mostly for the better. Who in his right mind would exchange this thrilling new world for battlefields soaked in blood? It felt so medieval.

War would be a catastrophe, for business, for everyone. Particularly those who had to fight it. He was probably too old to be called up, but you never knew—with the weapons they had now, the ranks of the young might be decimated in a matter of months. Whatever happened, he had no intention of renewing his acquaintance with Britain's military machine and finding himself once more at the mercy of some idiot general.

* * *

It rained that evening and for most of the next two days, a freezing rain that rendered the pavements and quaysides treacherous and obstinately refused to turn to snow. McColl divided his time among cafés, the hotel lounge, and his room, following Pip on his voyage of discovery and engaging all those he could in conversation.

On two occasions he slipped and slithered his way to the edge of the new harbor, drawn by some pointless urge to confirm that the fleet was still there. It was. The occasional sailor hurried along the rain-swept decks, but no tenders were moving, and the bars on the quayside were shuttered and closed.

On Friday morning a note arrived from the consulate reminding him to return the book, which seemed somewhat gratuitous. The beautiful mission-taught writing was clearly the work of the Chinese girl, the overwrought concern for property more likely the golf-playing consul's. He decided to have the note framed when he got home.

The weather changed that afternoon, the clouds moving out across the ocean like a sliding roof. He went for a long walk down the Pacific shoreline, ate dinner alone, and, once darkness had taken its grip, rode a rickshaw across town to the Blue Dragon. The old man was still hawking up phlegm, but the girl who'd rushed to greet him in the lobby was busy in the reception area, hovering over a young and nervous *Kriegsmarine* lieutenant. He was having trouble choosing and, seeing McColl, politely suggested he jump the line. "If you know which girl you want."

"English," McColl explained, shaking his head and gesturing that the other should proceed. The German threw up his hands, sighed, and turned back to the line of waiting females. "This one," he said eventually, pointing at a child of around fifteen. McColl could almost hear the eeny, meeny, miney, mo.

The child took the German's much larger hand in hers and led him away like a horse.

The other females all sat back down in unison, reminding McColl of church. "You want see Hsu Ch'ing-lan?" the girl asked McColl.

"Yes." After making sure that the German was behind a curtain, he walked down to the madam's room.

Hsu Ch'ing-lan was just the way he'd left her, sitting at her desk, holding a cigarette between two raised fingers, wearing the same blue silk. But this time she was reading an ancient copy of *Life* magazine—he recognized the cartoon of Woodrow Wilson.

She smiled when she saw him, which seemed promising.

They went through the usual ritual, exchanging small talk until the tea arrived, before getting down to business. "The girl I told you about," she began, "my cousin from Shanghai. She is very intelligent. She has been with an officer on the flagship and persuaded him to talk about their plans."

"How?" was McColl's immediate reaction.

"How do you think? There are many men—most of them, I think—who like to talk about themselves after sex. They feel good, and they want the woman to know how important they are."

"But . . ."

"Let her tell you herself." Ch'ing-lan rang her bell and told the answering girl to bring Hsu Mei-lien. "You will see how intelligent she is," she told McColl while they waited.

The girl who arrived was still a child, but every bit as bright as her cousin had said she was. She began in halting English, then switched to rapid-fire Shanghainese when Ch'ing-lan told her that McColl spoke that language. Her officer's name was Burchert, and they'd been together the last three nights. If she had understood him correctly, he was an *Oberleutnant* on the *Gneisenau*. Once he was in the mood, she had started by saying how she'd seen the big English battleships in Shanghai and how brave she thought the Germans in Tsingtau were, to think of fighting them. But surely just sailing out to meet them would be foolhardy. They must have a better plan than that.

And that was all she'd had to say—after that, nothing could stop him talking. As far as he was concerned, it was entirely about coal. They could keep their ships together if there was enough coal, while the English who were hunting them would have to split their fleet to search an ocean as wide as the Pacific. And that would give the Germans their chance, to destroy them a piece at a time. But only if they had the coal.

"And where will they find it?" McColl wondered. "Did you ask him?"

She gave him a derisive look. "I don't ask questions," she said. "I just let him talk. If I ask a question like that, he will suspect something."

"Yes. He probably would." McColl smiled at her—she really was quite remarkable. But had she told him anything new and useful? The East Asia Squadron's dependence on limited coal supplies seemed obvious enough, even for the British Admiralty. Where could the Germans find coal in the Pacific? If Japan entered a war against them, then not from the home islands or Formosa. Supplies from Australia and New Zealand would be cut off once war was declared. And the Germans would know that any colliers loading up in a time of deepening crisis would be followed. So they would have to build up stocks on various islands while peace continued—stocks that the Royal Navy would have to seek out and burn if and when a war broke out. "Anything else?" he asked her.

"He says their gunners are better than the English."

"I wouldn't be surprised." He smiled at the young girl. "Thank you."

Hsu Ch'ing-lan dismissed her. "Clever, yes?"

"Very," McColl agreed. Too clever to be working in a Tsingtau brothel. But then millions of Chinese people seemed to be shortchanging themselves, biding their time. "How about the man with the flying machines? Has he booked another spanking?"

"Pao-yu is seeing him tonight," Hsu Ch'ing-lan told him.

"Then I'll be back tomorrow."

As it happened, he saw her sooner than that. It was still dark on the following morning when a hand shook his shoulder and he woke to the smell of her perfume.

She said something in a dialect he didn't understand, and the gaslight flared to life. More words, and a familiar-looking member of the Chinese hotel staff slipped out the door and closed it behind him.

"This is a nice surprise," McColl said, hauling himself up onto his elbows. She was wearing a long black coat over the usual dress.

"I don't think so," she said, coldly. "Pao-yu—the girl who spanks the flying-machine man—has been arrested."

"When? Who by?" He swung himself out of bed and reached for his trousers.

"The Germans, of course. Her questions must have made the man suspicious, and they took her to their police building. Last night."

"But they haven't come to the Blue Dragon? I wonder why."

"Because the girl hasn't told them anything. Not yet. A friend came to let me know they have her. She knows not to say anything, but she's not as clever as my cousin—they'll trick it out of her. So you must leave. There's a train in an hour."

"Oh. Yes, I suppose I should." He found himself wondering why she had come to warn him. "What about you?" he asked. "Will they arrest you?"

She shrugged. "I shall say I know nothing. If you are gone, then all they have is guesses."

"I see." And he did. She was afraid he would be caught, would implicate her, and that once the white folks had patched things up between them, she would be left as the scapegoat. Given the history of the last century, it was a reasonable enough assumption for a Chinese person to make. "Well, thank you. But what about the girl?"

"I can probably buy her back, but I will need money."

"Ah." He reached for his wallet on the bedside table, checked the contents, and handed her a wad of notes, thinking that he had now given her more than Cumming had given him. Some businessman.

"This won't be enough," she said.

"I'll need the rest to pay my bill and reach Shanghai."

"All right," she agreed reluctantly, stuffing the notes into a coat pocket and walking toward the door. When she turned with her hand on the knob, he half expected her to wish him luck, but all she said was, "Don't miss the train."

He hurriedly crammed his few belongings into the battered suitcase, happily realized that there wasn't time to return *Great Expectations*, and went to the door. It was only when he opened it that he heard the commotion downstairs. One voice—male, German, and coldly insistent—was demanding a room number; the other—Hsu Ch'ing-lan's—was angrily protesting a client's right to discretion. She was almost shouting, presumably for McColl's benefit.

He hesitated for a second, wondering whether he should just walk down and bluff it out. He decided against it. If he were arrested, the Germans could probably make a case against him, and some sort of punishment would doubtless follow. Best not to give them the chance.

When he'd checked in a fortnight earlier, he had taken the precaution of exploring the hotel for possible exit routes. This had felt a touch histrionic at the time but now seemed pleasingly professional. Walking as quietly as he could, he headed down the long corridor toward the back staircase.

He met no one in the corridor or on the stairs, but one of the Chinese staff was lounging in the kitchen doorway, a hint of a smile in his eyes. McColl fished some coins from his tip pocket, raised a finger to his lips for silence, and opened the door leading out into the backyard. He didn't expect to find anyone stationed outside and wasn't disappointed—the German authorities had obviously assumed that they would find him asleep in his bed.

Hurrying across the yard and down the alley, he emerged onto Prinz Heinrich Strasse and into a bitter wind. The sky was lightening, and a Chinese man was working his way down the street, dousing the ornate gas lamps. The side of the station building was visible up ahead, but no smoke was rising above it—if Hsu Ch'ing-lan was right about the time of departure, he'd have at least forty-five minutes to wait.

Which was obviously out of the question. He might as well give himself up as sit in the station for that long.

Perhaps he could hide somewhere close by and then surreptitiously board the train at the moment of departure.

This possibility sustained him until he reached the corner across from the station and leaned his head around for a view of the forecourt. There were several uniformed Germans in evidence, and one was looking straight at him. "Halt!" the man shouted.

McColl's first instinct, which he regretted a moment later, was to turn and run. Better a few months in jail than a bullet in the back, he thought as Prinz Heinrich Strasse stretched out before him, looking too much like a shooting range for comfort. But it was a bit late now to take a chance on his pursuers' levelheadedness. He swerved off between two buildings and down the dark alley that divided them. He reckoned he had a fifty-meter start and must have run almost that far when a crossroads presented itself. Sparing a second to look back, he found the alley behind him still empty. But as he swung right, he heard shouts in the distance, which seemed to come from up ahead.

Staying put seemed the better of two poor options. A doorway offered a few inches of shelter, enough to conceal his body if not his valise. Hearing German voices nearby rendered this problem more acute, and the notion of perching the suitcase on his head occurred to him just in time. As the Germans drew nearer, he stood there holding his breath, feeling more than a little ridiculous.

He heard the feet stop some ten yards off, imagined the eyes looking this way and that.

"Hanke probably imagined it," one man said.

"He *is* getting fond of the pipe," a second man suggested.

The first man laughed.

"But we might as well go down to the end," his companion decided. "Then work our way back around the block."

"Beats just standing here," the first voice agreed. "Christ, it's cold this morning. And no fucking breakfast."

His voice was fading, and McColl gingerly lowered his suitcase to the ground. He decided he would give them ten minutes to abandon this particular search and then make a run for it before the wider search got under way. But how? The train was out of the question, and God only knew how he'd get on a ship.

He felt real anxiety for the first time. But it was not the prospect of captivity and consequent physical hardship that worried him so much as the personal failure it would represent. Getting caught now would likely destroy any future he might have had in Cumming's organization.

Was there any way he could go to ground in Tsingtau? Could he persuade Hsu Ch'ing-lan that finding him a bolt-hole was in her own best interests?

Considering her circumstances, she was more likely to give him up.

Still, the Chinese town seemed a better bet than the German, and once his ten minutes were up, he cautiously worked his way northward through the slowly waking streets. There were more people about now, but all of them were Chinese—the German police had vanished, their civilian counterparts still in bed.

Once in the Chinese town, he bent his knees to disguise his height and let habit draw him toward the Blue Dragon. There was no sign of the usual doorkeeper, but there was a coal cart standing outside, its horse pawing absentmindedly at the cobbles with a front hoof.

On its way into Tsingtau, McColl remembered, the train had stopped at a small station in the outskirts. Which couldn't be more than three miles from here. Or four at the most.

He was still weighing the pros and cons of theft and hire when the coal coolie emerged, a bowlegged Chinese man with a queue that reached down to his buttocks. McColl managed, with some difficulty, to explain what he wanted and then showed his incredulous audience the wad of German notes that should have paid his hotel bill. All doubts vanished from the coal-encrusted visage. Offered more money than he'd make in five years, the man bared his teeth in a grin of compliance and hustled McColl up onto the cart. After clambering up himself, he jerked the horse into motion with a tug of the woven-string reins.

A real stroke of luck, McColl thought as they clattered down the slope toward the railway line and harbor. Directly ahead, the four funnels of either *Scharnhorst* or *Gneisenau* loomed above the long line of storehouses; away to the right, a few desultory puffs of smoke were rising from the vicinity of the rail station. Just a shunter, he hoped—surely his train couldn't be leaving.

As they approached the railway tracks, the coal coolie turned onto the parallel maintenance road the Germans had laid on the landward side and cajoled the horse to increase its pace. Soon they were almost flying along. Looking back, McColl could see no telltale smoke behind them. Perhaps he really would escape.

One step at a time, he told himself—sooner or later the Germans were bound to pick up his trail. And if he were caught . . . well, truth be told, it probably wouldn't be all that bad. He would be questioned at length and most likely put on trial. And then they would likely deport him, with as much publicity as they could manage. He might even serve a few months in prison. Which would be unpleasant, but he'd survive it. Jed and Mac would have to get the Maia back to London. And he would miss the chance to renew his acquaintance with Caitlin Hanley.

Which was something he really wanted to do.

She was still uppermost in his thoughts when the road abruptly degenerated, smooth asphalt giving way to ridged and rutted frozen mud. McColl clung to his seat, only too aware of the creaking axles, and prayed that neither would snap. His driver showed no inclination to slacken their pace—either the promise of riches had rendered him oblivious to everything else or the cart was a good deal stronger than it sounded. As the minutes went by and nothing more serious occurred than the loss of several coal sacks, McColl allowed himself to hope it was the latter.

It felt as if they'd been traveling for hours, but his watch told him twenty-five minutes. If he hadn't underestimated the distance to the next station, they should reach it in time—the prospect of the train steaming past them didn't bear thinking about. What in heaven's name would he do then? Start walking toward Shanghai?

About ten minutes later, their track veered inland, away from the rails, but his chauffeur shrugged off his anxious questions. And sure enough, a few minutes more and they were back by the rails. By this time most of Tsingtau seemed behind them—they had to be nearly there.

They were. The stop he remembered came into view as they rounded a bend, its single platform facing out across the bay. The station building wouldn't have looked out of place in the Black Forest and had no need of the imperial flag that fluttered from its roof. European-style houses were clustered behind it, and beyond them was the famous brewery.

The station was still two hundred yards ahead, but McColl ordered a halt—he had no desire to show up on a coal cart. The driver pulled on the reins, brought them to a stop, and anxiously held out a hand for payment. He seemed almost surprised to receive it, but McColl could hardly blame him—with his face still wreathed in coal dust, he didn't seem a man accustomed to good fortune.

McColl wished him good-bye and started walking. The station ahead, he now realized, looked worryingly deserted. He hoped to God that the morning train was scheduled to stop there, because he didn't much fancy trying to flag the thing down.

But he needn't have worried. Several Chinese would-be travelers were sheltering from the wind on the far side of the building, and the German stationmaster was in his office, warming himself in front of a blazing coal fire. The man was consulting his pocketwatch when McColl appeared in his doorway, and as he snapped it shut, a whistle blew in the distance—the train was approaching.

His face flushed with alarm when he saw McColl, who thought for a moment that the game was up. But it was only the usual German annoyance at lateness and the wrecking of schedules that might ensue. Concealing his relief, McColl asked if the train's imminent arrival meant he should pay the guard, but that of course was against regulations, and the locomotive was hissing to a halt by the time the flustered official had written his ticket. "You'll reach Tsinan at five," the stationmaster told him. "And the connection to Pukow is at six."

Steeling himself, McColl walked out onto the platform, half expecting a posse of policemen to erupt from the two carriages. But there were none, only fifty or more Chinese men staring out of the open wagons hitched to the back of the coaches.

He entered an almost empty saloon. There were no other foreigners and only two Chinese men, both in Western suits. They stood up to bow and smile but offered no conversation, and McColl was happy to follow their lead. He took a window seat at the other end of the car and barely had time to place his luggage on the rack before the train slipped into motion.

If his memory of the local geography was accurate, they would be outside the Tsingtau concession in ten minutes or so and, theoretically at least, beyond German jurisdiction. Of course they owned and ran the railway and probably considered it part of their writ. The local Chinese population might argue the point, but he wouldn't like to bet on it. There was a British consulate in Tsinan, but also another German concession. This was much smaller than the one around Tsingtau but would still have some soldiers on hand.

He wouldn't feel safe until he was on the train to Pukow and Nanking, which was eleven long hours away.

The line was still following the shore of the bay, the train advancing at a satisfying pace. It occurred to him that cutting the telegraph wires that ran alongside the tracks would increase his chances by leaps and bounds, but even if granted an opportunity, he lacked the requisite tools.

And maybe there was no need. The train rattled past the concession's border post without even stopping, and there were no police or army officers waiting on the platform at Kiautschou, the first town in Chinese territory. It looked like he could relax until they reached Tsinan.

He got off for a stroll at Kiautschou and took a small clay pot of tea back to his seat. As the train got under way, the conductor sat down beside him with a pot of his own, clearly intent on conversation.

Over the next twenty minutes, McColl learned a lot about the man and his family. The wife who loved living in Tsingtau, who taught in the school there—the best school in China, according to some. The children liked it, too, though he sometimes thought they were missing much of their German heritage. But they could never have afforded servants in Germany.

It was clear that he loved his train and the pretty German stations, so out of place against the Chinese backdrop. He told McColl about the line's short history and how flat it was, with several hundred bridges and not a single tunnel. He pointed out kilns by the side of the line, where bricks had been baked and then broken for ballast, because Shantung province was devoid of suitable stones.

McColl responded with a wholly fictional life, which he located in Alsace to mask any linguistic mistakes. It was a relief to be speaking openly again, after a fortnight of pretending not to speak German, and he found himself liking the conductor. It was a strange place for a German to end up, but this one seemed at peace with himself and the world.

The man left after an hour or so, and McColl sat there watching the barely changing scene through his window—a wide valley dotted by small villages, an occasional row of planters in the winter fields, the distant line of brown mountains under a gray sky. He eventually woke with a jolt of alarm, but it was only a coal train rumbling past in the opposite direction, bound for Tsingtau and von Spee's ships. He imagined the colliers steaming out into the wide Pacific, dropping their loads on a hundred scattered islands for the future use of a fugitive fleet.

He thought about the girl the Germans had arrested. What would they do to her? If it had been Hsu Ch'ing-lan's cousin, then Ch'ing-lan would have moved heaven and earth to save her—that was the Chinese way. But Pao-yu wasn't family—at least not as far as McColl knew—and if not she'd probably just be abandoned. Which was also the Chinese way.

There was nothing he could do for her now.

After Wei, the mountains grew higher and the valley seemed less populated. It was almost a shock when a mining complex suddenly appeared in the window, complete with winding gear and mountains of glistening coal. Black-faced Chinese coolies were doing all the work, dragging carts of coal up ramps and tipping them into the railway wagons. Three German overseers were standing to one side, comparing notes about something or other.

The train soon stopped at a station, and two more Germans got on. They ignored the Chinese people who had bowed to McColl and then ignored him, too, as if intent on proving that race had no part in their arrogance. Which suited him well enough—if word of his escape were clicking along the telegraph wires, it clearly hadn't reached them.

But it had been clicking—he was almost certain of that. Failing to find him in Tsingtau, the Germans were bound to spread the net wider. They might not know he was headed their way, but the German authorities in Tsinan would certainly be on the lookout.

The last major stop was Tschou-tsun. After the train pulled out, the conductor stopped for another chat, and there was no change in his manner to suggest fresh intelligence, causing McColl to wonder whether he himself was in flight from a phantom. Maybe the girl was still refusing to speak or didn't know his name—that was something he should have asked Hsu Ch'ing-lan about. This wasn't his finest hour, he realized. His report to Cumming would need some glossing.

And he still had Tsinan to cope with. His best bet, he decided, was a variation on his departure from Tsingtau. On the journey down from Peking ten days earlier, he had noticed that Tsinan had two stations, one where travelers on the Peking–Pukow line changed for the Shan-tung Railway and another, closer to the town, that was served only by the latter. Any pursuers would assume he had a through ticket and would be waiting at the junction. If he got off at the town station and took a rickshaw across town, there was a reasonable chance he could sneak aboard the Pukow train without being seen.

The last stage of the journey seemed eternal, but the straggling outskirts of Tsinan finally appeared in his window, and almost immediately the train began to slow. He grabbed his suitcase and made for the vestibule farthest from the luggage car and the conductor.

The line was running along a slight embankment between a series of small lakes, the town visible beyond those to the south. The moment the train stopped, the Chinese passengers in the open wagons were dropping the sides, leaping down to the ground, and hurrying away. Cautiously inching an eye around the corner of his carriage, McColl saw the conductor sharing a convivial word with another German stationmaster. There were no other uniforms on display.

On the other side of the train, a team of coolies was transferring sacks of rice from a boxcar to a line of waiting carts. When the whistle blew and the train began to move, McColl stepped nimbly down and watched it steam away. It couldn't be much more than a mile to the other station, and for a moment he considered simply walking down the track. But the land on both sides was open, and there was still too much light in the sky—he would stick to his plan.

Which proved harder than expected. The rickshaw coolie he tried to engage spoke no dialect that McColl could understand and needed more than a little convincing from a better-traveled colleague that this foreigner wanted transport to the town's other station—a station he could have reached much more simply and cheaply by staying on his train. Once persuaded that his prospective passenger wasn't simply deranged—or at least not dangerously so—he allowed

McColl into the seat, picked up the bamboo shafts, and set off at a steady jog for the city gate some two hundred yards distant.

Passing through this, the rickshaw swayed along a narrow street that ran parallel to the town's crumbling wall. This was the old China, seemingly untouched by progress, its buildings dirty and decaying, its children half naked and clearly malnourished. Stares followed McColl, and one beggar ran after the rickshaw, stretching out a hand until he tripped on the uneven road.

The coolie crossed a stinking canal, turned through another gate behind a scurrying rat, and emerged onto a slightly more prosperous street. Several artisans were working outside their shops, making the most of the remaining light, and a brazier was burning in front of a small hardware emporium, the hanging copper pots reflecting the fire. The smell of food from a couple of cafés reminded McColl that he'd hardly eaten that day and started his stomach rumbling. Two more coolies ran by with a sedan chair, and he caught a glimpse of an old woman's face within.

They skirted a small lake and headed up a long, straight street toward what looked like a railway station. A column of smoke, dyed red by the sinking sun, rose up behind the German roof, confirming the fact. McColl waited until they were a short walk away, then shouted to the coolie to stop. The man did so with obvious reluctance but conjured up a toothless smile when the foreign devil overpaid him.

McColl walked toward the station, keeping to the rapidly deepening shadows on one side of the street. There was an automobile and at least a dozen rickshaws in the forecourt, all waiting, no doubt, for the train from the north. He ignored the gaslit booking hall, cautiously worked his way around the building, and found an area of shadow from which he could safely scan the platform. The first thing he noticed was a group of uniformed Germans, who seemed to be interrogating his friend the conductor. The train that had brought him from Tsingtau was sitting in the bay platform, lazily oozing steam.

So he hadn't been overreacting—they really were after him.

He took in the rest of the tableau. The platform lamps were glowing in the gloom, and there were several dozen Chinese people waiting for his train, many with several items of luggage. At the other end of the platform, four coolies were waiting with shovels beside a coal wagon, ready to refuel the incoming engine. One of the uniformed officers seemed to be staring straight at McColl, which gave him a moment of acute anxiety. But he soon looked away. The darkness was apparently enough of a cloak.

There was nothing to do but wait and take whatever chance was offered to get aboard the train. The minutes turned into an hour, and the temperature steadily dropped, but at least the darkness deepened.

There were several blows on the whistle before the headlight swam into view and the train steamed in alongside the low continental platform. It was more prepossessing than the one from Tsingtau, with five European-built carriages and no open wagons. The moment it clanked to a halt, scrimmages developed at all the vestibule doors as Chinese passengers trying to alight collided with those seeking entry. Above their heads the peaked caps of the German police were turning this way and that, looking for a British spy.

Up ahead the pipe from the water tank was being slewed across the tender, and beyond it the coolies were presumably shoveling coal. He had at least ten minutes, but there was no way he could cross the wide platform without being seen.

Two of the policemen were boarding the train, but the others were still keeping watch outside. He should have crossed the tracks out of sight of the platform and waited on the other side, but it was too late for that now.

He suddenly had an idea. He walked quickly back to the forecourt and up to the last rickshaw in line. "Hat," he said in Shanghainese, pointing it out for greater clarity and waving a note worth twenty times as much under the man's eyes. The coolie gave him an *Is this really Christmas?* look and slowly removed his conical headgear. McColl handed him the note, grabbed the hat, and walked back toward the platform. The police were still there, and the train seemed almost set to leave—there was nothing else for it. He put on the hat, arranged his suitcase so that it would be shielded by his body, and started the long, semicircular walk that would take him around the back of the train. He was too tall and the suitcase too big, but out where the light barely reached, he was hoping they'd see only the hat.

And it worked. Thirty nerve-racking seconds and he was behind the train, looking up at the dimly lit carriages. As he reached the inner end of the last carriage, the whistle sounded, and almost instantly the wheels began to turn. He stepped aboard and climbed up onto the vestibule platform. The temptation to stand and wave his coolie hat at the Germans was enormous, but discretion triumphed. He ducked inside what was clearly a third-class carriage and strode up the aisle in search of less crowded accommodation.

The Chinese passengers, noticing his bizarre souvenir, seemed relieved to see him pass. They were doubtless thinking that he would be more at home in first, with all the other inscrutable foreign devils.

OTHER TITLES IN THE SOHO CRIME SERIES